1974

# THE LUCIFER SOCIETY

Also edited by Peter Haining

THE GENTLEWOMEN OF EVIL
THE SATANISTS
A CIRCLE OF WITCHES
THE WILD NIGHT COMPANY
THE HOLLYWOOD NIGHTMARE
THE CLANS OF DARKNESS
GOTHIC TALES OF TERROR

# THE LUCIFER SOCIETY

MACABRE TALES BY GREAT MODERN WRITERS

Edited by Peter Haining

With a Foreword by Kingsley Amis

Taplinger Publishing Company : : New York

for a private society of friends
Judy, George, Joyce & Tony

: :     : :     : :     : :     : :

Second Printing

First published in the United States in 1972 by
Taplinger Publishing Co., Inc., New York, New York

Published simultaneously in the Dominion of Canada by
Burns & MacEachern, Ltd., Toronto

Library of Congress Catalog Card Number: 70-179949  ::  ISBN 0-8008-5042-4

## ACKNOWLEDGMENTS

The editor is grateful to the following authors, their agents, executors and publishers for permission to include copyright material in this book:

"Man Overboard" by Sir Winston Churchill. Copyright 1898 by *Harmsworth Magazine*. Reprinted by permission of Odhams Books Ltd., London.

"Timber" by John Galsworthy. Copyright 1920 by John Galsworthy. Reprinted from *Caravans* by permission of the publishers William Heinemann Ltd., London.

"The Angry Street" by G. K. Chesterton. Copyright 1936 by G. K. Chesterton. Reprinted from *Tremendous Rifles* by permission of the author's executors.

"The Call of Wings" by Agatha Christie. Copyright 1933 by Odhams Press from *The Hound of Death*. Reprinted by permission of Hughes Massie Ltd., London.

"The Cherries" by Lawrence Durrell. Copyright 1942 by *Daily Express* Publications, London, for *Masterpiece of Thrills*. Reprinted by permission of the author.

"A Man from Glasgow" by Somerset Maugham. Copyright 1947 by Somerset Maugham from *Creatures of Circumstance*. Reprinted by permission of William Heinemann Ltd., London.

# FOREWORD

What writers read (apart from their own works and the reviews of them) is an under-explored subject. We know well enough that Milton read Shakespeare and that Keats read Milton. We know nearly as well that George Eliot read Spinoza and Feuerbach and much else on that exalted level; but what did she read when she was not, so to speak, on her best behaviour? Did she revel in Jules Verne's *20,000 Leagues under the Sea*? Had she snapped up *Varney the Vampire* when he and a whole corps of fellow-fiends made their appearance round about 1850? Perhaps, with the earnestness of the self-educated, she scorned such delights, but, if so, I fancy she would have been something of an exception.

In more recent times, certainly, supposedly serious writers have shown a distinct propensity for rather unserious pursuits, for diversions of a sadly non-uplifting kind. Often, these go outside what could however loosely be called literature. Max Beerbohm was always laying down his critic's pen and ambling out to the music-hall; Wittgenstein would take time off from founding modern philosophy to gaze enraptured at whatever Western might be showing at the local cinema—in a front-row seat.

The reading-matter of writers tends to show a similar bent. However familiar he might have been with the work of other poets, Dylan Thomas was an avid reader of science fiction—including, incidentally, a lot of the pulpier sort. In a more discriminating spirit, W. H. Auden has given the highest praise to the novels of Raymond Chandler, creator of the most famous of all private eyes, Philip Marlowe. And it used to be said that you would have to go far to find a bishop who did not keep the latest Agatha Christie on his bedside table. Some people thought this showed that bishops were frivolous or bloodthirsty or both; to me it suggests humanity and a healthy inquisitiveness.

Several points emerge. My introduction of bishops, who are not really writers, except presumably of sermons and the like, may look like a mere attempt to lend respectability to the less

conventionally respectable forms of literature. Anybody prepared
to be seen reading this volume will hardly need that kind of
reassurance. All the same, there are plenty of other kinds of
reader, and plenty of critics, who knowingly or unknowingly
separate the written word into serious literature—lyric poetry,
verse drama, the traditional novel—on the one hand, and what I
can only call the *genres*—detective stories, science fiction, ghost
stories, fantasy, tales of horror and the macabre—on the other.
And the second category is often felt to be lower, cruder, less
imaginative, less (wait for it) relevant. To attack this position
properly would take a whole book, so I will end this modest
digression by saying simply that there would not be much hope
for anyone who thought M. R. James's ghost stories crude or
H. G. Wells's scientific romances unimaginative.

I was suggesting that writers are often adventurous in their
choice of reading-matter, inclined to stray off the beaten paths,
if not into the slums then at any rate into the more curious
suburbs of literature. Perhaps, after a day at the typewriter, they
just do not feel like taking on anybody as complex (or as dis-
mayingly good) as George Eliot. But perhaps, again, they find in
themselves a special professional curiosity, a desire to find out
how other kinds of writer operate, as a clarinettist in a symphony
orchestra, say, might find a particular interest in, and something
to learn from, the techniques of a jazz clarinettist. More than that:
every writer wants to extend his range, wants ideally to be able
to write about everything in any style. And to do that he must
study subjects new to him, styles he has never used, in the work
of writers whose field of activity is some distance away from
his own.

This would help to explain why a writer of ordinary fiction
may feel a peculiar attraction towards the *genres* as a whole. What
I have not touched on is the question why one *genre* in particular,
the macabre, has fascinated writers in the main stream of literature
from its beginnings. (A kind of science fiction did start off in the
seventeenth century, but, with rare exceptions like *Gulliver's
Travels,* it generates no more than academic interest until we reach
Verne and Wells.) Plainly, the macabre had the advantage
of a historical lead; there were no detectives to speak of in
Shakespeare's day, few if any cowboys in Jane Austen's. But the
fact remains that, until very recently, most of the writers one

can think of have shown their interest in the macabre by contri-
buting to it; and not only prose writers, as is testified by
Coleridge's *Christabel* and *Ancient Mariner* and Browning's *Childe
Roland*.

The reason for this involvement seems to me quite simple.
Writers (of ordinary fiction, ordinary poetry) do not have to be
exceptionally sensitive or suffering people, but their outlet, in the
sense of their means of getting rid of their personal tensions, is,
by definition, through writing. And ordinary fiction, etc., however broadly conceived, is still not quite broad enough to serve
as the outlet for all those tensions. There are awkward pieces of
obsession, neurotic anxiety, irrational fear, private nightmare and
so forth that cannot find release via any sort of conventional
narrative. Notice, for example, what a mess novelists make of
things when they try to portray the onset of madness or any
supposedly significant dream.

This is not an invariable rule: Dickens managed to incorporate
such matters successfully within the boundaries of the novel, or
of his novels, but he was a genius of a very rare and diverse kind.
The rest of us have had to make do with occasional forays into
the conveniently available macabre, producing a ghost story here,
a tale of horror there. No art can be adequately explained as
occupational therapy for the artist; nevertheless, the inner drives
of the artist help to explain the form as well as the content of
whatever he creates.

The appeal of the macabre, then, for writer and reader alike,
must lie very deep, as deep as the impulse that, thousands of years
before the invention of writing, led certain individuals to tell
stories and the mass of humanity to listen to them. Men and
women, by their nature, enjoy being stirred by accounts of
heroic deeds that never took place, being put in suspense by
imaginary dangers, being made to laugh at the predicaments of
people they know very well have no real existence. Why they
should just as much enjoy being frightened by what they hear or
read is less plain.

I am not qualified to attempt a psychological dissertation, and
it would bore me anyhow. All I can and need do is to draw certain
distinctions. A child will enjoy hearing about witches or ghosts
partly because he has the security of knowing that there are no
witches living in his street and that his house is not haunted. He

will not, on the whole, enjoy being told about a homicidal maniac currently on the loose. In the same sort of way, the normal adult, or the normal part of the adult's mind, lies gladly open to terrors of a more sophisticated and possibly more terrifying sort, to tales of delusion or demoniacal possession or hallucination. Here the enemy is to be found, not out in the open like a vampire or a werewolf, who can be dealt with decisively enough with a crucifix or intensified security on the night of the full moon. In this deeper kind of tale, the enemy is within, where no silver bullet can reach him. Yet even here our normal adult can conquer him, can lay the book aside, not without a qualm or two if the writer has done his job properly, but with his inner security unimpaired. This is not the case with some more recent writing, and recent films.

The macabre and the horror story (or horror film) are traditionally interchangeable terms. What is really meant by horror in this sense, though, is not so much horror as terror. The reader (or member of a cinema audience) is invited to feel a sense of foreboding, of dread, of anguished hope that the intolerable will not happen. What we are being increasingly faced with is something different and new, in which the reader (etc.) is invited to feel repulsion, shock, physical disgust, and here that normality of mind, that inner security, are threatened. To take a handy example: when, in the old Boris Karloff film of *Frankenstein*, made in 1931, the monster encounters the little girl, we feel dread, terror, or horror in the old sense; we discover later that he has thrown her into the water and so killed her. Today, we should be much more likely actually to see him tearing her to pieces with all the resources of modern cinematography. That is the new horror, and its literary parallels are obvious.

I do not want to start a moral harangue, but I am interested in pointing out a change of taste, more perhaps on the part of writers and film producers than among the public. Changes I strongly suspect of being related have taken place in other fields, such that science fiction has declined into whimsy or "experimental" flummery, the detective story is on the point of finally expiring, and avant-garde jazz is noise bereft of rhythm or melody. I could go on to be gloomy about developments, or degenerations, in major arts like poetry or painting, but I will confine myself here to indicating a sad falling-off in the *genres*.

This is nowhere more marked than in the macabre, the horror story in the traditional sense. I cannot help noticing that, of the authors in the present collection, very few of those still living are under fifty years old. This book may well turn out to be one of the last of its kind, an anthology of late-gathered blooms.

KINGSLEY AMIS
*February, 1972*

# CONTENTS

"I stare into the eyes
of devils
devils dark and foul
and look them down
and steal their ground."

NORMAN MAILER

# INTRODUCTION

The demands on the conscientious anthologist, while not often considered, can easily be defined: an abounding curiosity about the subject in question, the determined pursuit of rare stories in the remote corners of world literature, and a careful combination of personal choice with public taste. (A damn good pair of eyes are not a bad thing, either!) It is a pursuit I believe to need as much care, devotion and inspiration as that required by any novelist or biographer—for the *good anthology*, the anthology which is not just another collection of old favourites lifted, still warm, from a similar assemblage, is the blending of what is primarily individual into a special kind of uniformity. The taking of many varied talents and melding their work into a collection that can at best be read like a novel, enjoyed like a novel, yet still provide the many succinct moments of revelation and thrill that only the short story affords.

As one who has rooted through as many cob-webbed attics, dusty libraries and jumbled second-hand bookshops as probably anyone else in the past dozen years, the rewards of discovering an overlooked story or a lost tale are as keen now as they were when I first began this pursuit. The several anthologies which have resulted from my search have each brought their own pleasures both in the compiling and in the multi-volumed international publication which has followed. Without exception, though, these books have concentrated on the work of the accepted masters of the horror story: those men (and a few women) whose very names are synonymous with the tales they write, Edgar Allan Poe, M. R. James, E. F. Benson, Lord Dunsany, H. P. Lovecraft, August Derleth, Ray Bradbury and many, many more. In each instance I had delved into the writer's past and come up with some story that had either escaped the nets of other anthologists or proved to be of the last rarity. This was not to say, I hasten to add, that the quality of the item could be below standard or in a style no longer acceptable to modern readers.

During the endless hours of reading, re-reading, filing,

cross-referencing and pursuit of copyright that this kind of work has involved me in, I have occasionally come across an atypical story or two; a tale which fell outside the usual pattern of the macabre story. An important group of these are now the items which comprise *The Lucifer Society*. How their assembly came about might be of interest before we come to the stories themselves.

Although this book has developed as a result of the work of many writers, it was actually inspired by a single story which I unearthed during one of my forays. The story was *Man Overboard* by Sir Winston Churchill. This fine little macabre episode I found in one of the bound volumes of Victorian family magazines which proliferated (like "valambrosian leaves" according to one critic) for nearly a century and are now quite forgotten. My delight at the discovery can be imagined: a completely unknown story by one of the greatest modern Englishmen . . . and a tale of terror to boot! As I read the story an idea began to form in my mind for an anthology. If a man like Sir Winston Churchill, a distinguished writer among his many other attributes, had been inspired to write a macabre story, there must surely have been others. Men perhaps more totally involved in literature than Sir Winston, but known to an international reading audience in fields other than horror fiction. Even if their motivation to create such a story had been no more than a flash of dark inspiration once engendered and then never repeated, still, what a unique and entertaining assembly the tales would all make.

Before beginning my research I realised it was important to define and limit the scope of the collection. A rag-bag of stories—however distinguished the authors—would serve little purpose except in returning the items to print. I settled on covering a fifty-year period from the twenties, when the modern macabre story was going through a significant development at the hands of M. R. James, Arthur Machen and Lord Dunsany in this country, and A. Merritt, H. P. Lovecraft and the diverse contributors to *Weird Tales* magazine in America, to the present day. In this way the reader of outre fiction would have an opportunity of studying what an elite band of "general" writers produced during a critical half century in comparison to their

contemporaries working solely in the genre.* Finally, I decided
to restrict my selection to just English and American authors. In
those two countries, I was sure, there would prove to be a rich
enough cache of distinguished men and women who met the
requirements to more than fill a volume. Just how rich is now
evidenced by the book in your hands.

Perhaps the point to have emerged most forcefully from my
research is just how many great writers of this century have been
inspired to create macabre stories at one time or another.
Although they are not represented here (more for reasons of
space and total diversity of subject than actual quality) there *could*
have been contributions by such as Ernest Hemingway, Aldous
Huxley, Pearl S. Buck, Evelyn Waugh, Christopher Isherwood,
Mary McCarthy, Nicholas Monsarrat, Leslie Charteris, Erle
Stanley Gardner, Irwin Shaw, Herman Wouk, Anthony Burgess,
Norman Mailer, Mickey Spillane . . . the list is almost endless.
Together, whether represented here or not, this very special
circle of *Literateurs* form what I have called *The Lucifer Society*.

It has also become evident to me in reading the stories of these
masters what pleasure they got from writing them; one has only
to know a little of the style and scope of any contributor here to
appreciate his relish in plummeting the depths of the strange, the
macabre and the horrible. What was sad—but is in some measure
remedied by this book—was that once having been published,
most of their stories soon disappeared into obscurity while their
creators' more traditional work was endlessly reprinted and
discussed.

Finally, a word of caution. Don't expect to find traditional
tales of the macabre herein—we have a ghost or two, of course,
even the occasional "monster" of a sort, but these are stories by
major literary figures who innovate rather than copy and the
results promise some very strange sensations. So—pull up your
chair and join the Society!

PETER HAINING
Birch Green
Essex
March, 1972

* Editor's note: Although, obviously, Sir Winston Churchill's story does not fit
into this period, as it directly inspired the collection it would be wrong for it not
to be included.

# I

BRITISH

# MAN OVERBOARD

### WINSTON CHURCHILL

*Because of his achievements as a statesman and war leader, Sir Winston Churchill's earlier career as a journalist and author is hardly remembered any more. As a consequence, much of what he wrote as a young man of considerable gifts has gathered the dust of the forgotten years. Man Overboard, now seeing the light of print again, was written at the close of the last century and appeared in* The Harmsworth Magazine, *one of several popular family journals of the day. It is this story, a notable acquisition to the "terror tale" genre, that inspired the preparation of the present anthology.*

It was a little after half-past nine when the man fell overboard. The mail steamer was hurrying through the Red Sea in the hope of making up the time which the currents of the Indian Ocean had stolen.

The night was clear, though the moon was hidden behind clouds. The warm air was laden with moisture. The still surface of the waters was only broken by the movement of the great ship, from whose quarter the long, slanting undulations struck out like the feathers from an arrow shaft, and in whose wake the froth and air bubbles churned up by the propeller trailed in a narrowing line to the darkness of the horizon.

There was a concert on board. All the passengers were glad to break the monotony of the voyage and gathered around the piano in the companion-house. The decks were deserted. The man had been listening to the music and joining in the songs, but the room was hot and he came out to smoke a cigarette and enjoy a breath of the wind which the speedy passage of the liner created. It was the only wind in the Red Sea that night.

The accommodation-ladder had not been unshipped since leaving Aden and the man walked out on to the platform, as on to a balcony. He leaned his back against the rail and blew a puff of smoke into the air reflectively. The piano struck up a lively tune and a voice began to sing the first verse of "The Rowdy Dowdy Boys". The measured pulsations of the screw were a subdued but additional accompaniment. The man knew the song, it had been the rage at all the music halls when he had started for India seven years before. It reminded him of the brilliant and busy streets he had not seen for so long, but was soon to see again. He was just going to join in the chorus when the railing, which had been insecurely fastened, gave way suddenly with a snap and he fell backwards into the warm water of the sea amid a great splash.

For a moment he was physically too much astonished to think. Then he realised he must shout. He began to do this even before he rose to the surface. He achieved a hoarse, inarticulate, half-choked scream. A startled brain suggested the word, "Help!" and he bawled this out lustily and with frantic effort six or seven times without stopping. Then he listened.

"Hi! hi! clear the way
For the Rowdy Dowdy Boys."

The chorus floated back to him across the smooth water for the ship had already completely passed by. And as he heard the music a long stab of terror drove through his heart. The possibility that he would not be picked up dawned for the first time on his consciousness. The chorus started again:

"Then—I—say—boys,
Who's for a jolly spree?
Rum—tum—tiddley—um,
Who'll have a drink with me?"

"Help! Help! Help!" shrieked the man, now in desperate fear.

"Fond of a glass now and then,
Fond of a row or noise;
Hi! hi! clear the way
For the Rowdy Dowdy Boys!"

The last words drawled out fainter and fainter. The vessel was steaming fast. The beginning of the second verse was confused and broken by the ever-growing distance. The dark outline of the great hull was getting blurred. The stern light dwindled.

Then he set out to swim after it with furious energy, pausing every dozen strokes to shout long wild shouts. The disturbed waters of the sea began to settle again to their rest and the widening undulations became ripples. The aerated confusion of the screw fizzed itself upwards and out. The noise of motion and the sounds of life and music died away.

The liner was but a single fading light on the blackness of the waters and a dark shadow against the paler sky.

At length full realisation came to the man and he stopped swimming. He was alone—abandoned. With the understanding the brain reeled. He began again to swim, only now instead of shouting he prayed—mad, incoherent prayers, the words stumbling into one another.

Suddenly a distant light seemed to flicker and brighten.

A surge of joy and hope rushed through his mind. They were going to stop—to turn the ship and come back. And with the hope came gratitude. His prayer was answered. Broken words of thanksgiving rose to his lips. He stopped and stared after the light—his soul in his eyes. As he watched it, it grew gradually but steadily smaller. Then the man knew that his fate was certain. Despair succeeded hope; gratitude gave place to curses. Beating the water with his arms, he raved impotently. Foul oaths burst from him, as broken as his prayers—and as unheeded.

The fit of passion passed, hurried by increasing fatigue. He became silent—silent as was the sea, for even the ripples were subsiding into the glassy smoothness of the surface. He swam on mechanically along the track of the ship, sobbing quietly to himself in the misery of fear. And the stern light became a tiny speck, yellower but scarcely bigger than some of the stars, which here and there shone between the clouds.

Nearly twenty minutes passed and the man's fatigue began to change to exhaustion. The overpowering sense of the inevitable pressed upon him. With the weariness came a strange comfort—he need not swim all the long way to Suez. There was another course. He would die. He would resign his existence since he was thus abandoned. He threw up his hands impulsively and sank.

Down, down he went through the warm water. The physical death took hold of him and he began to drown. The pain of that savage grip recalled his anger. He fought with it furiously. Striking out with arms and legs he sought to get back to the air.

It was a hard struggle, but he escaped victorious and gasping to the surface. Despair awaited him. Feebly splashing with his hands, he moaned in bitter misery:

"I can't—I must. O God! let me die."

The moon, then in her third quarter, pushed out from behind the concealing clouds and shed a pale, soft glitter upon the sea. Upright in the water, fifty yards away, was a black triangular object. It was a fin. It approached him slowly.

His last appeal had been heard.

# TIMBER

JOHN GALSWORTHY

Timber, *which John Galsworthy wrote in 1920, is quite unique among his work and particularly fits the entry requirements for this anthology, as it was his only specific excursion into the macabre. Although the story is in some ways a parable of morality, it is also a study of the power of suggestion and the fear of darkness. To those who have come to know Galsworthy only through the lives of the Forsytes, the adventure of Sir Arthur Hirries will come as a chilling revelation. . . .*

SIR ARTHUR HIRRIES, Baronet, of Hirriehugh, in a northern county, came to the decision to sell his timber in that state of mind—common during the War—which may be called patrio-profiteering. Like newspaper proprietors, writers on strategy, shipbuilders, owners of works, makers of arms and the rest of the working classes at large, his mood was: "Let me serve my country, and if thereby my profits are increased, let me put up with it, and invest in National Bonds."

With an encumbered estate and some of the best coverts in that northern county, it had not become practical politics to sell his timber till the Government wanted it at all costs. To let his shooting had been more profitable, till now, when a patriotic action and a stroke of business had become synonymous. A man of sixty-five, but not yet grey, with a reddish tinge in his moustache, cheeks, lips, and eyelids, slightly knock-kneed, and with large, rather spreading feet, he moved in the best circles in a somewhat embarrassed manner. At the enhanced price, the timber at Hirriehugh would enfranchise him for the remainder of his days. He sold it therefore one day of April when the War news was bad, to a Government official on the spot. He sold it at half-past five in the afternoon, practically for cash down, and drank a stiff whisky and soda to wash away the taste of the transaction; for, though no sentimentalist, his great-great-grandfather had planted most of it, and his grandfather the rest. Royalty too had shot there in its time; and he himself (never much of a sportsman) had missed more birds in the rides and hollows of his fine coverts than he cared to remember. But the country was in need, and the price considerable. Bidding the Government official good-bye, he lighted a cigar, and went across the Park to take a farewell stroll among his timber.

He entered the home covert by a path leading through a group of pear trees just coming into bloom. Smoking cigars and drinking whisky in the afternoon in preference to tea, Sir Arthur Hirries had not much sense of natural beauty. But those pear trees impressed him, greenish white against blue sky and fleecy thick clouds which looked as if they had snow in them. They were deuced pretty, and promised a good year for fruit, if they escaped the late frosts, though it certainly looked like freezing tonight! He paused a moment at the wicket gate to glance back at them—like scantily-clothed maidens posing on the outskirts of his timber. Such, however, was not the vision of Sir Arthur Hirries, who was considering how he should invest the balance of the cash down after paying off his mortgages. National Bonds—the country was in need!

Passing through the gate he entered the ride of the home covert. Variety lay like colour on his woods. They stretched for miles, and his ancestors had planted almost every kind of tree— beech, oak, birch, sycamore, ash, elm, hazel, holly, pine; a lime tree and a hornbeam here and there, and further in among the winding coverts, spinneys and belts of larch. The evening air was sharp, and sleet showers came whirling from those bright clouds; he walked briskly, drawing at his richly fragrant cigar, the whisky still warm within him. He walked, thinking with a gentle melancholy slowly turning a little sulky, that he would never again be pointing out with his shooting stick to such a guest where he was to stand to get the best birds over him. The pheasants had been let down during the War, but he put up two or three old cocks who went clattering and whirring out to left and right; and rabbits crossed the rides quietly to and fro, within easy shot. He came to where Royalty had stood fifteen years ago during the last drive. He remembered Royalty saying: "Very pretty shooting at that last stand, Hirries; birds just about as high as I like them." The ground indeed rose rather steeply there, and the timber was oak and ash, with a few dark pines sprinkled into the bare greyish twiggery of the oaks, always costive in spring, and the just greening feather of the ashes.

"They'll be cutting those pines first," he thought—strapping trees, straight as the lines of Euclid, and free of branches, save at their tops. In the brisk wind those tops swayed a little and gave forth soft complaint. "Three times my age," he thought; "prime timber." The ride wound sharply and entered a belt of larch, whose steep rise entirely barred off the rather sinister sunset—a dark and wistful wood, delicate dun and grey, whose green shoots and crimson tips would have perfumed the evening coolness, but for the cigar smoke in his nostrils. "They'll have this spinney for pit props," he thought; and, taking a cross ride through it, he emerged in a heathery glen of birch trees. No forester, he wondered if they would make anything of those whitened, glistening shapes. His cigar had gone out now, and he leaned against one of the satin-smooth stems, under the lacery of twig and bud, sheltering the flame of a relighting match. A hare hopped away among the bilberry shoots; a jay, painted like a fan, squawked and flustered past him up the glen. Interested in birds, and wanting just one more jay to complete a fine stuffed group of them, Sir Arthur, though devoid of a gun, followed, to see where "the beggar's" nest was. The glen dipped rapidly, and the character of the timber changed, assuming greater girth and solidity. There was a lot of beech here—a bit he did not know, for though taken in by the beaters, no guns could be stationed there because of the lack of undergrowth. The jay had vanished, and light had begun to fail. "I must get back," he thought, "or I shall be late for dinner." He debated for a moment whether to retrace his steps or to cut across the beeches and regain the home covert by a loop. The jay, reappearing to the left, decided him to cross the beech grove. He did so, and took a narrow ride up through a dark bit of mixed timber with heavy undergrowth. The ride, after favouring the left for a little, bent away to the right; Sir Arthur followed it hurriedly, conscious that twilight was gathering fast. It must bend again to the left in a minute! It did, and then to the right, and, the undergrowth remaining thick, he could only follow on, or else retrace his steps. He followed on, beginning to get hot in spite of a sleet shower falling through the dusk. He was not framed by Nature for swift travelling—his

knees turning in and his toes turning out—but he went at a good
bat, uncomfortably aware that the ride was still taking him away
from home, and expecting it at any minute to turn left again. It
did not, and hot, out of breath, a little bewildered, he stood still
in three-quarter darkness, to listen. Not a sound save that of
wind in the tops of the trees, and a faint creaking of timber,
where two stems had grown athwart and were touching.

The path was a regular will-o'-the-wisp. He must make a bee
line of it through the undergrowth into another ride! He had
never before been amongst his timber in the dusk, and he found
the shapes of the confounded trees more weird, and more menacing, then he had ever dreamed of. He stumbled quickly on in and
out of them among the undergrowth, without coming to a ride.

"Here I am stuck in this damned wood!" he thought. To call
these formidably encircling shapes "a wood" gave him relief.
After all, it was *his* wood, and nothing very untoward could
happen to a man in his own wood, however dark it might get; he
could not be more than a mile and a half at the outside from his
dining-room! He looked at his watch, whose hands he could just
see—nearly half-past seven! The sleet had become snow, but it
hardly fell on him, so thick was the timber just here. But he had
no overcoat, and suddenly he felt that first sickening little drop in
his chest, which presages alarm. Nobody knew he was in this
damned wood! And in a quarter of an hour it would be black as
your hat! He *must* get on and out! The trees amongst which he
was stumbling produced quite a sick feeling now in one who
hitherto had never taken trees seriously. What monstrous
growths they were! The thought that seeds, tiny seeds or
saplings, planted by his ancestors, could attain such huge impending and imprisoning bulk—ghostly great growths mounting
up to heaven and shutting off this world, exasperated and
unnerved him. He began to run, caught his foot in a root and fell
flat on his face. The cursed trees seemed to have a down on him!
Rubbing elbows and forehead with his snow-wetted hands, he
leaned against a trunk to get his breath, and summon the sense
of direction to his brain. Once as a young man he had been
"bushed" at night in Vancouver Island; quite a scary business!
But he had come out all right, though his camp had been the
only civilised spot within a radius of twenty miles. And here he
was, on his own estate, within a mile or two of home, getting

into a funk. It was childish! And he laughed. The wind answered, sighing and threshing in the tree tops. There must be a regular blizzard blowing now, and, to judge by the cold, from the north—but whether north-east or north-west was the question. Besides, how to keep a definite direction without a compass, in the dark? The timber, too, with its thick trunks, diverted the wind into keen, directionless draughts. He looked up, but could make nothing of the two or three stars that he could see. It was a mess! And he lighted a second cigar with some difficulty, for he had begun to shiver. The wind in this blasted wood cut through his Norfolk jacket and crawled about his body, which had become hot from exertions, and now felt clammy and half-frozen. This would mean pneumonia, if he didn't look out! And, half feeling his way from trunk to trunk, he started on again, but for all he could tell he might be going round in a circle, might even be crossing rides without realising, and again that sickening drop occurred in his chest. He stood still and shouted. He had the feeling of shouting into walls of timber, dark and heavy, which threw the sound back at him.

"Curse you!" he thought; "I wish I'd sold you six months ago!" The wind fleered and mowed in the tree tops; and he started off again at a run in that dark wilderness; till, hitting his head against a low branch, he fell stunned. He lay several minutes unconscious, came to himself deadly cold, and struggled up on to his feet.

"By Jove!" he thought, with a sort of stammer in his brain; "this is a bad business! I may be out here all night!" For an unimaginative man, it was extraordinary what vivid images he had just then. He saw the face of the Government official who had bought his timber, and the slight grimace with which he had agreed to the price. He saw his butler, after the gong had gone, standing like a stuck pig by the sideboard, waiting for him to come down. What would they do when he didn't come? Would they have the *nous* to imagine that he might have lost his way in the coverts, and take lanterns and search for him? Far more likely they would think he had walked over to "Greenlands" or "Berrymoor", and stayed there to dinner. And, suddenly, he saw himself slowly freezing out here, in the snowy night, among this cursed timber. With a vigorous shake he butted again into the darkness among the tree trunks. He was angry now—with himself, with the night, with the trees; so angry that he actually let out with his fist at a trunk against which he had stumbled, and scored his knuckles. It was humiliating; and Sir Arthur Hirries was not accustomed to humiliation. In anybody else's wood—yes; but to be lost like this in one's own coverts! Well, if he had to walk all night, he would get out! And he plunged on doggedly in the darkness.

He was fighting with his timber now, as if the thing were alive and each tree an enemy. In the interminable stumbling exertion of that groping progress his angry mood gave place to half-comatose philosophy. Trees! His great-great-grandfather had planted them! His own was the fifth man's life, but the trees were almost as young as ever; they made nothing of a man's life! He sniggered: And a man made nothing of theirs! Did they know they were going to be cut down? All the better if they did, and were sweating in their shoes. He pinched himself—his thoughts were becoming so queer! He remembered that once, when his liver was out of order, trees had seemed to him like solid, tall diseases—bullbous, scarred, cavernous, witch-armed, fungoid emanations of the earth. Well, so they were! And he was among them, on a snowy pitch-black night, engaged in this death-struggle! The occurrence of the word death in his thoughts brought him up all standing. Why couldn't he concentrate his mind on getting out; why was he mooning about the life and nature of trees instead of trying to remember the conformation of his coverts, so as to re-kindle in himself some sense of general direction? He struck a number of matches to get a sight of his watch again. Great heaven! He had been walking nearly two hours since he last looked at it; and in what direction? They said a man in fog went round and round because of some kink in his brain! He began now to feel the trees, searching for a hollow trunk. A hollow would be some protection from the cold—his first conscious confession of exhaustion. He was not in training, and he was sixty-five. The thought: "I can't keep this up much longer," caused a second explosion of sullen anger. Damnation! Here he was—for all he could tell—standing where he had sat perhaps a dozen times on his spread shooting stick; watching sunlight on bare twigs, or the nose of his spaniel twitching beside him, listening to the tap of the beaters' sticks, and the shrill, drawn-out: "Marrk! Cock over!" Would they let the dogs out, to pick up his tracks? No! ten to one they would assume he was staying the night at the Summertons', or at Lady Mary's, as he had done before now, after dining there. And suddenly his strained heart leaped. He had struck a ride again! His mind slipped back into place like an elastic let-go, relaxed, quivering gratefully. He had only to follow this ride, and somewhere, somehow, he would come out. And be hanged if he would let them know what a fool he had made of himself! Right or left—which way? He turned so that the flying snow came on his back, hurrying forward between the denser darkness on either hand, where the timber stood in walls, moving his arms across and across his body, as if dragging a concertina to full stretch, to make sure that he was keeping in the path. He went what seemed an interminable way like this, till he was brought up all standing by trees, and could find no outlet, no continuation. Turning in his tracks, with the snow in his face now, he retraced his steps till once more he was brought up short by trees. He stood panting. It was ghastly—ghastly! And in a panic he dived this way and that to find the bend, the turning, the way on. The sleet stung his eyes, the wind fleered and whistled, the boughs sloughed and moaned. He struck matches, trying to shade them with his cold, wet hands, but one by one they went out, and still he found no turning. The ride must have a blind alley at either end, the turning be down the side somewhere! Hope revived in him. Never say die! He began a second retracing of his steps, feeling the trunks along one side, to find a gap. His breath came with difficulty. What would old Brodley say if he could see him, soaked, frozen, tired to death, stumbling along in the darkness among this cursed timber—old Brodley who had told him his heart was in poor case!... A gap? Ah! No trunks—a ride at last! He turned, felt a sharp pain in his knee and pitched forward. He could not rise—the knee dislocated six years ago was out again. Sir Arthur Hirries clenched his teeth. Nothing more could happen to him! But after a minute—blank and bitter—he began to crawl along the new ride. Oddly he felt less discouraged and alarmed on hands and knee—for he could use but one. It was a relief to have his eyes fixed on the ground, not peering at the tree trunks; or perhaps there was less strain for the moment on his heart. He crawled, stopping every minute or so to renew his strength. He crawled mechanically, waiting for his heart, his knee, his lungs to stop him. The earth was snowed over, and he could feel its cold wetness as he scraped along. Good tracks to follow, if anybody struck them! But in this dark forest—! In one of his halts, drying his hands as best he could, he struck a match, and sheltering it desperately, fumbled out his watch. Past ten o'clock! He wound the watch, and put it back against his heart. If only he could wind his heart! And squatting there he counted his matches—four! "Well," he thought grimly, "I won't light them to show me my blasted trees. I've got a cigar left; I'll keep them for that." And he crawled on again. He must keep going while he could!

He crawled till his heart and lungs and knee struck work; and, leaning his back against a tree, sat huddled together, so exhausted that he felt nothing save a sort of bitter heartache. He even dropped asleep, waking with a shudder, dragged from a dream armchair at the Club into this cold, wet darkness and the blizzard moaning in the trees. He tried to crawl again, but could not, and for some minutes stayed motionless, hugging his body with his arms. "Well," he thought vaguely, "I *have* done it!" His mind was in such lethargy that he could not even pity himself. His matches: could he make a fire? But he was no woodsman, and, though he groped around, could find no fuel that was not soaking wet. He scraped a hole and with what papers he had in his pockets tried to kindle the wet wood: No good! He had only two matches left now, and he remembered his cigar. He took it out, bit the end off, and began with infinite precautions to prepare for lighting it. The first burned, and the cigar drew. He had one match left, in case he dozed and let the thing go out. Looking up through the blackness he could see a star. He fixed his eyes on it, and leaning against the trunk, drew the smoke down into his lungs. With his arms crossed tightly on his breast he smoked very slowly. When it was finished—what? Cold, and the wind in the trees until the morning! Halfway through the cigar, he dozed off, slept a long time, and woke up so cold that he could barely summon vitality enough to strike his last match. By some miracle it burned, and he got his cigar to draw again. This time he smoked it nearly to its end, without mentality, almost without feeling, except the physical sense of bitter cold. Once with a sudden clearing of the brain, he thought faintly: "Thank God, I sold the trees, and they'll all come down!" The thought drifted away in frozen incoherence, drifted out like his cigar smoke into the sleet; and with a faint grin on his lips he dozed off again. . . .

An under-keeper found him at ten o'clock next morning, blue from cold, under a tall elm tree, within a mile of his bed, one leg stretched out, the other hunched up towards his chest, with its foot dug into the undergrowth for warmth, his head cuddled into the collar of his coat, his arms crossed on his breast. They said he must have been dead at least five hours. Along one side snow had drifted against him; but the trunk had saved his back and other side. Above him, the spindly top boughs of that tall tree were covered with green-gold clusters of tiny crinkled elm flowers, against a deep blue sky—gay as a song of perfect praise. The wind had dropped, and after the cold of the night the birds were singing their clearest in the sunshine.

They did not cut down the elm tree under which they found his body, with the rest of the sold timber, but put a little iron fence round it  and a little tablet on its trunk.

# THE ANGRY STREET

G. K. CHESTERTON

*Critic, poet and novelist, and one of the most colourful personalities of the Edwardian age, Gilbert Keith Chesterton made two distinguished excursions into the realms of fantasy fiction, firstly with his novel* The Man Who Was Thursday (1908), *about a group of seven men whose hobby is death, and* The Angry Street, *which he described as "a bad dream" and was written in the early 1930s. There is a timelessness about this piece that makes it an experience which might happen to anyone in any big city. If they should be that unlucky. . . .*

I CANNOT remember whether this tale is true or not. If I read it through very carefully I have a suspicion that I should come to the conclusion that it is not. But, unfortunately, I cannot read it through very carefully because, you see, it is not written yet. The image and idea of it clung to me through a great part of my boyhood; I may have dreamt it before I could talk; or told it to myself before I could read; or read it before I could remember. On the whole, however, I am certain that I did not read it. For children have very clear memories about things like that; and of the books of which I was really fond I can still remember not only the shape and bulk and binding, but even the position of the printed words on many of the pages. On the whole, I incline to the opinion that it happened to me before I was born.

At any rate, let us tell the story now with all the advantages of the atmosphere that has clung to it. You may suppose me, for the sake of argument, sitting at lunch in one of those quick-lunch restaurants in the City where men take their food so fast that it has none of the quality of food, and take their half-hour's vacation so fast that it has none of the qualities of leisure. To hurry through one's leisure is the most unbusiness-like of actions. They all wore tall shiny hats as if they could not lose an instant even to hang them on a peg, and they all had one eye a little off, hypnotised by the huge eye of the clock. In short, they were the slaves of the modern bondage, you could hear their fetters clanking. Each was, in fact, bound by a chain; the heaviest chain ever tied to a man—it is called a watch-chain.

Now, among these there entered and sat down opposite to me a man who almost immediately opened an uninterrupted monologue. He was like all the other men in dress, yet he was startlingly opposite to them all in manner. He wore a high shiny hat and a long frock coat, but he wore them as such solemn things were meant to be worn; he wore the silk hat as if it were a mitre, and the frock coat as if it were the ephod of a high priest. He not only hung his hat up on the peg, but he seemed (such was his stateliness) almost to ask permission of the hat for doing so, and to apologise to the peg for making use of it. When he had sat down on a wooden chair with the air of one considering its feelings and given a sort of slight stoop or bow to the wooden table itself, as if it were an altar, I could not help some comment springing to my lips. For the man was a big, sanguine-faced, prosperous-looking man, and yet he treated everything with a care that almost amounted to nervousness.

For the sake of saying something to express my interest I said, 'This furniture is fairly solid; but, of course, people do treat it much too carelessly.'

As I looked up doubtfully my eye caught his, and was fixed as his was fixed, in an apocalyptic stare. I had thought him ordinary as he entered, save for his strange, cautious manner; but if the other people had seen him they would have screamed and emptied the room. They did not see him, and they went on making a clatter with their forks, and a murmur with their conversation. But the man's face was the face of a maniac.

'Did you mean anything particular by that remark?' he asked at last, and the blood crawled back slowly into his face.

'Nothing whatever,' I answered. 'One does not mean anything here; it spoils people's digestion.'

He leaned back and wiped his broad forehead with a big handkerchief; and yet there seemed to be a sort of regret in his relief. 'I thought perhaps,' he said in a low voice, 'that another of them had gone wrong.'

'If you mean another digestion gone wrong,' I said, 'I never heard of one here that went right. This is the heart of the Empire, and the other organs are in an equally bad way.'

'No, I mean another street gone wrong,' and he said heavily and quietly, "but as I suppose that doesn't explain much to you, I think I shall have to tell you the story. I do so with all the less responsibility, because I know you won't believe it. For forty years of my life I invariably left my office, which is in Leadenhall Street, at half-past five in the afternoon, taking with me an umbrella in the right hand and a bag in the left hand. For forty years two months and four days I passed out of the side door, walked down the street on the left-hand side, took the first turning to the left and the third to the right, from where I bought an evening paper, followed the road on the right-hand side round two obtuse angles, and came out just outside a Metropolitan station, where I took a train home. For forty years two months and four days I fulfilled this course by accumulated habit: it was not a long street that I traversed, and it took me about four and a half minutes to do it. After forty years two months and four days, on the fifth day I went out in the same manner, with my umbrella in the right hand and my bag in the left, and I began to notice that walking along the familiar street tired me somewhat more than usual. At first I thought I must be breathless and out of condition; though this, again, seemed unnatural, as my habits had always been like clockwork. But after a little while I became convinced that the road was distinctly on a more steep incline than I had known previously; I was positively panting uphill. Owing to this no doubt the corner of the street seemed farther off than usual; and when I turned it I was convinced that I had turned down the wrong one. For now the street shot up quite a steep slant, such as one only sees in the hilly parts of London, and in this part there were no hills at all. Yet it was not the wrong street. The name written on it was the same; the shuttered shops were the same; the lamp-posts and the whole look of the perspective was the same; only it was tilted upwards like a lid. Forgetting any trouble about breathlessness or fatigue I ran furiously forward, and reached the second of my accustomed turnings, which ought to bring me almost within sight of the station. And as I turned that corner I nearly fell on the pavement. For now the street went up straight in front of my face like a steep staircase or the side of a pyramid.

There was not for miles around that place so much as a slope like that of Ludgate Hill. And this was a slope like that of the Matterhorn. The whole street had lifted itself like a single wave, and yet every speck and detail of it was the same, and I saw in the high distance, as at the top of an Alpine pass, picked out in pink letters, the name over my paper shop.

I ran on and on blindly now, passing all the shops, and coming to a part of the road where there was a long grey row of private houses. I had, I know not why, an irrational feeling that I was on a long iron bridge in empty space. An impulse seized me, and I pulled up the iron trap of a coal-hole. Looking down through it I saw empty space and the stars. When I looked up again a man was standing in his front garden, having apparently come out of his house; he was leaning over the railings and gazing at me. We were all alone on that nightmare road; his face was in shadow; his dress was dark and ordinary; but when I saw him standing so perfectly still I knew somehow that he was not of this world. And the stars behind his head were larger and fiercer than ought to be endured by the eyes of men.

"If you are a kind angel," I said, "or a wise devil, or have anything in common with mankind, tell me what is this street possessed of devils."

After a long silence he said, "What do you say it is?"

"It is Bumpton Street, of course," I snapped. "It goes to Oldgate Station."

"Yes," he admitted gravely, "it goes there sometimes. Just now, however, it is going to heaven."

"To heaven?" I said. "Why?"

"It is going to heaven for justice," he replied. "You must have treated it badly. Remember always there is one thing that cannot be endured by anybody or anything. That one unendurable thing is to be overworked and also neglected. For instance, you can overwork woman—everybody does. But you can't neglect women—I defy you to. At the same time, you can neglect tramps and gipsies and all the apparent refuse of the State, so long as you do not overwork them. But no beast of the field, no horse, no dog can endure long to be asked to do more than his work and yet have less than his honour.

"It is the same with streets. You have worked this street to death, and yet you have never remembered its existence. If you had owned a healthy democracy, even of pagans, they would have hung this street with garlands and given it the name of a god. Then it would have gone quietly. But at last the street has grown tired of your tireless insolence; and it is bucking and rearing its head to heaven. Have you never sat on a bucking horse?"

I looked at the long grey street, and for a moment it seemed to me to be exactly like the long grey neck of a horse flung up to heaven. But in a moment my sanity returned, and I said, "But this is all nonsense. Streets go to the place they have to go to. A street must always go to its end."

"Why do you think so of a street?" he asked, standing very still.

"Because I have always seen it do the same thing," I replied, in reasonable anger. "Day after day, year after year, it has always gone to Oldgate Station; day after. . . ."

I stopped, for he had flung up his head with the fury of the road in revolt.

"And you?" he cried terribly. "What do you think the road thinks of you? Does the road think you are alive? Are you alive? Day after day, year after year, you have gone to Oldgate Station. . . ." Since then I have respected the things called inanimate!'

And bowing slightly to the mustard-pot, the man in the restaurant withdrew.

# THE CALL OF WINGS

## AGATHA CHRISTIE

*Most of Agatha Christie's work has been in the traditional crime genre, but early in her career she wrote a selection of horror tales which appeared under the collective title* The Hound of Death *(1933). From this volume—now long out of print—I have selected the following item, which has a style and impact comparable to the very best in macabre fiction.*

### I

SILAS HAMER heard it first on a wintry night in February. He and Dick Borrow had walked from a dinner given by Bernard Selden, the nerve specialist. Borrow had been unusually silent, and Silas Hamer asked him with some curiosity what he was thinking about. Borrow's answer was unexpected.

"I was thinking, that of all these men tonight, only two amongst them could lay claim to happiness. And that these two, strangely enough, were you and I!"

The word "strangely" was apposite, for no two men could be more dissimilar than Richard Borrow, the hard-working east-end parson, and Silas Hamer, the sleek complacent man whose millions were a matter of household knowledge.

"It's odd, you know," mused Borrow, "I believe you're the only contented millionaire I've ever met."

Hamer was silent a moment. When he spoke his tone had altered.

"I used to be a wretched shivering little newspaper boy. I wanted then—what I've got now—the comfort and the luxury of money, not its power. I wanted money, not to wield as a force, but to spend lavishly—on myself! I'm frank about it, you see. Money can't buy everything, they say. Very true. But it can buy everything I want—therefore I'm satisfied. I'm a materialist, Borrow, out and out a materialist!"

The broad glare of the lighted thoroughfare confirmed this confession of faith. The sleek lines of Silas Hamer's body were amplified by the heavy fur-lined coat, and the white light emphasised the thick rolls of flesh beneath his chin. In contrast to him walked Dick Borrow, with the thin ascetic face and the star-gazing fanatical eyes.

"It's *you*," said Hammer with emphasis, "that I can't understand."

Borrow smiled.

"I live in the midst of misery, want, starvation—all the ills of the flesh! And a predominant Vision upholds me. It's not easy to understand unless you believe in Visions, which I gather you don't."

"I don't believe," said Silas Hamer stolidly, "in anything I can't see and hear and touch."

"Quite so. That's the difference between us. Well, good-bye, the earth now swallows me up!"

They had reached the doorway of a lighted tube station, which was Borrow's route home.

Hamer proceeded alone. He was glad he had sent away the car tonight and elected to walk home. The air was keen and frosty, his senses were delightfully conscious of the enveloping warmth of the fur-lined coat.

He paused for an instant on the kerbstone before crossing the road. A great motor bus was heavily ploughing its way towards him. Hamer, with the feeling of infinite leisure, waited for it to pass. If he were to cross in front of it he would have to hurry—and hurry was distasteful to him.

By his side a battered derelict of the human race rolled drunkenly off the pavement. Hamer was aware of a shout, an ineffectual swerve of the motor bus, and then—he was looking stupidly, with a gradually awakening horror, at a limp inert heap of rags in the middle of the road.

A crowd gathered magically, with a couple of policemen and the bus driver as its nucleus. But Hamer's eyes were riveted in horrified fascination on that lifeless bundle that had once been a man—a man like himself! He shuddered as at some menace.

"Dahn't yer blime yerself, guv'nor," remarked a rough-looking man at his side. "Yer couldn't 'a done nothin'. 'E was done for anyways."

Hamer stared at him. The idea that it was possible in any way
to save the man had quite honestly never occurred to him. He
scouted the notion now as an absurdity. Why, if he had been so
foolish, he might at this moment. . . . His thoughts broke off
abruptly, and he walked away from the crowd. He felt himself
shaking with a nameless unquenchable dread. He was forced to
admit to himself that he was *afraid*—horribly afraid—of
Death . . . Death that came with dreadful swiftness and remorse-
less certainty to rich and poor alike. . . .

He walked faster, but the new fear was still with him,
enveloping him in its cold and chilling grasp.

He wondered at himself, for he knew that by nature he was
no coward. Five years ago, he reflected, this fear would not
have attacked him. For then Life had not been so sweet. . . .
Yes, that was it; love of Life was the key to the mystery. The
zest of living was at its height for him; it knew but one
menace, Death, the destroyer!

He turned out of the lighted thoroughfare. A narrow passageway, between high walls, offered a short-cut to the Square
where his house, famous for its art treasures, was situated.

The noise of the streets behind him lessened and faded, the
soft thud of his own footsteps was the only sound to be heard.

And then out of the gloom in front of him came another
sound. Sitting against the wall was a man playing the flute. One
of the enormous tribe of street musicians, of course, but why
had he chosen such a peculiar spot? Surely at this time of night
the police— Hamer's reflections were interrupted suddenly as
he realised with a shock that the man had no legs. A pair of
crutches rested against the wall beside him. Hamer saw now
that it was not a flute he was playing but a strange instrument
whose notes were much higher and clearer than those of a flute.

The man played on. He took no notice of Hamer's approach.
His head was flung far back on his shoulders, as though
uplifted in the joy of his own music, and the notes poured out
clearly and joyously, rising higher and higher. . . .

It was a strange tune—strictly speaking, it was not a tune at
all, but a single phrase, not unlike the slow turn given out by
the violins of *Rienzi,* repeated again and again, passing from key
to key, from harmony to harmony, but always rising and
attaining each time to a greater and more boundless freedom.

It was unlike anything Hamer had ever heard. There was something strange about it, something inspiring—and uplifting . . . it . . . . He caught frantically with both hands to a projection in the wall beside him. He was conscious of one thing only—*that he must keep down*—at all costs he must *keep down*. . . .

He suddenly realised that the music had stopped. The legless man was reaching out for his crutches. And here was he, Silas Hamer, clutching like a lunatic at a stone buttress, for the simple reason that he had had the utterly preposterous notion—absurd on the face of it!—that he was rising from the ground—that the music was carrying him upwards. . . .

He laughed. What a wholly mad idea! Of course his feet had never left the earth for a moment, but what a strange hallucination! The quick tap-tapping of wood on the pavement told him that the cripple was moving away. He looked after him until the man's figure was swallowed up in the gloom. An odd fellow!

He proceeded on his way more slowly; he could not efface from his mind the memory of that strange impossible sensation when the ground had failed beneath his feet. . . .

And then on impulse he turned and followed hurriedly in the direction the other had taken. The man could not have gone far—he would soon overtake him.

He shouted as soon as he caught sight of the maimed figure swinging itself slowly along.

"Hi! One minute."

The man stopped and stood motionless until Hamer came abreast of him. A lamp burned just over his head and revealed every feature. Silas Hamer caught his breath in involuntary surprise. The man possessed the most singularly beautiful head he had ever seen. He might have been any age; assuredly he was not a boy, yet youth was the most predominant characteristic—youth and vigour in passionate intensity!

Hamer found an odd difficulty in beginning his conversation.

"Look here," he said awkwardly, "I want to know—what was that thing you were playing just now?"

The man smiled. . . . With his smile the world seemed suddenly to leap into joyousness. . . .

"It was an old tune—a very old tune. . . . Years old—centuries old."

He spoke with an odd purity and distinctness of enunciation, giving equal value to each syllable. He was clearly not an Englishman, yet Hamer was puzzled as to his nationality.

"You're not English? Where do you come from?"

Again the broad joyful smile.

"From over the sea, sir. I came—a long time ago—a very long time ago."

"You must have had a bad accident. Was it lately?"

"Some time now, sir."

"Rough luck to loose both legs."

"It was well," said the man very calmly. He turned his eyes with a strange solemnity on his interlocutor.

"They were evil."

Hamer dropped a shilling in his hand and turned away. He was puzzled and vaguely disquieted. "They were evil!" What a strange thing to say! Evidently an operation for some form of disease, but—how odd it had sounded.

Hamer went home thoughtful. He tried in vain to dismiss the incident from his mind. Lying in bed, with the first incipient sensation of drowsiness stealing over him, he heard a neighbouring clock strike one. One clear stroke and then silence—silence that was broken by a faint familiar sound. . . . Recognition came leaping. Hamer felt his heart beating quickly. It was the man in the passageway playing, somewhere not far distant. . . .

The notes came gladly, the slow turn with its joyful call, the same haunting little phrase. . . . "It's uncanny," murmured Hamer, "it's uncanny. It's got wings to it. . . ."

Clearer and clearer, higher and higher—each wave rising above the last, and catching *him* up with it. This time he did not struggle, he let himself go. . . . Up—up. . . . The waves of sound were carrying him higher and higher. . . . Triumphant and free, they swept on.

Higher and higher. . . . They had passed the limits of human sound now, but they still continued—rising, ever rising. . . . Would they reach the final goal, the full perfection of height?

Rising. . . .

*Something* was pulling—pulling him downwards. Something big and heavy and insistent. It pulled remorselessly—pulled him back, and down . . . down. . . .

He lay in bed gazing at the window opposite. Then, breathing heavily and painfully, he stretched an arm out of bed. The movement seemed curiously cumbrous to him. The softness of the bed was oppressive, oppressive too were the heavy curtains over the window that blocked out light and air. The ceiling seemed to press down upon him. He felt stifled and choked. He moved slightly under the bed clothes, and the weight of his body seemed to him the most oppressive of all. . . .

II

"I want your advice, Seldon."

Seldon pushed back his chair an inch or so from the table. He had been wondering what was the object of this tête-à-tête dinner. He had seen little of Hamer since the winter, and he was aware tonight of some indefinable change in his friend.

"It's just this," said the millionaire. "I'm worried about myself."

Seldon smiled as he looked across the table.

"You're looking in the pink of condition."

"It's not that." Hamer paused a minute, then added quietly. "I'm afraid I'm going mad."

The nerve specialist glanced up with a sudden keen interest. He poured himself out a glass of port with a rather slow movement, and then said quietly, but with a sharp glance at the other man: "What makes you think that?"

"Something that's happened to me. Something inexplicable, unbelievable. It can't be true, so I must be going mad."

"Take your time," said Seldon, "and tell me about it."

"I don't believe in the supernatural," began Hamer. "I never have. But this thing. . . . Well, I'd better tell you the whole story from the beginning. It began last winter one evening after I had dined with you."

Then briefly and concisely he narrated the events of his walk home and the strange sequel.

"That was the beginning of it all. I can't explain it to you properly—the feeling, I mean—but it was wonderful! Unlike anything I've ever felt or dreamed. Well, it's gone on ever since. Not every night, just now and then. The music, the feeling of being uplifted, the soaring flight . . . and then the terrible drag, the pull back to earth, and afterwards the pain, the actual physical pain of the awakening. It's like coming down from a high mountain—you know the pains in the ears one gets? Well, this is the same thing, but intensified—and with it goes the awful sense of *weight*—of being hemmed in, stifled. . . ."

He broke off and there was a pause.

"Already the servants think I'm mad. I couldn't bear the root and the walls—I've had a place arranged up at the top of the house, open to the sky, with no furniture or carpets, or any stifling things. . . . But even the houses all round are nearly as bad. It's open country I want, somewhere where one can breathe. . . ." He looked across at Seldon "Well what do you say? Can you explain it?"

"H'm," said Seldon. "Plenty of explanations. You've been hypnotised, or you've hypnotised yourself. Your nerves have gone wrong. Or it may be merely a dream."

Hamer shook his head. "None of those explanations will do."

"And there are others," said Seldon slowly, "but they're not generally admitted."

"*You* are prepared to admit them?"

"On the whole, yes! There's a great deal we can't understand which can't possibly be explained normally. We've any amount to find out still, and I for one believe in keeping an open mind."

"What do you advise me to do?" asked Hamer after a silence.

Seldon leaned forward briskly. "One of several things. Go away from London, seek out your 'open country'. The dreams may cease."

"I can't do that," said Hamer quickly. "It's come to this that I can't do without them. I don't want to do without them."

"Ah! I guessed as much. Another alternative, find this fellow, this cripple. You're endowing him now with all sorts of supernatural attributes. Talk to him. Break the spell."

Hamer shook his head again.

"Why not?"

"I'm afraid," said Hamer simply.

Seldon made a gesture of impatience. "Don't believe in it all so blindly! This tune now, the medium that starts it all, what is it like?"

Hamer hummed it, and Seldon listened with a puzzled frown.

"Rather like a bit out of the Overture to *Rienzi*. There *is* something uplifting about it—it had wings. But I'm not carried off the earth! Now, these flights of yours, are they all exactly the same?"

"No, no." Hamer leaned forward eagerly. "They develop. Each time I see a little more. It's difficult to explain. You see, I'm always conscious of reaching a certain point—the music carried me there—not direct, but by a succession of *waves,* each reaching higher than the last, until the highest point where one can go no further. I stay there until I'm dragged back. It isn't a place, it's more a *state*. Well, not just at first, but after a little while, I began to understand that there were other things all round me waiting until I was able to perceive them. Think of a kitten. It has eyes, but at first it can't see with them. It's blind and had to learn to see. Well, that was what it was to me. Mortal eyes and ears were no good to me, but there was something corresponding to them that hadn't. yet been developed—something that wasn't *bodily* at all. And little by little that grew ... there were sensationt of light ... then of sound ... then of colour. ... All very vague and unformulated. It was more the knowledge of things than seeing or hearing them. First it was light, a light that grew stronger and clearer ... then sand, great stretches of reddish sand. .. and here and there straight long lines of water like canals—"

Seldon drew in his breath sharply. "*Canals!* That's interesting. Go on."

"But these things didn't matter—they didn't count any longer. The real things were the things I couldn't see yet—but I heard them. ... It was a sound like the rushing of wings ... somehow I can't explain why, it was glorious! There's nothing like it here. And then came another glory—*I saw them*—the Wings! Oh, Seldon, the Wings!"

"But what were they? Men—angels—birds?"

"I don't know. I couldn't see—not yet. But the colour of them! *Wing colour*—we haven't got it here—it's a wonderful colour."

"Wing colour?" repeated Seldon. "What's it like?"

Hamer flung up his head impatiently. "How can I tell you? Explain the colour blue to a blind person! It's a colour you've never seen—Wing colour!"

"Well?"

"Well? That's all. That's as far as I've got. But each time the coming back has been worse—more painful. I can't understand that. I'm convinced my body never leaves the bed. In this place I get to I'm convinced I've got no *physical* presence. Why should it hurt so confoundedly then?"

Seldon shook his head in silence.

"It's something awful—the coming back. The *pull* of it—then the pain, pain in every limb and every nerve, and my ears feel as though they were bursting. Then everything *presses* so, the weight of it all, the dreadful sense of imprisonment. I want light, air, space—above all *space* to breathe in! And I want freedom."

"And what," asked Seldon, "of all the other things that used to mean so much to you?"

"That's the worst of it. I care for them still as much as, if not more than, ever. And these things, comfort, luxury, pleasure, seem to pull opposite ways to the Wings. It's a perpetual struggle between them—and I can't see how it's going to end."

Seldon sat silent. The strange tale he had been listening to was fantastic enough in all truth. Was it all a delusion, a wild hallucination—or could it by any possibility be true? And if so, why *Hamer*, of all men. . . ? Surely the materialist, the man who loved the flesh and denied the spirit, was the last man to see the sights of another world.

Across the table Hamer watched him anxiously.

"I suppose," said Seldon slowly, "that you can only wait. Wait and see what happens."

"I can't! I tell you I can't! Your saying that shows you don't understand. It's tearing me in two, this awful struggle—this killing long-drawn-out fight between—between—" He hesitated.

"The flesh and the spirit?" suggested Seldon.

Hamer stared heavily in front of him. "I suppose one might call it that. Anyway, it's unbearable. . . . I can't get free. . . ."

Again Bernard Seldon shook his head. He was caught up in the grip of the inexplicable. He made one more suggestion.

"If I were you," he advised. "I would get hold of that cripple."

But as he went home he muttered to himself: "*Canals*—I wonder."

### III

Silas Hamer went out of the house the following morning with a new determination in his step. He had decided to take Seldon's advice and find the legless man. Yet inwardly he was convinced that his search would be in vain and that the man would have vanished as completely as though the earth had swallowed him up.

The dark buildings on either side of the passageway shut out the sunlight and left it dark and mysterious. Only in one place, half-way up it, there was a break in the wall, and through it there fell a shaft of golden light that illuminated with radiance a figure sitting on the ground. A figure—yes, it was the man!

The instrument of pipes leaned against the wall beside his crutches, and he was covering the paving stones with designs in coloured chalk. Two were completed, sylvan scenes of marvellous beauty and delicacy, swaying trees and a leaping brook that seemed alive.

And again Hamer doubted. Was this man a mere street musician, a pavement artist? Or was he something more. . . .

Suddenly the millionaire's self-control broke down, and he cried fiercely and angrily: "Who are you? For God's sake, who are you?"

The man's eyes met his, smiling.

"Why don't you answer? Speak, man, speak!"

Then he noticed that the man was drawing with incredible rapidity on a bare slab of stone. Hamer followed the movement with his eyes. . . . A few bold strokes, and giant trees took form. Then, seated on a boulder . . . a man . . . playing an instrument of pipes. A man with a strangely beautiful face—*and goat's legs*. . . .

The cripple's hand made a swift movement. The man still sat on the rock, but the goat's legs were gone. Again his eyes met Hamer's.

"They were evil," he said.

Hamer stared, fascinated. For the face before him was the face of the picture, but strangely and incredibly beautified. . . . Purified from all but an intense and exquisite joy of living.

Hamer turned and almost fled down the passageway into the bright sunlight, repeating to himself incessantly: "It's impossible. Impossible. . . . I'm mad—dreaming!" But the face haunted him—the face of Pan. . . .

He went into the Park and sat on a chair. It was a deserted

hour. A few nursemaids with their charges sat in the shade of the trees, and dotted here and there in the stretches of green, like islands in the sea, lay the recumbent forms of men. . . .

The words "a wretched tramp" were to Hamer an epitome of misery. But suddenly, today, he envied them. . . .

They seemed to him of all created beings the only free ones. The earth beneath them, the sky above them, the world to wander in . . . they were not hemmed in or chained.

Like a flash it came to him that that which bound him so remorselessly was the thing he had worshipped and prized above all others—wealth! He had thought it the strongest thing on earth, and now, wrapped round by its golden strength, he saw the truth of his words. It was his money that held him in bondage. . . .

But was it? Was that really it? Was there a deeper and more pointed truth that he had not seen? Was it the money or was it his own love of money? He was bound in fetters of his own making; not wealth itself, but love of wealth was the chain.

He knew now clearly the two forces that were tearing at him, the warm composite strength of materialism that enclosed and surrounded him, and, opposed to it, the clear imperative call—he named it to himself the Call of the Wings.

And while the one fought and clung the other scorned war and would not stoop to struggle. It only called—called unceasingly. . . . He heard it so clearly that it almost spoke in words.

"You cannot make terms with Me," it seemed to say. "For I am above all other things. If you follow my call you must give up all else and cut away the forces that hold you. For only the Free shall follow where I lead. . . ."

"I can't," cried Hamer. "I can't. . . ."

A few people turned to look at the big man who sat talking to himself.

So sacrifice was being asked of him, the sacrifice of that which was most dear to him, that which was part of himself.

*Part of himself*—he remembered the man without legs. . . .

IV

"What in the name of Fortune brings you here?" asked Borrow.

Indeed the east-end mission was an unfamiliar background to Hamer.

"I've listened to a good many sermons," said the millionaire, "all saying what could be done if you people had funds. I've just come to tell you this: you can have the funds."

"Very good of you," answered Borrow, with some surprise. " A big subscription, eh?"

Hamer smiled dryly. "I should say so. Just every penny I've got."

"*What?*"

Hamer rapped out details in a brisk businesslike manner. Borrow's head was whirling.

"You—you mean to say that you're making over your entire fortune to be devoted to the relief of the poor in the East-End, with myself appointed as trustee?"

"That's it."

"But why—*why*?"

"I can't explain," said Hamer slowly. "Remember our talk about visions last February? Well, a vision has got hold of me."

"It's splendid!" Borrow leaned forward, his eyes gleaming.

"There's nothing particularly splendid about it," said Hamer grimly. "I don't care a button about poverty in the East-End. All they want is grit! *I* was poor enough—and I got out of it. But I've got to get rid of the money, and these tom-fool societies shan't get hold of it. You're a man I can trust. Feed bodies or souls with it—preferably the former. I've been hungry, but you can do as you like."

"There's never been such a thing known," stammered Borrow.

"The whole thing's done and finished with," continued Hamer. "The lawyers have fixed it up at last, and I've signed everything. I can tell you I've been busy this last fortnight. It's almost as difficult getting rid of a fortune as making one."

"But you—you've kept *something*?"

"Not a penny," said Hamer cheerfully. "At least—that's not quite true. I've just twopence in my pocket." He laughed.

He said good-bye to his bewildered friend, and walked out of the mission into the narrow evil-smelling streets. The words he had said so gaily just now came back to him with an aching sense of loss. "Not a penny!" Of all his vast wealth he had kept nothing. He was afraid now—afraid of poverty and hunger and cold. Sacrifice had no sweetness for him.

Yet behind it all he was conscious that the weight and menace of things had lifted, he was no longer oppressed and bound down. The severing of the chain had seared and torn him, but the vision of freedom was there to strengthen him. His material needs might dim the Call, but they could not deaden it, for he knew it to be a thing of immortality that could not die.

There was a touch of autumn in the air, and the wind blew chill. He felt the cold and shivered, and then, too, he was hungry—he had forgotten to have any lunch. It brought the future very near to him. It was incredible that he should have given it all up; the ease, the comfort, the warmth! His body cried out impotently.... And then once again there came to him a glad and uplifting sense of freedom.

Hamer hesitated. He was near a Tube station. He had twopence in his pocket. The idea came to him to journey by it to the Park where he had watched the recumbent idlers a fortnight ago. Beyond this whim he did not plan for the future. He believed honestly enough now that he was mad—sane people did not act as he had done. Yet, if so, madness was a wonderful and amazing thing.

Yes, he would go now to the open country of the Park, and there was a special significance to him in reaching it by Tube. For the Tube represented to him all the horrors of buried, shut-in life.... He would ascend from its imprisonment free to the wide green and the trees that concealed the menace of the pressing houses.

The lift bore him swiftly and relentlessly downward. The air was heavy and lifeless. He stood at the extreme end of the platform, away from the mass of people. On his left was the opening of the tunnel from which the train, snakelike, would presently emerge. He felt the whole place to be subtly evil. There was no one near him but a hunched-up lad sitting on a seat, sunk, it seemed, in a drunken stupor.

In the distance came the faint menacing roar of the train. The lad rose from his seat and shuffled unsteadily to Hamer's side, where he stood on the edge of the platform peering into the tunnel.

Then—it happened so quickly as to be almost incredible—he lost his balance and fell. . . .

A hundred thoughts rushed simultaneously to Hamer's brain. He saw a huddled heap run over by a motor bus, and heard a hoarse voice saying: "Dahn't yer blime yerself, guv'nor Yer couldn't 'a done nothin'." And with that came the knowledge that *this* life could only be saved, if it were saved, by himself. There was no one else near, and the train was close. . . . It all passed through his mind with lightning rapidity. He experienced a curious calm lucidity of thought.

He had one short second in which to decide, and he knew in that moment that his fear of Death was unabated. He was horribly afraid. And then—was it not a forlorn hope? A useless throwing away of two lives?

To the terrified spectators at the other end of the platform there seemed no gap between the boy's fall and the man's jump after him—and then the train, rushing round the curve of the tunnel, powerless to pull up in time.

Swiftly Hamer caught up the lad in his arms. No natural gallant impulse swayed him, his shivering flesh was but obeying the command of the alien spirit that called for sacrifice. With a last effort he flung the lad forward on to the platform, falling himself. . . .

Then suddenly his Fear died. The material world held him down no longer. He was free of his shackles. He fancied for a moment that he heard the joyous piping of Pan. Then—nearer and louder—swallowing up all else—came the glad rushing of innumerable Wings . . . enveloping and encircling him. . . .

# THE CHERRIES

### LAWRENCE DURRELL

*Although there are macabre elements in several of Lawrence Durrell's novels, it came as something of a surprise to me—as it doubtless will be to the reader—that he should have written such an out-and-out weird tale as* The Cherries. *It is therefore my pleasure to revive here an extraordinary little story (written in the 1940s) which may well be the strangest thing you'll ever read. . . .*

I LIVED in the smallest room, right at the very top of the stairs. There was a white apple on the door which I had to take in my hand and turn before I could get inside. On the walls were strings of cherries: from top to bottom. In the summer they made me feel thirsty. Once I tried to take some of the picture to eat, but that wasn't much of a success. Plaster and lime tasted very sharp. Afterwards, of course, I laughed to think of my silliness; but my tongue was very sore. That lasted for a long time: but, then, I was there for a long time.

I remember the streets: very long and full of stones that fitted smoothly together. They looked like black water. The lamps wet me with their yellow water as I passed. That was real. Often I had to change my clothes, and I was very cold. My pyjamas were dry, with a red stripe and a blue one. I loved them. Sometimes I stayed awake rubbing my chest against them and pressing down my arms to try to make them tickle me. I liked the red stripe much better than the blue, but I never took them outside, for fear of the lamps. Oh! I was much too clever to go and get them wet.

I used to walk very slowly in the night-time, and feel my coat dragging on my shoulders. Sometimes that seemed funny, too, and I laughed out loud; but I could never laugh at the sound my feet made on the streets. They were dull and sober, and, as they went on and on, they slapped the stones. The noise reminded me of solemn things. You cannot laugh out loud in a church, can you? So I used to look down at them, watching them go on and on under me, as if I didn't really own them. I was as quiet as a little mouse.

There were lots of people in the house where I lived, and they all had a key. She gave me a key too, and I enjoyed putting it in the lock. The door was beautiful. It had a sign of figures on it: like this—33. Sometimes I knew it was just thirty-three, but at others it seemed to be a sign, not a number. Once in the night I stared at it until it looked like a face. I wrote it on the wall in my room, but she came in the morning and was very angry. Her voice was rusty. It worried me. She said I was not to lick the wall-paper, even if I did feel thirsty. I was afraid of her. She looked mad. I tried not to meet her on the landing, where the glass window made her face look green.

I went out, mostly to a small house with lights and tables; always at night. I was happy there. I had lots of pretty things to eat. My hands would feel quiet when I was there, and not as if they wanted to be touching things, or moving among each other.

It was here I first saw her.

She sat with the man Boris, whose voice was clockwork, like his face. He did not laugh, ever. When I saw her I began to shiver, and the inside of my thighs felt cold. She smiled and took her eyes away. She was sitting with the man Boris. She took her eyes away.

I went to their table then, taking her some flowers from a vase, and she was happy, looking at me with wide eyes. But the man Boris put his hand on my arm and spoke with his fingers. I said "If music be the food of love," right out loud, again and again: "If music be the food of love." But when she turned her head away my hands felt restless.

I ate the food, but 1 was clever. 1 watched them. When they got up I got up too and followed them. I walked very slowly behind them for a little while. I had nothing to give her, so I tore off my fingernail and ran to the man Boris.

"Give it to her," I said. "Give her a present."

His eyes played hide-and-seek in his beard, which seemed funny. So I laughed just a bit as I sucked my hand. She opened her mouth so as to let me see the little teeth in it. After that I went away very quickly.

That night I saw her face. I drew it on the wall above my bed. Like this: 33. It was pretty, and I felt a pain in my side. It stopped me from sleeping, so I read a book which said, at the top of the page:

> And I will make a sharp knife of my love,
> To turn upon myself, to search among my body
> For the vessel that pains,
> Pains me forever with a sense of her.

The next day 1 went there again, among the lights. I ran quickly, with my coat dangling round me. I was happy. My shoes were yellow and noisy.

But she was not there. I waited and waited, but she did not come. The man Boris did not come. Every time I remembered her open mouth with the small teeth in it I shivered, and it hurt me on the left side. It hurt me. But she did not come. And again that night I could not sleep. I saw her on the wall.

For many days after that I waited, but she did not come. I still had the pain, low down on the left side, and I still couldn't sleep much. Sometimes I sang moony songs in the night, but the man across the landing said I sounded like a dog or something. I did not tell him of the pain.

I said, pretending: "It must be the window creaking." Of course I was only pretending. "It's a hinge," I said.

I think he believed me, because he turned round and went away.

How very long I waited! What a long time it was! It went on and on and on, I don't know how long for; but I always waited for her. Neither she nor the man Boris came. The night became a very long time. One night I read the book again:

> And I will make a sharp knife of my love,
> To turn upon myself, to search among my body
> For the vessel that pains,
> Pains me forever with a sense of her.

Of course it seemed very solemn. I drank my crying as it came out of my eyes. Then I took off my clothes and stood in front of the mirror. I looked thin, but I had stopped crying. I put my hand on my left side, over the pain, so that I couldn't miss the right place. I could see the cherries behind my reflection in the mirror. The razor whispered, as if it were cutting silk. Then I sat on the bed because I felt just a little bit tired. Somehow I felt a bit open, too. But I could still see myself in the mirror, with the cherries behind my reflection. I felt thirsty, but I knew I mustn't lick them.

I was very careful. My hands got a bit slippery, but I didn't mind. Everything seemed to get a little further away from me. I looked up, but there were no vessels; only red tubes curled up. I looked carefully.

Then they all came in from outside, making a noise, and stood at the door. I noticed how big their eyes were. They shouted and moved their hands very quickly. I began to hiccup a lot.

I said: "I haven't licked the cherries again. Please, I haven't licked the cherries. . . ."

They didn't seem to understand me, and I was afraid, so I hid my face in my hands. There was a noise on the landing, and everything seemed to get farther away. I peeped through my fingers once. The cherries were still there.

# A MAN FROM GLASGOW

W. SOMERSET MAUGHAM

*Throughout his life Somerset Maugham was deeply interested in the super-
natural and in 1908 wrote a novel based on the activities of the notorious
occultist, Aleister Crowley, entitled* The Magician, *following this in
1945 with a rather more significant work on mysticism,* The Razor's
Edge. *It is perhaps appropriate, then, that it should be Somerset
Maugham who introduces us for the first time in this book to that
traditional figure of the macabre story, the ghost. Take note, though, A
Man From Glasgow (1947) is only a ghost story in that it recounts
the experiences of a "haunted" man; in all other aspects it is the kind
of finely wrought piece that makes it unlike any other "strange
experience" story you might encounter.*

IT IS not often that anyone entering a great city for the first time
has the luck to witness such an incident as engaged the poet
Shelley's attention when he drove into Naples. A youth ran out
of a shop pursued by a man armed with a knife. The man
overtook him and with one blow in the neck laid him dead on
the road. Shelley had a tender heart. He didn't look upon it as a
bit of local colour; he was seized with horror and indignation.
But when he expressed his emotions to a Calabrian priest who
was travelling with him, a fellow of gigantic strength and stature,
the priest laughed heartily and attempted to quiz him. Shelley
says he never felt such an inclination to beat anyone.

I have never seen anything so exciting as that, but the first
time I went to Algeciras I had an experience that seemed to me
far from ordinary. Algeciras was then an untidy, neglected town.
I arrived somewhat late at night and went to an inn on the quay.
It was rather shabby, but it had a fine view of Gibraltar, solid
and matter of fact, across the bay. The moon was full. The office
was on the first floor, and a slatternly maid, when I asked for a
room, took me upstairs. The landlord was playing cards. He

seemed little pleased to see me. He looked me up and down, curtly gave me a number, and then, taking no further notice of me, went on with his game.

When the maid had shown me to my room I asked her what I could have to eat.

"What you like," she answered.

I knew well enough the unreality of the seeming profusion.

"What have you got in the house?"

"You can have eggs and ham."

The look of the hotel had led me to guess that I should get little else. The maid led me to a narrow room with whitewashed walls and a low ceiling in which was a long table laid already for the next day's luncheon. With his back to the door sat a tall man, huddled over a *brasero,* the round brass dish of hot ashes which is erroneously supposed to give sufficient warmth for the temperate winter of Andalusia. I sat down at the table and waited for my scanty meal. I gave the stranger an idle glance. He was looking at me, but meeting my eyes he quickly turned away. I waited for my eggs. When at last the maid brought them he looked up again.

"I want you to wake me in time for the first boat," he said.

"*Si, señor.*"

His accent told me that English was his native tongue, and the breadth of his build, his strongly marked features, led me to suppose him a northerner. The hardy Scot is far more often found in Spain than the Englishman. Whether you go to the rich mines of Rio Tinto, or to the bodegas of Jerez, to Seville or to Cadiz, it is the leisurely speech of beyond the Tweed that you hear. You will meet Scotsmen in the olive groves of Carmona, on the railway between Algeciras and Bobadilla, and even in the remote cork woods of Merida.

I finished eating and went over to the dish of burning ashes. It was midwinter and the windy passage across the bay had chilled my blood. The man pushed his chair away as I drew mine forwards.

"Don't move," I said. "There's heaps of room for two."

I lit a cigar and offered one to him. In Spain the Havana from Gib is never unwelcome.

"I don't mind if I do," he said, stretching out his hand.

I recognised the singing speech of Glasgow. But the stranger

was not talkative, and my efforts at conversation broke down
before his monosyllables. We smoked in silence. He was even
bigger than I had thought, with great broad shoulders and
ungainly limbs; his face was sunburned, his hair short and
grizzled. His features were hard; mouth, ears and nose were large
and heavy and his skin much wrinkled. His blue eyes were pale.
He was constantly pulling his ragged, grey moustache. It was a
nervous gesture that I found faintly irritating. Presently I felt
that he was looking at me, and the intensity of his stare grew so
irksome that I glanced up expecting him, as before, to drop his
eyes. He did, indeed, for a moment, but then raised them again.
He inspected me from under his long, bushy eyebrows.

"Just come from Gib?" he asked suddenly.

"Yes."

"I'm going back tomorrow—on my way home. Thank God."

He said the last two words so fiercely that I smiled.

"Don't you like Spain?"

"Oh, Spain's all right."

"Have you been here long?"

"Too long. Too long."

He spoke with a kind of gasp. I was surprised at the emotion
my casual inquiry seemed to excite in him. He sprang to his feet
and walked backwards and forwards. He stamped to and fro like
a caged beast, pushing aside a chair that stood in his way, and
now and again repeated the words in a groan. "Too long. Too
long." I sat still. I was embarrassed. To give myself countenance
I stirred the *brasero* to bring the hotter ashes to the top, and he
stood suddenly still, towering over me, as though my movement
had brought back my existence to his notice. Then he sat down
heavily in his chair.

"Do you think I'm queer?" he asked.

"Not more than most people," I smiled.

"You don't see anything strange in me?"

He leant forward as he spoke so that I might see him well.

"No."

"You'd say so if you did, wouldn't you?"

"I would."

I couldn't quite understand what all this meant. I wondered
if he was drunk. For two or three minutes he didn't say anything
and I had no wish to interrupt the silence.

"What's your name?" he asked suddenly. I told him.

"Mine's Robert Morrison."

"Scotch?"

"Glasgow. I've been in this blasted country for years. Got any baccy?"

I gave him my pouch and he filled his pipe. He lit it from a piece of burning charcoal.

"I can't stay any longer. l've stayed too long. Too long."

He had an impulse to jump up again and walk up and down, but he resisted it, clinging to his chair. I saw on his face the effort he was making. I judged that his restlessness was due to chronic alcoholism. I find drunks very boring, and I made up my mind to take an early opportunity of slipping off to bed.

"I've been managing some olive groves," he went on. "I'm here working for the Glasgow and South of Spain Olive Oil Company Limited."

"Oh, yes."

"We've got a new process for refining oil, you know. Properly treated, Spanish oil is every bit as good as Lucca. And we can sell it cheaper."

He spoke in a dry, matter-of-fact, business-like way. He chose his words with Scotch precision. He seemed perfectly sober.

"You know, Ecija is more or less the centre of the olive trade, and we had a Spaniard there to look after the business. But I found he was robbing us right and left, so I had to turn him out. I used to live in Seville; it was more convenient for shipping the oil. However, I found I couldn't get a trustworthy man to be at Ecija, so last year I went there myself. D'you know it?"

"No."

"The firm has got a big estate two miles from the town, just outside the village of San Lorenzo, and it's got a fine house on it. It's on the crest of a hill, rather pretty to look at, all white, you know, and straggling, with a couple of storks perched on the roof. No one lived there, and I thought it would save the rent of a place in town if I did."

"It must have been a bit lonely," I remarked.

"It was."

Robert Morrison smoked on for a minute or two in silence. I wondered whether there was any point in what he was telling me.

I looked at my watch.

"In a hurry?" he asked sharply.

"Not particularly. It's getting late."

"Well, what of it?"

"I suppose you didn't see many people?" I said, going back.

"Not many. I lived there with an old man and his wife who looked after me, and sometimes I used to go down to the village and play *tresillo* with Fernandez, the chemist, and one or two men who met at his shop. I used to shoot a bit and ride."

"It doesn't sound such a bad life to me."

"I'd been there two years last spring. By God, I've never known such heat as we had in May. No one could do a thing. The labourers just lay about in the shade and slept. Sheep died and some of the animals went mad. Even the oxen couldn't work. They stood around with their backs all humped up and gasped for breath. That blasted sun beat down and the glare was so awful, you felt your eyes would shoot out of your head. The earth cracked and crumbled, and the crops frizzled. The olives went to rack and ruin. It was simply hell. One couldn't get a wink of sleep. I went from room to room, trying to get a breath of air. Of course I kept the windows shut and had the floors watered, but that didn't do any good. The nights were just as hot as the days. It was like living in an oven.

"At last I thought I'd have a bed made up for me downstairs on the north side of the house in a room that was never used because in ordinary weather it was damp. I had an idea that I might get a few hours' sleep there at all events. Anyhow it was worth trying. But it was no damned good; it was a washout. I turned and tossed and my bed was so hot that I couldn't stand it. I got up and opened the doors that led to the veranda and walked out. It was a glorious night. The moon was so bright that I swear you could read a book by it. Did I tell you the house was on the crest of a hill? I leant against the parapet and looked at the olive-trees. It was like the sea. I suppose that's what made me think of home. I thought of the cool breeze in the fir-trees and the racket of the streets in Glasgow. Believe it or not, I could smell them, and I could smell the sea. By God, I'd have given every bob I had in the world for an hour of that air. They say it's a foul climate in Glasgow. Don't you believe it. I like the rain and the grey sky and that yellow sea and the waves. I forgot that I was in Spain, in the middle of the olive country, and I opened my mouth and took a long breath as though I were breathing in the sea-fog.

"And then all of a sudden I heard a sound. It was a man's voice. Not loud, you know, low. It seemed to creep through the silence like—well, I don't know what it was like. It surprised me. I couldn't think who could be down there in the olives at that hour. It was past midnight. It was a chap laughing. A funny sort of laugh. I suppose you'd call it a chuckle. It seemed to crawl up the hill—disjointedly."

Morrison looked at me to see how I took the odd word he used to express a sensation that he didn't know how to describe.

"I mean, it seemed to shoot up in little jerks, something like shooting stones out of a pail. I leant forward and stared. With the full moon it was almost as light as day, but I'm dashed if I could see a thing. The sound stopped, but I kept on looking at where it had come from in case somebody moved. And in a minute it started off again, but louder. You couldn't have called it a chuckle any more, it was a real belly laugh. It just rang through the night. I wondered it didn't wake my servants. It sounded like someone who was roaring drunk.

"Who's there?" I shouted.

"The only answer I got was a roar of laughter. I don't mind telling you I was getting a bit annoyed. I had half a mind to go down and see what it was all about. I wasn't going to let some drunken swine kick up a row like that on my place in the middle of the night. And then suddenly there was a yell. By God, I was startled. Then cries. The man had laughed with a deep bass voice, but his cries were—shrill, like a pig having his throat cut.

" 'My God,' I cried.

"I jumped over the parapet and ran down towards the sound. I thought somebody was being killed. There was silence and then one piercing shriek. After that sobbing and moaning. I'll tell you what it sounded like, it sounded like someone at the point of death. There was a long groan and then nothing. Silence. I ran from place to place. I couldn't find anyone. At last I climbed the hill again and went back to my room.

"You can imagine how much sleep I got that night. As soon as it was light, I looked out of the window in the direction from which the row had come and I was surprised to see a little white house in a sort of dale among the olives. The ground on that side didn't belong to us and I'd never been through it. I hardly ever went to that part of the house and so I'd never seen the house before. I asked Josè who lived there. He told me that a madman had inhabited it, with his brother and a servant."

"Oh, was that the explanation?" I said. "Not a very nice neighbour."

The Scot bent over quickly and seized my wrist. He thrust his face into mine and his eyes were staring out of his head with terror.

"The madman had been dead for twenty years," he whispered.

He let go my wrist and leant back in his chair panting.

"I went down to the house and walked all round it. The windows were barred and shuttered and the door was locked. I knocked. I shook the handle and rang the bell. I heard it tinkle, but no one came. It was a two-storey house and I looked up. The shutters were tight closed, and there wasn't a sign of life anywhere."

"Well, what sort of condition was the house in?" I asked.

"Oh, rotten. The whitewash had worn off the walls and there was practically no paint left on the door or the shutters. Some of the tiles off the rooff were lying on the ground. They looked as though they'd been blown away in a gale."

"Queer," I said.

"I went to my friend Fernandez, the chemist, and he told me the same story as Josè. I asked about the madman and Fernandez said that no one ever saw him. He was more or less comatose ordinarily, but now and then he had an attack of acute mania and then he could be heard from ever so far laughing his head off and then crying. It used to scare people. He died in one of his attacks and his keepers cleared out at once. No one had ever dared to live in the house since.

"I didn't tell Fernandez what I'd heard. I thought he'd only laugh at me. I stayed up that night and kept watch. But nothing happened. There wasn't a sound. I waited about till dawn and then I went to bed."

"And you never heard anything more?"

"Not for a month. The drought continued and I went on sleeping in the lumber-room at the back. One night I was fast asleep, when something seemed to happent to me; I don't exactly

know how to describe it, it was a funny feeling as though
someone had given me a little nudge, to warn me, and suddenly I
was wide awake. I lay there in my bed and then in the same way
as before I heard a long, low gurgle, like a man enjoying an old
joke. It came from away down in the valley and it got louder. It
was a great bellow of laughter. I jumped out of bed and went to
the window. My legs began to tremble. It was horrible to stand
there and listen to the shouts of laughter that rang through the
night. Then there was the pause, and after that a shriek of pain
and that ghastly sobbing. It didn't sound human. I mean, you
might have thought it was an animal being tortured. I don't
mind telling you I was scared stiff. I couldn't have moved if I'd
wanted to. After a time the sounds stopped, not suddenly, but
dying away little by little. I strained my ears, but I couldn't hear
a thing. I crept back to bed and hid my face.

"I remembered then that Fernandez had told me that the
madman's attacks only came at intervals. The rest of the time he
was quite quiet. Apathetic, Fernandez said. I wondered if the fits
of mania came regularly. I reckoned out how long it had been
between the two attacks I'd heard. Twenty-eight days. It didn't
take me long to put two and two together; it was quite obvious
that it was the full moon that set him off. I'm not a nervous man
really and I made up my mind to get to the bottom of it, so I
looked out in the calendar which day the moon would be full
next and that night I didn't go to bed. I cleaned my revolver and
loaded it. I prepared a lantern and sat down on the parapet of my
house to wait. I felt perfectly cool. To tell you the truth, I was
rather pleased with myself because I didn't feel scared. There was
a bit of a wind, and it whistled about the roof. It rustled over the
leaves of the olive trees like waves shishing on the pebbles of the
beach. The moon shone on the white walls of the house in
the hollow. I felt particularly cheery.

"At last I heard a little sound, the sound I knew, and I almost
laughed. I was right; it was the full moon and the attacks came as
regular as clockwork That was all to the good. I threw myself
over the wall into the olive grove and ran straight to the house.
The chuckling grew louder as I came near. I got to the house and
looked up. There was no light anywhere. I put my ears to the
door and listened. I heard the madman simply laughing his
bloody head off. I beat on the door with my fist and I pulled the

bell. The sound of it seemed to amuse him. He roared with laughter. I knocked again, louder and louder, and the more I knocked the more he laughed Then I shouted at the top of my voice.

" 'Open the blasted door, or I'll break it down.'

"I stepped back and kicked at the latch with all my might. I flung myself at the door with the whole weight of my body. It cracked. Then I put all my strength into it and the damned thing smashed open.

"I took the revolver out of my pocket and held my lantern in the other hand. The laughter sounded louder now that the door was opened. I stepped in. The stink nearly knocked me down. I mean, just think, the windows hadn't been opened for twenty years. The row was enough to raise the dead, but for a moment I didn't know where it was coming from. The walls seemed to throw the sound backwards and forwards. I pushed open a door by my side and went into a room. It was bare and white and there wasn't a stick of furniture in it. The sound was louder and I followed it. I went into another room, but there was nothing there. I opened a door and found myself at the foot of a staircase. The madman was laughing just over my head. I walked up, cautiously, you know, I wasn't taking any risks, and at the top of the stairs there was a passage. I walked along it, throwing my light ahead of me, and I came to a room at the end. I stopped. He was in there. I was only separated from the sound by a thin door.

"It was awful to hear it. A shiver passed through me and I cursed myself because I began to tremble. It wasn't like a human being at all. By Jove, I very nearly took to my heels and ran. I had to clench my teeth to force myself to stay. But I simply couldn't bring myself to turn the handle. And then the laughter was cut, cut with a knife you'd have said, and I heard a hiss of pain. I hadn't heard that before, it was too low to carry to my place, and then a gasp.

" 'Ay!' I heard the man speak in Spanish. 'You're killing me. Take it away. O God, help me!'

"He screamed. The brutes were torturing him. I flung open the door and burst in. The draught blew a shutter back and the moon streamed in so bright that it dimmed my lantern. In my ears, as clearly as I hear you speak and as close, I heard the wretched chap's groans. It was awful, moaning and sobbing, and frightful gasps. No one could survive that. He was at the point of death. I tell you I heard his broken, choking cries right in my ears. And the room was empty."

Robert Morrison sank back in his chair. That huge solid man had strangely the look of a lay figure in a studio. You felt that if you pushed him he would fall over in a heap on to the floor.

"And then?" I asked.

He took a rather dirty handkerchief out of his pocket and wiped his forehead.

"I felt I didn't want to sleep in that room on the north side so, heat or no heat, I moved back to my own quarters. Well, exactly four weeks later, about two in the morning, I was waked up by the madman's chuckle. It was almost at my elbow. I don't mind telling you that my nerve was a bit shaken by then, so next time the blighter was due to have an attack, next time the moon was full, I mean, I got Fernandez to come and spend the night with me. I didn't tell him anything. I kept him up playing cards till two in the morning, and then I heard it again. I asked him if he heard anything. 'Nothing,' he said. 'There's somebody laughing,' I said. 'You're drunk, man,' he said, and he began laughing too. That was too much. 'Shut up, you fool,' I said. The laughter grew louder and louder. I cried out. I tried to shut it out by putting my hands to my ears, but it wasn't a damned bit of good. I heard it and I heard the scream of pain. Fernandez thought I was mad. He didn't dare say so, because he knew I'd have killed him. He said he'd go to bed, and in the morning I found he'd slunk away. His bed hadn't been slept in. He'd taken himself off when he left me.

"After that I couldn't stop in Ecija. I put a factor there and went back to Seville. I felt myself pretty safe there, but as the time came near I began to get scared. Of course I told myself not to be a damned fool, but you know, I damned well couldn't help myself. The fact is, I was afraid the sounds had followed me, and I knew if I heard them in Seville I'd go on hearing them all my life. I've got as much courage as any man, but damn it all, there are limits to everything. Flesh and blood couldn't stand it. I knew I'd go stark staring mad. I got in such a state that I began drinking, the suspense was so awful, and I used to lie awake counting the days. And at last I knew it'd come. And it came. I heard those sounds in Seville—sixty miles away from Ecija."

I didn't know what to say. I was silent for a while.

"When did you hear the sounds last?" I asked.

"Four weeks ago."

I looked up quickly. I was startled.

"What d'you mean by that? It's not full moon tonight?"

He gave me a dark, angry look. He opened his mouth to speak and then stopped as though he couldn't. You would have said his vocal cords were paralysed, and it was with a strange croak that at last he answered.

"Yes, it is."

He stared at me and his pale blue eyes seemed to shine red. I have never seen in a man's face a look of such terror. He got up quickly and stalked out of the room, slamming the door behind him.

I must admit that I didn't sleep any too well that night myself.

# EARTH TO EARTH

ROBERT GRAVES

*One of the most distinguished poets and novelists of the day, Robert Graves has lived in Majorca for many years. Earth to Earth was written in the early 1950s and is assuredly the author's moment of macabre inspiration. The dénouement is brilliantly contrived to chill the blood.*

ELSIE AND Roland Hedge—she a book illustrator, he an architect with suspect lungs—had been warned against Dr Eugen Steinpilz. "He'll bring you no luck," I told them. "My little finger says so decisively."

"You too?" asked Elsie indignantly. (This was at Brixham, South Devon, in March, 1940.) "I suppose you think that because of his foreign accent and his beard he must be a spy?"

"No," I said coldly, "that point hadn't occurred to me. But I won't contradict you." I was annoyed.

The very next day Elsie deliberately picked a friendship—I don't like the phrase, but that's what she did—with the Doctor, an Alsatian with an American passport, who described himself as a *Naturphilosoph*; and both she and Roland were soon immersed in Steinpilzeri up to the nostrils. It began when he invited them to lunch and gave them cold meat and two rival sets of vegetable dishes—potatoes (baked), carrots (creamed), bought from the local fruiterer; and potatoes (baked) and carrots (creamed), grown on compost in his own garden.

The superiority of the latter over the former in appearance, size, and especially flavour came as an eye-opener to Elsie and Roland; and so Dr Steinpilz soon converted the childless and devoted couple to the Steinpilz method of composting. It did not, as a matter of fact, vary greatly from the methods you read about in the *Gardening Notes* of your favourite national

newspaper, except that it was far more violent. Dr Steinpilz
had invented a formula for producing extremely fierce bacteria,
capable (Roland claimed) of breaking down an old boot or the
family Bible or a torn woollen vest into beautiful black humus
almost as you watched.

The formula could not be bought, however, and might be
communicated under oath of secrecy only to members of the
Eugen Steinpilz Fellowship—which I refused to join. I won't
pretend therefore to know the formula myself, but one night I
overheard Elsie and Roland arguing as to whether the plan-
etary influences were favourable; and they also mentioned a
ram's horn in which, it seems, a complicated mixture of tri-
turated animal and vegetable products—technically called "the
Mother"—was to be cooked up. I gather also that a bull's foot
and a goat's pancreas were part of the works, because Mr
Pook, the butcher, afterward told me that he had been puzzled
by Roland's request for these unusual cuts. Milkwort and
pennyroyal and bee-orchid and vetch certainly figured among
"the Mother's" herbal ingredients; I recognised these one day
in a gardening basket Elsie had left in the post office.

The Hedges soon had their first compost heap cooking away
in the garden, which was about the size of a tennis court and
consisted mostly of well-kept lawn. Dr Steinpilz, who super-
vised, now began to haunt the cottage like the smell of drains;
I had to give up calling on them. Then, after the Fall of
France, Brixham became a war zone whence everyone but we
British and our Free French or Free Belgian allies was ex-
cluded. Consequently Dr Steinpilz had to leave; which he did
with very bad grace, and was killed in a Liverpool air raid the
day before he should have sailed back to New York.

I think Elsie must have been in love with the Doctor, and
certainly Roland had a hero worship for him. They treasured a
signed collection of all his esoteric books, each titled after a
different semi-precious stone; and used to read them out loud
to each other at meals, in turns. And to show that this was a
practical philosophy, not just a random assembly of beautiful
thoughts about Nature, they began composting in a deeper
and even more religious way than before. The lawn had come
up, of course; but they used the sods to sandwich layers of
kitchen waste, which they mixed with the scrapings of an

abandoned pigsty, two barrowfuls of sodden poplar leaves from the recreation ground, and a sack of rotten turnips. Once I caught the fanatic gleam in Elsie's eye as she turned the hungry bacteria loose on the heap, and could not repress a premonitory shudder.

So far, not too bad, perhaps. But when serious bombing started and food became so scarce that housewives were fined for not making over their swill to the national pigs, Elsie and Roland grew worried. Having already abandoned their ordinary sanitary system and built an earth-closet in the garden, they now tried to convince neighbours of their duty to do the same, even at the risk of catching cold and getting spiders down the neck. Elsie also sent Roland after the slow-moving Red Devon cows as they lurched home along the lane at dusk, to rescue the precious droppings with a kitchen shovel; while she visited the local ash dump with a packing case mounted on wheels, and collected whatever she found there of an organic nature—dead cats, old rags, withered flowers, cabbage stalks, and such household waste as even a national wartime pig would have coughed at. She also saved every drop of their bath water for sprinkling the heaps; because it contained, she said, valuable animal salts.

The test of a good compost heap, as every illuminate knows, is whether a certain revolting-looking, if beneficial, fungus sprouts from it. Elsie's heaps were grey with this crop, and so hot inside that they could be used for haybox cookery; which must have saved her a deal of fuel. I called them "Elsie's heaps", because she now considered herself Dr Steinpilz's earthly delegate; and loyal Roland did not dispute this claim.

A critical stage in the story came during the Blitz. It will be remembered that trainloads of Londoners, who had been evacuated to South Devon when War broke out, thereafter de-evacuated and re-evacuated and re-de-evacuated themselves, from time to time, in a most disorganised fashion. Elsie and Roland, as it happened, escaped having evacuees billeted on them, because they had no spare bedroom; but one night an old naval pensioner came knocking at their door and demanded lodging for the night. Having been burned out of Plymouth, where everything was chaos, he had found himself

walking away and blundering along in a daze until he fetched
up here, hungry and dead-beat. They gave him a meal and
bedded him on the sofa; but when Elsie came down in the
morning to fork over the heaps, she found him dead of heart
failure.

Roland broke a long silence by coming, in some embarrassment, to ask my advice. Elsie, he said, had decided that it
would be wrong to trouble the police about the case; because
the police were so busy these days, and the poor old fellow
had claimed to possess neither kith nor kin. So they'd read
the burial service over him and, after removing his belt
buckle, trouser buttons, metal spectacle case, and a bunch of
keys, which were irreducible, had laid him reverently in the
new compost heap. Its other contents, Roland added, were a
cartload of waste from the cider factory and salvaged cow
dung.

"If you mean 'Will I report you to Civil Authorities?' the
answer is no," I assured him. "I wasn't looking at the
relevant hour, and, after all, what you tell me is only hear-
say."

The War went on. Not only did the Hedges convert the
whole garden into serried rows of Eugen Steinpilz memorial
heaps, leaving no room for planting the potatoes or carrots
to which they had been prospectively devoted, but they
regularly scavenged offal from the fish market. Every Spring,
Elsie used to pick big bunches of primroses and put them
straight on the compost, without even a last wistful sniff;
virgin primroses were supposed to be particularly relished by
the fierce bacteria.

Here the story becomes a little painful for readers of a
delicate disposition, but I will soften it as much as possible.
One morning a policeman called on the Hedges with a
summons, and I happened to see Roland peep anxiously out
of the bedroom window, but quickly pull his head in again.

The policeman rang and knocked and waited, then tried
the back door; and presently went away. The summons was
for a blackout offence, but apparently the Hedges did not
know this.

Next morning the policeman called again, and when nobody answered, forced the lock of the back door. They were

found dead in bed together, having taken an overdose of sleeping tablets. A note on the coverlet ran simply:

*Please lay our bodies on the heap nearest the pigsty. Flowers by request. Strew some on the bodies, mixed with a little kitchen waste, and then fork the earth lightly over.*

George Irks, the new tenant, proposed to grow potatoes and dig for victory. He hired a cart and began throwing the compost into the River Dart, "not liking the look of them toadstools". The five beautifully clean human skeletons which George unearthed in the process were still awaiting identification when the War ended.

# THE GREY ONES

J. B. PRIESTLEY

*John Boynton Priestley has evinced an interest in macabre fiction on a number of occasions, and of his handful of stories in the genre* The Grey Ones *(1953) is, in my opinion, the most outstanding. Through the medium of confession it hurls us into a terrifying situation which is, thankfully, no more than a nightmare. Or is it?*

"AND YOUR occupation, Mr Patson?" Dr Smith asked, holding his beautiful fountain pen a few inches from the paper.

"I'm an exporter," said Mr Patson, smiling almost happily. Really this wasn't too bad at all. First, he had drawn Dr Smith instead of his partner Dr Meyenstein. Not that he had anything against Dr Meyenstein, for he had never set eyes on him, but he had felt that it was at least a small piece of luck that Dr Smith had been free to see him and Dr Meyenstein hadn't. If he had to explain himself to a psychiatrist, then he would much rather have one simply and comfortingly called Smith. And Dr Smith, a broad-faced man about fifty with giant rimless spectacles, had nothing forbidding about him, and looked as if he might have been an accountant, a lawyer or a dentist. His room too was reassuring, with nothing frightening in it; rather like a sitting-room in a superior hotel. And that fountain pen really was a beauty. Mr Patson had already made a mental note to ask Dr Smith where he had bought that pen. And surely a man who could make such a mental note, right off, couldn't have much wrong with him?"

"It's a family business," Mr Patson continued, smiling away. "My grandfather started it. Originally for the Far East. Firms abroad, especially in rather remote places, send us orders for all manner of goods, which we buy here on commission for them. It's not the business it was fifty years ago, of course, but on the other hand we've been helped to some extent by all these trade restrictions and systems of export licences, which people a long way off simply can't cope with. So we cope for them. Irritating work often, but not uninteresting. On the whole I enjoy it."

"That is the impression you've given me," said Dr Smith, making a note. "And you are reasonably prosperous, I gather? We all have our financial worries these days, of course. I know I have." He produced a mechanical sort of laugh, like an actor in a comedy that had been running too long, and Mr Patson echoed him like another bored actor. Then Dr Smith looked grave and pointed his pen at Mr Patson as if he might shoot him with it. "So I think we can eliminate all that side, Mr Patson—humph?"

"Oh yes—certainly—certainly," said Mr Patson hurriedly, not smiling now.

"Well now," said Dr Smith, poising his pen above the paper again, "tell me what's troubling you."

Mr. Patson hesitated. "Before I tell you the whole story. can I ask you a question?"

Dr Smith frowned, as if his patient had made an improper suggestion. "If you think it might help—"

"Yes, I think it would," said Mr Patson, "because I'd like to know roughly where you stand before I begin to explain." He waited a moment. "Dr Smith, do you believe there's a kind of Evil Principle in the universe, a sort of super-devil, that is working hard to ruin humanity, and has its agents, who must really be minor devils or demons, living among us as people? Do you believe that?"

"Certainly not," replied Dr Smith without any hesitation at all. "That's merely a superstitious fancy, for which there is no scientific evidence whatever. It's easy to understand—though we needn't go into all that now—why anybody, even today, suffering from emotional stress, might be possessed by such an absurd belief, but of course it's mere fantasy, entirely subjective in origin. And the notion that this Evil Principle could have its agents among us might be very dangerous indeed. It could produce very serious anti-social effects. You realise that, Mr Patson?"

"Oh—yes—I do. I mean, at certain times when—well,

when I've been able to look at it as you're looking at it, doctor. But most times I can't. And that, I suppose," Mr Patson added, with a wan smile, "is why I'm here."

"Quite so," Dr Smith murmured, making some notes. "And I think you have been well advised to ask for some psychiatric treatment. These things are apt to be sharply progressive, although their actual progress might be described as regressive. But I won't worry you with technicalities, Mr Patson. I'll merely say that you—or was it Mrs Patson?—or shall I say both of you?—are to be congratulated on taking this very sensible step in good time. And now you know, as you said, where I stand, perhaps you had better tell me all about it. Please don't omit anything for fear of appearing ridiculous. I can only help you if you are perfectly frank with me, Mr Patson. I may ask a few questions, but their purpose will be to make your account clearer to me. By the way, here we don't adopt the psycho-analytic methods—we don't sit behind our patients while they relax on a couch—but if you would find it easier not to address me as you have been doing—face to face—"

"No, that's all right," said Mr Patson, who was relieved to discover he would not have to lie on the couch and murmur at the opposite wall. "I think I can talk to you just like this. Anyhow, I'll try."

"Good! And remember, Mr Patson, try to tell me everything relevant. Smoke if it will help you to concentrate."

"Thanks, I might later on." Mr Patson waited a moment, surveying his memories as if they were some huge glittering sea, and then waded in. "It began about a year ago. I have a cousin who's a publisher, and one night he took me to dine at his club—the Burlington. He thought I might like to dine there because it's a club used a great deal by writers and painters and musicians and theatre people. Well, after dinner we played bridge for an hour or two, then we went down into the lounge for a final drink before leaving. My cousin was claimed by another publisher, so I was left alone for about quarter of an hour. It was then that I overheard Firbright—you know, the famous painter—who was obviously full of drink, although you couldn't exactly call him drunk, and was holding forth to a little group at the other side of the fireplace. Apparently he'd just come back from Syria or somewhere around there, and he'd picked this idea up from somebody there, though he said it only confirmed what he'd been thinking himself for some time."

Dr Smith gave Mr Patson a thin smile. "You mean the idea of an Evil Principle working to ruin humanity?"

"Yes," said Mr Patson. "Firbright said that the old notion of a scarlet-and-black sulphuric Satan, busy tempting people, was of course all wrong, though it might have been right at one time, perhaps in the Middle Ages. Then the devils were all fire and energy. Firbright quoted the poet Blake—I've read him since—to show that these weren't real devils and their Hell wasn't the real Hell. Blake, in fact, according to Firbright, was the first man here to suggest we didn't understand the Evil Principle, but in his time it had hardly made a start. It's during the last few years, Firbright said, that the horrible thing has really got to work on us."

"Got to work on us?" Dr Smith raised his eyebrows. "Doing what?"

"The main object, I gathered from what Firbright said," Mr Patson replied earnestly, "is to make mankind go the way the social insects went, to turn us into automatic creatures, mass beings without individuality, soulless machines of flesh and blood."

The doctor seemed amused. "And why should the Evil Principle want to do that?"

"To destroy the soul of humanity," said Mr Patson, without an answering smile. "To eliminate certain states of mind that belong essentially to the Good. To wipe from the face of this earth all wonder, joy, deep feeling, the desire to create, to praise life. Mind you, that is what Firbright said."

"But you believed him?"

"I couldn't help feeling, even then, that there was something in it. I'd never thought on those lines before—I'm just a plain business man and not given to fancy speculation—but I had been feeling for some time that things were going wrong and that somehow they seemed to be out of our control. In theory I suppose we're responsible for the sort of lives we lead, but in actual practice we find ourselves living more and more the kind of life we don't like. It's as if," Mr

Patson continued rather wildly, avoiding the doctor's eye,
"we were all compelled to send our washing to one huge
sinister laundry, which returned everything with more and
more colour bleached out of it until it was all a dismal grey."

"I take it," said Dr Smith, "that you are now telling me
what you thought and felt yourself, and not what you overheard this man Firbright say?"

"About the laundry—yes. And about things never going
the right way. Yes, that's what I'd been feeling. As if the
shape and colour and smell of things were going. Do you
understand what I mean, doctor?"

"Oh—yes—it's part of a familiar pattern. Your age may
have something to do with it—"

"I don't think so," said Mr Patson sturdily. "This is
something quite different. I've made all allowance for that."

"So far as you can, no doubt," said Dr Smith smoothly,
without any sign of resentment. "You must also remember
that the English middle class, to which you obviously belong,
has suffered recently from the effects of what has been virtually an economic and social revolution. Therefore any member of that class—and I am one myself—can't help feeling
that life does not offer the same satisfactions as it used to do,
before the War."

"Doctor Smith," cried Mr Patson, looking straight at him
now, "I know all about that—my wife and her friends have
enough to say about it, never stop grumbling. But this is something
else. I may tell you, I've always been a Liberal and believed in social
reform. And if this was a case of one class getting a bit less, and
another class getting a bit more, my profits going down and my
clerk's and warehousemen's wages going up, I wouldn't lose
an hour's sleep over it. But what I'm talking about is
something quite different. Economics and politics and social
changes may come into it, but *they're just being used*."

"I don't follow you there, Mr Patson."

"You will in a minute, doctor. I want to get back to what
I overheard Firbright saying, that night. I got away from it
just to make the point that I couldn't help feeling at once
there was something in what he said. Just because for the
first time somebody had given me a reason why these things
were happening." He regarded the other man earnestly.

Smiling thinly, Dr Smith shook his head. "The hypothesis of a mysterious but energetic Evil Principle, Mr Patson, doesn't offer us much of a reason."

"It's a start," replied Mr Patson, rather belligerently. "And of course that wasn't all, by any means. Now we come to these agents."

"Ah—yes—the agents." Dr Smith looked very grave now. "It was Firbright who gave you that idea, was it?"

"Yes, it would never have occurred to me, I'll admit. But if this Evil Principle was trying to make something like insects out of us, it could do it in two ways. One—by a sort of remote control, perhaps by a sort of continuous radio programme, never leaving our minds alone, telling us not to attempt anything new, to play safe, not to have any illusions, to keep to routine, nor to waste time and energy wondering and brooding and being fanciful, and all that."

"Did Firbright suggest something of that sort was happening?"

"Yes, but it wasn't his own idea. The man he'd been talking about before I listened to him, somebody he'd met in the Near East, had told him definitely all that non-stop propaganda was going on. But the other way—direct control, you might call it—was by the use of these agents—a sort of Evil Fifth Column—with more and more of 'em everywhere, hard at work."

"Devils?" enquired the doctor, smiling. "Demons? What?"

"That's what they amount to," said Mr Patson, not returning the smile but frowning a little. "Except that it gives one a wrong idea of them—horns and tails and that sort of thing. These are quite different, Firbright said. All you can definitely say is that they're not human. They don't belong to us. They don't like us. They're working against us. They have their orders. They know what they're doing. They work together in teams. They arrange to get jobs for one another, more and more influence and power. So what chance have we against them?" And Mr Patson asked this question almost at the top of his voice.

"If such beings existed," Dr Smith replied calmly, "we should soon be at their mercy, I agree. But then they don't exist—except of course as figures of fantasy, although in that capacity they can do a great deal of harm. I take it, Mr Patson, that you have thought about—or shall we say *brooded over*—these demonic creatures rather a lot lately? Quite so. By the way, what do you call them? It might save time and possible confusion if we can give them a name."

"They're the Grey Ones," said Mr Patson without any hesitation.

"Ah—The Grey Ones." Dr Smith frowned again and pressed his thin lips together, perhaps to show his disapproval of such a prompt reply. "You seem very sure about this, Mr Patson."

"Well, why shouldn't I be? You ask me what I call them, so I tell you. Of course, I don't know what they call themselves. And I didn't invent the name for them."

"Oh—this is Firbright again, is it?"

"Yes, that's what I heard him calling them, and it seemed to me a very good name for them. They're trying to give everything a grey look, aren't they? And there's something essentially grey about these creatures themselves—none of your gaudy, red and black, Mephistopheles stuff about *them*. Just quiet grey fellows busy greying everything—that's them."

"Is it indeed? Now I want to be quite clear about this, Mr Patson. As I suggested earlier, this idea of the so-called Grey Ones is something I can't dismiss lightly, just because it might have very serious anti-social effects. It is one thing to entertain a highly fanciful belief in some mysterious Evil Principle working on us for its own evil ends. It is quite another thing to believe that actual fellow-citizens, probably highly conscientious and useful members of the community, are not human beings at all but so many masquerading demons. You can see that, can't you?"

"Of course I can," said Mr Patson, with a flick of impatience. "I'm not stupid, even though I may have given you the impression that I am. This idea of the Grey Ones—well, it brings the whole thing home to you, doesn't it? Here they are, busy as bees, round every corner, you might say."

The doctor smiled. "Yet you've never met one. Isn't that highly suggestive? Doesn't that make you ask yourself what truth there can be in this absurd notion? All these Grey Ones, seeking power over us, influencing our lives, and yet

you've never actually come into contact with one. Now—
now—Mr Patson—" And he wagged a finger.

"Who says I've never met one?" Mr Patson demanded
indignantly. "Where did you get that idea from, doctor?"

"Do you mean to tell me—"

"Certainly I mean to tell you. I know at least a dozen of
'em. My own brother-in-law is one."

Dr Smith looked neither shocked nor surprised. He merely
stared searchingly for a moment or two, then rapidly made
some notes. And now he stopped sounding like a rather
playful schoolmaster and became a doctor in charge of a
difficult case. "So that's how it is, Mr Patson. You know at
least a dozen Grey Ones, and one of them is your brother-in-
law. That's correct, isn't it? Good! Very well, let us begin
with your brother-in-law. When and how did you make the
discovery that he is a Grey One?"

"Well, I'd wondered about Harold for years," said Mr
Patson slowly. "I'd always disliked him but I never quite
knew why. He'd always puzzled me too. He's one of those
chaps who don't seem to have any centre you can understand. They don't act from ordinary human feeling. They
haven't motives you can appreciate. It's as if there was
nothing inside 'em. They seem to tick over like automatic
machines. Do you know what I mean, doctor?"

"It would be better now if you left me out of it. Just tell
me what you thought and felt—about Harold, for instance."

".Yes, Harold. Well, he was one of them. No centre, no
feeling, no motives. I'd try to get closer to him, just for my
wife's sake, although they'd never been close. I'd talk to him
at home, after dinner, and sometimes I'd take him out. You
couldn't call him unfriendly—that at least would have been
*something*. He'd listen, up to a point, while I talked. If I asked
him a question, he'd make some sort of reply. He'd talk
himself in a kind of fashion, rather like a leading article in
one of the more cautious newspapers. Chilly stuff, grey stuff.
Nothing exactly wrong with it, but nothing right about it
either. And after a time, about half an hour or so, I'd find it
hard to talk to him, even about my own affairs. I'd begin
wondering what to say next. There'd be a sort of vacuum
between us. He had a trick, which I've often met elsewhere,

of deliberately not encouraging you to go on, of just staring, waiting for you to say something silly. Now I put this down to his being a public official. When I first knew him, he was one of the assistants to the Clerk of our local Borough Council. Now he's the Clerk, quite a good job, for ours is a big borough. Well, a man in that position has to be more careful than somebody like me has. He can't let himself go, has too many people to please—or rather, not to offend. And one thing was certain about Harold—and that ought to have made him more human, but somehow it didn't—and that was that he meant to get on. He had ambition, but there again it wasn't an ordinary human ambition, with a bit of fire and nonsense in it somewhere, but a sort of cold determination to keep on moving up. You see what I mean? Oh—I forgot—no questions. Well, that's how he was—and is. But then I noticed another thing about Harold. And even my wife had to agree about this. He was what we called a damper. If you took him out to enjoy something, he not only didn't enjoy it himself but he contrived somehow to stop you enjoying it. I'm very fond of a good show—and don't mind seeing a really good one several times—but if I took Harold along then it didn't matter what it was, I couldn't enjoy it. He wouldn't openly attack or sneer at it, but somehow by just being there, sitting beside you, he'd cut it down and take all the colour and fun out of it. You'd wonder why you'd wasted your evening and your money on such stuff. It was the same if you tried him with a football or cricket match, you'd have a boring afternoon. And if you asked him to a little party, it was fatal. He'd be polite, quite helpful, do whatever you asked him to do, but the party would never get going. It would be just as if he was invisibly spraying us with some devilish composition that made us all feel tired and bored and depressed. Once we were silly enough to take him on a holiday with us, motoring through France and Italy. It was the worst holiday we ever had. He killed it stone dead. Everything he looked at seemed smaller and duller and greyer than it ought to have been. Chartres, the Loire country, Provence, the Italian Riviera, Florence, Siena—they were all cut down and greyed over, so that we wondered why we'd ever bothered to arrange such a trip and hadn't

stuck to Torquay and Bournemouth. Then, before I'd learnt
more sense, I'd talk to him about various plans I had for
improving the business, but as soon as I'd described any
scheme to Harold I could feel my enthusiasm ebbing away. I
felt—or he made me feel—any possible development wasn't
worth the risk. Better stick to the old routine. I think I'd
have been done for now if I hadn't had sense enough to stop
talking to Harold about the business. If he asked me about
any new plans, I'd tell him I hadn't any. Now all this was
long before I knew about the Grey Ones. But I had Harold
on my mind, particularly as he lived and worked so close to
us. When he became Clerk to the Council, I began to take
more interest in our municipal affairs, just to see what influence Harold was having on them. I made almost a detective job of it. For instance, we'd had a go-ahead youngish
Chief Education Officer, but he left and in his place a dull
timid fellow was appointed. And I found out that Harold had
worked that. Then we had a lively chap as Entertainments
Officer, who'd brightened things up a bit, but Harold got rid
of him too. Between them, he and his friend, the Treasurer,
who was another of them, managed to put an end to everything that added a little colour and sparkle to life round our
way. Of course they always had a good excuse—economy and
all that. But I noticed that Harold and the Treasurer only
made economies in one direction, on what you might call the
anti-grey side, and never stirred themselves to save money in
other directions, in what was heavily official, pompous, inter-
fering, irritating, depressing, calculated to make you lose
heart. And you must have noticed yourself that we never do
save money in those directions, either in municipal or
national affairs, and that what I complained of in our borough
was going on all over the country—yes, and as far as I can
make out, in a lot of other countries too."

Dr Smith waited a moment of two, and then said rather
sharply: "Please continue, Mr Patson. If I wish to make a
comment or ask a question, I will do so."

"That's what I meant earlier," said Mr Patson, "when I
talked about economics and politics and social changes just
being used. I've felt all the time there was something behind
'em. If we're doing it for ourselves, it doesn't make sense.

But the answer is of course that we're not doing it for ourselves, we're just being manipulated. Take Communism. The Grey Ones must have almost finished the job in some of those countries—they hardly need to bother any more. All right, we don't like Communism. We must make every possible effort to be ready to fight it. So what happens? More and more of the Grey Ones take over. This is their chance. So either way they win and we lose. We're further along the road we never wanted to travel. Nearer the bees, ants, termites. Because we're being pushed. My God—doctor—can't you feel it yourself?"

"No, I can't, but never mind about me. And don't become too general, please. What about your brother-in-law, Harold? When did you decide he was a Grey One?"

"As soon as I began thinking over what Firbright said," replied Mr Patson. "I'd never been able to explain Harold before—and God knows I'd tried often enough. Then I saw at once he was a Grey One. He wasn't born one, of course, for that couldn't possibly be how it works. My guess is that sometime while he was still young, the soul or essence of the real Harold Sothers was drawn out and a Grey One slipped in. That must be going on all the time now, there are so many of them about. Of course they recognise each other and help each other, which makes it easy for them to handle us humans. They know exactly what they're up to. They receive and give orders. It's like having a whole well-disciplined secret army working against us. And our only possible chance now is to bring 'em out into the open and declare war on 'em."

"How can we do that," asked Mr Smith, smiling a little, "if they're secret?"

"I've thought a lot about that," said Mr Patson earnestly, "and it's not so completely hopeless as you might think. After a time you begin to recognise a few. Harold, for instance. And our Borough Treasurer. I'm certain he's one. Then, as I told you at first, there are about a dozen more that I'd willingly stake a bet on. Yes, I know what you're wondering, doctor. If they're all officials, eh? Well no, they aren't, though seven or eight of 'em are—and you can see why—because that's where the power is now. Another two are up-and-coming politicians—and not in the same Party neither. One's a banker I know in the City—and he's a Grey One all right. I wouldn't have been able to spot them if I hadn't spent so much time either with Harold or wondering about him. They all have the same cutting-down and bleaching stare, the same dead touch. Wait till you see a whole lot of 'em together, holding a conference." Then Mr Patson broke off abruptly, as if he felt he had said too much.

Dr Smith raised his eyebrows so that they appeared above his spectacles, not unlike hairy caterpillars on the move. "Perhaps you would like a cigarette now, Mr Patson. No, take one of these. I'm no smoker myself but I'm told they're excellent. Ah—you have a light. Good! Now take it easy for a minute or two because I think you're tiring a little. And it's very important you should be able to finish your account of these—er—Grey Ones, if possible without any hysterical over-emphasis. No, no—Mr Patson—I didn't mean to suggest there'd been any such over-emphasis so far. You've done very well indeed up to now, bearing in mind the circumstances. And it's a heavy sort of day, isn't it? We seem to have too many days like this, don't we? Or is it simply that we're not getting any younger?" He produced his long-run actor's laugh. Then he brought his large white hands together, contrived to make his lips smile without taking the hard stare out of his eyes, and said finally: "Now then, Mr Patson. At the point you broke off your story, shall we call it, you had suggested that you had seen a whole lot of Grey Ones together, holding a conference. I think you might very usefully enlarge that rather astonishing suggestion, don't you?"

Mr. Patson looked and sounded troubled. "I'd just as soon leave that, if you don't mind, doctor. You see, if it's all nonsense, then there's no point in my telling you about that business. If it isn't all nonsense—"

"Yes," said Dr Smith, after a moment, prompting him, "if it isn't all nonsense—"

"Then I might be saying too much." And Mr Patson looked about for an ashtray as if to hide his embarrassment.

"There—at your elbow, Mr Patson. Now please look at me. And remember what I said earlier. I am not interested in

fanciful theories of the universe or wildly imaginative interpretations of present world conditions. All I'm concerned
with here, in my professional capacity, is your state of mind,
Mr Patson. That being the case, it's clearly absurd to suggest
that you might be saying too much. Unless you are perfectly
frank with me, it will be very difficult for me to help you.
Come now, we agreed about that. So far you've followed my
instructions admirably. All I ask now is for a little more
cooperation. Did you actually attend what you believed to be
a conference of these Grey Ones?"

"Yes, I did," said Mr Patson, not without some reluctance.
"But I'll admit I can't prove anything. The important part
may be something I imagined. But if you insist, I'll tell you
what happened. I overheard Harold and our Borough
Treasurer arranging to travel together to Maundby Hall,
which is about fifteen miles north of where I live. I'd never
been there myself but I'd heard of it in connection with
various summer schools and conferences and that sort of
thing. Perhaps you know it, Dr Smith?"

"As a matter of fact, I do. I had to give a paper there one
Saturday night. It's a rambling Early Victorian mansion, with
a large ballroom that's used for the more important meetings."

"That's the place. Well, it seems they were going there to
attend a conference of the New Era Community Planning
Association. And when I overheard them saying that, first I
told myself how lucky I was not to be going too. Then
afterwards, thinking it over, I saw that if you wanted to hold
a meeting that no outsider in his senses would want to
attend, you couldn't do better than hold it in a country
house that's not too easy to get at, and call it a meeting or
conference of the New Era Community Planning Association.
I know if anybody said to me 'Come along with me and
spend the day listening to the New Era Community Planning
Association', I'd make any excuse to keep away. Of course
it's true that anybody like Harold couldn't be bored. The
Grey Ones are never bored, which is one reason why they
are able to collar and hold down so many jobs nowadays, the
sort of jobs that reek of boredom. Well, this New Era
Community Planning Association might be no more than one

of the usual societies of busybodies, cranks and windbags. But then again it might be something very different, and I kept thinking about it in connection with the Grey Ones. Saturday was the day of the conference. I went down to my office in the morning, just to go through the post and see if there was anything urgent, and then went home to lunch. In the middle of the afternoon I felt I had to know what was happening out at Maundby Hall, so off I went in my car. I parked it just outside the grounds, scouted round a bit, then found an entrance through a little wood at the back. There was nobody about, and I sneaked into the house by way of a servants' door near the pantries and larders. There were some catering people around there, but nobody bothered me. I went up some back stairs and after more scouting, which I enjoyed as much as anything I've done this year, I was guided by the sound of voices to a small door in a corridor upstairs. This door was locked on the inside, but a fellow had once shown me how to deal with a locked door when the key's still in the lock on the other side. You slide some paper under the door, poke the key out so that it falls on to the paper and then slide the paper back with the key on it. Well, this trick worked and I was able to open the door, which I did very cautiously. It led to a little balcony over-looking the floor of the ballroom. There was no window near this balcony so that it was rather dark up there and I was able to creep down to the front rail without being seen. There must have been between three and four hundred of them in that ballroom, sitting on little chairs. This balcony was high above the platform, so I had a pretty good view of them as they sat facing it. They looked like Grey Ones, but of course I couldn't be sure. And for the first hour or so, I couldn't be sure whether this really was a meeting of the New Era Community Planning Association or a secret confer-ence of Grey Ones. The stuff they talked would have done for either. That's where the Grey Ones are so damnably clever. They've only to carry on doing what everybody expects them to do, in their capacity as sound conscientious citizens and men in authority, to keep going with their own hellish task. So there I was, getting cramp, no wiser. Another lot of earnest busybodies might be suggesting new ways of robbing us of our individuality. Or an organized covey of masquerading devils and demons might be making plans to bring us nearer to the insects, to rob us of our souls. Well, I was just about to creep back up to the corridor, giving it up as a bad job, when something happened." He stopped, and looked dubiously at his listener.

"Yes, Mr Patson," said Dr Smith encouragingly, "then something happened?"

"This is the part you can say I imagined, and I can't prove I didn't. But I certainly didn't dream it, because I was far too cramped and aching to fall asleep. Well, the first thing I noticed was a sudden change in the atmosphere of the meeting. It was as if somebody very important had arrived, although I didn't see anybody arriving. And I got the impression that the *real* meeting was about to begin. Another thing—I knew for certain now that this was no random collection of busybodies and windbags, that they were all Grey Ones. If you asked me to tell you in detail how I knew, I couldn't begin. But I noticed something else, after a minute or two. These Grey Ones massed together down there had now a positive quality of their own, which I'd never discovered before. It wasn't that they were just negative, not human, as they were at ordinary times; they had this positive quality, which I can't describe except as a sort of chilly hellishness. As if they'd stopped pretending to be human and were letting themselves go, recovering their demon natures. And here I'm warning you, doctor, that my account of what happened from then is bound to be sketchy and peculiar. For one thing, I wasn't really well placed up in that balcony, not daring to show myself and only getting hurried glimpses; and for another thing, I was frightened. Yes, doctor, absolutely terrified. I was crouching there just above three or four hundred creatures from some cold hell. That quality I mentioned, that chilly hellishness, seemed to come rolling over me in waves. I might have been kneeling on the edge of a pit of iniquity a million miles deep. I felt the force of this hellishness not on the outside but inside, as if the very essence of me was being challenged and attacked. One slip, a black-out, and then I might waken up to find myself running a concentration camp, choosing skins for lampshades. Then somebody, something, arrived. Whoever or whatever they'd been waiting for was down there on the platform. I knew that definitely. But I couldn't see him or it. All I could make out was a sort of thickening and whirling of the air down there. Then out of that a voice spoke, the voice of the leader they had been expecting. But this voice didn't come from outside, through my ears. It spoke inside me, right in the centre, so that it came out to my attention, if you see what I mean. Rather like a small, very clear voice on a good telephone line, but coming from inside. I'll tell you frankly I didn't want to stay there and listen, no matter what big secrets were coming out; all I wanted to do was to get away from there as soon as I could; but for a few minutes I was too frightened to make the necessary moves."

"Then you heard what this—er—voice was saying, Mr Patson?" the doctor asked.

"Some of it—yes."

"Excellent! Now this is important." And Dr Smith pointed his beautiful fountain pen at Mr Patson's left eye. "Did you learn from it anything you hadn't known before? Please answer me carefully."

"I'll tell you one thing you won't believe," cried Mr Patson. "Not about the voice—we'll come to that—but about those Grey Ones. I risked a peep while the voice was talking, and what I saw nearly made me pass out. There they were—three or four hundred of 'em—not looking human at all, not making any attempt; they'd all gone back to their original shapes. They looked—this is the nearest I can get to it—like big semi-transparent toads—and their eyes were like six hundred electric lamps burning under water, all greeny, unblinking, and shining out of Hell."

"But what did you hear the voice say?" Dr Smith was urgent now. "How much can you remember? That's what I want to know. Come along, man."

Mr Patson passed a hand across his forehead and then looked at the edge of this hand with some astonishment, as if he had not known it would be so wet. "I heard it thank them in the name of Adaragraffa—Lord of the Creeping Hosts. Yes, I could have imagined it—only I never knew I'd that sort of imagination. And what is imagination anyhow?"

"What else—what else—did you hear, man?"

"Ten thousand more were to be drafted into the Western Region. There would be promotions for some there who'd been on continuous duty longest. There was to be a swing over from the assault by way of social conditions, which could almost look after itself now, to the draining away of character, especially in the young of the doomed species. Yes, those were the very words," Mr Patson shouted, jumping up and waving his arms. "Especially in the young of the doomed species. Us—d'you understand—us. And I tell you—we haven't a chance unless we start fighting back now—*now*—yes, and with everything we've got left. Grey Ones. And more and more of them coming, taking charge of us, giving us a push here, a shove there—down—down—down—"

Mr Patson found his arms strongly seized and held by the doctor, who was clearly a man of some strength. The next moment he was being lowered into his chair. "Mr Patson," said the doctor sternly, "you must not excite yourself in this fashion. I cannot allow it. Now I must ask you to keep still and quiet for a minute while I speak to my partner, Dr Meyenstein. It's for your own good. Now give me your promise."

"All right, but don't be long," said Mr Patson, who suddenly felt quite exhausted. As he watched the doctor go out, he wondered if he had not said either too much or not enough. Too much, he felt, if he was to be accepted as a sensible business man who happened to be troubled by some neurotic fancies. Not enough, perhaps, to justify, in view of the doctor's obvious scepticism, the terrible shaking excitement that had possessed him at the end of their interview. No doubt, round the corner, Doctors Smith and Meyenstein were having a good laugh over this rubbish about Grey Ones. Well, they could try and make him laugh too. He would be only too delighted to join them, if they could persuade him he had been deceiving himself. Probably that is what they would do now.

"Well, Mr Patson," said Dr Smith, at once brisk and grave, as he returned with two other men, one of them Dr Meyenstein and the other a bulky fellow in white who might be a male nurse. All three moved forward slowly as Dr Smith spoke to him. "You must realise that you are a very sick man—sick in mind if not yet sick in body. So you must put yourself in our hands."

Even as he nodded in vague agreement, Mr Patson saw what he ought to have guessed before, that Dr Smith was a Grey One and that now he had brought two more Grey Ones with him. There was a fraction of a moment, as the three of them bore down upon him to silence his warning forever, when he thought he caught another glimpse of the creatures in the ballroom, three of them now like big semi-transparent toads, six eyes like electric lamps burning under water, all greeny, unblinking, shining triumphantly out of Hell. . . .

# THE MAN WHO DIDN'T ASK WHY

C. S. FORESTER

*Cecil Scott Forester's interest in the fearsome was apparently aroused by a story once told to him by his grandfather about the awesome fate of a relative of the family, an elderly spinster. It encouraged the writing of a few weird tales, among them the one now presented. Briefly, it concerns a man who dabbled in the Black Arts and got more than he bargained for.*

IT WAS inevitable that Carpmael should ask those questions eventually. He could not restrain himself in the end from making use of his peculiar gift to seek the answers.

He had looked into the future a hundred times, always with satisfactory results.

Even his earlier excursions, timid and unskilful, had brought enormous financial profit, which was not surprising, seeing that they had revealed to him stock exchange prices and racing results a week ahead.

Now he was rich, he was successful, he was famous—or notorious—as the most successful gambler of the century, and he was happily married.

In fact, by practically any standard, and most certainly by his own, he was a very happy man.

He cannot be blamed for wanting to know how long his happiness would endure. While he was resisting the temptation to find out he did at least argue with himself regarding the desirability of knowing the time, the place and the manner of his dying.

The knowledge might not help his happiness, but on the other hand once his curiosity had been roused he could not be happy until he had gratified it. He had to know.

He made his preparations. He did those things which he believed to be black magic but which the unbeliever might consider to be a convenient ritual to induce self-hypnosis.

He made the great effort of will which carried him into the billowing grey clouds, the further effort which opened a peep-hole in them for him, and the further effort still which widened the peep-hole.

He was looking into a hospital room—nothing surprising about that; there was even reassurance to be found in knowing he would die in a hospital bed.

There was a nurse beside the bed, and as the peep-hole widened he could see that she was talking to Viola, his wife.

It was not very distinct, as yet. He had to crane round the peep-hole to see that lying on the bed was a Thing. That Thing was himself, and he looked anxiously at it, to find the answers to his questions.

The sprouting beard on the unshaven cheeks was black; the expressionless face was unlined, the hair—several inches long— was thick and dark and curly still. But the Thing was a Thing. It was not human.

He could see that it was blind. He could see that this slobbering Thing was completely and utterly helpless, horrible to look at with all the muscles of the face useless.

He made the effort to listen to what was being said—it was harder, in these excursions, to hear than to see.

"*I can't help but say that it's a merciful release,*" said *Viola*.

"He is feeling nothing in any case," said the nurse. Her fingers were on the Thing's pulse.

"*Do you think he has known anything at all?*" asked *Viola*.

"I don't think so," said the nurse. "With complete paralysis like this it is hard to say, cut off from all communication, but he cannot know much, blind and helpless, poor fellow."

It was important that Carpmael should discover the date. He strained to find out.

He realised that Viola was wearing a coat and skirt that he knew well. That and the hair of the Thing told him that it could not be far off in the future.

Then he thought of the notes above the bed. They would be dated; they were a daily record. He strained and strained to get a glimpse of them.

One final convulsive effort revealed them to him. Just for a second they were before his eyes, just long enough to read the date.

The effort broke the spell—terminated the self-hypnosis, and he was back in his chair with the sweat running down him in streams, and in his mind the knowledge that he had only a year to live—51 weeks to be exact, he worked out, as he checked on today's date.

He had 51 weeks to live, and he was going to die blind and paralysed, a dreadful, horrible Thing. And it would take many—most—of those 51 weeks for that Thing to die.

He had heard that paralysis cases died in the end of exhaustion resulting from bedsores.

And this would be in 51 weeks' time. If he were going to forestall it he did not have much time to spare. He could not doubt the accuracy of what he had seen.

He had only to look round him, at all the evidence of wealth and success, to know that he had never been wrong, that his gift had never failed him. He could be quite sure of it.

If he were going to forestall his fate he must act immediately, before the paralysis came to prevent him. The motives of suicide, like those of murder, are usually inadequate in the estimation of the onlooker.

He got out his pistol; it was only a .22 but it would do his business for him. He saw that it was loaded. He looked once more round at the evidence of wealth and success. Then he pushed the muzzle up under his chin and pulled the trigger. He went out into darkness.

He came back into darkness again, not remembering. The darkness was intense, darker than any darkness he had ever known.

He tried to see—he could not even be sure if his eyes were open or not. He tried again to look through the darkness. He tried to raise his hand to his eyes, and his hand would not move.

Then he realised that he was blind and paralysed, cut off from all communication, and he still had 51 weeks to live.

*It was perhaps typical that Carpmael had sought answers to the questions when and where and how. He had not asked why.*

# ALL BUT EMPTY

GRAHAM GREENE

*Death remains the most mysterious of all phenomena, and the degree of fascination it exercises on the minds of the curious depends on how grim and inexplicable are the circumstances. The subject is explored in* All But Empty, *a stark and compelling tale by Graham Greene. It is less well known than some of the author's other short stories but as superbly written as any of them.*

IT IS not often that one finds an empty cinema, but this one I used to frequent in the early '30s because of its almost invariable, almost total emptiness. I speak only of the afternoons, the heavy grey afternoons of late winter; in the evenings, when the lights went up in the Edgware Road and the naphtha flares, and the peep-shows were crowded, this cinema may have known prosperity. But I doubt it.

It had so little to offer. There was no talkie apparatus, and the silent films it showed did not appeal to the crowd by their excitement or to the connoisseur by their unconscious humour.

I suspect that the cinema kept open only because the owner could not sell or let the building and he could not afford to close it. I went to it because it was silent, because it was all but empty, and because the girl who sold the tickets had a bright, common, venal prettiness.

One passed out of the Edgware Road and found it in a side street. It was built of boards like a saloon in an American western, and there were no posters. Probably no posters existed of the kind of films it showed. One paid one's money to the girl of whom I spoke, taking an unnecessarily expensive seat in the drab emptiness on the other side of the red velvet curtains, and she would smile, charming and venal, and address one by a name of her own.

I remember I went in one afternoon and found myself quite alone. There was not even a pianist; blurred metallic music was relayed from a gramophone in the pay-box. I hoped the girl would soon leave her job and come in. I sat almost at the end of a row with one seat free as an indication that I felt like company, but she never came. An elderly man got entangled in the curtain and billowed his way through it and lost himself in the dark. He tried to get past me, though he had the whole cinema to choose from, and brushed my face with a damp beard. Then he sat down in the seat I had left, and there we were, close together in the darkness.

The flat figures passed and repassed, their six-year-old gestures as antique as designs on a Greek coin. They were emotional in great white flickering letters, but their emotions were not comic nor to me moving. I was surprised when I heard the old man next to me crying to himself—so much to himself and not to me, not a trace of histrionics in those slow, carefully stifled sobs that I felt sorry for him. I said:

"Can I do anything?"

He may not have heard me, but he spoke: "I can't hear what they are saying."

The loneliness of the old man was extreme; no one had warned him that he would find only silent pictures here. I tried to explain, but he did not listen, whispering gently, "I can't see them."

I thought that he was blind and asked him where he lived, and when he gave an address in Seymour Terrace, I felt such pity for him that I offered to show him the way to another cinema and then to take him home. It was because we shared a desolation, sitting in the dark and stale air, when all around us people were lighting lamps and making tea and gas fires glowed. But no! He wouldn't move. He said that he always came to this cinema of an evening, and when I said that it was only afternoon, he remarked that afternoon and evening were now to him "much of a muchness." I still didn't realise what he was enduring.

Only a hint of it came to me a moment after, when he turned suddenly towards me, and whispered:

"No one could expect me to see, not after I've seen what I've seen," and then in a lower voice, talking to himself, "From ear to ear."

That startled me because there were only two things he could mean, and I did not believe that he referred to a smile.

"Leave them to it," he said, "at the bottom of the stairs. The black-beetles always came out of that crack."

It was extraordinary how he seemed to read my thoughts, because I had already begun to comfort myself with the fact of his age and that he must be recalling something very far away, when he spoke again: "Not a minute later than this morning. The clock had just struck two and I came down the stairs, and there he was. Oh, I was angry. He was smiling."

"From ear to ear," I said lightly.

"That was later," he corrected me, and then he startled me by reading out suddenly from the screen the words, "I love you. I will not let you go." He laughed and said, "I can see a little now. But it fades, it fades."

I was quite sure then that the man was mad, but I did not go. For one thing, I thought that at any moment the girl might come and two people could deal with him more easily than one; for another, stillness seemed safest. So I sat very quietly.

After a while he spoke again so low that his words were lost in the tin blare of the relayed record, but I caught the words "serpent's tooth" and guessed that he must have been quoting scripture. He did not leave me much longer in doubt, however, of what had happened at the bottom of the stairs, for he said quite casually, his tears forgotten in curiosity:

"I never thought the knife was so sharp. I had forgotten I had had it reground."

Then he went on speaking, his voice gaining strength and calmness: "I had just put down the borax for the black-beetles that morning. How could I have guessed? I must have been very angry coming downstairs. The clock struck two, and there he was, smiling at me. I must have sent it to be reground when I had the joint of pork for Sunday dinner. Oh, I was angry when he laughed: the knife trembled. And there the poor body lay with the throat cut from ear to ear," and hunching up his shoulders and dropping his bearded chin towards his hands, the old man began again to cry.

It needed courage to stand up and press by him into the gangway, and then turn the back and be lost in the blind velvet folds of the curtains which would not part, knowing that he might have the knife still with him. I got out into the grey afternoon light at last, and startled the girl in the box with my white face. I opened the door of the kiosk and shut it again behind me with immeasurable relief.

"The police station," I called softly into the telephone, afraid that he might hear me where he sat alone in the cinema, and when a voice answered, I said hurriedly, "That murder in Seymour Terrace this morning."

The voice at the other end became brisk and interested, telling me to hold the line.

All the while I held the receiver I watched the curtain, and presently it began to shake and billow, as if somebody was fumbling for the way out. "Hurry, hurry," I called down the telephone, and then as the voice spoke I saw the old man wavering in the gap of the curtain. "Hurry. The murderer's here," I called, stumbling over the name of the cinema and so intent on the message I had to convey that I could not take in for a moment the puzzled and puzzling reply: "We've got the murderer. It's the body that's disappeared."

# ANIMALS OR HUMAN BEINGS

## ANGUS WILSON

*The creative talents of novelist and playwright Angus Wilson first became known to the public through* The Wrong Set (*1949*), *a collection of short stories satirising the middle classes, but he has written one or two others of a much more bizarre character, including* Animals or Human Beings *published in 1955.*

FRAULEIN PARTENKIRCHEN was a reserved girl. At twenty-seven she was still unmarried, and her quiet blonde prettiness was fading; her skin had a sallow look, her hair if not constantly cared for quickly became dry and scurfy, about her heavy eye-lids there hung a mauve, translucent look. She was not very strong. The feeling that she had been left on the shelf preoccupied her and made her unresponsive in company. The many changes in the German political scene in her youth and the experiences of heavy air raids had somehow startled her into permanent stillness. She never knew what to expect of people and so she never committed herself to expressing opinions.

It had cost her family a determined and united effort to make her accept the post of housekeeper to Miss Ingelow in Wales. To her, they pretended that the acquisition of fluency in English would help her to get a higher post in the secretarial world. Among themselves, they agreed that this was highly unlikely, but they asserted that in England she might perhaps find a husband. An easily adaptable, acquisitive, noisy, small shop-keeping family, they found her presence an irksome restraint, and they sent her to England because they wanted to be rid of her.

Since Miss Ingelow lived in the remote fastness of the Welsh Marches, Fraulein Partenkirchen was to be met at Liverpool Street by another English lady, a friend of Miss Ingelow's, Mrs Gosport, who was to put her on the train for the little town of Montgomery. Mrs Gosport was a big, motherly woman whose figure seemed to be coming to pieces. Childless, she had devoted her life to girls' clubs. She was pleasantly impressed by Fraulein Partenkirchen's neat appearance, nothing vulgar yet not dowdy, and with just enough lipstick to make one feel that she was a nice human girl. Mrs Gosport hoped that she was not too delicate for the post, but attributed her faded appearance to the long journey.

They had breakfast together at the Great Western Hotel before Fraulein Partenkirchen left for Wales. "I don't know how you'll find Alice Ingelow. I haven't seen her for over three years. Of course, she's quite a character," said Mrs Gosport, "but she's a wonderful woman. She's given her life for others. In the last years before she retired to Wales, I'm afraid we drifted apart a bit. I can't really feel as strongly about animals as about human beings, can you?" Mrs Gosport's large, cowlike eyes appealed to Fraulein Partenkirchen, but if the German girl had any preference in the matter she did not express it. "Well, perhaps you don't agree with me," said Mrs Gosport, "but it seemed such a waste when Alice Ingelow who had done such wonderful work for girls and women became entirely absorbed with animals. She was the first, you know, to get the canteens going for women munition workers in the '14 war. And so wonderfully human and cheerful. And then the last time I went to see her, in a big house outside London, the place was filled with cats and dogs. I felt it terribly. It was vivisection that did it, of course. She became quite crazy about the subject. Well, of course, I *don't* care for the idea. I can't believe they couldn't make just the same discoveries without cruelty to animals, but all the same when there's so much *human* material in need of help. . . . But there you are, dear, I don't want to say too much. Alice Ingelow is a wonderful woman, one of our pioneers, but I did just want to warn you. Because if you didn't like animals, it wouldn't be a very happy post for you. You see she's a very old lady and she's always been used to having her own way." Once again Fraulein Partenkirchen did not say whether she liked animals or not, she only said that she would like another cup of tea.

When Fraulein Partenkirchen arrived at Montgomery station, there was no one to meet her, but she seemed to make little of the half-hour walk that lay in front of her to reach Miss Ingelow's house in the hills. The little town square was unusually crowded that evening, and people were standing in the columned doorways of the square red brick houses enjoying the last gleams of the September sunshine. Fraulein Partenkirchen's neat figure and the heavy suitcase she was carrying attracted quite a lot of attention, but she went on her way without appearing to notice anyone. The little drive that led up to Miss Ingelow's house was quite a steep ascent, and the girl paused once or twice to lay down her heavy load. The house itself was a rather elegant long white-stuccoed house of about 1840, with a verandah. The stucco, however, was peeling everywhere and the garden was a tangle of overgrown nettles and convolvulus among which a few hardy Michaelmas daisies and montbretia alone survived. Everything was dead and dusty. Except for Miss Ingelow who came out to meet her. It was true that she was a very old lady, but she was also a very bright birdlike one. Despite the mannish crop and the heavy tweed skirt and coat, her old, wrinkled weatherbeaten face was so small and well-rounded and her blue eyes were so alive and twinkling that she seemed intensely feminine, like a little wrinkled kitten that had got wrapped in a heavy rug by mistake. Her voice, too, when it came was not the deep bark that one would have expected, but a light, intensely cultured, almost over-modulated noise like an actress trained in the old school. She was at once brisk and cheerful and kind, and yet remote and dreamy. She took quick and entire charge of her new housekeeper, giving her tea and cossetting her after the long journey, and yet not explaining why she had done nothing to provide her with transport. "Now *I* shall make the supper this evening," she said, "and then tomorrow you can take over. I'm getting very old, you see, and I don't want to do much but potter in the garden and look after the animals. I hope you won't get too bored with an old woman. There's nobody else, you know, but you and me." "But the animals?" asked Fraulein Partenkirchen, looking around the neat little dining room with its refectory table and its horse brasses.

"Well, I've only got the two now, you know. Rufus and Maria. Or I *did* have, but Maria's just got a lot of little babies, so I'm afraid we're going to be rather a large family party."

Fraulein Partenkirchen gave a wan smile, "But where are they?" she asked.

"Oh! I have to keep them in upstairs. They will go after the little birds and we can't have that, can we?" Miss Ingelow said.

"At the moment Rufus has to be in his little house all by himself, he's jealous of his own children. Naughty Rufus! Come and see them," she said, springing up most agilely from her pseudo-Jacobean chair. As they mounted the stairs, Miss Ingelow looked back at Fraulein Partenkirchen with rather a worried smile. "I do hope you *like* animals," she said. "Some foreigners aren't very fond of them, I think." Fraulein Partenkirchen did not reply.

"Well," Miss Ingelow cried, throwing open the door of her bedroom, "There's Rufus. Isn't he fine?"

Fraulein Partenkirchen did not reply to this question, she only said, "He is very big."

"Yes," said Miss Ingelow, "Have you ever seen a more beautiful coat or a finer tail? We're talking about you, Rufus, but you mustn't listen or you'll get conceited. He knows every word we say and he's got a bit of a swollen head already. And now we must say how do you do to Maria. There she is, a picture of mother love. Thirsty little things, aren't they? Poor Maria! But she doesn't mind, she knows it's Nature's way."

"The big one is quite angry, I think," said Fraulein Partenkirchen.

"Yes," said Miss Ingelow, "Wicked Rufus! He's so jealous! He bit me the other day. Yes, you, Rufus! Look at his magnificent whiskers. I call him Rufus because of the red colour of his lovely fur." She jangled the little bell on Rufus's house. "Yes, I know. Dinner time," she said, "They always know and they eat such a lot of meat, but that's better than the little birds. Auntie will go and get dinner," she said to her pets.

"And to think," she told Fraulein Partenkirchen, as they descended the stairs, "I only just saved them from those wicked vivisectionists. The dustman was going to sell them to the hospital." They went into the little drawing room where all Miss Ingelow's little treasures were—her Crown Derby service and her Chinese ivory chess set and her two Ostrich eggs. With its striped wallpaper and its bright chintzes it seemed quite homely and cheerful. A fire was burning in the grate. "The evenings get so chilly now," said Miss Ingelow. "Now you sit and rest and I'll get their dinner. And then we can have our supper in peace."

After Miss Ingelow had gone out of the room, Fraulein Partenkirchen waited a moment, then she crossed the hall and went into the dining room. She opened her suitcase and took out a pad of writing paper. She tore off one sheet and in pencil she wrote on it, "I am going away again. I do not like animals." She seemed more cheerful now that she had expressed her opinion. Then, picking up her suitcase, she walked out of the house. As she passed along the path through the high, waving Michaelmas daisies and the grubby Montbretia, she heard Miss Ingelow go upstairs. Then as she reached the dusty beech hedge and the little gate, she heard one after another two loud shrieks. She was not surprised and she went on her way. There was no-one in the little town square to watch her leave. At the station, she was told that she would have to wait an hour for the return train, but she sat quite reserved and silent in the waiting room.

It was as well that she had not returned to the house, for she had seen quite enough that was horrible in the air-raids on Hamburg as a young girl. Upstairs, Miss Ingelow lay on the floor with her throat torn open. An enormous buck rat was hissing and scratching at the wires of a cage. It wanted to get to its doe and devour the young ones. Soon it would have eaten all the raw meat that Miss Ingelow had brought with her; and as she had closed the door of the room behind her, there would be nothing then for Rufus to devour except Miss Ingelow herself. But the little bells she had put on his cage jangled merrily.

Fraulein Partenkirchen's family were not at all pleased to see her back again. If anything, she seemed more reserved and her skin more sallow. As to this story of hers, it promised ill for her chances of marrying. Such hallucinations were the mark of hysterical old maids, not of desirable brides. Of course, there was always the chance that she had seen ghosts. A certain amount of sixth sense could be very attractive in a woman. It was an *echt Deutsch* quality uniting her with all the old *Legenden* and *Marchen*. But hardly if all she could see was ghost rats! Now if only she had said the old Englishwoman had been carried off by the *Niebelungen* or lured to her death by the *Lorelei*. As it was, it was all very disappointing.

# SOMETHING STRANGE

KINGSLEY AMIS

*Kingsley Amis as the final contributor to the first part of this book, appropriately looks to the future with a strange tale on the border-land of fantasy and SF. A novelist, whose work is highly regarded, he is equally capable of writing with vision and originality in the field of speculative fiction.*

SOMETHING STRANGE happened every day. It might happen during the morning, while the two men were taking their readings and observations and the two women busy with the domestic routine; the big faces had come during the morning. Or, as with the little faces and the coloured fires, the strange thing would happen in the afternoon, in the middle of Bruno's maintenance pro-gramme and Clovis's transmission to Base, Lia's rounds of the garden and Myri's work on her story. The evening was often undisturbed, the night less often.

They all understood that ordinary temporal expressions had no meaning for people confined indefinitely, as they were, to a motionless steel sphere hanging in a region of space so empty that the light of the nearest star took some hundreds of years to reach them. The Standing Orders devised by Base, however, recom-mended that they adopt a twenty-four-hour unit of time, as was the rule on the Earth they had not seen for many months. The arrangement suited them well: their work, recreation and rest seemed to fall naturally into the periods provided. It was only the prospect of year after year of the same routine, stretching further into the future than they could see, that was a source of strain.

Bruno commented on this to Clovis after a morning spent repairing a fault in the spectrum analyser they used for investigat-ing and classifying the nearer stars. They were sitting at the main observation port in the lounge, drinking the midday cocktail and waiting for the women to join them.

"I'd say we stood up to it extremely well," Clovis said in answer to Bruno. "Perhaps too well."

Bruno hunched his fat figure upright. "How do you mean?"

"We may be hindering our chances of being relieved."

"Base has never said a word about our relief."

"Exactly. With half a million stations to staff, it'll be a long time before they get round to one like this, where everything runs smoothly. You and I are a perfect team, and you have Lia and I have Myri, and they're all right together—no real conflict at all. Hence no reason for a relief."

Myri had heard all this as she laid the table in the alcove. She wondered how Clovis could not know that Bruno wanted to have her instead of Lia, or perhaps as well as Lia. If Clovis did know, and was teasing Bruno, then that would be a silly thing to do, because Bruno was not a pleasant man. With his thick neck and pale fat face he would not be pleasant to be had by, either, quite unlike Clovis, who was no taller but whose straight, hard body and soft skin were always pleasant. He could not think as well as Bruno, but on the other hand many of the things Bruno thought were not pleasant. She poured herself a drink and went over to them.

Bruno had said something about it being a pity they could not fake their personnel report by inventing a few quarrels, and Clovis had immediately agreed that that was impossible. She kissed him and sat down at his side. "What do you think about the idea of being relieved?" he asked her.

"I never think about it."

"Quite right," Bruno said, grinning. "You're doing very nicely here. Fairly nicely, anyway."

"What are you getting at?" Clovis asked him with a different kind of grin.

"It's not a very complete life, is it? For any of us. I could do with a change, anyway. A different kind of job, something that isn't testing and using and repairing apparatus. We do seem to have a lot of repairing to do, don't we? That analyser breaks down almost every day. And yet. . . ."

His voice tailed off and he looked out of the port, as if to assure himself that all that lay beyond it was the familiar starscape of points and smudges of light.

"And yet what?" Clovis asked, irritably this time.

"I was just thinking that we really ought to be thankful for having plenty to do. There's the routine, and the fruits and vegetables to look after, and Myri's story. . . . How's that going, by the way? Won't you read us some of it? This evening, perhaps?"

"Not until it's finished, if you don't mind."

"Oh, but I do mind. It's part of our duty to entertain one another. And I'm very interested in it personally."

"Why?"

"Because you're an interesting girl. Bright brown eyes and a healthy, glowing skin—how do you manage it after all this time in space? And you've more energy than any of us."

Myri said nothing. Bruno was good at making remarks there was nothing to say to.

"What's it about, this story of yours?" he pursued. "At least you can tell us that."

"I have told you. It's about normal life. Life on Earth before there were any space stations, lots of different people doing different things, not this—"

"That's normal life, is it, different people doing different things? I can't wait to hear what the things are. Who's the hero, Myri? Our dear Clovis?"

Myri put her hand on Clovis's shoulder. "No more, please, Bruno. Let's go back to your point about the routine. I couldn't understand why you left out the most important part, the part that keeps us busiest of all."

"Ah, the strange happenings." Bruno dipped his head in a characteristic gesture, half laugh, half nervous tremor. "And the hours we spend discussing them. Oh yes. How could I have failed to mention all that?"

"If you've got any sense you'll go on not mentioning it," Clovis snapped. "We're all fed up with the whole business."

"You may be, but I'm not. I want to discuss it. So does Myri, don't you, Myri?"

"I do think perhaps it's time we made another attempt to find a pattern," Myri said. This was a case of Bruno not being pleasant but being right.

"Oh, not again." Clovis bounded up and went over to the drinks table. "Ah, hallo, Lia," he said to the tall, thin blonde woman who had just entered with a tray of cold dishes. "Let me get you a drink. Bruno and Myri are getting philosophical—looking for patterns. What do you think? I'll tell you what I think. I think we're doing enough already. I think patterns are Base's job."

"We can make it ours too," Bruno said. "You agree, Lia?"

"Of course," Lia said in the deep voice that seemed to Myri to carry so much more firmness and individuality in its tone than any of its owner's words or actions.

"Very well. You can stay out of this if you like, Clovis. We start from the fact that what we see and hear need not be illusions, although they may be."

"At least that they're illusions that any human being might have, they're not special to us, as we know from Base's reports of what happens to other stations."

"Correct, Myri. In any event, illusions or not, they are being directed at us by an intelligence and for a purpose."

"We don't know that," Myri objected. "They may be natural phenomena, or the by-product of some intelligent activity not directed at us."

"Correct again, but let us reserve these less probable possibilities until later. Now, as a sample, consider the last week's strange happenings. I'll fetch the log so that there can be no dispute."

"I wish you'd stop it," Clovis said when Bruno had gone out to the apparatus room. "It's a waste of time."

"Time's the only thing we're not short of."

"I'm not short of anything," he said, touching her thigh. "Come with me for a little while."

"Later."

"Lia always goes with Bruno when he asks her."

"Oh yes, but that's my choice," Lia said. "She doesn't want to now. Wait until she wants to."

"I don't like waiting."

"Waiting can make it better."

"Here we are," Bruno said briskly, returning. "Right. . . . Monday. *Within a few seconds the sphere became encased in a thick brownish damp substance that tests revealed to be both impermeable and infinitely thick. No action by the staff suggested itself. After three hours and eleven minutes the substance disappeared.* It's the *infinitely thick* thing that's interesting. That must have been an illusion, or something would have happened to all the other stations at the same time, not to speak of the stars and planets. A total or partial illusion, then. Agreed?"

"Go on."

"Tuesday. *Metallic object of size comparable to that of the sphere approaching on collision course at 500 kilometres per second. No counter-measures available. Object appeared instantaneously at 35 million kilometres' distance and disappeared instantaneously at 1500 kilometres.* What about that?"

"We've had ones like that before," Lia put in. "Only thing this was the longest time it's taken to approach and the nearest it's come before disappearing."

"Incomprehensible or illusion," Myri suggested.

"Yes, I think that's the best we can do at the moment. Wednesday: a very trivial one, not worth discussing. *A being apparently constructed entirely of bone approached the main port and made beckoning motions.* Whoever's doing this must be running out of ideas. Thursday. *All bodies external to the sphere vanished to all instruments simultaneously, reappearing to all instruments simultaneously two hours later.* That's not a new one either, I seem to remember. Illusion? Good. Friday. *Beings resembling terrestrial reptiles covered the sphere, fighting ceaselessly and eating portions of one another. Loud rustling and slithering sounds.* The sounds at least must have been an illusion, with no air out there, and I never heard of a reptile that didn't breathe. The same sort of thing applies to yesterday's perfor-mance. *Human screams of pain and extreme astonishment approaching and receding. No visual or other accompaniment.*" He paused and looked round at them. "Well? Any uniformities suggest themselves?"

"No," Clovis said, helping himself to salad, for they sat now at the lunch table. "And I defy any human brain to devise any. The whole thing's arbitrary."

"On the contrary, the very next happening—today's when it comes—might reveal an unmistakable pattern."

"The one to concentrate on," Myri said, "is the approaching object. Why did it vanish before striking the sphere?"

Bruno stared at her. "It had to, if it was an illusion."

"Not at all. Why couldn't we have had an illusion of the sphere being struck? And supposing it wasn't an illusion?"

"Next time there's an object, perhaps it will strike," Lia said.

Clovis laughed. "That's a good one. What would happen if it did, I wonder? And it wasn't an illusion?"

They all looked at Bruno for an answer. After a moment or two he said: "I presume the sphere would shatter and we'd all be thrown into space. I simply can't imagine what that would be like. We should be . . . Never to see one another again, or anybody or anything else, to be nothing more than a senseless lump floating in space for ever. The chances of—"

"It would be worth something to be rid of your conversation," Clovis said, amiable again now that Bruno was discomfited. "Let's be practical for a change. How long will it take you to run off your analyses this afternoon? There's a lot of stuff to go out to Base and I shan't be able to give you a hand."

"An hour, perhaps, after I've run the final tests."

"Why run tests at all? She was lined up perfectly when we finished this morning."

"Fortunately."

"Fortunately indeed. One more variable and we might have found it impossible."

"Yes," Bruno said abstractedly. Then he got to his feet so abruptly that the other three started. "But we didn't did we? There wasn't one more variable, was there? It didn't quite happen, you see, the thing we couldn't handle."

Nobody spoke.

"Excuse me, I must be by myself."

"If Bruno keeps this up,' Clovis said to the two women, "Base will send us a relief sooner than we think."

Myri tried to drive a thought of Bruno's strange behaviour out of her head when, half an hour later, she sat down to work on her story. The expression on his face as he left the table had been one she could not name. Excitement? Dislike? Surprise? That was the nearest—a kind of persistent surprise. Well, he was certain, being Bruno, to set about explaining it at dinner. She wished he were more pleasant, because he did think well.

Finally expelling the image of Bruno's face, she began rereading the page of manuscript she had been working on when the screams had interrupted her the previous afternoon. It was part of a difficult scene, one in which a woman met by chance a man who had been having her ten years earlier, with the complication that she was at the time in the company of the man who was currently having her. The scene was an eating alcove in a large city.

*"Go away," Volsci said, "Or I'll hit you."*

*Norbu smiled in a not-pleasant way. "What good would that do? Irmy likes me better than she likes you. You are more pleasant, no doubt, but she likes me better. She remembers me having her ten years ago more clearly than she remembers you having her last night. I am good at thinking, which is better than any amount of being pleasant."*

*"She's having her meal with me," Volsci said, pointing to the cold food and drinks in front of them. "Aren't you, Irmy?"*

*"Yes, Irmy," Norbu said. "You must choose. If you can't let both of us have you, you must say which one of us you like better."*

*Irmy looked from one man to the other. There was so much difference between them that she could hardly begin to choose: the one more pleasant, the other better at thinking, the one slim, the other plump. She decided being pleasant was better. It was more important and more significant —better in every way that made a real difference. She said: "I'll have Volsci."*

*Norbu looked surprised and sorry. "I think you're wrong."*

*"You might as well go now," Volsci said. "Ila will be waiting."*

*"Yes," Norbu said. He looked extremely sorry now.*

*Irmy felt quite sorry too. "Goodbye, Norbu," she said.*

Myri smiled to herself. It was good, even better than she had remembered—there was no point in being modest inside one's own mind. She must be a real writer in spite of Bruno's scoffing, or how could she have invented these characters, who were so utterly unlike anybody she knew, and then put them into a situation that was so completely outside her experience? The only thing she was not sure about was whether she might not have overplayed the part about feeling or dwelt on it at too great length. Perhaps *extremely sorry* was a little heavy; she replaced it by *sorrier than before.* Excellent: now there was just the right touch of restraint in the middle of all the feeling. She decided she could finish off the scene in a few lines.

*"Probably see you at some cocktail hour," Volsci said,* she wrote, then looked up with a frown as the buzzer sounded at her door. She crossed her tiny wedged-shaped room—its rear wall was part of the outer wall of the sphere, but it had no port—threw the lock and found Bruno on the threshold. He was breathing fast, as if he had been hurrying or lifting a heavy weight, and she saw with distaste that there were drops of sweat on his thick skin. He pushed past her and sat down on her bed, his mouth open.

"What is it?" she asked, displeased. The afternoon was a private time unless some other arrangement were made at lunch.

"I don't know what it is. I think I must be ill."

"Ill? But you can't be. Only people on Earth get ill. Nobody on a station is ever ill: Base told us that. Illness is caused by—"

"I don't think I believe some of the things that Base says."

"But who can we believe if we don't believe Base?"

Bruno evidently did not hear her question. He said: "I had to come to you—Lia's no good for this. Please let me stay with you, I've got so much to say."

"It's no use, Bruno. Clovis is the one who has me. I thought you understood that I didn't—"

"That's not what I mean," he said impatiently. "Where I need you is in thinking. Though that's connected with the other, the having. I don't expect you to see that. I've only just begun to see it myself."

Myri could make nothing of this last part. "Thinking? Thinking about what?"

He bit his lip and shut his eyes for a moment. "Listen to this," he said. "It was the analyser that set my mind going. Almost every other day it breaks down. And the computer, the counters, the repellers, the scanners and the rest of them—they're always breaking down too, and so are their power supplies. But not the purifier of the fluid-reconstitutor or the fruit and vegetable growers or the heaters or the main power source. Why not?"

"Well, they're less complicated. How can a fruit grower go wrong? A chemical tank and a water tank is all there is to it. You ask Lia about that."

"All right. Try answering this, then. The strange happenings. If they're illusions, why are they always outside the sphere? Why are there never any inside?"

"Perhaps there are," Myri said.

"Don't. I don't want that. I shouldn't like that. I want everything in here to be real. Are you real? I must believe you are."

"Of course I'm real." She was now thoroughly puzzled.

"And it makes a difference, doesn't it? It's very important that you and everything else should be real, everything in the sphere. But tell me: whatever's arranging these happenings must be pretty powerful if it can fool our instruments and our senses so completely and consistently, and yet it can't do anything—anything we recognise as strange, that is—inside this puny little steel skin. Why not?"

"Presumably it has its limitations. We should be pleased."

"Yes. All right, next point. You remember the time I tried to sit up in the lounge after midnight and stay awake?"

"That was silly. Nobody can stay awake after midnight. Standing Orders were quite clear on that point."

"Yes, they were, weren't they?" Bruno seemed to be trying to grin. "Do you remember my telling you how I couldn't account for being in my own bed as usual when the music woke us—you remember the big music? And—this is what I'm really after—do you remember how we all agreed at breakfast that life in space must have conditioned us in such a way that falling asleep at a fixed time had become an automatic mechanism? You remember that?"

"Naturally I do."

"Right. Two questions, then. Does that strike you as a likely explanation? That sort of complete self-conditioning in all four of us after . . . just a number of months?"

"Not when you put it like that."

"But we all agreed on it, didn't we? Without hesitation."

Myri, leaning against a side wall, fidgeted. He was being not pleasant in a new way, one that made her want to stop him talking even when he was thinking at his best. "What's your other question, Bruno?" Her voice sounded unusual to her.

"Ah, you're feeling it too, are you?"

"I don't know what you mean."

"I think you will in a minute. Try my other question. The night of the music was a long time ago, soon after we arrived here, but you remember it clearly. So do I. And yet when I try to remember what I was doing only a couple of months earlier, on Earth, finishing up my life there, getting ready for this, it's just a vague blur. Nothing stands out."

"It's all so remote."

"Maybe. But I remember the trip clearly enough, don't you?"

Myri caught her breath. I feel surprised, she told herself. Or something like that. I feel the way Bruno looked when he left the lunch table. She said nothing.

"You're feeling it now all right, aren't you?" He was watching her closely with his narrow eyes. "Let me try to describe it. A surprise that goes on and on. Puzzlement. Symptoms of physical exertion or strain. And above all a . . . a sort of discomfort, only in the mind. Like having a sharp object pressed against a tender part of your body, except that this is in your mind."

"What are you talking about?"

"A difficulty of vocabulary."

The loudspeaker above the door clicked on and Clovis's voice said: "Attention. Strange happening. Assemble in the lounge at once. Strange happening."

Myri and Bruno stopped staring at each other and hurried out along the narrow corridor. Clovis and Lia were already in the lounge, looking out of the port.

Apparently only a few feet beyond the steelhard glass, and illuminated from some invisible source, were two floating figures. The detail was excellent, and the four inside the sphere could distinguish without difficulty every fold in the naked skin of the two caricatures of humanity presented, it seemed, for their thorough inspection, a presumption given added weight by the slow rotation of the pair that enabled their every portion to be scrutinised. Except for a scrubby growth at the base of the skull, they were hairless. The limbs were foreshortened, lacking the normal narrowing at the joints, and the bellies protuberant. One had male characteristics, the other female, yet in neither case were these complete. From each open, wet, quivering toothless mouth there came a loud, clearly audible yelling, higher in pitch than any those in the sphere could have produced, and of an unfamiliar emotional range.

"Well, I wonder how long this will last," Clovis said.

"Is it worth trying the repellers on them?" Lia asked. "What does the radar say? Does it see them?"

"I'll go and have a look."

Bruno turned his back on the port. "I don't like them."

"Why not?" Myri saw he was sweating again.

"They remind me of something."

"What?"

"I'm trying to think."

But although Bruno went on trying to think for the rest of that day, with such obvious seriousness that even Clovis did his best to help with suggestions, he was no nearer a solution when they parted, as was their habit, at five minutes to midnight. And when, several times in the next couple of days, Myri mentioned the afternoon of the caricatures to him, he showed little interest.

"Bruno, you are extraordinary," she said one evening. "What happened to those odd feelings of yours you were so eager to describe to me just before Clovis called us into the lounge?"

He shrugged his narrow shoulders in the almost girlish way he had. "Oh, I don't know what could have got into me," he said. "I expect I was just angry with that confounded analyser and the way it kept breaking down. It's been much better recently."

"And all that thinking you used to do."

"That was a complete waste of time."

"Surely not."

"Yes, I agree with Clovis, let Base do all the thinking."

Myri was disappointed. To hear Bruno resigning the task of thought seemed like the end of something. This feeling was powerfully underlined for her when, a little later, the announcement came over the loudspeaker in the lounge. Without any preamble at all, other than the usual click on, a strange voice said: "Your attention, please. This is Base calling over your intercom."

They all looked up in great surprise, especially Clovis, who said quickly to Bruno: "Is that possible?"

"Oh yes, they've been experimenting," Bruno replied as quickly.

"It is perhaps ironical," the voice went on, "that the first transmission we have been able to make to you by the present means is also the last you will receive by any. For some time the maintenance of space stations has been uneconomic, and the decision has just been taken to discontinue them altogether. You will therefore make no further reports of any kind, or rather you may of course continue to do so on the understanding that nobody will be listening. In many cases it has fortunately been found possible to arrange for the collection of station staffs and their return to Earth; in others, those involving a journey to the remoter parts of the galaxy, a prohibitive expenditure of time and effort would be entailed. I am sorry to have to tell you that your own station is one of these. Accordingly, you will never be relieved. All of us here are confident that you will respond to this new situation with dignity and resource.

"Before we sever communication for the last time, I have one more point to make. It involves a revelation which may prove so unwelcome that only with the greatest reluctance can I bring myself to utter it. My colleagues, however, insisted that those in your predicament deserve, in your own interests, to hear the whole truth about it. I must tell you, then, that contrary to your earlier information we have had no reports from any other station whose contents resembles in the slightest degree your accounts of the strange happenings you claim to have witnessed. The deception was considered necessary so that your morale might be maintained, but the time for deceptions is over. You are unique, and in the variety of mankind that is no small distinction. Be proud of it. Goodbye for ever."

They sat without speaking until five minutes to midnight. Try as she would, Myri found it impossible to conceive their future, and the next morning she had no more success. That was as long as any of them had leisure to come to terms with their permanent isolation, for by midday a quite new phase of strange happenings had begun. Myri and Lia were preparing lunch in the kitchen when Myri, opening the cupboard where the dishes were kept, was confronted by a flattish, reddish creature with many legs and a pair of unequally-sized pincers. She gave a gasp, almost a shriek, of astonishment.

"What is it?" Lia said, hurrying over, and then in a high voice: "Is it alive?"

"It's moving. Call the men."

Until the others came, Myri simply stared. She found her lower lip shaking in a curious way. *Inside* now, she kept thinking. Not just outside. *Inside.*

"Let's have a look," Clovis said. "I see. Pass me a knife or something." He rapped at the creature, making a dry, bony sound. "Well, it works for tactile and aural as well as visual, anyway. A thorough illusion. If it is one."

"It must be," Bruno said. "Don't you recognise it?"

"There is something familiar about it. I suppose."

"You suppose? You mean you don't know a crab when you see one?"

"Oh, of course," Clovis looked slightly sheepish. "I remember now. A terrestrial animal, isn't it? Lives in the water. And so it must be an illusion. Crabs don't cross space as far as I know, and even if they could they'd have a tough time carving their way through the skin of the sphere."

His sensible manner and tone helped Myri to get over her astonishment, and it was she who suggested that the crab be disposed of down the waste chute. At lunch she said: "It was a remarkably specific illusion, don't you think? I wonder how it was projected."

"No point in wondering about that," Bruno told her. "How can we ever know? And what use would the knowledge be to us if we did know?"

"Knowing the truth has its own value."

"I don't understand you."

Lia came in with the coffee just then. "The crab's back," she said. "Or there's another one there, I can't tell."

More crabs, or simulacra thereof, appeared at intervals for the rest of the day, eleven of them in all. It seemed, as Clovis put it, that the illusion-producing technique had its limitations, inasmuch as none of them saw a crab actually materialise: the new arrival would be "discovered" under a bed or behind a bank of apparatus. On the other hand, the depth of illusion produced was very great, as they all agreed when Myri, putting the eighth crab down the chute, was nipped in the finger, suffered pain and exuded a few drops of blood.

"Another new departure," Clovis said. "An illusory physical process brought about on the actual person of one of us. They're improving."

Next morning there were the insects. The main apparatus room was found to be infested with what, again on Bruno's prompting, they recognised as cockroaches. By lunch-time there were moths and flying beetles in all the main rooms, and a number of large flies became noticeable towards the evening. The whole of their attention became concentrated upon avoiding these creatures as far as possible. The day passed without Clovis asking Myri to go with him. This had never happened before.

The following afternoon a fresh problem was raised by Lia's announcement that the garden now contained no fruits or vegetables—none, at any rate, that were accessible to her senses. In this the other three concurred. Clovis put the feelings of all of them into words when he said: "If this is an illusion, it's as efficient as the reality, because fruits and vegetables you can never find are the same as no fruits and vegetables."

The evening meal used up all the food they had. Soon after two o'clock in the morning Myri was aroused by Clovis's voice saying over the loudspeaker: "Attention, everyone. Strange happening. Assemble in the lounge immediately."

She was still on her way when she became aware of a new quality in the background of silence she had grown used to. It was a deeper silence, as if some sound at the very threshold of audibility had ceased. There were unfamiliar vibrations underfoot.

Clovis was standing by the port, gazing through it with interest. "Look at this, Myri," he said.

At a distance impossible to gauge, an oblong of light had become visible, a degree or so in breadth and perhaps two and a half times as high. The light was of comparable quality to that illuminating the inside of the sphere. Now and then it flickered.

"What is it?" Myri asked.

"I don't know, it's only just appeared." The floor beneath them shuddered violently. "That was what woke me, one of those tremors. Ah, here you are, Bruno. What do you make of it?"

Bruno's large eyes widened further, but he said nothing. A moment later Lia arrived and joined the silent group by the port. Another vibration shook the sphere. Some vessel in the kitchen fell to the floor and smashed. Then Myri said: "I can see what looks like a flight of steps leading down from the lower edge of the light. Three or four of them, perhaps more."

She had barely finished speaking when a shadow appeared before them, cast by the rectangle of light on to a surface none of them could identify. The shadow seemed to them of a stupefying vastness, but it was beyond question that of a man. A moment later the man came into view, outlined by the light, and descended the steps. Another moment or two and he was evidently a few feet from the port, looking in at them, their own lights bright on the upper half of him. He was a well-built man wearing a grey uniform jacket and a metal helmet. An object recognisable as a gun of some sort was slung over his shoulder. While he watched them, two other figures, similarly accoutred, came down the steps and joined him. There was a brief interval, then he moved out of view to their right, doing so with the demeanour of one walking on a level surface.

None of the four inside spoke or moved, not even at the sound of heavy bolts being drawn in the section of outer wall directly in front of them, not even when that entire section swung away from them like a door opening outwards and the three men stepped through into the sphere. Two of them had unslung the guns from their shoulders.

Myri remembered an occasion, weeks ago, when she had risen from a stooping position in the kitchen and struck her head violently on the bottom edge of a cupboard door Lia had happened to leave open. The feeling Myri now experienced was similar, except that she had no particular physical sensations. Another memory, a much fainter one, passed across the far background of her mind: somebody had once tried to explain to her the likeness between a certain mental state and the bodily sensation of discomfort, and she had not understood. The memory faded sharply.

The man they had first seen said: "All roll up your sleeves."

Clovis looked at him with less curiosity than he had been showing when Myri first joined him at the port, a few minutes earlier. "You're an illusion," he said.

"No I'm not. Roll up your sleeves, all of you."

He watched them closely while they obeyed, becoming impatient at the slowness with which they moved. The other man whose gun was unslung, a younger man, said: "Don't be hard on them, Allen. We've no idea what they've been through."

"I'm not taking any chances," Allen said. "Not after that crowd in the trees. Now this is for your own good," he went on, addressing the four. "Keep quite still. All right, Douglas."

The third man came forward, holding what Myri knew to be a hypodermic syringe. He took her firmly by her bare arm and gave her an injection. At once her feelings altered, in the sense that, although there was still discomfort in her mind, neither this nor anything else seemed to matter.

After a time she heard the young man say: "You can roll your sleeves down now. You can be quite sure that nothing bad will happen to you."

"Come with us," Allen said.

Myri and the others followed the three men out of the sphere, across a gritty floor that might have been concrete and up the steps, a distance of perhaps thirty feet. They entered a corridor with artificial lighting and then a room into which the sun was streaming. There were twenty or thirty people in the room, some of them wearing the grey uniform. Now and then the walls shook as the sphere had done, but to the accompaniment of distant explosions. A faint shouting could also be heard from time to time.

Allen's voice said loudly: "Let's try and get a bit of order going. Douglas, they'll be wanting you to deal with the people in the tank. They've been conditioned to believe they're congenitally aquatic, so you'd better give them a shot that'll knock them out straight away. Holmes is draining the tank now. Off you go. Now you, James, you watch this lot while I find out some more about them. I wish those psycho chaps would turn up—we're just working in the dark." His voice moved further away. "Sergeant— get these five out of here."

"Where to, sir?"

"I don't mind where—just out of here. And watch them."

"They've all been given shots, sir."

"I know, but look at them, they're not human any more. And it's no use talking to them, they've been deprived of language. That's how they got the way they are. Now get them out right away."

Myri looked slowly at the young man who stood near them: James. "Where are we?" she asked.

James hesitated. "I was ordered to tell you nothing," he said. "You're supposed to wait for the psychological team to get to you and treat you."

"Please."

"All right. This much can't hurt you, I suppose. You four and a number of other groups have been the subject of various experiments. This building is part of Special Welfare Research Station No. 4. Or rather it was. The government that set it up no longer exists. It has been removed by the revolutionary army of which I'm a member. We had to shoot our way in here and there's fighting still going on."

"Then we weren't in space at all."

"No."

"Why did they make us believe we were?"

"We don't know yet."

"And how did they do it?"

"Some new form of deep-level hypnosis, it seems, probably renewed at regular intervals. Plus various apparatus for producing illusions. We're still working on that. Now, I think that's enough questions for the moment. The best thing you can do is sit down."

"Thank you. What's hypnosis?"

"Oh, of course they'd have removed knowledge of that. It'll all be explained to you later."

"James, come and have a look at this, will you?" Allen's voice called. "I can't make much of it."

Myri followed James a little way. Among the clamour of voices, some speaking languages unfamiliar to her, others speaking none, she heard James ask: "Is this the right file? Fear Elimination?"

"Must be," Allen answered. "Here's the last full entry. *Removal of Bruno V and substitution of Bruno VI accomplished, together with memory-adjustment of other three subjects. Memo to Preparation Centre: avoid repetition of Bruno V personality-type with strong curiosity-drives.* Started catching up to the set-up, eh? Wonder what they did with him."

"There's that psycho hospital across the way they're still investigating; perhaps he's in there."

"With Brunos I to IV, no doubt. Never mind that for the moment. Now. *Procedures: penultimate phase. Removal of all ultimate confidence: severance of communication, total denial of prospective change, inculcation of "uniqueness" syndrome, environment shown to be violable, unknowable crisis in prospect (food deprivation).* I can understand that last bit. They don't look starved, though."

"Perhaps they've only just started them on it."

"We'll get them fed in a minute. Well, all this still beats me, James. *Reactions. Little change. Responses poor. Accelerating impoverishment of emotional life and its vocabulary: compare portion of novel written by Myri VII with contributions of predecessors. Prognosis: further affective deterioration: catatonic apathy: failure of experiment.* That's a comfort, anyway. But what has all this got to do with fear elimination?"

They stopped talking suddenly and Myri followed the direction of their gaze. A door had been opened and the man called Douglas was supervising the entry of a number of others, each supporting or carrying a human form wrapped in a blanket.

"This must be the lot from the tank," Allen or James said.

Myri watched while those in the blankets were made as

comfortable as possible on benches or on the floor. One of them, however, remained totally wrapped in his blanket and was being paid no attention.

"He's had it, has he?"

"Shock, I'm afraid." Douglas's voice was unsteady. "There was nothing we could do. Perhaps we shouldn't have . . ."

Myri stooped and turned back the edge of the blanket. What she saw was much stranger than anything she had experienced in the sphere. "What's the matter with him?" she asked James.

"Matter with him? You can die of shock, you know."

"I can do what?"

Myri, staring at James, was aware that his face had become distorted by a mixture of expressions. One of them was under-standing: all the others were painful to look at. They were renderings of what she herself was feeling. Her vision darkened and she ran from the room, back the way they had come, down the steps, across the floor, back into the sphere.

James was unfamiliar with the arrangement of the rooms there and did not reach her until she had picked up the manuscript of the novel, hugged it to her chest with crossed arms and fallen on to her bed, her knees drawn up as far as they would go, her head lowered as it had been before her birth, an event of which she knew nothing.

She was still in the same position when, days later, somebody sat heavily down beside her. "Myri. You must know who this is. Open your eyes, Myri. Come out of there."

After he had said this, in the same gentle voice, some hundreds of times, she did open her eyes a little. She was in a long, high room, and near her was a fat man with a pale skin. He reminded her of something to do with space and thinking. She screwed her eyes shut.

"Myri. I know you remember me. Open your eyes again."

She kept them shut while he went on talking.

"Open your eyes. Straighten your body."

She did not move.

"Straighten your body, Myri. I love you."

Slowly her feet crept down the bed and her head lifted. . . .

# II

## AMERICAN

# THE POST-MORTEM MURDER

SINCLAIR LEWIS

*Once described as the author's solitary excursion into the realms of wonder, this story by Sinclair Lewis, the first American to win the Nobel Prize for Literature, was published in the weekly journal* The Century Magazine *in 1921. It has lain forgotten in the periodical's archives ever since and as far as can be ascertained has been reprinted only once—in a specialist magazine. It is an intriguing and strangely disturbing tale. . . .*

I WENT to Kennuit to be quiet through the summer vacation. I was tired after my first year as associate professor, and I had to finish my "Life of Ben Jonson". Certainly the last thing I desired was that dying man in the hot room and the pile of scrawled booklets.

I boarded with Mrs Nickerson in a cottage of silver-grey shingles under silver-grey poplars, heard only the harsh fiddling of locusts and the distant rage of the surf, looked out on a yard of bright wild grass and a jolly windmill weather-vane, and made notes about Ben Jonson. I was as secluded and happy as old Thoreau raising beans and feeling superior at Walden.

My fiancee—Quinta Gates, sister of Professor Gates, and lovelier than ever in the delicate culture she had attained at thirty-seven—Quinta urged me to join them at Fleet Harbour. It is agreeable to be with Quinta. While I cannot say that we are stirred to such absurd manifestations as kissing and hand-holding—why any sensible person should care to hold a damp female hand is beyond me—we do find each other inspiring. But Fleet Harbour would be full of "summerites", dreadful young people in white flannels, singing their jazz ballads.

No, at thought of my spacious, leafy freedom I wriggled with luxury and settled down to an absorbed period when night and day glided into one ecstasy of dreaming study. Naturally, then, I was angry when I heard a puckery voice outside in the tiny hallway:

"Well, if he's a professor, I got to see him."

A knock. I affected to ignore it. It was irritatingly repeated until I roared, "Well, well, well?" I am normally, I trust, a gentle person, but I desired to give them the impression of annoyance.

Mrs Nickerson billowed in, squeaking:

"Mis' White from Lobster Pot Neck wants to see you."

Past her wriggled a pinch-faced, humourless-looking woman. She glared at Mrs Nickerson, thrust her out, and shut the door. I could hear Mrs Nickerson protesting, "Well, upon my word!"

I believe I rose and did the usual civilities. I remember this woman, Miss or Mrs White, immediately asking me, with extraordinary earnestness:

"Are you a professor?"

"I teach English."

"You write books?"

I pointed to a box of manuscript.

"Then, please, you got to help us. Byron Sanders is dying. He says he's got to see a learned man to give him some important papers." Doubtless I betrayed hesitation, for I can remember her voice rising in creepy ululation: "Please! He's dying—that good old man that never hurt nobody!"

I fluttered about the room to find my cap. I fretted that her silly phrase of "important papers" sounded like a melodrama, with maps of buried treasure, or with long-lost proofs that the chore boy is really the kidnapped son of royalty. But these unconscious defences against the compulsion expressed in her face, with its taut and terrified oval of open mouth, were in vain. She mooned at me, she impatiently waited. I dabbled at my collar and lapels with my fingers, instead of decently brushing off the stains of smoking and scribbling. I came stumbling and breathless after her.

She walked rapidly, unspeaking, intense, and I followed six inches behind, bespelled by her red-and-black gingham waist and her chip of a brown hat. We slipped among the grey houses of the town, stumped into country still and shimmering with late afternoon. By a trail among long salty grasses we passed an inlet where sandpipers sprinted and horseshoe-crabs bobbed on the crisping ripples. We crossed a moorland to a glorious point of blowing grasses and sharp salt odour, with the waves of the harbour flickering beyond. In that resolute place my embarrassed awe was diluted, and I almost laughed as I wondered:

"What is this story-book errand? Ho, for the buried treasure! I'll fit up a fleet, out of the six hundred dollars I have in the savings bank, and find the pirates' skellingtons. 'Important papers!' I'll comfort the poor dying gentleman, and be back in time for another page before supper. The harbour is enchanting. I really must have a sail this summer or go swimming."

My liveliness, uneasy at best in the presence of that frightened, fleeing woman, wavered when we had dipped down through a cranberry-bog and entered a still, hot wood of dying pines. They were dying, I tell you, as that old man in there was dying. The leaves were of a dry colour of brick dust; they had fallen in heaps that crunched beneath my feet; the trunks were lean and black, with an irritation of branches; and all the dim alleys were choking with a dusty odour of decay. It was hot and hushed, and my throat tickled, my limbs dragged in a hopeless languor.

Through ugly trunks and red needles we came to a restrained dooryard and an ancient, irregular house, a dark house, very sullen. No one had laughed there these many years. The windows were draped. The low porch between the main structure and a sagging ell was drifted with the pine-needles. My companion's tread was startling and indecent on the flapping planks. She held open the door. I hesitated. I was not annoyed now; I was afraid, and I knew not of what I was afraid.

Prickly with unknown disquietude, I entered. We traversed a hall choked with relics of the old shipping days of Kennuit: a whale's vertebra, a cribbage-board carved in a walrus-tusk, a Chinese screen of washed-out gold pagodas on faded, weary black. We climbed a narrow stair over which jutted, like a secret trap-door, the corner of a mysterious chamber above. My companion opened a door in the upper hall and croaked, "In there."

I went in slowly. I am not sure now, after two years, but I think I planned to run out again, to flee downstairs, to defend myself with that ivory tusk if I should be attacked by— whatever was lurking in that shadowy, silent place. As I edged in, about me crept an odour of stale air and vile medicines and ancient linen. The shutters were fast; the light was grudging. I was actually relieved when I saw in the four-poster bed a pitiful, vellum-faced old man, and the worst monster I had to face was normal illness.

I have learned that Byron Sanders was only seventy-one then, but he seemed ninety. He was enormous. He must have been hard to care for. His shoulders, in the mended linen nightgown thrust above the patchwork comforter, were bulky; his neck was thick; his head a shiny dome—an Olympian, majestic even in dissolution.

The room had been lived in too long. It was a whirl of useless things: staggering chairs, clothes in piles, greasy medicine-bottles, and a vast writing-desk pouring out papers, and dingy books with bindings of speckled brown. Amid the litter, so still that she seemed part of it, I was startled to discern another woman. Who she may have been I have never learned.

The man ponderously turning in bed, peering at me through the shaky light.

"You are a professor?" he wheezed.

"That depends upon what you mean, sir. I teach English. I am not—"

"You understand poetry, essays, literary history?"

"I am supposed to."

"I'm a kind of a colleague of yours. Byron—" He stopped, choked frightfully. The repressed woman beside the bed, moving with stingy patience, wiped his lips. "My name is Byron Sanders. For forty years, till a year ago, I edited the *Kennuit Beacon.*"

The nauseating vanity of man! In that reverent hour, listening to the entreaties of a dying man, I was yet piqued at having my stripped athletic scholarship compared to editing the *Beacon,* with its patent-medicine advertisements, its two straggly columns of news about John Brown's cow and Jim White's dory.

His eyes trusting me, Byron Saunders went on:

"Can't last long. It's come quicker—no time to plan. I want you to take the literary remains of my father. He was not a good man, but he was a genius. I have his poetry here, and the letters. I haven't read them for years, and—too late—give them to the world. You must—"

He was desperately choking. The still woman crept up, thrust into my hands a box of papers and a pile of notebooks which had been lying on the bed.

"You must go," she muttered. "Say, 'Yes', and go. He can't stand any more."

"Will you?" the broken giant wailed to me, a stranger!

"Yes, yes, indeed; I'll give them to the world," I mumbled, while the woman pushed me towards the door.

I fled down the stairs, through the coppery pine-woods, up to the blithe headland that was swept by the sea-breeze.

I knew of course, what the "poetry" of that poor "genius" his father would be—Christmas doggerel and ditties about "love" and "dove", "heart" and "must part". I was, to be honest, irritated. I wanted to take this debris back to Mr Sanders, and that was the one thing I could not do. For once I was sensible: I took it home and tried to forget it.

In the next week's *Kennuit Beacon,* discovered on Mrs Nickerson's parlour-table, crowning a plush album, I read that Byron Sanders, "the founder and for many years the highly esteemed editor of this paper", had died.

I sought relatives to whom I could turn over his father's oddments. There was no one; he was a widower and childless. For months the bothersome papers were lost in my desk, back at the university. On the opening day of the Christmas vacation I remembered that I had not read a word of them. I was to go to Quinta Gates's for tea at a quarter to five, and to her serene companionship I looked forward as, in a tired, after-term desultoriness, I sat down to glance at Jason Sanders's caterwaulings. That was at four. It was after nine when the flabby sensation of hunger brought me back to my room and the dead fire.

In those five hours I had discovered a genius. The poetry at which I had so abominably sneered was minted glory.

I stood up, and in that deserted dormitory I shouted, and listened to the tremour of the lone sound and defiantly shouted again. That I was "excited" is too pallid a word. My life of Jonson could go hang! I was selfish about it: it meant fame for me. But I think something higher than selfishness had already come into my devotion to Jason Sanders; something of the creator's passion and the father's pride.

I was hungry enough, but I walked the room contemptuous of

it. I felt unreal. 1918 was fantastically unreal. I had for hours
been veritably back in 1850. It was all there; manuscripts which
had not been touched since 1850, which still held in their
wrinkles the very air of seventy years ago: a diary; daguerreotypes; and letters, preserved like new in the darkness, from
Poe, Emerson, Thoreau, Hawthorne, and the young Tennyson!

The diary had been intermittently kept for fifteen years. It was
outline enough for me to reconstruct the story of Jason Sanders,
born at Kennuit in 1825, probably died in Greece in 1853.


Between Cape Cod and the ocean is a war sinister and incessant. Here and there the ocean has gulped a farm, or a lighthouse
reared on a cliff, but at Kennuit the land has been the victor.
Today there are sandy flats and tepid channels where a hundred
years ago was an open harbour brilliant with a hundred sails,
crackling with tidings from the Banks, proud of whalers back
from years of cruising off Siberia and of West Indiamen pompous
with rum and sugar and the pest.

Captain Bethuel Sanders, master and owner of the *Sally S.*, was
on a voyage out of Kennuit to Pernambuco when his only child,
Jason Sanders, was born. He never came back. In every Cape
Cod burying-ground, beside the meeting-house, there are a score
of headstones with "Lost at sea". There is one, I know now, at
Kennuit for Bethuel Sanders.

His widow, daughter of a man of God who for many years had
been pastor at Truro, was a tight, tidy, capable woman. Bethuel
left her a competence. She devoted herself to keeping house and
to keeping her son from going to sea. He was not to die as his
father had, perhaps alone, last man on a wave-smashed brig.
Theirs was a neat, unkindly cottage with no windows on the
harbour side. The sailors' women-folks did not greatly esteem
the view to sea, for thither went the strong sons who would
never return. In a cottage with a low wall blank towards the
harbour lived Mrs Sanders, ardently loving her son, bitterly
restraining him. Jason was obsessed by her. She was mother,
father, sweetheart, teacher, tyrant. He stroked her cheeks, and he
feared her eye, which was a frozen coal when she caught him
lying.

In the first pages of Jason's diary, when he was only thirteen, he raged that while his schoolmates were already off to the Banks or beholding, as cabin-boys, the shining Azores, he was kept at his lessons, unmanned, in apron-strings. Resources of books he had from his parson grandsire: Milton, Jeremy Taylor, Pope. If the returned adventurers sneered at him, he dusted their jackets, He must have been hardy and reasonably vicious. He curtly records that he beat Peter Williams, son of the Reverend Abner Williams, "till he could scarce move", and that for this ferocity he was read out of meeting. He became a hermit, the village "bad boy".

He was at once scorned as a "softy" by his mates because he did not go to sea, dreaded by their kin because he was a marking fighter, bombarded by his Uncle Ira because he would not become a grocer, and chided by his mother because he had no calling to the ministry. Nobody, apparently, took the trouble to understand him. The combination of reading and solitude led him inevitably to scribbling. On new-washed Cape Cod afternoons, when grasses rustled on the cream-shadowed dunes, he sat looking out to sea, chin in hand, staring at ardent little waves and lovely sails that bloomed and vanished as the schooners tacked; and through evenings rhythmic with the surf he sought with words which should make him enviable to justify himself and his mocked courage.

At twenty he ran off to sea on a fishing schooner.

Twenty he was and strong, but when he returned his mother larruped him. Apparently he submitted; his comment in the famous diary is: "Mother kissed me in welcome, then, being a woman of whimsies somewhat distasteful to a man of my sober nature, she stripped off my jacket and lashed me with a strip of whalebone long and surprisingly fanged. I shall never go a-whaling if so very little of a whale can be so very unamiable."

This process neatly finished, Mrs Sanders—she was a swift and diligent woman—immediately married the young bandit off to a neighbour woman four years his senior, a comely woman, pious, and gifted with dullness. Within the year was born a son, the Byron Sanders whom I saw dying as a corpulent elder.

That was in 1847, and Jason was twenty-two.

He went to work—dreaming and the painful carving of beautiful words not being work—in the Mammoth Store and Seamen's Outfitters. He was discharged for, imprimis, being drunk and abusive; further, stealing a knife of the value of two shillings. For five or six years he toiled in a sail-loft. I fancy that between stitchings of thick canvas he read poetry, a small book hidden in the folds of a topsail, and with a four-inch needle he scratched on shingles a plan of Troy. He was discharged now and then for roistering, and now and then was grudgingly hired again.

I hope that nothing I have said implies that I consider Jason a young man of virtue. I do not. He drank Jamaica rum, he stole strawberries, his ways with the village girls were neither commendable nor in the least commended, and his temper was such that he occasionally helped himself to a fight with sailors, and regularly, with or without purpose, thrashed the unfortunate Peter Williams, son of the Reverend Abner.

Once he betrayed a vice far meaner. A certain Boston matron, consort of a highly esteemed merchant, came summering to Kennuit, first of the tennis-yelping hordes who now infest the cape and interrupt the meditations of associate professors. This worthy lady was literary, and doubtless musical and artistic. She discovered that Jason was a poet. She tried to patronise him; in a highfalutin way she commanded him to appear next Sunday, to read aloud and divert her cousins from Boston. For this she would give him a shilling and what was left of the baked chicken. He gravely notes: "I told her to go to the devil. She seemed put out." The joke is that three weeks later he approached the good matron with a petition to be permitted to do what he had scorned. She rightly, he records without comment, "showed me the door".

No, he was virtuous save in bellicose courage, and he was altogether casual about deserting his wife and child when, the year after his mother died, he ran away to the Crimean War. But I think one understands that better in examining, as I have examined with microscope and aching eye, the daguerreotypes of Jason and his wife and boy.

Straight-nosed and strong-lipped was Jason at twenty-six or -seven. Over his right temple hung an impatient lock. He wore the high, but open and flaring, collar of the day, the space in front filled with the soft folds of a stock. A fluff of side-whiskers along the jaw set off his resoluteness of chin and brow. His coat was long-skirted and heavy, with great collar and wide lapels, a cumbrous garment, yet on him as graceful as a cloak. But his wife! Her eyes stared, and her lips, though for misery and passionate

prayer they had dark power, seem in the mirrory old picture to
have had no trace of smiles. Their son was dumpy. As I saw him
dying there in the pine woods, Byron Sanders appeared a godly
man and intelligent; but at six or seven he was pudding-faced,
probably with a trick of howling. In any case, with or without
reason, Jason foully deserted them.

In 1853, at the beginning of the struggle between Russia and
Turkey that was to develop into the Crimean War, Greece
planned to invade Turkey. Later, to prevent alliance between
Greece and Russia, the French and English forces held Piraeus;
but for a time Greece seemed liberated.

Jason's diary closes with a note:

*Tomorrow I leave this place of sand and sandy brains; make by friend
Bearse's porgy boat for Long Island, thence to New York and ship
for Piraeus, for the glory of Greece and the memory of Byron. How
better can a man die? And perhaps some person of intelligence there
will comprehend me. Thank fortune my amiable spouse knows naught.
If ever she finds this, may she grant forgiveness, as I grant it to her!*

That is all—all save a clipping from the *Lynmouth News Letter*
of seven years later announcing that as no word of Mr Jason
Sanders had come since his evanishment, his widow was peti-
tioning the court to declare him legally dead.

This is the pinchbeck life of Jason Sanders. He lived not in
life, but in his writing, and that is tinct with genius. Five years
before Whitman was known he was composing what today we
call "free verse". There are in it impressions astoundingly like
Amy Lowell. The beauty of a bitter tide-scourged garden and
of a bitter sea-scourged woman who walks daily in that sterile
daintiness is one of his themes, and the poem is as radiant and
as hard as ice.

Then the letters.

Jason had sent his manuscripts to the great men of the day.
From most of them he had noncommittal acknowledgments.
His only encouragement came from Edgar Allan Poe, who in
1849, out of the depths of his own last discouragement, wrote
with sympathy:

*I pledge you my heart that you have talent. You will go far if
you can endure hatred and disgust, forgetfulness and bitter bread,*

*blame for your most valorous and for your weakness and meekness, the praise of matrons and the ladylike.*

That letter was the last thing I read before dawn on Christmas day.

On the first train after Christmas I hastened down to the winter-clutched cape.


As Jason had died sixty-five years before, none but persons of eighty or more would remember him. One woman of eighty-six I found, but beyond, "Heh? Whas sat?" she confided only: "Jassy Sanders was a terror to snakes. Run away from his family, that's what he done! Poetry? Him write poetry? Why, he was a sail-maker!"

I heard then of Abiathar Gould, eighty-seven years old, and already become a myth streaked with blood and the rust of copper bottoms. He had been a wrecker, suspected of luring ships ashore with false lights in order that he might plunder them with his roaring mates. He had had courage enough, plunging in his whaleboat through the long swells after a storm, but mercy he had not known. He was not in Kennuit itself; he lived down by the Judas Shoals, on a lean spit of sand running seven miles below Lobster Pot Neck.

How could one reach him? I asked Mrs Nickerson.

Oh, that was easy enough: one could walk! Yes, and one did walk, five miles against a blast whirling with snow, grinding with teeth of sand. I cursed with surprising bitterness, and planned to give up cigarettes and to do patent chest exercises. I wore Mr Aaron Bloomer's coonskin coat, Mrs Nickerson's grey flannel muffler, David Dill's fishing-boots, and Mrs Antonia Sparrow's red flannel mittens; but, by the gods, the spectacles were my own, and mine the puffing, the cramped calves, and the breath that froze white on that itchy collar! Past an inlet with grasses caught in the snow-drifted ice; along the frozen beach, which stung my feet at every pounding step; among sand-dunes, which for a moment gave blessed shelter; out again into the sweep of foam-slavering wind, the bellow of the surf, I went.

I sank all winded on the icy step of Captain Abiathar Gould's bachelor shack.

He was not deaf and he was not dull at eighty-seven. He came to the door, looked down on me, and grunted:

"What do you want? D'yuh bring me any hootch?"

I hadn't. There was much conversation bearing on that point while I broiled and discovered new muscles by his stove. He had only one bunk, a swirl of coiled blankets and comforters and strips of gunny-sacking. I did not care to spend the night; I had to be back. I opened:

"Cap'n, you knew Jason Sanders?"

"Sanders? I knew Byron Sanders, and Gideon Sanders of Wellfleet and Cephas Sanders of Falmouth and Bessie Sanders, but I never knew no Jason—oh, wa'n't he Byron's pa? Sure I remember him. Eight or nine years old 'n I was. Died in foreign parts. I was a boy on the *Dancing Jig* when he went fishing. Only time he ever went. W'a'n't much of a fisherman."

"Yes, but do you remember—"

"Don't remember nothing. Jassy never went with us fellows; had his nose in a book. Some said he was a good fighter; I dunno."

"But didn't you—how did he talk, for instance?"

"Talk? Talked like other folks, I suppose. But he wa'n't a fisherman, like the rest of us. Oh, one time he tanned my hide for tearing up some papers with writin' on 'em that I swiped for gun-wadding."

"What did he say then?"

"He said—"

On second thought it may not be discreet to report what Jason said.

Beyond that Captain Gould testified only:

"Guess I kind of get him mixed up with the other fellows; good many years ago. But"—he brightened—"I recollect he wa'n't handy round a schooner. No, he wa'n't much of a fisherman."

When I got back to Kennuit my nose was frozen.

No newspaper had been published in Kennuit before 1877, and I unearthed nothing more. Yet this very blankness made Jason Sanders my own province. I knew incomparably more about him than any other living soul. He was at once my work, my spiritual ancestor, and my beloved son. I had a sense of the importance and nobility of all human life such as—I acknowledge sadly—I had never acquired in dealing with cubbish undergraduates. I wondered how many Jasons might be lost in the routine of my own classes. I forgot my studies of Ben Jonson. I was obsessed by Jason.

Quinta Gates—I don't know—when I met her at the president's reception in February, she said I had been neglecting her. At the time I supposed that she was merely teasing; but I wonder now. She was—oh, too cool; she hadn't quite the frankness I had come to depend on in her. I don't care. Striding the dunes with Jason, I couldn't return to Quinta and the discussion of sonatas in a lavender twilight over thin tea-cups.

I gave Jason Sanders to the world in a thumping article in *The Weekly Gonfalon*.

Much of it was reprinted in the New York *Courier's* Sunday literary section, with Jason's picture, and—I note it modestly—with mine, the rather interesting picture of me in knickers sitting beside Quinta's tennis court. Then the New York *Gem* took him up. It did not mention me or my article. It took Jason under its own saffron wing and crowed, at the head of a full-page Sunday article:

## VICIOUS EUROPEAN CONSPIRACY HIDES DEATH OF GREATEST AMERICAN BARD

I was piqued by their theft, but I was also amused to see the creation of a new mythical national hero. *The Gem* had Jason sailing nine of the seven seas, and leading his crew to rescue a most unfortunate Christian maiden who had been kidnapped by the Turks—at Tangier! About the little matter of deserting his wife and son *The Gem* was absent-minded. According to them, Jason's weeping helpmate bade him, "Go where duty calls you", whereupon he kissed her, left her an agreeable fortune, and departed with banners and bands. But *The Gem's* masterpiece was the interview with Captain Abiathar Gould, whose conversational graces I have portrayed. In *The Gem* Captain Gould rhapsodises:

> *We boys was a wild lot, sailing on them reckless ships. But Captain Jason Sanders was, well, sir, he was like a god to us. Not one of the crew would have dared, like he done, to spring overboard in a wintry*

*blast to rescue the poor devils capsized in a dory, and yet he was so quiet
and scholarly, always a-reading at his poetry books between watches.
Oh, them was wonderful days on the barkantine* Dancing Jig!

The *Gem* reporter must have taken down to Abiathar some of
the "hootch" I failed to bring with me.

I was—to be honest, I was un-academically peeved. My hero
was going out of my hands, and I wanted him back. I got him
back. No one knew what had happened to Jason after he went to
Greece, but I found out. With a friend in the European history
department I searched all available records of Greek history in
1853–54. I had faith that the wild youngster would tear his way
through the dryest pages of reports.

We discovered that in '54, when the French and English
occupied Piraeus, a mysterious Lieutenant Jasmin Sandec appeared as a popular hero in Athens. Do you see the resemblance?
Jasmin Sandec—Jason Sanders. The romantic boy had coloured
his drab Yankee name. Nobody quite knew who Lieutenant
Sandec was. He was not Greek. The French said he was English;
the English said he was French. He led a foray of rollicking
young Athenians against the French lines; he was captured and
incontinently shot. After his death an American sea captain
identified Lieutenant Sandec as a cousin of his! He testified that
Sandec was not his name, though what his name was the skipper
did not declare. He ended with:

"My cousin comes from the town of Kennebunkport, and has
by many people been thought to be insane."

Need I point out how easily the Greek scribe confused
Kennebunkport with Kennuit? As easily as the miserable cousinly
captain confused insanity with genius.

Do you see the picture of Jason's death? Was it not an end
more fitting than moulding away in a sail-loft, or becoming a
grocer, a parson, an associate professor? The Grecian afternoon
sun glaring on the whitewashed wall, the wine-dark sea, the
marble-studded hills of Sappho, and a youth, perhaps in a crazy
uniform, French shako and crimson British coat, Cape Cod
breeches and Grecian boots, lounging dreamily, not quite understanding; a line of soldiers with long muskets; a volley, and that
fiery flesh united to kindred dust from the bright body of Helen
and the thews of Ajax.

The report of these facts about Jason's fate I gave in my second article in *The Gonfalon*. By this time people were everywhere discussing Jason.

It was time for my book.

Briefly, it was a year's work. It contained all his writing and the lives of three generations of Sanderses. It had a reasonable success, and it made of Jason's notoriety a solid fame. So, in 1919, sixty-five years after his death, he began to live.

An enterprising company published his picture in a large carbon print which appeared on school-room walls beside portraits of Longfellow, Lowell, and Washington. So veritably was he living that I saw him! In New York, at a pageant representing the great men of America, he was enacted by a clever young man made up to the life, and shown as talking to Poe. That, of course, was inaccurate. Then he appeared as a character in a novel; he was condescendingly mentioned by a celebrated visiting English poet; his death was made the subject of a painting; a motion-picture person inquired as to the possibilities of "filming" him, and he was, in that surging tide of new living, suddenly murdered!


The poison which killed Jason the second time was in a letter to *The Gonfalon* from Whitney A. Edgerton, PhD, adjunct professor of English literature in Melanchthon College.

Though I had never met Edgerton, we were old combatants. The dislike had started with my stern, but just, review of his edition of Herrick. Edgerton had been the only man who had dared to sneer at Jason. In a previous letter in *The Gonfalon* he had hinted that Jason had stolen his imagery from Chinese lyrics, a pretty notion, since Jason probably never knew that the Chinese had any literature save laundry checks. But now I quote his letter:

> *I have seen reproductions of a very bad painting called "The Death of Jason Sanders", portraying that admirable young person as being shot in Greece. It happens that Mr Sanders was not shot in Greece. He deserved to be, but he wasn't. Jason Sanders was not Jasmin Sandec. The changing of his own honest name to such sugar-candy was the sort of thing he would have done. But he didn't do it. What kept Jason from*

*heroically dying in Greece in 1845 was the misfortune that from December, '53, to April, '58, he was doing time in the Delaware State Penitentiary for the proved crimes of arson and assault with intent to kill. His poetic cell in Delaware was the nearest he ever, in his entire life, came to Greece. Yours, etc.*

*Whitney Edgerton.*

The editor of *The Gonfalon* telegraphed me the contents of the letter just too late for me to prevent its printing, and one hour later I was bound for Delaware, forgetting, I am afraid, that Quinta had invited me to dinner. I knew that I would "show up" this Edgerton.

The warden of the penitentiary was interested. He helped me. He brought out old registers. We were thorough. We were too thorough. We read that Jason Sanders of Kennuit, Massachusetts, married, professional sailmaker, was committed to the penitentiary in December, 1853, for arson and murderous assault, and that he was incarcerated for over four years.

In the Wilmington library, in the files of a newspaper long defunct, I found an item dated, November, 1853:

*What happens to have been a piece of wretched scoundrelism was perpetrated at the house of Mr Palatinus, a highly esteemed farmer residing near Christiansburg, last Thursday. Mr Palatinus gave food and shelter to a tramp calling himself Sanders, in return for some slight labour. The second evening the fellow found some spirits concealed in the barn, became intoxicated, demanded money from Mr Palatinus, struck him, cast the lamp upon the floor, and set fire to the dwelling. He has been arrested and is held for trial. He is believed to have been a sailor on Cape Cod.*

I did not make any especial haste to communicate my discoveries.

It was New York *Gem* correspondent who did that. His account was copied rather widely.

The pictures of Jason were taken down from school-room walls.

I returned to the university. I was sustained only by Quinta's faith. As she sat by the fire, chin resting against fragile fingers, she asserted, "Perhaps there has been some mistake." That inspired me. I left her, too hastily, it may be, but she is ever one to understand and forgive me. I fled to my rooms, stopping only

to telephone to my friend of the history department. He assured
me that there was a common Greek family name, Palatainos!
You will note its resemblance to Palatinus! At this I jigged in the
drug-store telephone-booth and joyfully beat on the resounding
walls, and looked out to see one of my own students, purchasing
a bar of chocolate, indecently grinning at me. I sought to stalk
out, but I could not quiet my rejoicing feet.

I began my new letter to *The Gonfalon* at ten in the evening. I
finished it at five of a cold morning. I remember myself as
prowling through the room with no dignity, balancing myself
ridiculously on the brass bar at the foot of my bed, beating my
desk with my fists, lighting and hurling down cigarettes.

In my letter I pointed out—I virtually proved—that the
Delaware farmer's name was not Palatinus, but Palatainos. He
was a Greek. He could not have sheltered Jason "in return for
some slight labour", because this was December, when farm-
work was slackest. No, this Palatainos was an agent of the Greek
revolutionists. Jason was sent from New York to see him. Can
you not visualise it?

The ardent youngster arrives, is willing to take from
Palatainos any orders, however desperate. And he finds that
Palatainos is a traitor, is in the pay of the Turks! Sitting in the
kitchen, by a fireplace of whitewashed bricks, Palatainos leers
upon the horrified Yankee lad with the poisonous sophistication
of an international spy. He bids Jason spy upon the Greeks in
America. Staggered, Jason goes feebly up to bed. All next day he
resists the traitor's beguilement. Palatainos plies him with
brandy. The poet sits brooding; suddenly he springs up, righ-
teously attacks Palatainos, the lamp is upset, the house partly
burned, and Jason, a stranger and friendless, is arrested by the
besotted country constable. He was, in prison, as truly a martyr
to freedom as if he had veritably been shot in a tender-coloured
Grecian afternoon!

My reconstruction of the history was—though now I was so
distressed that I could take but little pride in it—much quoted
from *The Gonfalon* not only in America, but abroad. The *Mercure de
France* mentioned it, inexcusably misspelling my name. I turned
to the tracing of Jason's history after his release from the
penitentiary, since now I did not know when and where he
actually had died. I was making plans when there appeared

another letter from Whitney Edgerton, the secret assassin of Jason. He snarled that Palatinus's name was not Palatainos. It was Palatinus. He was not Greek; he was a Swede.

I wrote to Edgerton, demanded his proofs, his sources for all this information. He did not answer. He answered none of my half-dozen letters.

*The Gonfalon* announced that it had been deceived in regard to Jason, that it would publish nothing more about him. So for the third time Jason Sanders was killed, and this time he seemed likely to remain dead.

Shaky, impoverished by my explorations on Cape Cod and in Delaware, warned by the dean that I should do well to stick to my teaching and cease "these unfortunate attempts to gain notoriety", I slunk into quiet classwork, seemingly defeated. Yet all the while I longed to know when and where Jason really had died. Might he not have served valorously in the American Civil War? But how was I to know? Then came my most extraordinary adventure in the service of Jason Sanders.

I went to Quinta's for tea. I have wondered sometimes if Quinta may not have become a bit weary of my speculations about Jason. I did not mean to bore her; I tried not to: but I could think of nothing else, and she alone was patient with me.

"How—how—how can I force Edgerton to tell all he knows?" I said with a sigh.

"Go see him!" Quinta was impatient.

"Why, you know I can't afford to, with all my savings gone, and Edgerton way out in Nebraska."

She shocked me by quitting the room. She came back holding out a cheque—for three hundred dollars! The Gateses are wealthy, but naturally I could not take this. I shook my head.

"Please!" she said sharply. "Let's get it over."

I was suddenly hopeful.

"Then you do believe in Jason? I'd thought you were almost indifferent to him."

"I—" It flared out, that sound. She went on compactly: "Let's not talk about it, please. Now tell me, didn't you think they made a mistake at the symphony—"

I had a not at all pleasant conference with the dean before I took my train for Melanchthon, Nebraska.

I had a plan. This was towards the end of the academic year

1919–20. I would pretend to be a chap who, after working in offices, that sort of thing, desired to begin graduate work in English, but had first to make up for the courses he had forgotten since college. I wanted the celebrated Dr Whitney Edgerton to tutor me. I would lure him into boarding me at his house; a young professor like Edgerton would be able to use the money. Once dwelling there, it would be easy enough to search his study, to find what histories or letters had furnished his secret knowledge of Jason.

I adopted as *nom de guerre* the name Smith. That was, perhaps, rather ingenious, since it is a common name, and therefore unlikely to arouse attention. It was all reasonable, and should have been easy.

But when, in Melanchthon, I was directed to Edgerton's house, I perceived that, instead of being a poor devil, he was uncomfortably rich. His was a monstrous Georgian house, all white columns and dormers and iron window-railings and brick terrace and formal gardens. Reluctantly, I gained entrance, and addressed myself to Edgerton.

He was a square-built, pompous, rimless-eyeglassed, youngish man. His study was luxurious, with velvet curtains at the windows, with a vast desk, with built-in cases containing books I yearned to possess; a vast apartment, all white and tender blue, against which my two patchy rooms in Hendrik Hall seemed beggary. I had expected to have to conceal hatred, but instead I was embarrassed. Yet by the gods it was I, the shabby scholar, who had created Jason, and this silken, sulky dilettante who without reason had stabbed him!

While I peeped about, I was telling Edgerton, perhaps less deftly than I had planned, of my desire to be tutored.

He answered:

"You're very complimentary, I'm sure, but I'm afraid it's impossible. I'll recommend you to someone— By the way, what was your college?"

Heaven knows how it popped into my head, but I recalled an obscure and provincial school, Titus College, of which I knew nothing.

He lightened.

"Oh, really? Did you know I had my first instructorship in Titus? Haven't had any news from there for years. How is

President Dolson, and Mrs Siebel? Oh, and how is dear old Cassaworthy?"

May the trustees of Titus College forgive me! I had President Dolson sick of a fever, and Cassaworthy—professor, janitor, village undertaker, or whatever he was—taking to golf. As for Mrs Siebel, she'd given me a cup of tea only a few months ago. Edgerton seemed astonished. I have often wondered whether Mrs Siebel would actually be most likely to serve tea, gin, or vitriol.

Edgerton got rid of me. He amiably kicked me out. He smiled, gave me the name of a "suitable tutor", mesmerised me towards the door, and did not invite me to return. I sat on a bench in the Melanchthon station. Apparently I had come from the Atlantic seaboard to Nebraska to sit on this broken bench and watch an undesirable citizen spit at a box of sawdust.

I spent the night at a not agreeable tavern or hotel, and next day I again called on Edgerton. I had surmised that he would be bored by the sight of me. He was. I begged him to permit me to look over his library. Impatiently, he left me alone, hinting, "When you go out, be sure and close the front door."

With the chance of someone entering, it would not have been safe to scurry through his desk and his ingenious cabinets in search of data regarding Jason. But while I stood apparently reading, with a pen-knife I so loosened the screws in a window-catch that the window could be thrust up from outside.

I was going to burglarise the study.

That night, somewhat after twelve, I left my room in the hotel, yawned about the office, pretended to glance at the ragged magazines, sighed to the drowsy night clerk, "I think I'll have some fresh air before I retire," and sauntered out. In my inner pocket were a screw-driver and a small electric torch which I had that afternoon purchased at a hardware shop. I knew from the fiction into which I had sometimes dipped that burglars find these torches and screw-drivers, or "jimmies", of value in their work.

I endeavoured, as I stole about the streets, to assume an expression of ferocity, to intimidate whoever might endeavour to interrupt me. For this purpose I placed my spectacles in my pocket and disarrayed my bow-tie.

I was, perhaps, thrown off my normal balance. For the good

name of Jason Sanders I would risk all of serene repute that had been precious to me. So I, who had been a lecturer to respectful students, edged beneath the cottonwoods, slipped across a lawn, crawled over a wire fence, and stood in the garden of Whitney Edgerton. It was fenced and walled on all sides save towards the street. That way, then, I should have to run in case of eruption— out into the illumination of a street lamp. I might be very prettily trapped. Suddenly I was a-tremble, utterly incredulous that I should be here.

I couldn't do it.

I was menaced from every side. Wasn't that someone peering from an upper window of the house? Didn't a curtain move in the study? What was that creak behind me? I, who had never in my life spoken to a policeman save to ask a direction, had thrust myself in here, an intruder, to be treated like a common vagrant, to be shamed and roughly handled. As I grudgingly swayed towards the study windows I was uneasy before imaginary eyes. I do not remember a fear of being shot. It was something vaguer and more enfeebling: it was the staring disapproval of all my civilisation, schools, churches, banks, the courts, and Quinta. But I came to the central window of the study, the window whose catch I had loosened.

I couldn't do it.

It had seemed so easy in fiction; but crawl in there? Into the darkness? Face the unknown? Shin over the sill like a freshman? Sneak and pilfer like a mucker?

I touched the window; I think I tried to push it up. It was beyond my strength.

Disgust galvanised me. I to thieve from the thief who had slain Jason Sanders? Never! I had a right to know his information; I had a right. By heavens! I'd shake it out of him; I'd face, beat, kill that snobbish hound. I remember running about the corner of the house, jabbing the button of the bell, bumping the door panels with sore palms.

A light, and Edgerton's voice:

"What is it? What is it?"

"Quick! A man hurt! Motor accident!" I bellowed.

He opened the door. I was on him, pushing him back into the hall, demanding:

"I want everything you have about Jason Sanders!" I noticed

then that he had a revolver. I am afraid I hurt his wrist. Somewhat after, when I had placed him in a chair in the study, I said: "Where did you get your data? And where did Sanders die?"

"You must be this idiot that's been responsible for the Sanders folderol," he was gasping.

"Will you be so good as to listen? I am going to kill you unless you give me what I wish, and immediately."

"Wh-what! See here!"

I don't remember. It's curious; my head aches when I try to recall that part. I think I must have struck him, yet that seems strange, for certainly he was larger than I and better fed. But I can hear him piping:

"This is an outrage! You're insane! But if you insist, I had all my facts about Sanders from Peter Williams, a clergyman out in Yancey, Colorado."

"Let me see your letters from him."

"Is that necessary?"

"Do you think I'd trust you?"

"Well, I have only one letter here. The others are in my safe-deposit vault. Williams first wrote to me when he read my letter criticising your articles. He has given me a good many details. He apparently has some reason to hate the memory of Sanders. Here's his latest epistle, some more facts about Sander's delightful poetic career."

One glance showed me that this was indeed the case. The sheet which Edgerton handed me had inartistically printed at the top, "Rev. Peter F. Williams, Renewalist Brotherhood Congregation, Yancey, Colo.", and one sentence was, "Before this, Sanders's treatment of women in Kennuit was disgraceful—can't be too strongly condem'd."

I had the serpent of whose venom Edgerton was but the bearer!

I backed out, left Edgerton. He said a silly thing, which shows that he was at least as flustered as I was:

"Goodbye, Lieutenant Sandec!"

I was certain that he would have me apprehended if I returned to my hotel, even for so long as would be needed to gather my effects. Instantly, I decided to abandon my luggage, hasten out of town. Fortunately, I had with me neither my other suit nor the fitted bag which Quinta had given me. Traversing only side streets, I sped out of town by the railway track. Then I was glad of the pocket flashlight which, outside the study window, had seemed absurd. I sat on the railway embankment. I can still feel the grittiness of sharp-cornered cinders and cracked rock, still see the soggy pile of rotting logs beside the embankment upon which my flashlight cast a milky beam as I switched it on in order that I might study Peter Williams's letter.

Already I had a clue.

Peter Williams was also the name of that son of the Reverend Abner Williams of Kennuit whom Jason had often trounced. I wished that he had trounced him oftener and more roundly. The Reverend Abner had hurled Jason out of his church. All this would naturally institute a feud between Jason and the Williamses. There might have been additional causes, perchance rivalry for a girl.

Well! The Reverend Peter Williams's letter to Edgerton was typewritten. That modernity would indicate, in a village parson, a man not over forty years old. Was it not logical to guess that Peter Williams of Colorado was the grandson of Peter Williams of Kennuit, and that he had utilised information long possessed by the whole tribe of the Williamses to destroy his grandsire's enemy, Jason?

By dawn I was on a way-train; in the afternoon of the next day I was in Yancey, Colorado.

I found the Renewalist parsonage, residence of the Reverend Peter Williams, to be a small, dun-coloured cottage on a hill-crest. I strode thither, vigorous with rage. I knocked. I faced a blank Teutonic maid. I demanded to see Mr Williams.

I was admitted to his rustic study. I saw a man not of forty, as his letter had suggested, but astoundingly old, an ancient dominie, as sturdy as a bison, with a bursting immensity of white beard. He was sitting in a hollowed rocker close by the stove.

"Well?" said he.

"Is this the Reverend Peter Williams?"

"It be."

"May I sit down?"

"You can."

I sat calmly in a small, mean chair. My rage was sated by perceiving that I had to deal not with any grandson of Jason's foe, but with the actual original Peter Williams himself! I was beholding one who had been honoured by the fists of Jason Sanders. He was too precious a serpent not to draw him with cunning. Cautiously, I pursued:

"I was told—I once spent a summer on Cape Cod—"

"Who are you, young man?"

"Smith, William Smith."

"Well, well, let's have it."

"I was told you came from the Cape—from Kennuit."

"Well, what of it?"

"I just wondered if you weren't the son of the Reverend Abner Williams who used to be pastor in Kennuit."

"I be. I am the son in the spirit of that man of holiness."

Cautiously, oh, so cautiously, simulating veneration, I hinted:

"Then you must have known this fellow I've been reading about; this Jason—what was it?—Sandwich?"

"Jason Sanders. Yes, sir, I knew him well, too well. A viler wretch never lived. A wine-bibber, a man of wrath, blind to the inner grace, he was all that I seek to destroy." Williams's voice loomed like a cathedral service. I hated him, yet I was impressed. I ventured:

"One thing I've often wondered. They say this Sanders fellow didn't really die in Greece. I wonder when and where he did die."

The old man was laughing; he was wrinkling his eyes at me; he was shaking.

"You're daft, but you have grit. I know who you be. Edgerton telegraphed me you were coming. So you like Jason, eh?"

"I do."

"He was a thief, a drunkard—"

"And I tell you he was a genius!"

"You tell me! Huh!"

"See here, what reason has there been for your dogging Jason? It wasn't just your boyish fighting and—how did you find out what became of him after he left Kennuit?"

The old man looked at me as though I were a bug. He answered slowly, with a drawl maddening to my impatience.

"I know it because in his prison—" he stopped, yawned,

rubbed his jaw—"in his cell I wrestled with the evil spirit in him."

"You won?"

"I did."

"But after that—when did he die?" I asked.

"He didn't."

"You mean Jason is alive now—"

"He's ninety-five years old. You see, I'm—I was till I rechristened myself Williams—I'm Jason Sanders," he replied.

Then for two thousand miles, by village street and way-train and limited, sitting unmoving in berths and silent in smoking-rooms, I fled to the cool solace of Quinta Gates.

# THE DANCE

## F. SCOTT FITZGERALD

*While most of Scott Fitzgerald's work has remained in print from the time of publication, it is surprising to discover that the following splendid "thriller", written in 1926, has never been included in the popular collections of his stories. The reason for the omission is not easy to explain. The Dance is a study of the dark forces below the surface of everyday life and has remarkable power.*

ALL MY life I have had a rather curious horror of small towns: not suburbs; they are quite a different matter—but the little lost cities of New Hampshire and Georgia and Kansas, and upper New York. I was born in New York City, and even as a little girl I never had any fear of the streets of the strange foreign faces—but on the occasions when I've been in the sort of place I'm referring to, I've been oppressed with the consciousness that there was a whole hidden life, a whole series of secret implications, significances and terrors, just below the surface, of which I knew nothing. In the cities everything good or bad eventually comes out, comes out of people's hearts, I mean. Life moves about, moves on, vanishes. In the small towns—those of between 5,000 and 25,000 people—old hatreds, old and unforgotten affairs, ghostly scandals and tragedies, seem unable to die, but live on all tangled up with the ebb and flow of outward life.

Nowhere has this sensation come over me more insistently than in the South. Once out of Atlanta and Birmingham and New Orleans, I often have the feeling that I can no longer communicate with the people around me. The men and the girls speak a language wherein courtesy is combined with violence, fanatic morality with corn-drinking recklessness, in a fashion which I can't understand. In *Huckleberry Finn* Mark Twain described some of those towns perched along the Mississippi

River, with their fierce feuds and their equally fierce revivals—
and some of them haven't fundamentally changed beneath their
new surface of flibbers and radios. They are deeply uncivilised
to this day.

I speak of the South because it was in a small southern city of
this type that I once saw the surface crack for a minute and
something savage, uncanny and frightening rear its head. Then
the surface closed again—and when I have gone back there
since, I've been surprised to find myself as charmed as ever by
the magnolia trees and the singing darkies in the street and the
sensuous warm nights. I have been charmed, too, by the
bountiful hospitality and the languorous easy-going outdoor life
and the almost universal good manners. But all too frequently I
am the prey of a vivid nightmare that recalls what I experienced
in that town five years ago.

Davis—that is not its real name—has a population of about
20,000 people, one-third of them coloured. It is a cotton-mill
town, and the workers of that trade, several thousand gaunt and
ignorant "poor whites", live together in an ill-reputed section
known as "Cotton Hollow". The population of Davis has
varied in its seventy-five years. Once it was under consideration
for the capital of the State, and so the older families and their
kin form a little aristocracy, even when individually they have
sunk to destitution.

That winter I'd made the usual round in New York until
about April, when I decided I never wanted to see another
invitation again. I was tired and I wanted to go to Europe for a
rest; but the baby panic of 1921 hit father's business, and so it
was suggested that I go South and visit Aunt Musidora Hale
instead.


Vaguely I imagined that I was going to the country, but on
the day I arrived the *Davis Courier* published a hilarious old
picture of me on its society page, and I found I was in for
another season. On a small scale, of course: there were
Saturday-night dances at the little country-club with its nine-
hole golf-course, and some informal dinner parties and several
attractive and attentive boys. I didn't have a dull time at all, and
when after three weeks I wanted to go home, it wasn't because

I was bored. On the contrary I wanted to go home because I'd allowed myself to get rather interested in a young man named Charley Kincaid, without realising that he was engaged to another girl.

We'd been drawn together from the first because he was almost the only boy in town who'd gone North to college, and I was still young enough to think that America revolved around Harvard and Princeton and Yale. He liked me too—I could see that; but when I heard that his engagement to a girl named Marie Bannerman had been announced six months before, there was nothing for me except go away. The town was too small to avoid people, and though so far there hadn't been any talk, I was sure that—well, that if we kept meeting, the emotion we were beginning to feel would somehow get into words. I'm not mean enough to take a man away from another girl.

Marie Bannerman was almost a beauty. Perhaps she would have been a beauty if she'd had any clothes, and if she hadn't used bright pink rouge in two high spots on her cheeks and powdered her nose and chin to a funeral white. Her hair was shining black; her features were lovely; and an affliction of one eye kept it always half-closed and gave an air of humorous mischief to her face.

I was leaving on a Monday, and on Saturday night a crowd of us dined at the country-club as usual before the dance. There was Joe Cable, the son of a former governor, a handsome dissipated and yet somehow charming young man; Catherine Jones, a pretty, sharp-eyed girl with an exquisite figure, who under her rouge might have been any age from eighteen to twenty-five; Marie Bannerman; Charley Kincaid; myself and two or three others.

I loved to listen to the genial flow of bizarre neighbourhood anecdote at this kind of party. For instance, one of the girls, together with her entire family, had that afternoon been evicted from her house for non-payment of rent. She told the story wholly without self-consciousness, merely as something trouble-some but amusing. And I loved the banter which presumed every girl to be infinitely beautiful and attractive, and every man to have been secretly and hopelessly in love with every girl present from their respective cradles.

"We liked to die laughin' ". . . "—said he was fixin' to shoot him without he stayed away." The girls "clared to heaven"; the men "took oath" on inconsequential statements. "How come you nearly forgot to come by for me—" and the incessant Honey, Honey, Honey, Honey, until the word seemed to roll like a genial liquid from heart to heart.

Outside, the May night was hot, a still night, velvet, soft-pawed, splattered thick with stars. It drifted heavy and sweet into the large room where we sat and where we would later dance, with no sound in it except the occasional long crunch of an arriving car on the drive. Just at that moment I hated to leave Davis as I never had hated to leave a town before—I felt that I wanted to spend my life in this town, drifting and dancing forever through these long, hot, romantic nights.

Yet horror was already hanging over that little party, was waiting tensely among us, an unived guest, and telling off the hours until it could show its pale and blinding face. Beneath the chatter and laughter something was going on, something secret and obscure that I didn't know.

Presently the coloured orchestra arrived, followed by the first trickle of the dance crowd. An enormous red-faced man in muddy knee boots and with a revolver strapped around his waist, clumped in and paused for a moment at our table before going upstairs to the locker-room. It was Bill Abercrombie, the sheriff, the son of Congressman Abercrombie. Some of the boys asked him half-whispered questions, and he replied in an attempt at an undertone.

"Yes. . . . He's in the swamp all right; farmer saw him near the crossroads store. . . . Like to have a shot at him myself."

I asked the boy next to me what was the matter.

"Nigger case," he said, "over in Kisco, about two miles from here. He's hiding in the swamp, and they're going in after him tomorrow."

"What'll they do to him?"

"Hang him, I guess."

The notion of the forlorn darky crouching dismally in a desolate bog waiting for dawn and death depressed me for a moment. Then the feeling passed and was forgotten.

After dinner Charley Kincaid and I walked out on the veranda—he had just heard that I was going away. I kept as close to the others as I could, answering his words but not his eyes—something inside me was protesting against leaving him on such a casual note. The temptation was strong to let something flicker up between us here at the end. I wanted him to kiss me—my heart promised that if he kissed me, just once, it would accept with equanimity the idea of never seeing him any more; but my mind knew it wasn't so.

The other girls began to drift inside and upstairs to the dressing-room to improve their complexions, and with Charley still beside me, I followed. Just at that moment I wanted to cry—perhaps my eyes were already blurred, or perhaps it was my haste lest they should be, but I opened the door of a small card-room by mistake and with my error the tragic machinery of the night began to function. In the card-room, not five feet from us, stood Marie Bannerman, Charley's fiancee, and Joe Cable. They were in each other's arms, absorbed in a passionate and oblivious kiss.

I closed the door quickly and without glancing at Charley opened the right door and ran upstairs.

A few minutes later Marie Bannerman entered the crowded dressing-room. She saw me and came over, smiling in a sort of mock despair, but she breathed quickly, and the smile trembled a little on her mouth.

"You won't say a word, honey, will you?" she whispered.

"Of course not." I wondered how that could matter, now that Charley Kincaid knew.

"Who else was it that saw us?"

"Only Charley Kincaid and I."

"Oh!" She looked a little puzzled; then she added: "He didn't wait to say anything, honey. When we came out, he was just going out the door. I thought he was going to wait and romp all over Joe."

"How about his romping all over you?" I couldn't help asking.

"Oh, he'll do that." She laughed wryly. "But, honey, I know how to handle him. It's just when he's first mad that I'm scared of him—he's got an awful temper." She whistled reminiscently. "I know, because this happened once before."

I wanted to slap her. Turning my back, I walked away on the pretext of borrowing a pin from Katie, the Negro maid. Catherine Jones was claiming the latter's attention with a short gingham garment which needed repair.

"What's that?" I asked.

"Dancing dress," she answered shortly, her mouth full of pins. When she took them out, she added: "It's all come to pieces— I've used it so much."

"Are you going to dance here tonight?"

"Going to try."

Somebody had told me that she wanted to be a dancer—that she had taken lessons in New York.

"Can I help you fix anything?"

"No, thanks—unless—can you sew? Katie gets so excited Saturday night that she's no good for anything except fetching pins. I'd be everlasting grateful to you, honey."

I had reasons for not wanting to go downstairs just yet, and so I sat down and worked on her dress for half an hour. I wondered if Charley had gone home, if I would ever see him again—I scarcely dared to wonder if what he had seen would set him free, ethically. When I went down finally he was not in sight.

The room was now crowded; the tables had been removed and dancing was general. At that time, just after the war, all Southern boys had a way of agitating their heels from side to side, pivoting on the ball of the foot as they danced, and to acquiring this accomplishment I had devoted many hours. There were plenty of stags, almost all of them cheerful with corn-liquor; I refused on an average at least two drinks a dance. Even when it is mixed with a soft drink, as is the custom, rather than gulped from the neck of a warm bottle, it is a formidable proposition. Only a few girls like Catherine Jones took an occasional sip from some boy's flask down at the dark end of the veranda.

I liked Catherine Jones—she seemed to have more energy than these other girls, though Aunt Musidora sniffed rather contemptuously whenever Catherine stopped for me in her car to go to the movies, remarking that she guessed "the bottom rail had gotten to be the top rail now". Her family were "new and common", but it seemed to me that perhaps her very commonness was an asset. Almost every girl in Davis confided in me at one time or another that her ambition was to "get away to New York", but only Catherine Jones had actually taken the step of studying stage dancing with that end in view.

She was often asked to dance at these Saturday night affairs, something "classic" or perhaps an acrobatic clog—on one memorable occasion she had annoyed the governing board by a "shimee" (then the scape-grace of jazz), and the novel and somewhat startling excuse made for her was that she was "so tight she didn't know what she was doing, anyhow". She impressed me as a curious girl, and I was eager to see what she would produce tonight.

At 12 o'clock the music always ceased, as dancing was forbidden on Sunday morning. So at 11.30 a vast fanfaronade of drum and cornet beckoned the dancers and the couples on the verandas, and the ones in the cars outside, and the stragglers from the bar, into the ballroom. Chairs were brought in and galloped up en masse and with a great racket to the slightly raised platform. The orchestra had evacuated this and taken a place beside. Then, as the rearward lights were lowered, they began to play a tune accompanied by a curious drum-beat that I had never heard before, and simultaneously Catherine Jones appeared upon the platform. She wore the short, country girl's dress upon which I had lately laboured, and a wide sun-bonnet under which her face, stained yellow with powder, looked out at us with rolling eyes and a vacant negroid leer. She began to dance.

I had never seen anything like it before, and until five years later, I wasn't to see it again. It was the Charleston—it must have been the Charleston. I remember the double drum-beat like a shouted "Hey! Hey!" and the swing of the arms and the odd knock-kneed effect. She had picked it up, heaven knows where.

Her audience, familiar with Negro rhythms, leaned forward eagerly—even to them it was something new, but it is stamped on my mind as clearly and indelibly as though I had seen it yesterday. The figure on the platform swinging and stamping, the excited orchestra, the waiters grinning in the doorway of the bar, and all around, through many windows, the soft languorous Southern night seeping in from the swamp and cottonfield and lush foliage and brown, warm streams. At what point a feeling of tense uneasiness began to steal over me I don't know. The dance could scarcely have taken ten minutes; perhaps the first beats of the barbaric music disquieted me—long before it was over, I was sitting rigid in my seat, and my eyes were wandering here and there around the hall, passing along the rows of shadowy faces as if seeking some security that was no longer there.

I'm not a nervous type; nor am I given to panic; but for a moment I was afraid that if the music and the dance didn't stop, I'd be hysterical. Something was happening all about me. I knew it as well as if I could see into these unknown souls. Things were happening, but one thing especially was leaning over so close that it almost touched us, that it did touch us. . . . I almost screamed as a hand brushed accidentally against my back.

The music stopped. There was applause and protracted cries of encore, but Catherine Jones shook her head definitely at the orchestra leader and made as though to leave the platform. The appeals for more continued—again she shook her head, and it seemed to me that her expression was rather angry. Then a strange incident occurred. At the protracted pleading of someone in the front row, the coloured orchestra leader began the vamp of the tune, as if to lure Catherine Jones into changing her mind. Instead she turned towards him, snapped out: "Didn't you hear me say no?" and then, surprisingly, slapped his face. The music stopped, and an amused murmur terminated abruptly as a muffled but clearly audible shot rang out.

Immediately we were on our feet, for the sound indicated that it had been fired within or near the house. One of the chaperons gave a little scream, but when some wag called out: "Caesar's in that henhouse again", the momentary alarm dissolved into laughter. The club manager, followed by several curious couples, went out to have a look about, but the rest were already moving around the floor to the strains of "Good Night, Ladies", which traditionally ended the dance.

I was glad it was over. The man with whom I had come went to get his car, and calling a waiter, I sent him for my golf-clubs, which were upstairs. I strolled out on the porch and waited, wondering again if Charley Kincaid had gone home.

Suddenly I was aware, in that curious way in which you become aware of something that has been going on for several minutes, that there was a tumult inside. Women were shrieking; there was a cry of "Oh, my God!", then the sounds of a stampede on the inside stairs, and footsteps running back and forth across the ballroom. A girl appeared from somewhere and pitched forward in a dead faint—almost immediately another girl did the same, and I heard a frantic male voice shouting into a telephone. Then, hatless and pale, a young man rushed out on the porch, and with hands that were cold as ice, seized my arm.

"What is it?" I cried. "A fire? What's happened?"

"Marie Bannerman's dead upstairs in the women's dressing room. Shot through the throat!"

The rest of that night is a series of visions that seem to have no connection with one another, that follow each other with the sharp instantaneous transitions of scenes in the movies. There was a group who stood arguing on the porch, in voices now raised, now hushed, about what should be done and how every waiter in the club, "even old Moses", ought to be given the third degree tonight. That a "nigger" had shot and killed Marie Bannerman was the instant and unquestioned assumption—in the first unreasoning instant, anyone who doubted it would have been under suspicion. The guilty one was said to be Katie Golstein, the coloured maid, who had discovered the body and fainted. It was said to be "that nigger they were looking for at Kisco." It was any darky at all.

Within half an hour people began to drift out, each with his little contribution of new discoveries. The crime had been committed with Sheriff Abercrombie's gun—he had hung it, belt and all, in full view on the wall before coming down to dance. It was missing—they were hunting for it now. Instantly killed, the doctor said—bullet had been fired from only a few feet away.

Then a few minutes later another young man came out and made the announcement in a loud, grave voice: "They've arrested Charley Kincaid."

My head reeled. Upon the group gathered on the veranda fell an awed, stricken silence.

"Arrested Charley Kincaid!"

"Charley Kincaid!"

Why, he was one of the best, one of themselves.

"That's the craziest thing I ever heard of!"

The young man nodded, shocked like the rest, but self-important with his information.

"He wasn't downstairs, when Catherine Jones was dancing—he says he was in the men's locker-room. And Marie Bannerman told a lot of girls that they'd had a row, and she was scared of what he'd do."

Again an awed silence.

"That's the craziest thing I ever heard!" someone said again.

"Charley Kincaid!"

The narrator waited a moment. Then he added:

"He caught her kissing Joe Cable—"

I couldn't keep silence a minute longer.

"What about it?" I cried out. "I was with him at the time. He wasn't—he wasn't angry at all."

They looked at me, their faces startled, confused, unhappy. Suddenly the footsteps of several men sounded loud through the ballroom, and a moment later Charley Kincaid, his face dead white, came out the front door between the Sheriff and another man. Crossing the porch quickly, they descended the steps and disappeared in the darkness. A moment later there was the sound of a starting car.

When an instant later far away down the road I heard the eerie scream of an ambulance, I got up desperately and called to my escort, who formed part of the whispering group.

"I've got to go," I said. "I can't stand this. Either take me home or I'll find a place in another car." Reluctantly he shouldered my clubs—the sight of them made me realise that I now couldn't leave on Monday after all—and followed me down the steps just as the black ambulance curved in at the gate—a ghastly shadow on the bright, starry night.


The situation after the first wild surmises, the first burst of unreasoning loyalty to Charley Kincaid, had died away, was outlined by the *Davis Courier* and by most of the State newspapers in this fashion: Marie Bannerman died in the women's dressing-room of the Davis Country Club from the effects of a shot fired at close quarters from a revolver just after 11.45 o'clock on Saturday night. Many persons had heard the shot; moreover, it had undoubtedly been fired from the revolver of

Sheriff Abercrombie, which had been hanging in full sight on the wall of the next room. Abercrombie himself was in the ballroom when the murder took place, as many witnesses could testify. The revolver was not found.

So far as was known, the only man who had been upstairs at the time the shot was fired was Charley Kincaid. He was engaged to Miss Bannerman, but according to several witnesses they had quarrelled seriously that evening. Miss Bannerman herself had mentioned the quarrel, adding that she was afraid and wanted to keep away from him until he cooled off.

Charles Kincaid asserted that at the time the shot was fired he was in the men's locker-room—where, indeed, he was found, immediately after the discovery of Miss Bannerman's body. He denied having had any words with Miss Bannerman at all. He had heard the shot but if he thought anything of it, he thought that "someone was potting cats outdoors."

Why had he chosen to remain in the locker-room during the dance?

No reason at all. He was tired. He was waiting until Miss Bannerman wanted to go home.

The body was discovered by Katie Golstein, the coloured maid, who herself was found in a faint when the crowd of girls surged upstairs for their coats. Returning from the kitchen, where she had been getting a bite to eat, Katie had found Miss Bannerman, her dress wet with blood, already dead on the floor.

Both the police and the newspapers attached importance to the geography of the country-club's second storey. It consisted of a row of three rooms—the women's dressing-room and the men's locker-room at either end, and in the middle a room which was used as a cloak-room and for the storage of golf-clubs. The women's and men's rooms had no outlet except into this chamber, which was connected by one stairs with the ballroom below, and by another with the kitchen. According to the testimony of three Negro cooks and the white caddy-master, no one but Katie Golstein had gone up the kitchen stairs that night.

As I remember if after five years, the foregoing is a pretty accurate summary of the situation when Charley Kincaid was accused of first-degree murder and committed for trial. Other people, chiefly Negroes, were suspected (at the loyal instigation of Charley Kincaid's friends), and several arrests were made, but nothing ever came of them, and upon what grounds they were based I have long forgotten. One group, in spite of the disappearance of the pistol, claimed persistenly that it was a suicide and suggested some ingenious reasons to account for the absence of the weapon.

Now when it is known Marie Bannerman happened to die so savagely and so violently, it would be easy for me, of all people, to say that I believed in Charley Kincaid all the time. But I didn't. I thought that he had killed her, and at the same time I knew that I loved him with all my heart. That it was I who first happened upon the evidence which set him free was due not to any faith in his innocence but to a strange vividness with which, in moods of excitement, certain scenes stamp themselves on my memory, so that I can remember every detail and how that detail struck me at the time.

It was one afternoon early in July, when the case against Charley Kincaid seemed to be at its strongest, that the horror of the actual murder slipped away from me for a moment and I began to think about other incidents of that same haunted night. Something Marie Bannerman had said to me in the dressing-room persistently eluded me, bothered me—not because I believed it to be important, but simply because I couldn't remember. It was gone from me, as if it had been a part of the fantastic undercurrent of small-town life which I had felt so strongly that evening, the sense that things were in the air, old secrets, old loves and feuds, and unresolved situations, that I could never fully understand. Just for a minute it seemed to me that Marie Bannerman had pushed aside the curtain; then it had dropped into place again—the house into which I might have looked was dark now forever.

Another incident, perhaps less important, also haunted me. The tragic events of a few minutes after had driven it from everyone's mind, but I had a strong impression that for a brief space of time I wasn't the only one to be surprised. When the audience had demanded an encore from Catherine Jones, her unwillingness to dance again had been so acute that she had been driven to the point of slapping the orchestra leader's face. The discrepancy between his offence and the venom of the rebuff recurred to me again and again. It wasn't natural—or, more important, it hadn't seemed natural. In view of the fact that Catherine Jones had been drinking, it was explicable, but it worried me now as it had worried me then. Rather to lay its ghost than to do any investigating, I pressed an obliging young man into service and called on the leader of the band.

His name was Thomas, a very dark, very simple-hearted virtuoso of the traps, and it took less than ten minutes to find out that Catherine Jones' gesture had surprised him as much as it had me. He had known her a long time, seen her at dances since she was a little girl—why, the very dance she did that night was one she had rehearsed with his orchestra a week before. And a few days later she had come to him and said she was sorry.

"I knew she would," he concluded. "She's a right good-hearted girl. My sister Katie was her nurse from when she was born up to the time she went to school."

"Your sister?"

"Katie. She's the maid out at the country-club. Katie Golstein. You been reading about her in the papers in 'at Charley Kincaid case. She's the maid. Katie Golstein. She's the maid at the country-club what found the body of Miss Bannerman."

"So Katie was Miss Catherine Jones' nurse?"

"Yes ma'am."

Going home, stimulated but unsatisfied, I asked my companion a quick question.

"Were Catherine and Marie good friends?"

"Oh, yes," he answered without hesitation. "All the girls are good friends here, except when two of them are tryin' to get hold of the same man. Then they warm each other up a little."

"Why do you suppose Catherine hasn't married? Hasn't she got lots of beaux?"

"Off and on. She only likes people for a day or so at a time. That is—all except Joe Cable."

Now a scene burst upon me, broke over me like a dissolving wave. And suddenly, my mind shivering from the impact, I remembered what Marie Bannerman had said to me in the dressing-room: "Who else was it that saw?" She had caught a glimpse of someone else, a figure passing so quickly that she could not identify it, out of the corner of her eye.

And suddenly I seemed to see that figure, as if I too had been vaguely conscious of it at the time, just as one is aware of a familiar gait or outline on the street long before there is any flicker of recognition. On the corner of my own eye was stamped a hurrying figure—that might have been Catherine Jones.

But when the shot was fired, Catherine Jones was in full view of over fifty people. Was it credible that Katie Golstein, a woman of fifty, who as a nurse had been known and trusted by three generations of Davis people, would shoot down a young girl in cold blood at Catherine Jones' command?

"But when the shot was fired, Catherine Jones was in full view of over fifty people."

That sentence beat in my head all night, taking on fantastic variations, dividing itself into phrases, segments, individual words.

"But when the shot was fired—Catherine Jones was in full view—of over fifty people."

When the shot was fired! What shot? The shot we heard. When the shot was fired. . . . When the shot was fired. . . .

The next morning at 9 o'clock, with the pallor of sleeplessness buried under a quantity of paint such as I had never worn before or have since, I walked up a rickety flight of stairs to the Sheriff's office.

Abercrombie, engrossed in his morning's mail, looked up curiously as I came in the door.

"Catherine Jones did it," I cried, struggling to keep the hysteria out of my voice. "She killed Marie Bannerman with a shot we didn't hear because the orchestra was playing and everybody was pushing up the chairs. The shot we heard was when Katie fired the pistol out of the window after the music was stopped. To give Catherine an alibi!"

I was right—as everyone now knows, but for a week, until Katie Golstein broke down under a fierce and ruthless inquisition, nobody believed me. Even Charley Kincaid, as he afterwards confessed, didn't dare to think it could be true.

What had been the relations between Catherine and Joe Cable no one ever knew, but evidently she had determined that his clandestine affair with Marie Bannerman had gone too far.

Then Marie chanced to come into the women's room while

Catherine was dressing for her dance—and there again there is a certain obscurity, for Catherine always claimed that Marie got the revolver, threatened her with it and that in the ensuing struggle the trigger was pulled. In spite of everything, I always rather liked Catherine Jones, but in justice it must be said that only a simple-minded and very exceptional jury would have let her off with five years.

And in just about five years from her commitment my husband and I are going to make a round of the New York musical shows and look hard at all the members of the chorus from the very front row.

After the shooting she must have thought quickly. Katie was told to wait until the music stopped, fire the revolver out of the window and then hide it—Catherine Jones neglected to specify where. Katie, on the verge of collapse, obeyed instructions, but she was never able to specify where she had hid the revolver. And no one ever knew until a year later, when Charley and I were on our honeymoon and Sheriff Abercrombie's ugly weapon dropped out of my golf-bag on to a Hot Springs golf-links. The bag must have been standing just outside the dressing-room door; Katie's trembling hand had dropped the revolver into the first aperture she could see.

We live in New York. Small towns make us both uncomfortable. Every day we read about the crimewaves in the big cities, but at least a wave is something tangible that you can provide against. What I dread above all things is the unknown depths, the incalculable ebb and flow, the secret shapes of things that drift through opaque darkness under the surface of the sea.

# A ROSE FOR EMILY

WILLIAM FAULKNER

*It is no irreverence to describe William Faulkner as one of the old masters of American literature. He returned to his homeland, the deep south, after being wounded in the First World War while serving with the Royal Flying Corps, and over the years his novels of the darker side of life inevitably reflect the passions of white and black alike. Written in 1930,* A Rose for Emily *is a sombre story of a woman's withdrawal from the main stream of life.*

I

WHEN MISS EMILY GRIERSON died, our whole town went to her funeral: the men through a sort of respectful affection for a fallen monument, the women mostly out of curiosity to see the inside of her house, which no one save an old manservant—a combined gardener and cook—had seen in at least ten years.

It was a big, squarish frame house that had once been white, decorated with cupolas and spires and scrolled balconies in the heavily lightsome style of the seventies, set on what had once been our most select street. But garages and cotton gins had encroached and obliterated even the august names of that neighbourhood; only Miss Emily's house was left, lifting its stubborn and coquettish decay above the cotton wagons and the gasoline pumps—an eyesore among eyesores. And now Miss Emily had gone to join the representatives of those august names where they lay in the cedar-bemused cemetery among the ranked and anonymous graves of Union and Confederate soldiers who fell at the battle of Jefferson.

Alive, Miss Emily had been a tradition, a duty, and a care; a sort of hereditary obligation upon the town, dating from that day in 1894 when Colonel Sartoris, the mayor—he who fathered the edict that no Negro woman should appear on the streets without an apron—remitted her taxes, the dispensation dating from the death of her father on into perpetuity. Not that Miss Emily

would have accepted charity. Colonel Sartoris invented an involved tale to the effect that Miss Emily's father had loaned
money to the town, which the town, as a matter of business,
preferred this way of repaying. Only a man of Colonel Sartoris'
generation and thought could have invented it, and only a
woman could have believed it.

When the next generation, with its more modern ideas, became
mayors and aldermen, this arrangement created some little dis-
satisfaction. On the first of the year they mailed her a tax notice.
February came, and there was no reply. They wrote her a formal
letter, asking her to call at the sheriff's office at her convenience.
A week later the mayor wrote her himself, offering to call or to
send his car for her, and received in reply a note on paper of an
archaic shape, in a thin, flowing calligraphy in faded ink, to the
effect that she no longer went out at all. The tax notice was also
enclosed, without comment.

They called a special meeting of the Board of Aldermen. A
deputation waited upon her, knocked at the door through which
no visitor had passed since she ceased giving china-painting
lessons eight or ten years earlier. They were admitted by the old
Negro into a dim hall from which a stairway mounted into still
more shadow. It smelled of dust and disuse—a close, dank smell.
The Negro led them into the parlour. It was furnished in heavy,
leather-covered furniture. When the Negro opened the blinds of
one window, they could see that the leather was cracked; and
when they sat down, a faint dust rose sluggishly about their
thighs, spinning with slow motes in the single sunray. On a
tarnished gilt easel before the fireplace stood a crayon portrait of
Miss Emily's father.

They rose when she entered—a small, fat woman in black,
with a thin gold chain descending to her waist and vanishing into
her belt, leaning on an ebony cane with a tarnished gold head.
Her skeleton was small and spare; perhaps that was why what
would have been merely plumpness in another was obesity in her.
She looked bloated, like a body long submerged in motionless
water, and of that pallid hue. Her eyes, lost in the fatty ridges of
her face, looked like two small pieces of coal pressed into a lump
of dough as they moved from one face to another while the
visitors stated their errand.

She did not ask them to sit. She just stood in the door and

listened quietly until the spokesman came to a stumbling halt. Then they could hear the invisible watch ticking at the end of the gold chain.

Her voice was dry and cold. "I have no taxes in Jefferson. Colonel Sartoris explained it to me. Perhaps one of you can gain access to the city records and satisfy yourselves."

"But we have. We are the city authorities, Miss Emily. Didn't you get a notice from the sheriff, signed by him?"

"I received a paper, yes," Miss Emily said. "Perhaps he considers himself the sheriff . . . I have no taxes in Jefferson."

"But there is nothing on the books to show that, you see. We must go by the—"

"See Colonel Sartoris. I have no taxes in Jefferson."

"But, Miss Emily—"

"See Colonel Sartoris." (Colonel Sartoris had been dead almost ten years.) "I have no taxes in Jefferson. Tobe!" The Negro appeared. "Show these gentlemen out."

II

So she vanquished them, horse and foot, just as she had vanquished their fathers thirty years before about the smell. That was two years after her father's death and a short time after her sweetheart—the one we believed would marry her—had deserted her. After her father's death she went out very little; after her sweetheart went away, people hardly saw her at all. A few of the ladies had the temerity to call, but were not received, and the only sign of life about the place was the Negro man—a young man then—going in and out with a market basket.

"Just as if a man—any man—could keep a kitchen properly," the ladies said; so they were not surprised when the smell developed. It was another link between the gross, teeming world and the high and mighty Griersons.

A neighbour, a woman, complained to the mayor, Judge Stevens, eighty years old.

"But what will you have me do about it, madam?" he said.

"Why, send her word to stop it," the woman said. "Isn't there a law?"

"I'm sure that won't be necessary," Judge Stevens said. "It's probably just a snake or a rat that nigger of hers killed in the yard. I'll speak to him about it."

The next day he received two more complaints, one from a man who came in diffident deprecation. "We really must do something about it, Judge. I'd be the last one in the world to bother Miss Emily, but we've got to do something." That night the Board of Aldermen met—three greybeards and one younger man, a member of the rising generation.

"It's simple enough," he said. "Send her word to have her place cleaned up. Give her a certain time to do it in, and if she don't . . ."

"Dammit, sir," Judge Stevens said, "will you accuse a lady to her face of smelling bad?"

So the next night, after midnight, four men crossed Miss Emily's lawn and slunk about the house like burglars, sniffing along the base of the brickwork and at the cellar openings while one of them performed a regular sowing motion with his hand out of a sack slung from his shoulder. They broke open the cellar door and sprinkled lime there, and in all the outbuildings. As they recrossed the lawn, a window that had been dark was lighted and Miss Emily sat in it, the light behind her, and her upright torso motionless as that of an idol. They crept quietly across the lawn and into the shadow of the locusts that lined the street. After a week or two the smell went away.

That was when people had begun to feel really sorry for her. People in our town, remembering how old lady Wyatt, her great-aunt, had gone completely crazy at last, believed that the Griersons held themselves a little too high for what they really were. None of the young men were quite good enough to Miss Emily and such. We had long thought of them as a tableau: Miss Emily a slender figure in white in the background, her father a spraddled silhouette in the foreground, his back to her and clutching a horse-whip, the two of them framed by the back-flung front door. So when she got to be thirty and was still single, we were not pleased exactly, but vindicated; even with insanity in the family she wouldn't have turned down all of her chances if they had really materialised.

When her father died, it got about that the house was all that was left to her; and in a way, people were glad. At last they could pity Miss Emily. Being left alone, and a pauper, she had become humanised. Now she too would know the old thrill and the despair of a penny more or less.

The day after his death all the ladies prepared to call at the house and offer condolence and aid, as is our custom. Miss Emily met them at the door, dressed as usual and with no trace of grief on her face. She told them that her father was not dead. She did that for three days, with the ministers calling on her, and the doctors, trying to persuade her to let them dispose of the body. Just as they were about to resort to law and force, she broke down, and they buried her father quickly.

We did not say she was crazy then. We believed she had to do that. We remembered all the young men her father had driven away, and we knew that with nothing left, she would have to cling to that which had robbed her, as people will.

## III

She was sick for a long time. When we saw her again, her hair was cut short, making her look like a girl, with a vague resemblance to those angels in coloured church windows—sort of tragic and serene.

The town had just let the contracts for paving the sidewalks, and in the summer after her father's death they began the work. The construction company came with niggers and mules and machinery, and a foreman named Homer Barron, a Yankee—a big, dark, ready man, with a big voice and eyes lighter than his face. The little boys would follow in groups to hear him cuss the niggers, and the niggers singing in time to the rise and fall of picks. Pretty soon he knew everybody in town. Whenever you heard a lot of laughing anywhere about the square, Homer Barron would be in the centre of the group. Presently we began to see him and Miss Emily on Sunday afternoons driving in the yellow-wheeled buggy and the matched team of bays from the livery stable.

At first we were glad that Miss Emily would have an interest, because the ladies all said, "Of course a Grierson would not think seriously of a Northerner, a day labourer." But there were still others, older people, who said that even grief could not cause a real lady to forget *noblesse oblige*—without calling it *noblesse oblige*. They just said, "Poor Emily. Her kinsfolk should come to her." She had some kin in Alabama; but years ago her father had fallen out with them over the estate of old lady Wyatt, the crazy woman, and there was no communication between the two families. They had not even been represented at the funeral.

And as soon as the old people said, "Poor Emily," the whispering began. "Do you suppose it's really so?" they said to one another. "Of course it is. What else could. . . ." This behind their hands; rustling of craned silk and satin behind jalousies closed upon the sun of Sunday afternoon as the thin, swift clop-clop-clop of the matched team passed: "Poor Emily."

She carried her head high enough—even when we believed that she was fallen. It was as if she demanded more than ever the recognition of her dignity as the last Grierson; as if it had wanted that touch of earthiness to re-affirm her imperviousness. Like when she bought the rat poison, the arsenic. That was over a year after they had begun to say "Poor Emily", and while the two female cousins were visiting her.

"I want some poison," she said to the druggist. She was over thirty then, still a slight woman, though thinner than usual, with cold, haughty black eyes in a face the flesh of which was strained across the temples and about the eye-sockets as you imagine a lighthouse-keeper's face ought to look. "I want some poison," she said.

"Yes, Miss Emily. What kind? For rats and such? I'd recom—"

"I want the best you have. I don't care what kind."

The druggist named several. "They'll kill anything up to an elephant. But what you want is—"

"Arsenic," Miss Emily said. "Is that a good one?"

"Is . . . arsenic? Yes, ma'am. But what you want—"

"I want arsenic."

The druggist looked down at her. She looked back at him, erect, her face like a strained flag. "Why, of course," the druggist said. "If that's what you want. But the law requires you to tell what you are going to use it for."

Miss Emily just stared at him, her head tilted back in order to look him eye for eye, until he looked away and went and got the arsenic and wrapped it up. The Negro delivery boy brought her the package; the druggist didn't come back. When she opened the package at home there was written on the box, under the skull and bones: "For rats."

IV

So the next day we all said, "She will kill herself"; and we said it would be the best thing. When she had first begun to be seen with Homer Barron, we had said, "She will marry him." Then we said, "She will persuade him yet," because Homer himself had remarked—he liked men, and it was known that he drank with the younger men in the Elks' Club—that he was not a marrying man. Later we said, "Poor Emily" behind the jalousies as they passed on Sunday afternoon in the glittering buggy, Miss Emily with her head high and Homer Barron with his hat cocked and a cigar in his teeth, reins and whip in a yellow glove.

Then some of the ladies began to say that it was a disgrace to the town and a bad example to the young people. The men did not want to interfere, but at last the ladies forced the Baptist minister—Miss Emily's people were Episcopal—to call upon her. He would never divulge what happened during that interview, but he refused to go back again. The next Sunday they again drove about the streets, and the following day the minister's wife wrote to Miss Emily's relations in Alabama.

So she had blood-kin under her roof again and we sat back to watch developments. At first nothing happened. Then we were sure that they were to be married. We learned that Miss Emily had been to the jeweller's and ordered a man's toilet set in silver, with the letters H.B. on each piece. Two days later we learned that she had bought a complete outfit of men's clothing, including a nightshirt, and we said, "They are married." We were really glad. We were glad because the two female cousins were even more Grierson than Miss Emily had ever been.

So we were not surprised when Homer Barron—the streets had been finished some time since—was gone. We were a little disappointed that there was not a public blowing-off, but we believed that he had gone on to prepare for Miss Emily's coming, or to give her a chance to get rid of the cousins. (By that time it was a cabal, and we were all Miss Emily's allies to help circumvent the cousins.) Sure enough, after another week they departed. And, as we had expected all along, within three days Homer Barron was back in town. A neighbour saw the Negro man admit him at the kitchen door at dusk one evening.

And that was the last we saw of Homer Barron. And of Miss Emily for some time. The Negro man went in and out with the market basket, but the front door remained closed. Now and then we would see her at a window for a moment, as the men did that night when they sprinkled the lime, but for almost six months she did not appear on the streets. Then we knew that this was to be expected too; as if that quality of her father which had thwarted her woman's life so many times had been too virulent and too furious to die.

When we next saw Miss Emily, she had grown fat and her hair was turning grey. During the next few years it grew greyer and greyer until it attained an even pepper-and-salt iron-grey, when it ceased turning. Up to the day of her death at seventy-four it was still that vigorous iron-grey, like the hair of an active man.

From that time on her front door remained closed, save for a period of six or seven years, when she was about forty, during which she gave lessons in china-painting. She fitted up a studio in one of the downstairs rooms, where the daughters and granddaughters of Colonel Sartoris' contemporaries were sent to her with the same regularity and in the same spirit that they were sent to church on Sundays with a twenty-five-cent piece for the collection plate. Meanwhile her taxes had been remitted.

Then the newer generation became the backbone and the spirit of the town, and the painting pupils grew up and fell away and did not send their children to her with boxes of colour and tedious brushes and pictures cut from the ladies' magazines. The front door closed upon the last one and remained closed for good. When the town got free postal delivery, Miss Emily alone refused to let them fasten the metal numbers above her door and attach a mailbox to it. She would not listen to them.

Daily, monthly, yearly we watched the Negro grow greyer and more stooped, going in and out with the market basket. Each December we sent her a tax notice, which would be returned by the post office a week later, unclaimed. Now and then we would see her in one of the downstairs windows—she had evidently shut up the top floor of the house—like the carven torso of an idol in a niche, looking or not looking at us, we could never tell which. Thus she passed from generation to generation—dear, inescapable, impervious, tranquil and perverse.

And so she died. Fell ill in the house filled with dust and shadows, with only a doddering Negro man to wait on her. We did not even know she was sick; we had long since given up trying to get any information from the Negro. He talked to no one, probably not even to her, for his voice had grown harsh and rusty, as if from disuse.

She died in one of the downstairs rooms, in a heavy walnut bed with a curtain, her grey head propped on a pillow yellow and mouldy with age and lack of sunlight.

v

The Negro met the first of the ladies at the front door and let them in, with their hushed, sibilant voices and their quick, curious glances, and then he disappeared. He walked right through the house and out the back and was not seen again.

The two female cousins came at once. They held the funeral on the second day, with the town coming to look at Miss Emily beneath a mass of bought flowers, with the crayon face of her father musing profoundly above the bier and the ladies sibilant and macabre; and the very old men—some in their brushed Confederate uniforms—on the porch and the lawn, talking of Miss Emily as if she had been a contemporary of theirs, believing that they had danced with her and courted her perhaps, confusing time with its mathematical progression, as the old do, to whom all the past is not a diminishing road but, instead, a huge meadow which no winter ever quite touches, divided from them now by the narrow bottle-neck of the most recent decade of years.

Already we knew that there was one room in that region above stairs which no one had seen in forty years, and which would have to be forced. They waited until Miss Emily was decently in the ground before they opened it.

The violence of breaking down the door seemed to fill this room with pervading dust. A thin, acrid pall as of the tomb seemed to lie everywhere upon this room decked and furnished as for a bridal: upon the valence curtains of faded rose colour, upon the rose-shaded lights, upon the dressing table, upon the delicate array of crystal and the man's toilet things backed with tarnished silver, silver so tarnished that the monogram was obscured. Among them lay a collar and tie, as if they had just been removed, which, lifted, left upon the surface a pale crescent in the dust. Upon a chair hung the suit, carefully folded; beneath it the two mute shoes and the discarded socks.

The man himself lay in the bed.

For a long while we just stood there, looking down at the profound and fleshless grin. The body had apparently once lain in the attitude of an embrace, but now the long sleep that outlasts love, that conquers even the grimace of love, had cuckolded him. What was left of him, rotted beneath what was left of the nightshirt, had become inextricable from the bed in which he lay; and upon him and upon the pillow beside him lay that even coating of the patient and biding dust.

Then we noticed that in the second pillow was the indentation of a head. One of us lifted something from it, and leaning forward, that faint and invisible dust dry and acrid in the nostrils, we saw a long strand of iron-grey hair.

# THE BRONZE DOOR

RAYMOND CHANDLER

*Raymond Chandler was a confirmed devotee of fantasy fiction and his biographers have disclosed that he wrote quite a number of "strange" stories during his lifetime—primarily for his own satisfaction. Of these tales he allowed only a handful to be published, among them* The Bronze Door, *which was the very first and appeared as early as 1939. It recalls the dying flicker of London's gaslit years with remarkable fidelity, and although it is worlds apart in time and space from such novels as* The Big Sleep *and* Farewell, My Lovely *displays an identical mastery in the great art of story telling.*

THE LITTLE man was from the Calabar coast or from Papua or Tongatabu, some such remote place like that. An empire-builder frayed at the temples, thin and yellow, and slightly drunk at the club bar. And he was wearing a faded school tie he had probably kept year after year in a tin box so the centipedes wouldn't eat it.

Mr Sutton-Cornish didn't know him, at least not then, but he knew the tie because it was his own school tie. So he spoke to the man timidly, and the man talked to him, being a little drunk and not knowing anybody. They had drinks and talked of the old school, in that peculiar, remote way the English have, without exchanging names, but friendly underneath.

It was a big thrill for Mr Sutton-Cornish, because nobody ever talked to him at the club except the servants. He was too ingrowing, and you don't have to talk to people in London clubs. That's what they're for.

Mr Sutton-Cornish got home to tea a little thick-tongued, for the first time in fifteen years. He sat there blankly in the upstairs drawing room, holding his cup of tepid tea and going over the man's face in his mind, making it younger and

chubbier, a face that would go over an Eton collar or under a
school cricket cap.

Suddenly he got it, and chuckled. That was something he
hadn't done in a good few years either.

"Llewellyn, m'dear," he said. "Llewellyn Minor. Had an
elder brother. Killed in the War, in the horse artillery."

Mrs Sutton-Cornish stared at him bleakly across the heavily
embroidered tea cosy. Her chestnut-coloured eyes were dull
with disdain—dried-out chestnuts, not fresh ones. The rest of
her large face looked grey. The late October afternoon was
grey, and the heavy, full-bottomed, monogrammed curtains
across the windows. Even the ancestors on the walls were
grey—all except the bad one, the general.

The chuckle died in Mr Sutton-Cornish's throat. The long
grey stare took care of that. Then he shivered a little, and as
he wasn't very steady, his hand jerked. He emptied his tea on
the rug, almost delicately, cup and all.

"Oh, rot," he said thickly. "Sorry, m'dear. Missed me
trousers, though. Awfully sorry, m'dear."

For a minute Mrs Sutton-Cornish made only the sound of a
large woman breathing. Then suddenly things began to tinkle
on her—to tinkle and rustle and squeak. She was full of quaint
noises, like a haunted house, but Mr Sutton-Cornish shuddered, because he knew she was trembling with rage.

"Ah-h-h," she breathed out very, very slowly, after a long
time in her firing-squad manner. "Ah-h-h. Intoxicated,
James?"

Something stirred suddenly at her feet. Teddy, the
Pomeranian, stopped snoring and lifted his head and smelled
blood. He let out a short snapping bark, merely a ranging
shot, and waddled to his feet. His protuberant brown eyes
stared malignantly at Mr Sutton-Cornish.

"I'd better ring the bell, m'dear," Mr Sutton-Cornish said
humbly, and stood up. "Hadn't I?"

She didn't answer him. She spoke to Teddy instead, softly.
A sort of doughy softness, with something sadistic in it.

"Teddy," she said softly, "look at that man. Look at that
man, Teddy."

Mr Sutton-Cornish said thickly: "Now don't let him snap at
me, m'dear. D-don't let him snap at me, please, m'dear."

No answer. Teddy braced himself and leered. Mr Sutton-Cornish tore his eyes away and looked up at the bad ancestor, the general. The general wore a scarlet coat with a diagonal blue sash across it, rather like a bar sinister. He had the flushed complexion generals used to have in his day. He had a lot of very fruity-looking decorations and a bold stare, the stare of an unrepentant sinner. The general was no violet. He had broken up more homes than he had fought duels, and he had fought more duels than he had won battles, and he had won plenty of battles.

Looking up at the bold-veined face, Mr Sutton-Cornish braced himself, leaned down and took a small triangular sandwich from the tea table.

"Here, Teddy," he gulped. "Catch, boy, catch!"

He threw the sandwich. It fell in front of Teddy's little, brown paws. Teddy snuffled it languidly and yawned. He had his meals served to him on china, not thrown at him. He sidled innocently over to the edge of the rug and suddenly pounced on it, snarling.

"At table, James?" Mrs Sutton-Cornish said slowly and dreadfully.

Mr Sutton-Cornish stood on his teacup. It broke into thin light slivers of fine china. He shuddered again.

But now was the time. He started quickly towards the bell. Teddy let him get almost there, still pretending to worry the fringe of the rug. Then he spat out a piece of fringe, and charged low and soundlessly, his small feet like feathers in the nap of the rug. Mr Sutton-Cornish was just reaching for the bell.

Small bright teeth tore rapidly and expertly at a pearl-grey spat.

Mr Sutton-Cornish yelped, pivoted swiftly—and kicked. His neat shoe flashed in the grey light. A silky brown object sailed through the air and landed gobbling.

Then there was a quite indescribable stillness in the room, like the silence in the innermost room of a cold-storage warehouse, at midnight.

Teddy whimpered once, artfully, crept along the floor with his body close to it, crept under Mrs Sutton-Cornish's chair. Her purplish-brown skirts moved and Teddy's face emerged slowly, framed in silk, the face of a nasty old woman with a shawl over her head.

"Caught me off balance," Mr Sutton-Cornish mumbled, leaning against the mantelpiece. "Didn't mean . . . never intended—"

Mrs Sutton-Cornish rose. She rose with the air of gathering a retinue about her. Her voice was the cold bleat of a foghorn on an icy river.

"Chinverly," she said. "I shall leave at once for Chinverly. At once. This hour . . . Drunk! Filthily drunk in the middle of the afternoon. Kicking little inoffensive animals. Vile! Utterly vile! *Open the door!*"

Mr Sutton-Cornish staggered across the room and opened the door. She went out. Teddy trotted beside her, on the side away from Mr Sutton-Cornish, and for once he didn't try to trip her in the doorway.

Outside she turned, slowly, as a liner turns.

"James," she said, "have you anything to say to me?"

He giggled—from pure nervous strain.

She looked at him horribly, turned again, said over her shoulder: "This is the end, James. The end of our marriage."

Mr Sutton-Cornish said appallingly: "Goodness, m'dear—are we married?"

She started to turn again, but didn't. A sound like somebody being strangled in a dungeon came from her. Then she went on.

The door of the room hung open like a paralysed mouth. Mr Sutton-Cornish stood just inside it, listening. He didn't move until he heard steps on the floor above—heavy steps—hers. He sighed and looked down at his torn spat. Then he crept downstairs, into his long, narrow study beside the entrance hall, and got at the whisky.

He hardly noticed the sounds of departure, luggage being descended, voices, the throbbing of the big car out in front, voices, the last bark from Teddy's iron-old throat. The house grew utterly silent. The furniture waited with its tongue in its cheek. Outside the lamps were lit in a light fog. Taxis hooted along the wet street. The fire died low in the grate.

Mr Sutton-Cornish stood in front of it, swaying a little, looking at his long grey face in the wall mirror.

"Take a little stroll," he whispered wryly. "You and me. Never was anyone else, was there?"

He sneaked out into the hall without Collins, the butler, hearing him. He got his scarf and overcoat and hat on, grasped his stick and gloves, let himself out silently into the dusk.

He stood a little while at the bottom of the steps and looked up at the house. No. 14 Grinling Crescent. His father's house, his grandfather's house, his great-grandfather's house. All he had left. The rest was hers. Even the clothes he wore, the money in his bank account. But the house was still his—at least in name.

Four white steps, as spotless as the souls of virgins, leading up to an apple-green, deep-panelled door, painted as things used to be painted long ago, in the age of leisure. It had a brass knocker and a thumb latch above the handle and one of those bells you twisted, instead of pushing or pulling them, and it rang just on the other side of the door, rather ridiculously, if you were not used to it.

He turned and looked across the street at the little railed-in park always kept locked, where on sunny days the small, prim children of Grinling Crescent walked along the smooth paths, around the little ornamental lake, beside the rhododendron bushes, holding the hands of their nursemaids.

He looked at all this a little wanly, then he squared his thin shoulders and marched off into the dusk, thinking of Nairobi and Papua and Tongatabu, thinking of the man in the faded school tie who would go back there presently, wherever it was he came from, and lie awake in the jungle, thinking of London.


"Keb, sir?"

Mr Sutton-Cornish halted, stood on the edge of the kerb and stared. The voice came from above, one of those wind-husked, beery voices you don't hear very often any more. It came from the driver's seat of a hansom cab.

The hansom cab had come out of the darkness, sliding oilily along the street on high rubber-tyred wheels, the horse's hoofs making a slow, even *clop-clop* that Mr Sutton-Cornish hadn't noticed until the driver called down to him.

It looked real enough. The horse had time-worn black blinkers and the characteristic well-fed and yet somehow dilapidated look that cab horses used to have. The half doors of the handsom were folded back and Mr Sutton-Cornish could see the quilted grey upholstery inside. The long reins were riddled with cracks and following them upward he saw the beefy driver, the wide-brimmed coachman's "topper" he wore, the huge buttons on the upper part of his greatcoat, and the well-worn blanket that swathed the lower part of him round and round. He held his long whip lightly and delicately, as a hansom driver should hold his whip.

The trouble was that there weren't any more hansom cabs.

Mr Sutton-Cornish gulped, slipped a glove off and reached out to touch the wheel. It was very cold, very solid, wet with the muddy slime of the city streets.

"Doubt if I've ever seen one of these since the War," he said out loud, very steadily.

"Wot war, guv'nor?"

Mr Sutton-Cornish started. He touched the wheel again. Then he smiled, slowly and carefully drew his glove on again.

"I'm getting in," he said.

"Steady there, Prince," the driver wheezed.

The horse switched his long tail contemptuously. Telling *him* to be steady, Mr Sutton-Cornish climbed in over the wheel, rather clumsily, because one had lost the knack of that art these many years. He closed the half doors around in front of him, leaned back against the seat in the pleasant harness-room smell.

The trap opened over his head and the driver's large nose and alchoholic eyes made an improbable picture in the opening, like a deep-sea fish staring you down through the glass wall of an aquarium.

"Where to, guv'nor?"

"Well . . . Soho." It was the most foreign place he could think of—for a hansom cab to go to.

The cabman's eyes stared down at him.

"Won't like it there, guv'nor."

"I don't have to like it," Mr Sutton-Cornish said bitterly.

The cabman stared down at him a little longer. "Yus," he said. "Soho. Wardour Street like. Right you are, guv'nor."

The trap slammed shut, the whip flicked delicately beside the horse's right ear, and motion came to the hansom cab.

Mr Sutton-Cornish sat perfectly still, his scarf tight around his thin neck and his stick between his knees and his gloved hands clasped on the crook of the stick. He stared mutely out into the mist, like an animal on the bridge. The horse *clop-clopped* out of Grinling Crescent, through Belgrave Square, over to Whitehall, up to Trafalgar Square, across that to St. Martin's Lane.

It went neither fast nor slow, and yet it went as fast as anything else went. It moved without sound, except for the *clop-clop,* across a world that stank of gasoline fumes, and charred oil, that shrilled with whistles and hooted with horns.

And nobody seemed to notice it and nothing seemed to get in its way. That was rather amazing, Mr Sutton-Cornish thought. But after all a hansom cab had nothing to do with that world. It was a ghost, an underlayer of time, the first writing on a palimpsest, brought out by ultra-violet light in a darkened room.

"Y'know," he said, speaking to the horse's rump, because there wasn't anything else there to speak to, "things might happen to a man, if a man would just let them happen."

The long whip flicked by Prince's ear as lightly as a trout fly flicking at a small dark pool under a rock.

"They already have," he added glumly.

The cab slowed along a kerb, and the trap snapped open again.

"Well, 'ere we are, guv'nor. 'Ow about one of them little French dinners for eighteen pence? You know, guv'nor. Six courses of nothink at all. You 'ave one on me and then I 'ave one on you and we're still 'ungry. 'Ow about it?"

A very chill hand clutched at Mr Sutton-Cornish's heart. Six-course dinners for eighteen pence? A hansom cab driver who said: "Wot war, guv'nor?" Twenty years ago, perhaps—

"Let me out here!" he said shrilly.

He threw the doors open, thrust money up at the face in the trap, hopped over the wheel to the sidewalk.

He didn't quite run, but he walked pretty fast and close to a dark wall and a little slinkingly. But nothing followed him, not even the *clop-clop* of the horse's hoofs. He swung around a corner into a narrow crowded street.

The light came from the open door of a shop. CURIOS AND ANTIQUES it said on the façade, in letters once gold, heavily Gothic in style. There was a flare on the sidewalk to attract attention and by this light he read the sign. The voice came from inside, from a little, plump man standing on a box who chanted over the heads of a listless crowd of silent, bored foreign-looking men. The chanting voice held a note of exhaustion and futility.

"Now what am I bid, gents? Now what am I bid on this magnificent example of Oriental art? One pound starts the ball rolling, gents. One pound note coin of the realm. Now 'oo says a pound, gents? 'Oo says a pound?"

Nobody said anything. The little plump man on the box shook his head, wiped his face with a dirty handkerchief and drew a long breath. Then he saw Mr Sutton-Cornish standing on the fringe of the little crowd.

" 'Ow about you, sir?" he pounced. "You look as if you'd a country 'ouse. Now that door's made for a country 'ouse. 'Ow about you, sir? Just give me a start like."

Mr Sutton-Cornish blinked at him. "Eh? What's that?" he snapped.

The listless men smiled faintly and spoke among themselves without moving their thick lips.

"No offence, sir," the auctioneer chirped. "If you did 'ave a country 'ouse, that there door might be just what you could use."

Mr Sutton-Cornish turned his head slowly, following the auctioneer's pointing hand, and looked for the first time at the bronze door.

It stood all by itself over against the left-hand wall of the nearly stripped shop. It stood about two feet from the side wall, on its own base. It was a double door, apparently of cast bronze, although from its size that seemed impossible. It was heavily scrolled over with a welter of Arabic script in relief, an endless story that here found no listener, a procession of curves and dots that might have expressed anything from an anthology of the Koran to the by-laws of a well-organised harem.

The two leaves of the door were only part of the thing. It had a wide, heavy base below and a superstructure topped by a Moorish arch. From the meeting edge of the two leaves a huge key stuck out of a huge key-hole, the sort of key a medieval jailer used to wear in enormous clanking bunches on a leather belt around his waist. A key from *The Yeoman of the Guard*—a comic-opera key.

"Oh . . . that," Mr Sutton-Cornish said in the stillness. "Well, really, you know. I'm afraid not that, you know."

The auctioneer sighed. No hope had ever been smaller, probably, but at least it was worth a sigh. Then he picked up something which might have been carved ivory, but wasn't, stared at it pessimistically, and burst out again:

"Now 'ere, gents, I 'old in my 'and one of the finest examples—"

Mr Sutton-Cornish smiled faintly and skimmed along the cluster of men until he came close to the bronze door.

He stood in front of it leaning on his stick, which was a section of polished rhinoceros hide over a steel core, dull mahogany in colour, and a stick even a heavy man could have leaned on. After a while he reached forward idly and twisted the great key. It turned stubbornly, but it turned. A ring beside it was the doorknob. He twisted that, too, and tugged one half of the door open.

He straightened, and with a pleasantly idle gesture thrust his stick forward through the opening. And then, for the second time that evening, something incredible happened to him.

He wheeled sharply. Nobody was paying any attention. The auction was dead on its feet. The silent men were drifting out into the night. In a pause, hammering sounded at the back of the shop. The plump little auctioneer looked more and more as of he were eating a bad egg.

Mr Sutton-Cornish looked down at his gloved right hand. There was no stick in it. There was nothing in it. He stepped to one side and looked behind the door. There was no stick there, on the dusty floor.

He had felt nothing. Nothing had jerked him. The stick had merely passed part way through the door and then—it had merely ceased to exist.

He leaned down and picked up a piece of torn paper, wadded it swiftly into a ball, glanced behind him again and tossed the ball through the open part of the door.

Then he let out a slow sigh in which some neolithic rapture struggled with his civilised amazement. The ball of paper didn't fall to the floor behind the door. It fell, in mid-air, clean out of the visible world.

Mr Sutton-Cornish reached his empty right hand forward and very slowly and carefully pushed the door shut. Then he just stood there, and licked his lips.

After a while: "Harem door," he said very softly. "Exit door of a harem. Now, that's an idea."

A very charming idea, too. The silken lady, her night of pleasure with the sultan over, would be conducted politely to that door and would casually step through it. Then nothing. No sobbing in the night, no broken hearts, no blackamoor with cruel eyes and a large scimitar, no knotted silk cord, no blood, no dull splash in the midnight Bosphorus. Merely nothing. A cool, clean, perfectly timed, and perfectly irrevocable absence of existence. Someone would close the door and lock it and take the key out, and for the time being that would be that.

Mr Sutton-Cornish didn't notice the emptying of the shop. Faintly he heard its street door close, but without giving it any meaning. The hammering at the back stopped for a moment, voices spoke. Then steps came near. They were weary steps in the silence, the steps of a man who had had enough of that day, and of many such days. A voice spoke at Mr Sutton-Cornish's elbow, an end-of-the-day voice.

"A very fine piece of work, sir. A bit out of my line—to be frank."

Mr Sutton-Cornish didn't look at him, not yet. "Quite a bit out of anybody's line," he said gravely.

"I see it interests you, sir, after all."

Mr Sutton-Cornish turned his head slowly. Down on the floor, off his box, the auctioneer was a mere wisp of a man. A shabby, unpressed red-eyed little man who had found life no picnic.

"Yes, but what would one *do* with it?" Mr Sutton-Cornish asked throatily.

"Well—it's a door like any other, sir. Bit 'eavy. Bit queer-like. But still a door like any other."

"I wonder," Mr Sutton-Cornish said, still throatily.

The auctioneer gave him a swift appraising glance, shrugged and gave it up. He sat down on an empty box, lit a cigarette and relaxed sloppily into private life.

"What are you asking for it?" Mr Sutton-Cornish inquired, quite suddenly. "What are you asking for it, Mr—"

"Skimp, sir. Josiah Skimp. Well, a £20 note, sir? Bronze alone ought to be worth that for art work." The little man's eyes were glittering again.

Mr Sutton-Cornish nodded absently. "I don't know much about that."

" 'Ell of a lot of it, sir." Mr Skimp hopped off his box, patted over and heaved the leaf of the door open, grunting. "Beats me 'ow it ever got 'ere. For seven-footers. No door for shrimps like me. Look, sir."

Mr Sutton-Cornish had a rather ghastly presentiment, of course. But he didn't do anything about it. He couldn't. His tongue stuck in his throat and his legs were like ice. The comical contrast between the massiveness of the door and his own wisp of a body seemed to amuse Mr Skimp. His little, round face threw back the shadow of a grin. Then he lifted his foot and hopped.

Mr Sutton-Cornish watched him—as long as there was anything to watch. In fact he watched much longer. The hammering at the back of the shop seemed to get quite thunderous in the silence.

Once more, after a long time, Mr Sutton-Cornish bent forward and closed the door. This time he twisted the key and dragged it out and put it in his overcoat pocket.

"Got to do something," he mumbled. "Got to do—Can't let this sort of thing—" His voice trailed off and then he jerked violently, as though a sharp pain had shot through him. Then he laughed out loud, off key. Not a natural laugh. Not a very nice laugh.

"That was beastly," he said under his breath. "But amazingly funny."

He was still standing there rooted when a pale young man with a hammer appeared at his elbow.

"Mr Skimp step out, sir—or did you notice? We're supposed to be closed up, sir."

Mr Sutton-Cornish didn't look up at the pale young man with the hammer. Moving a clammy tongue he said:

"Yes . . . Mr Skimp . . . stepped out."

The young man started to turn away. Mr Sutton-Cornish made a gesture. "I've bought this door—from Mr Skimp," he said. "Twenty pounds. Will you take the money—and my card?"

The pale young man beamed, delighted at personal contact with a sale. Mr Sutton-Cornish drew out a note case, extracted four five-pound notes from it, also a formal calling card. He wrote on the card with a small, gold pencil. His hand seemed surprisingly steady.

"No 14 Grinling Crescent," he said. "Have it sent tomorrow without fail. It's . . . it's very heavy. I shall pay the drayage, of course. Mr Skimp will—" His voice trailed off again. Mr Skimp wouldn't.

"Oh, that's all right, sir. Mr Skimp is my uncle."

"Ah, that's too—I mean, well, take this ten-shilling note for yourself, won't you?"

Mr Sutton-Cornish left the shop rather rapidly, his right hand clutching the big key down in his pocket.

An ordinary taxi took him home to dinner. He dined alone—after three whiskies. But he wasn't as much alone as he looked. He never would be any more.


It came the next day, swathed in sacking and bound about with cords, looking like nothing on earth.

Four large men in leather aprons perspired it up the four front steps and into the hall, with a good deal of sharp language back and forth. They had a light hoist to help them get it off their dray, but the steps almost beat them. Once inside the hall they got it on two dollies and after that it was just an average heavy, grunting job. They set it up at the back of Mr Sutton-Cornish's study, across a sort of alcove he had an idea about.

He tipped them liberally, they went away, and Collins, the butler, left the front door open for a while to air the place through.

Carpenters came. The sacking was stripped off, and a frame-work was built around the door, so that it became part of a partition wall across the alcove. A small door was set in the partition. When the work was done and the mess cleared up Mr Sutton-Cornish asked for an oil-can, and locked himself into his study. Then and only then he got out the big bronze key and fitted it again into the huge lock and opened the bronze door wide, both sides of it.

He oiled the hinges from the rear, just in case. Then he shut it again and oiled the lock, removed the key and went for a good long walk, in Kensington Gardens, and back. Collins and the first parlourmaid had a look at it while he was out. Cook hadn't been upstairs yet.

"Beats me what the old fool's after," the butler said stonily. "I give him another week, Bruggs. If *she's* not back by then, I give him my notice. How about you, Bruggs?"

"Let him have his fun," Bruggs said, tossing her head. "That old sow he's married to—"

"Bruggs!"

"Tit-tat to you, Mr Collins," Bruggs said and flounced out of the room.

Mr Collins remained long enough to sample the whisky in the big square decanter on Mr Sutton-Cornish's smoking table.

In a shallow, tall cabinet in the alcove behind the bronze door, Mr Sutton-Cornish arranged a few odds and ends of old china and bric-a-brac and carved ivory and some idols in shiny black wood, very old and unnecessary. It wasn't much of an excuse for so massive a door. He added three statuettes in pink marble. The alcove still had an air of not being quite on to itself. Naturally the bronze door was never open unless the room door was locked.

In the morning Bruggs, or Mary the housemaid, dusted in the alcove, having entered, of course, by the partition door. That amused Mr Sutton-Cornish slightly, but the amusement began to wear thin. It was about three weeks after his wife and Teddy left that something happened to brighten him up.

A large, tawny man with a waxed moustache and steady grey eyes called on him and presented a card that indicated he was Detective-sergeant Thomas Lloyd of Scotland Yard.

He said that one Josiah Skimp, an auctioneer, living in Kennington, was missing from his home to the great concern of his family, and that his nephew, one George William Hawkins, also of Kennington, had happened to mention that Mr Sutton-Cornish was present in a shop in Soho on the very night when Mr Skimp vanished. In fact, Mr Sutton-Cornish might have been the last person known to have spoken to Mr Skimp.

Mr Sutton-Cornish laid out the whisky and cigars, placed his fingertips together and nodded gravely.

"I recall him perfectly, sergeant. In fact I bought that funny door over there from him. Quaint, isn't it?"

The detective glanced at the bronze door, a brief and empty glance.

"Out of my line, sir, I'm afraid. I do recall now something was said about the door. They had quite a job moving it. Very smooth whisky, sir. Very smooth indeed."

"Help yourself, sergeant. So Mr Skimp has run off and lost himself. Sorry I can't help you. I really didn't know him, you know."

The detective nodded his large tawny head. "I didn't think you did, sir. The Yard only got the case a couple of days ago. Routine call, you know. Did he seem excited, for instance?"

"He seemed tired," Mr Sutton-Cornish mused. "Very fed up—with the whole business of auctioneering, perhaps. I only spoke to him a moment. About that door, you know. A nice little man—but tired."

The detective didn't bother to look at the door again. He finished his whisky and allowed himself a little more.

"No family trouble," he said. "Not much money, but who has these days? No scandal. Not a melancholy type, they say. Odd."

"Some very queer types in Soho," Mr Sutton-Cornish said mildly.

The detective thought it over. "Harmless, though. A rough district once, but not in our time. Might I ask what you was doing over there?"

"Wandering," Mr Sutton-Cornish said. "Just wandering. A little more of this?"

"Well, now, really, sir, three whiskies in a morning . . . well, just this once and many thanks to you, sir."

Detective-sergeant Lloyd left—rather regretfully.

After he had been gone ten minutes or so, Mr Sutton-Cornish got up and locked the study door. He walked softly down the long, narrow room and got the big bronze key out of his inside breast pocket, where he always carried it now.

The door opened noiselessly and easily now. It was well-balanced for its weight. He opened it wide, both sides of it.

"Mr Skimp," he said very gently into the emptiness, "you are wanted by the police, Mr Skimp."

The fun of that lasted him well on to lunch time.

In the afternoon Mrs Sutton-Cornish came back. She appeared quite suddenly before him in the study, sniffed harshly at the smell of tobacco and scotch, refused a chair, and stood very solid and lowering just inside the closed door. Teddy stood beside her for a moment, then hurled herself at the edge of the rug.

"Stop that, you little beast. Stop that at once, darling," Mrs Sutton-Cornish said. She picked Teddy up and stroked him. He lay in her arms and licked her nose and sneered at Mr Sutton-Cornish.

"I find," Mrs Sutton-Cornish said, in a voice that had brittleness of dry suet, "after numerous very boring interviews with my solicitor, that I can do nothing without your help. Naturally, I dislike asking for that."

Mr Sutton-Cornish made ineffectual motions towards a chair and when they were ignored he leaned resignedly against the mantelpiece. He said he supposed that was so.

"Perhaps it has escaped your attention that I am still comparatively a young woman. And these are modern days, James."

Mr Sutton-Cornish smiled wanly and glanced at the bronze door. She hadn't noticed it yet. Then he put his head on one side and wrinkled his nose and said mildly, without much interest:

"You're thinking of a divorce?"

"I'm thinking of very little else," she said brutally.

"And you wish me to compromise myself in the usual manner, at Brighton, with a lady who will be described in court as an actress?"

She glared at him. Teddy helped her glare. Their combined

glare failed even to perturb Mr Sutton-Cornish. He had other resources now.

"Not with that dog," he said carelessly, when she didn't answer.

She made some kind of furious noise, a snort with a touch of snarl in it. She sat down then, very slowly and heavily, a little puzzled. She let Teddy jump to the floor.

"Just what are you talking about, James?" she asked witheringly.

He strolled over to the bronze door, leaned his back against it and explored its rich protuberances with a fingertip. Even then she didn't see the door.

"You want a divorce, my dear Louella," he said slowly, "so that you may marry another man. There's absolutely no point in it—with that dog. I shouldn't be asked to humiliate myself. Too useless. No man would marry that dog."

"James—are you attempting to blackmail me?" Her voice was rather dreadful. She almost bugled. Teddy sneaked across to the window curtains and pretended to lie down.

"And even if he would," Mr Sutton-Cornish said with a peculiar quiet in his tone, "I oughtn't to make it possible. I ought to have enough human compassion—"

"James! How dare you! you make me physically sick with your insincerity!"

For the first time in his life James Sutton-Cornish laughed in his wife's face.

"Those are two or three of the silliest speeches I ever had to listen to," he said. "You're an elderly, ponderous and damn dull woman. Now run along and take your miserable brown beetle with you."

She got up quickly, very quickly for her, and stood a moment almost swaying. Her eyes were as blank as a blind man's eyes. In the silence Teddy tore fretfully at a curtain, with bitter, preoccupied growls that neither of them noticed.

She said very slowly and almost gently: "We'll see how long you stay in your father's house, James Sutton-Cornish—*pauper*."

She moved very quickly the short distance to the door, went through and slammed it behind her.

The slamming of the door, an unusual event in that household, seemed to awaken a lot of echoes that had not been called upon to perform for a long time. So that Mr Sutton-Cornish was not instantly aware of the small peculiar sound at his own side of the door, a mixture of sniffing and whimpering, with just a dash of growl.

Teddy. Teddy hadn't made the door. The sudden, bitter exit had for once caught him napping. Teddy was shut in—with Mr Sutton-Cornish.

For a little while Mr Sutton-Cornish watched him rather absently, still shaken by the interview, not fully realising what had happened. The small, wet, black snout explored the crack at the bottom of the closed door. At moments, while the whimpering and sniffing went on, Teddy turned a reddish brown outjutting eye, like a fat wet marble, towards the man he hated.

Mr Sutton-Cornish snapped out of it rather suddenly. He straightened and beamed. "Well, well, old man," he purred. "Here we are, and for once without the ladies."

Cunning dawned in his beaming eye. Teddy read it and slipped off under a chair. He was silent now, very silent. And Mr Sutton-Cornish was silent as he moved swiftly along the wall and turned the key in the study door. Then he sped back toward the alcove, dug the key of the bronze door out of his pocket, unlocked and opened that—wide.

He sauntered back toward Teddy, beyond Teddy, as far as the window.

"Here we are, old man. Jolly, eh? Have a shot of whisky, old man?"

Teddy made a small sound under the chair, and Mr Sutton-Cornish sidled towards him delicately, bent down suddenly and lunged. Teddy made another chair, farther up the room. He breathed hard and his eyes stuck out rounder and wetter than ever, but he was silent, except for his breathing. And Mr Sutton-Cornish, stalking him patiently from chair to chair, was as silent as the last leaf of autumn, falling in slow eddies in a windless copse.

At about that time the doorknob turned sharply. Mr Sutton-Cornish paused to smile and click his tongue. A sharp knock followed. He ignored it. The knocking went on, sharper and sharper, and an angry voice accompanied it.

Mr Sutton-Cornish went on stalking Teddy. Teddy did the best he could, but the room was narrow and Mr Sutton-Cornish was patient and rather agile when he wanted to be. In the interests of agility he was quite willing to be undignified.

The knocking and calling out beyond the door went on, but inside the room things could only end one way. Teddy reached the sill of the bronze door, sniffed at it rapidly, almost lifted a contemptuous hind leg, but didn't because Mr Sutton-Cornish was too close to him. He sent a low snarl back over his shoulder and hopped that disastrous sill.

Mr Sutton-Cornish raced back to the room door, turned the key swiftly and silently, crept over to a chair and sprawled in it laughing. He was still laughing when Mrs Sutton-Cornish thought to try the knob again, found the door yielded this time, and stormed into the room. Through the mist of his grisly, solitary laughter he saw her cold stare, then he heard her rustling about the room, heard her calling Teddy.

Then, "What's that thing?" he heard her snap suddenly. "What utter foolishness—Teddy! Come, mother's little lamb! Come, Teddy!"

Even in his laughter Mr Sutton-Cornish felt the wing of a regret brush his cheek. Poor little Teddy. He stopped laughing and sat up, stiff and alert. The room was too quiet.

"Louella!" he called sharply.

No sound answered him.

He closed his eyes, gulped, opened them again, crept along the room staring. He stood in front of his little alcove for a long time, peering, peering through that bronze portal at the innocent little collection of trivia beyond.

He locked the door with quivering hands, stuffed the key down in his pocket, poured himself a stiff peg of whisky.

A ghostly voice that sounded something like his own, and yet unlike it, said out loud, very close to his ear:

"I didn't really intend anything like that . . . never . . . never . . . oh, never . . . or . . ."—after a long pause—"did I?"


Braced by the scotch he sneaked out into the hall and out of the front door without Collins seeing him. No car waited outside. As luck would have it she had evidently come up from Chinverly by train and taken a taxi. Of course they could trace the taxi—later on, when they tried. A lot of good that would do them.

Collins was next. He thought about Collins for some time, glancing at the bronze door, tempted a good deal, but finally shaking his head negatively.

"Not that way," he muttered. "Have to draw the line somewhere. Can't have a procession—"

He drank some more whisky and rang the bell. Collins made it rather easy for him.

"You rang sir?"

"What did it sound like?" Mr Sutton-Cornish asked, a little thick-tongued. "Canaries?"

Collins' chin snapped back a full two inches.

"The dowager won't be here to dinner, Collins. I think I'll dine out. That's all."

Collins stared at him. A greyness spread over Collins' face, with a little flush at the cheekbones.

"You allude to Mrs Sutton-Cornish, sir?"

Mr Sutton-Cornish hiccupped. "Who d'you suppose? Gone back to Chinverly to stew in her own juice some more. Ought to be plenty of it."

With deadly politeness Collins said: "I had meant to ask you, sir, whether Mrs Sutton-Cornish would return here—permanently. Otherwise—"

"Carry on." Another hiccup.

"Otherwise I should not care to remain myself, sir."

Mr Sutton-Cornish stood up and went close to Collins and breathed in his face. Haig & Haig. A good breath, of the type.

"Get out!" he rasped. "Get out now! Upstairs with you and pack your things. Your cheque will be ready for you. A full month. Thirty-two pounds in all, I believe."

Collins stepped back and moved towards the door. "That will suit me perfectly, sir. Thirty-two pounds is the correct amount." He reached the door, spoke again before he opened it. "A reference from *you,* sir, will not be desired."

He went out, closing the door softly.

"Ha!" Mr Sutton-Cornish said.

Then he grinned slyly, stopped pretending to be angry or drunk, and sat down to write the cheque.

He dined out that night, and the next night, and the next.

Cook left on the third day, taking the kitchenmaid with her. That left Bruggs and Mary, the housemaid. On the fifth day Bruggs wept when she gave her notice.

"I'd rather go at once, sir, if you'll let me," she sobbed. "There's something creepylike about the house since cook and Mr Collins and Teddy and Mrs Sutton-Cornish left."

Mr Sutton-Cornish patted her arm. "Cook and Mr Collins and Teddy and Mrs Sutton-Cornish," he repeated. "If only she could hear *that* order of precedence."

Bruggs stared at him, red-eyed. He patted her arm again. "Quite all right, Bruggs. I'll give you your month. And tell Mary to go, too. Think I'll close the house up and live in the south of France for a while. Now don't cry, Bruggs."

"No, sir." She bawled her way out of the room.

He didn't go to the south of France, of course. Too much fun being right where he was—alone at last in the home of his fathers. Not quite what they would have approved of, perhaps, except possibly the general. But the best he could do.

Almost overnight the house began to have the murmurs of an empty place. He kept the windows closed and the shades down. That seemed to be a gesture of respect he could hardly afford to omit.


Scotland Yard moves with the deadly dependability of a glacier, and at times almost as slowly. So it was a full month and nine days before Detective-sergeant Lloyd came back to No. 14 Grinling Crescent.

By that time the front steps had long since lost their white serenity. The apple-green door had acquired a sinister shade of grey. The brass saucer around the bell, the knocker, the big latch, all these were tarnished and stained, like the brass work of an old freighter limping around the Horn. Those who rang the bell departed slowly, with backward glances, and Mr Sutton-Cornish would be peeping out at them from the side of a drawn window shade.

He concocted himself weird meals in the echoing kitchen, creeping in after dark with ragged-looking parcels of food. Later he would slink out again with his hat pulled low and his overcoat collar up, give a quick glance up and down the street, then scramble off around the corner. The police constable on duty saw him occasionally at these manoeuvres and rubbed his chin a good deal over the situation.

No longer a study even in withered elegance, Mr Sutton-Cornish became a customer in obscure eating houses where draymen blew their soup on naked tables in compartments like horse stalls; in foreign cafés where men with blue-black hair and pointed shoes dined interminably over minute bottles of wine; in crowded, anonymous tea shops where the food looked and tasted as tired as the people who ate it.

He was no longer a perfectly sane man. In his dry, solitary, poisoned laughter there was the sound of crumbling walls. Even the pinched loafers under the arches of the Thames Embankment, who listened to him because he had sixpences, even these were glad when he passed on, stepping carefully in unshined shoes and lightly swinging the stick he no longer carried.

Then, late one night, returning softly, out of the dull-grey darkness, he found the man from Scotland Yard lurking near the dirty front steps with an air of thinking himself hidden behind a lampost.

"I'd like a few words with you, sir," he said, stepping forth briskly and holding his hands as though he might have to use them suddenly.

"Charmed, I'm sure," Mr Sutton-Cornish chuckled. "Trot right in."

He opened the door with his latchkey, switched the light on, and stepped with accustomed ease over a pile of dusty letters on the floor.

"Got rid of the servants," he explained to the detective. "Always did want to be alone some day."

The carpet was covered with burned matches, pipe ash, torn paper, and the corners of the hall had cobwebs in them. Mr Sutton-Cornish opened his study door, switched the light on in there and stood aside. The detective passed him warily, staring hard at the condition of the house.

Mr Sutton-Cornish pushed him into a dusty chair, thrust a cigar at him, reached for the whisky decanter.

"Business or pleasure this time?" he inquired archly.

Detective-sergeant Lloyd held his hard hat on his knee and looked the cigar over dubiously. "Smoke it later, thank you, sir . . . Business, I take it. I'm instructed to make inquiries as to the whereabouts of Mrs Sutton-Cornish."

Mr Sutton-Cornish sipped whisky amiably and pointed at the decanter. He took his whisky straight now. "Haven't the least idea," he said. "Why? Down at Chinverly, I suppose. Country place. She owns it."

"It so 'appens she ain't," Detective-sergeant Lloyd said, slipping on an "h", which he seldom did any more. "Been a separation, I'm told," he added grimly.

"That's *our* business, old man."

"Up to a point, yes, sir. Granted. Not after her solicitor can't find her and she ain't anywhere anybody can find her. Not *then*, it ain't just your business."

Mr Sutton-Cornish thought it over. "You might have something there—as the Americans say," he conceded.

The detective passed a large pale hand across his forehead and leaned forward.

"Let's 'ave it, sir," he said quickly. "Best in the long run. Best for all. Nothing to gain by foolishness. The law's the law."

"Have some whisky," Mr Sutton-Cornish said.

"Not tonight I won't," Detective-sergeant Lloyd said grimly.

"She left me." Mr Sutton-Cornish shrugged. "And because of that the servants left me. You know what servants are nowadays. Beyond that I haven't an idea."

"Oh yus I think you 'ave," the detective said, losing a little more of his West End manner. "No charges have been preferred, but I think you know all right, all right."

Mr Sutton-Cornish smiled airily. The detective scowled and went on: "We've taken the liberty of watching you, and for a gentleman of your position—you've been living a damn queer life, if I may say so."

"You may say so, and then you may get to hell out of my house," Mr Sutton-Cornish said suddenly.

"Not so fast. Not yet I won't."

"Perhaps you would like to search the house."

"Per'aps I should. Per'aps I shall. No hurry there. Takes

time. Sometimes takes shovels." Detective-sergeant Lloyd permitted himself to leer rather nastily. "Seems to me like people does a bit of disappearin' when you 'appen to be around. Take that Skimp. Now take Mrs Sutton-Cornish."

Mr Sutton-Cornish stared at him with lingering malice. "And in your experience, sergeant, where do people go when they disappear?"

"Sometimes they don't disappear. Sometimes somebody disappears them." The detective licked his strong lips, with a cat-like expression.

Mr Sutton-Cornish slowly raised his arm and pointed to the bronze door. "You wanted it, sergeant," he said suavely. "You shall have it. There is where you should look for Mr Skimp, for Teddy the Pomeranian, and for my wife. There—behind that ancient door of bronze."

The detective didn't shift his gaze. For a long moment he didn't change expression. Then, quite amiably, he grinned. There was something else behind his eyes, but it was behind them.

"Let's you and me take a nice little walk," he said breezily. "The fresh air would do you a lot of good, sir. Let's—"

"There," Mr Sutton-Cornish announced, still pointing with his arm rigid, "behind that door."

"Ah-ah," Detective-sergeant Lloyd waggled a large finger roguishly. "Been alone too much, you 'ave, sir. Thinkin' about things. Do it myself once in a while. Gets a fellow balmy in the crumpet like. Take a nice little walk with me, sir. We could stop somewhere for a nice—" The big tawny man planted a forefinger on the end of his nose and pushed his head back and wiggled his little finger in the air at the same time. But his steady grey eyes remained in another mood.

"We look at my bronze door first."

Mr Sutton-Cornish skipped out of his chair. The detective had him by the arm in a flash. "None of that," he said in a frosty voice. "Hold still."

"Key in here," Mr Sutton-Cornish said, pointing at his breast pocket but not trying to get his hand into it.

The detective got it out for him, stared at it heavily.

"All behind the door—on meathooks," Mr Sutton-Cornish

said. "All three. Little meathook for Teddy. Very large meathook for my wife. *Very* large meathook."

Holding him with his left hand, Detective-sergeant Lloyd thought it over. His pale brows were drawn tight. His large weathered face was grim—but sceptical.

"No harm to look," he said finally.

He marched Mr Sutton-Cornish across the floor, pushed the bronze key into the huge antique lock, twisted the ring, and opened the door.

He opened both sides of it. He stood looking into that very innocent alcove with its cabinets of knick-knacks and absolutely nothing else. He became genial again.

"Meathooks, did you say, sir? Very cute, if I may say so."

He laughed, released Mr Sutton-Cornish's arm and teetered on his heels.

"What the hell's it for?" he asked.

Mr Sutton-Cornish doubled over very swiftly and launched his thin body with furious speed at the big detective.

"Take a little walk yourself—and find out!" he screamed.

Detective-sergeant Lloyd was a big and solid man and probably used to being butted. Mr Sutton-Cornish could hardly have moved him six inches, even with a running start. But the bronze door had a high sill. The detective moved with the deceptive quickness of his trade, swayed his body just enough, and jarred his foot against the bronze sill.

If it hadn't been for that he would have plucked Mr Sutton-Cornish neatly out of the air and held him squirming like a kitten, between his large thumb and forefinger. But the sill jarred him off balance. He stumbled a little, and swayed his body completely out of Mr Sutton-Cornish's way.

Mr Sutton-Cornish butted empty space—the empty space framed by that majestic door of bronze. He sprawled forward clutching—falling—clutching—across the sill—

Detective-sergeant Lloyd straightened up slowly, twisted his thick neck and stared. He moved back a little from the sill so that he could be perfectly certain the side of the door hid nothing from him. It didn't. He saw a cabinet of odd pieces of china, odds and ends of carved ivory and shiny black wood, and on top of the cabinet three little statuettes of pink marble.

He saw nothing else. There was nothing else in there to see.

"Gorblimey!" he said at last, violently. At least he thought he said it. Somebody said it. He wasn't quite sure. He was never absolutely sure about anything—after that night.

The whisky looked all right. It smelled all right, too. Shaking so that he could hardly hold the decanter, Detective-sergeant Lloyd poured a little into a glass and took a sip in his dry mouth and waited.

After a little while he drank another spoonful. He waited again. Then he drank a stiff drink—a very stiff drink.

He sat down in the chair beside the whisky and took his large folded cotton handkerchief out of his pocket and unfolded it slowly and mopped his face and neck behind his ears.

In a little while he wasn't shaking quite so much. Warmth began to flow through him. He stood up, drank some more whisky, then slowly and bitterly moved back down the room. He swung the bronze door shut, locked it, put the key down in his pocket. He opened the partition door at the side, braced himself and stepped through into the alcove. He looked at the back of the bronze door. He touched it. It wasn't very light in there, but he could see that the place was empty, except for the silly-looking cabinet. He came out again shaking his head.

"Can't be," he said out loud. "Not a chance. Not 'arf a chance."

Then, with the sudden unreasonableness of the reasonable man, he flew into a rage.

"If I get 'ooked for this," he said between his teeth, "I get 'ooked."

He went down to the dark cellar, rummaged around until he found a hand axe and carried it back upstairs.

He hacked the woodwork to ribbons. When he was done, the bronze door stood alone on its base, jaggled wood all around it, but not holding it any longer. Detective-sergeant Lloyd put the hand axe down, wiped his hands and face on his big handkerchief, and went on behind the door. He put his shoulder to it and set his strong, yellow teeth.

Only a brutally determined man of immense strength could

have done it. The door fell forward with a heavy rumbling crash that seemed to shake the whole house. The echoes of that crash died away slowly, along infinite corridors of un-belief.

Then the house was silent again. The big man went out into the hall and had another look out of the front door.

He put his coat on, adjusted his hard hat, folded his damp handkerchief carefully and put it in his hip pocket, lit the cigar Mr Sutton-Cornish had given him, took a drink of whisky and swaggered to the door.

At the door he turned and deliberately sneered at the bronze door, lying fallen but still huge in the welter of splintered wood.

"To 'ell with you, 'ooever you are," Detective-sergeant Lloyd said. "I ain't no bloody primrose."

He shut the house door behind him. A little high fog outside, a few dim stars, a quiet street with lighted windows. Two or three cars of expensive appearance, very likely chauffeurs loung-ing in them, but no one in sight.

He crossed the street at an angle and walked along beside the tall iron railing of the park. Faintly through the rhododendron bushes he could see the dull glimmer of the little ornamental lake. He looked up and down the street and took the big bronze key out of his pocket.

"Make it a good 'un," he told himself softly.

His arm swept up and over. There was a minute splash in the ornamental lake, then silence. Detective-sergeant Lloyd walked on calmly, puffing at his cigar.

Back at C.I.D. he gave his report steadily, and for the first and last time in his life, there was something besides truth in it. Couldn't raise anybody at the house. All dark. Waited three hours. Must all be away.

The inspector nodded and yawned.


The Sutton-Cornish heirs eventually pried the estate out of Chancery and opened up No. 14 Grinling Crescent and found the bronze door lying in a welter of dust and splintered wood and matted cobwebs. They stared at it goggle-eyed, and when they found out what it was, sent for dealers, thinking there might be a little money in it. But the dealers sighed and said no, no money in that sort of thing now. Better ship it off to a foundry and have it melted down for the metal. Get so much a pound. The dealers departed noiselessly with wry smiles.

Sometimes when things are a little dull in the Missing Persons section of the C.I.D. they take out the Sutton-Cornish file out and dust it off and look through it sourly and put it away again.

Sometimes when Inspector—formerly Detective-sergeant—Thomas Lloyd is walking along an unusually dark and quiet street he will whirl suddenly, for no reason at all, and jump to one side with a swift anguished agility.

But there isn't really anybody there, trying to butt him.

# A MAN WHO HAD NO EYES

*MacKinlay Kantor was reared in a rural area of Iowa and while working there as a newspaper reporter developed an interest in fantasy by collecting local legends. Some of these he used as the basis for a number of short stories. The success he achieved later as a novelist* (Andersonville, *etc.*) *and screenwriter made it impossible for him to return to his former interest, but from his early writing has been located this short exercise in horror (written in 1943) which is a prime example of how to stun your unsuspecting reader with the last line. But don't look first!*

A BEGGAR was coming from the avenue just as Mr Parsons emerged from the hotel. He was a blind beggar, carrying the traditional battered cane, and thumping his way before him with the cautious, half-furtive effort of the sightless. He was a shaggy, thick-necked fellow; his coat was greasy about the lapels and pockets, and his hands splayed over the cane's crook with a futile sort of clinging. He wore a black pouch slung over his shoulder. Apparently he had something to sell.

The air was rich with spring; sun was warm and yellowed on the asphalt. Mr Parsons, standing there in front of his hotel and noting the *clack-clack* approach of the sightless man, felt a sudden and foolish sort of pity for all blind creatures.

And, thought Mr Parsons, he was very glad to be alive. A few years ago he had been little more than a skilled labourer; now he was successful, respected, admired. Insurance. And he had done it alone, unaided, struggling beneath handicaps. And he was still young. The blue air of spring, fresh from its memories of windy pools and lush shrubbery, could thrill him with eagerness.

He took a step forward just as the tap-tapping blind man passed him by. Quickly the shabby fellow turned.

"Listen, guv'nor. Just a minute of your time."

Mr Parsons said, "It's late. I have an appointment. Do you want me to give you something?"

"I ain't no beggar, guv'nor. You bet I ain't. I got a handy little article here"—he fumbled until he could press a small object into Mr Parsons' hand—"that I sell. One buck. Best cigarette lighter made."

Mr Parsons stood there, somewhat annoyed and embarrassed. He was a handsome figure with his immaculate grey suit and grey hat and malacca stick. Of course the man with the cigarette lighters could not see him. . . . "But I don't smoke," he said.

"Listen. I bet you know plenty of people who smoke. Nice little present," wheedled the man. "And, mister, you wouldn't mind helping a poor guy out?" He clung to Mr Parsons' sleeve.

Mr Parsons sighed and felt in his vest pocket. He brought out two half-dollars and pressed them into the man's hand. "Certainly. I'll help you out. As you say, I can give it to someone. Maybe the elevator boy would—" He hesitated, not wishing to be boorish and inquisitive, even with a blind pedlar. "Have you lost your sight entirely?"

The shabby man pocketed the two half-dollars. "Fourteen years, guv'nor." Then he added with an insane sort of pride: "Westbury, sir. I was one of 'em."

"Westbury," repeated Mr Parsons. "Ah, yes. The chemical explosion. The papers haven't mentioned it for years. But at the time it was supposed to be one of the greatest disasters in—"

"They've all forgot about it." The fellow shifted his feet wearily. "I tell you, guv'nor, a man who was in it don't forget about it. Last thing I ever saw was C shop going up in one grand smudge, and that damn gas pouring in at all the busted windows."

Mr Parsons coughed. But the blind pedlar was caught up with the train of his one dramatic reminiscence. And, also, he was thinking that there might be more half-dollars in Mr Parsons' pocket.

"Just think about it, guv'nor. There was a hundred and eight people killed, about two hundred injured, and over fifty of them lost their eyes. Blind as bats—" He groped forward until his dirty hand rested against Mr Parsons' coat. "I tell you, sir, there wasn't nothing worse than that in the war. If I had lost my eyes in the war, okay. I would have been well took care of. But I was just a workman, working for what was in it. And I got it. You're damn right I got it, while the capitalists were making their dough! They was insured, don't worry about that. They—"

"Insured," repeated his listener. "Yes. That's what I sell—"

"You want to know how I lost my eyes?" cried the man. "Well, here it is!" His words fell with the bitter and studied drama of a story often told, and told for money. "I was there in C shop, last of all the folks rushing out. Out in the air there was a chance, even with buildings exploding right and left. A lot of guys made it safe out the door and got away. And just when I was about there, crawling along between those big vats, a guy behind me grabs my leg. He says, 'Let me past, you—!' Maybe he was nuts. I dunno. I try to forgive him in my heart, guv'nor. But he was bigger than me. He hauls me back and climbs right over me! Tramples me into the dirt. And he gets out, and I lie there with all that poison gas pouring down on all sides of me and flame and stuff—" He swallowed—a studied sob—and stood dumbly expectant. He could imagine the next words: *Tough luck, my man. Damned tough. Now I want to*— "That's the story, guv'nor."

The spring wind shrilled past them, damp and quivering.

"Not quite," said Mr Parsons.

The blind peddlar shivered crazily. "Not quite? What do you mean, you—?"

"The story is true," Mr Parsons said, "except that it was the other way around."

"Other way around?" He croaked unamiably. "Say, guv'nor—"

"I was in C shop," said Mr Parsons. "It was the other way around. You were the fellow who hauled back on me and climbed over me. You were bigger than I was, Markwardt."

The blind man stood there for a long time swallowing hoarsely. He gulped: "Parsons. By God. By God! I thought you—" And then he screamed fiendishly: "Yes. Maybe so.

Maybe so. But I'm blind! I'm blind, and you've been standing here letting me spout to you, and laughing at me every minute! I'm blind!"

People in the street turned to stare at him.

"You got away, but I'm blind! Do you hear? I'm—"

"Well," said Mr Parsons, "don't make such a row about it, Markwardt. So am I."

# THE AFFAIR AT 7 RUE DE M——

JOHN STEINBECK

*While many of John Steinbeck's short stories are pervaded by elements of cruelty and suffering, it is none the less surprising to find him sitting down to write a piece of weird fantasy such as* The Affair at 7 Rue De M——, *obviously for his own entertainment as much as the reader's. This story dates from one of his trips to Paris and may well have been inspired by something out of the ordinary which happened to him there. Steinbeck remains as one of the most widely read of all modern American writers and the reprinting of the following forgotten tale can only underline the exceptional versatility of his talent.*

I HAD hoped to withhold from public scrutiny those rather curious events which had given me some concern for the past month. I knew, of course, that there was talk in the neighbourhood; I have even heard some of the distortions current in my district—stories, I hasten to add, in which there is no particle of truth. However, my desire for privacy was shattered yesterday by a visit of two members of the fourth estate who assured me that the story, or rather, a story, had escaped the boundaries of my *arrondissement*.

In the light of impending publicity I think it only fair to issue the true details of those happenings which have come to be known as The Affair at 7 rue de M——, in order that nonsense may not be added to a set of circumstances which are not without their *bizarrerie*. I shall set down the events as they happened without comment, thereby allowing the public to judge of the situation.

At the beginning of the summer I carried my family to Paris and took up residence in a pretty little house at 7 rue de M——, a building which in another period had been the mews of the great house beside it. The whole property is now owned and part of it inhabited by a noble French family of such age and purity that its members still consider the Bourbons unacceptable as claimants to the throne of France.

To this pretty little converted stable with three floors of rooms above a well-paved courtyard, I brought my immediate family, consisting of my wife, my three children (two small boys and a grown daughter), and of course, myself. Our domestic arrangement in addition to the concierge who, as you might say, came with the house, consists of a French cook of great ability, a Spanish maid, and my own secretary, a girl of Swiss nationality whose high attainments and ambitions are only equalled by her moral altitude. This then was our little family group when the events I am about to chronicle were ushered in.

If one must have an agency in this matter, I can find no alternative to placing not the blame but rather the authorship, albeit innocent, on my younger son John who has only recently attained his eighth year, a lively child of singular beauty and buck teeth.

This young man has, during the last several years in America, become not so much an addict as an aficionado of that curious American practice, the chewing of bubble gum, and one of the pleasanter aspects of the early summer in Paris lay in the fact that the Cadet John had neglected to bring any of the atrocious substance with him from America. The child's speech became clear and unobstructed and the hypnotised look went out of his eyes.

Alas, this delightful situation was not long to continue. An old family friend travelling in Europe brought as a present to the children a more than adequate supply of this beastly gum, thinking to do them a kindness. Thereupon the old familiar situation reasserted itself. Speech fought its damp way past a huge wad of the gum and emerged with the sound of a faulty water tap. The jaws were in constant motion, giving the face at best a look of agony, while the eyes took on a glaze like those of a pig with a recently severed jugular. Since I do not believe in inhibiting my children I resigned myself to a summer not quite so pleasant as I had at first hoped.

On occasion I do not follow my ordinary practice of *laissez-faire*. When I am composing the material for a book or play or essay, in a word, when the utmost of concentration is required, I am prone to establish tyrannical rules for my own comfort and effectiveness. One of these rules is that there shall be neither chewing nor bubbling while I am trying to concentrate. This rule is so thoroughly understood by the Cadet John that he accepts it as one of the laws of nature and does not either complain or attempt to evade the ruling. It is his pleasure and my solace for my son to come sometimes into my workroom, there to sit quietly beside me for a time. He knows he must be silent and when he has remained so for as long a time as his character permits, he goes out quietly, leaving us both enriched by the wordless association.

Two weeks ago in the late afternoon, I sat at my desk composing a short essay for *Figaro Litteraire,* an essay which later roused some controversy when it was printed under the title "Sartre Resartus". I had come to that passage concerning the proper clothing for the soul when to my astonishment and chagrin I heard the unmistakable soft plopping sound of a bursting balloon of bubble gum. I looked sternly at my offspring and saw him chewing away. His cheeks were coloured with embarrassment and the muscles of his jaws stood rigidly out.

"You know the rule," I said coldly.

To my amazement tears came into his eyes and while his jaws continued to masticate hugely, his blubbery voice forced its way past the huge lump of bubble gum in his mouth. "I didn't do it!"

"What do you mean, you didn't do it?" I demanded in a rage. "I distinctly heard and now I distinctly see."

"Oh, sir!" he moaned. "I really didn't. I'm not chewing it, sir. It's chewing me."

For a moment I inspected him closely. He is an honest child, only under the greatest pressure of gain permitting himself an untruth. I had the horrible thought that the bubble gum had finally had its way and that my son's reason was tottering. If this were so, it were better to tread softly. Quietly I put out my hand. "Lay it here," I said kindly.

My child manfully tried to disengage the gum from his jaws. "It won't let me go," he sputtered.

"Open up." I said and then inserting my fingers in his mouth I seized hold of the large lump of gum and, after a struggle in which my fingers slipped again and again, managed to drag it forth and to deposit the ugly blob on my desk on top of a pile of white manuscript paper.

For a moment it seemed to shudder there on the paper and then with an easy slowness began to undulate, to swell and recede with the exact motion of being chewed while my son and I regarded it with popping eyes.

For a long time we watched it while I drove through my mind for some kind of explanation. Either I was dreaming or some principle as yet unknown had taken its seat in the pulsing bubble gum on the desk. I am not unintelligent; while I considered the indecent thing, a hundred little thoughts and glimmerings of understanding raced through my brain. At last I asked, "How long has it been chewing you?"

"Since last night," he replied.

"And when did you first notice, this, this propensity on its part?"

He spoke with perfect candour. "I will ask you to believe me, sir," he said. "Last night before I went to sleep I put it under my pillow as is my invariable custom. In the night I was awakened to find that it was in my mouth. I again placed it under my pillow and this morning it was again in my mouth, lying very quietly. When, however, I became thoroughly awakened, I was conscious of a slight motion and shortly afterwards the situation dawned on me that I was no longer master of the gum. It had taken its head. I tried to remove it, sir, and could not. You yourself with all your strength have seen how difficult it was to extract. I came to your study to wait till you were free, wishing to acquaint you with my difficulty. Oh, Daddy, what do you think has happened?"

The cancerous thing held my complete attention.

"I must think," I said. "This is something a little out of the ordinary, and I do not believe it should be passed over without some investigation."

As I spoke a change came over the gum. It ceased to chew itself and seemed to rest for a while, and then with a flowing movement like those monocellular animals of the order Paramecium, the gum slid across the desk straight in the direction of my son. For a moment I was stricken with astonishment and for an even longer time I failed to discern its intent. It dropped to his knee, climbed horribly up his shirt front. Only then did I understand. It was trying to get back into his mouth. He looked down on it paralysed with fright.

"Stop," I cried, for I realised that my third-born was in danger and at such times I am capable of a violence which verges on the murderous. I seized the monster from his chin and striding from my study, entered the sitting-room, opened the window and hurled the thing into the busy traffic on the rue de M—

I believe it is the duty of a parent to ward off those snocks which may cause dreams or trauma whenever possible. I went back to my study to find young John sitting where I had left him. He was staring into space. There was a troubled line between his brows.

"Son," I said, "you and I have seen something which, while we know it to have happened, we might find difficult to describe with any degree of success to others. I ask you to imagine the scene if we should tell this story to the other members of the family. I greatly fear we should be laughed out of the house."

"Yes, sir," he said passively.

"Therefore I am going to propose to you, my son, that we lock the episode deep in our memories and never mention it to a soul as long as we live." I waited for his assent and when it did not come, glanced up at his face to see it a ravaged field of terror. His eyes were staring out of his head. I turned in the direction of his gaze. under the door there crept a paper-thin sheet which, once it had entered the room, grew to a grey blob and rested on the rug, pulsing and chewing. After a moment it moved again by pseudo-podian progression towards my son.

I fought down panic as I rushed at it. I grabbed it up and flung it on my desk, then seizing an African war club from among the trophies on the wall, a dreadful instrument studded with brass, I beat the gum until I was breathless and it a torn piece of plastic fabric. The moment I rested, it drew itself together and for a few moments chewed very rapidly, as though it chuckled at my impotence, and then inexorably it moved towards my son, who by this time was crouched in a corner moaning with terror.

Now a coldness came over me. I picked up the filthy thing and wrapped it in my handkerchief, strode out of the house, walked three blocks to the Seine and flung the handkerchief into the slowly moving current.

I spent a good part of the afternoon soothing my son and trying to reassure him that his fears were over. But such was his nervousness that I had to give him half a barbiturate tablet to get him to sleep that night, while my wife insisted that I call a doctor.

I did not at that time dare to tell her why I could not obey her wish.

I was awakened, indeed the whole house was awakened, in the night by a terrified, muffled scream from the children's room. I took the stairs two at a time and burst into the room, flicking the light switch as I went. John sat up in bed squalling, while with his fingers he dug at his half-open mouth, a mouth which horrifyingly went right on chewing. As I looked a bubble emerged between his fingers and burst with a wet plopping sound.

What chance of keeping our secret now! All had to be explained, but with the plopping gum pinned to a breadboard with an ice pick the explanation was easier than it might have been. And I am proud of the help and comfort given me. There is no strength like that of the family. Our French cook solved the problem by refusing to believe it even when she saw it. It was not reasonable, she explained, and she was a reasonable member of a reasonable people. The Spanish maid ordered and paid for an exorcism by the parish priest who, poor man, after two hours of strenuous effort went away muttering that this was more a matter of the stomach than the soul.

For two weeks we were besieged by the monster. We burned it in the fireplace, causing it to splutter in blue flames and melt in a nasty mess among the ashes. Before morning it had crawled through the keyhole of the children's room, leaving a trail of wood ash on the door, and again we were awakened by screams from the Cadet.

In despair I drove far into the country and threw it from my automobile. It was back before morning. Apparently it had crept to the highway and placed itself in the Paris traffic until picked up by a truck tyre. When we tore it from John's mouth it had still the nonskid marks of Michelin imprinted in its side.

Fatigue and frustration will take their toll. In exhaustion, with my will to fight back sapped, and after we had tried every possible method to lose or destroy the bubble gum, I placed it at last under a bell jar which I ordinarily use to cover my microscope. I collapsed in a chair to gaze at it with weary, defeated eyes. John slept in his little bed under the influence of sedatives, backed by my assurance that I would not let the Thing out of my sight.

I lighted a pipe and settled back to watch it. Inside the bell jar the grey tumorous lump moved restlessly about searching for some means of exit from its prison. Now and then it paused as though in thought and emitted a bubble in my direction. I could feel the hatred it had for me. In my weariness I found my mind slipping into an analysis which had so far escaped me.

The background I had been over hurriedly. It must be that from constant association with the lambent life which is my son, the magic life had been created in the bubble gum. And with life had come intelligence, not the manly open intelligence of the boy, but an evil calculating wiliness.

How could it be otherwise? Intelligence without the soul to balance it must of necessity be evil; the gum had not absorbed any part of John's soul.

Very well, said my mind, now that we have a hypothesis of its origin, let us consider its nature. What does it think? What does it want? What does it need? My mind leaped like a terrier. It needs and wants to get back to its host, my son. It wants to be chewed. It must be chewed to survive.

Inside the bell jar the gum inserted a thin wedge of itself under the heavy glass foot and constricted so that the whole jar lifted a fraction of an inch. I laughed as I drove it back. I laughed with almost insane triumph. I had the answer.

In the dining-room I procured a clear plastic plate, one of a dozen my wife had bought for picnics in the country. Then turning the bell jar over and securing the monster in its bottom, I smeared the mouth of it with a heavy plastic cement guaranteed to be water-, alcohol- and acid-proof. I forced the plate over the opening and pressed it down until the glue took hold and bound the plate to the glass, making an airtight container. And last I turned the jar upright again and adjusted the reading light so that I could observe every movement of my prisoner.

Again it searched the circle for escape. Then it faced me and emitted a great number of bubbles very rapidly. I could hear the little bursting plops through the glass.

"I have you, my beauty," I cried. "I have you at last."

That was a week ago. I have not left the side of the bell jar since, and have only turned my head to accept a cup of coffee. When I go to the bathroom, my wife takes my place. I can now report the following hopeful news.

During the first day and night, the bubble gum tried every means to escape. Then for a day and a night it seemed to be agitated and nervous as though it had for the first time realised its predicament. The third day it went to work with its chewing motion, only the action was speeded up greatly, like the chewing of a baseball fan. On the fourth day it began to weaken and I observed with joy a kind of dryness on its once slick and shiny exterior.

I am now in the seventh day and I believe it is almost over. The gum is lying in the centre of the plate. At intervals it heaves and subsides. Its colour has turned to a nasty yellow. Once today when my son entered the room, it leaped up excitedly, then seemed to realise its hopelessness and collapsed on the plate. It will die tonight, I think, and only then will I dig a deep hole in the garden, and I will deposit the sealed bell jar and cover it up and plant geraniums over it.

It is my hope that this account will set straight some of the silly tales that are being hawked in the neighbourhood.

# THE SNAIL WATCHER

### PATRICIA HIGHSMITH

*The following nightmarish story about a wealthy man's preoccupation with the courtship and reproductive habits of snails may serve as a reminder that in macabre fiction women have absolutely nothing to learn from the opposite sex. This is certainly true of Miss Highsmith, one of whose novels provided a screenplay for a Hitchcock thriller. The sting in this tale, however, is that Patricia Highsmith is herself not only a breeder of snails but has been known to travel abroad with her "pets".*

WHEN MR PETER Knoppert began to make a hobby of snail watching, he had no idea that his handful of specimens would become hundreds in no time. Only two months after the original snails were carried up to the Knoppert study, some thirty glass tanks and bowls, all teeming with snails, lined the walls, rested on the desk and windowsills, and were beginning even to cover the floor. Mrs Knoppert disapproved strongly, and would no longer enter the room. It smelled, she said, and besides she had once stepped on a snail by accident, a horrible sensation she would never forget. But the more his wife and friends deplored his unusual and vaguely repellent pastime, the more pleasure Mr Knoppert seemed to find in it.

"I never cared for nature before in my life," Mr Knoppert often remarked—he was a partner in a brokerage firm, a man who had devoted all his life to the science of finance—"but snails have opened my eyes to the beauty of the animal world."

If his friends commented that snails were not really animals, and their slimy habitats hardly the best example of the beauty of nature, Mr Knoppert would tell them with a superior smile that they simply didn't know all that *he* knew about snails.

And it was true. Mr Knoppert had witnessed an exhibition that was not described, certainly not adequately described, in any encyclopaedia or zoology book that he had been able to find. Mr Knoppert had wandered into the kitchen one evening for a bite of something before dinner, and had happened to notice that a couple of snails in the china bowl on the draining-board were behaving very oddly. Standing more or less on their tails, they were weaving before each other for all the world like a pair of snakes hypnotised by a flute player. A moment later, their faces came together in a kiss of voluptuous intensity. Mr Knoppert bent closer and studied them from all angles. Something else was happening: a protuberance like an ear was appearing on the right side of the head of either snail. His instinct told him that he was watching a sexual activity of some sort.

The cook came in and said something to him, but Mr Knoppert silenced her with an impatient wave of his hand. He couldn't take his eyes from the enchanted little creatures in the bowl.

When the earlike excrescences were precisely together rim to rim, a whitish rod like another small tentacle shot out from one ear and arched over towards the ear of the other snail. Mr Knoppert's first surmise was dashed when a tentacle sallied from the other snail, too. Most peculiar, he thought. The two tentacles withdrew, then shot forth again, one after the other, and then as if they had found some invisible mark, remained fixed in the other snail. Mr Knoppert peered intently closer. So did the cook.

"Did you ever see anything like this?" Mr Knoppert asked.

"No. They must be fighting," the cook said indifferently and went away.

That was a sample of the ignorance on the subject of snails that he was later to discover everywhere.

Mr Knoppert continued to observe the pair of snails for nearly an hour, until first the ears, then the rods withdrew, and the snails themselves relaxed their attitudes and paid no further attention to each other. But by that time, a different pair of snails had begun a flirtation, and were slowly rearing themselves to get into a position for kissing. Mr Knoppert told the cook that the snails were not to be served that evening. He took the whole bowl of them up to his study.

And snails were never again served in the Knoppert household.

That night, he searched his encyclopaedias and a few general science books he happened to possess, but there was absolutely nothing on snails' breeding habits, though the oyster's dull reproductive cycle was described in detail. Perhaps it hadn't been a mating he had seen after all, Mr Knoppert decided after a day or two. His wife Edna told him either to eat the snails or get rid of them—it was at this time she stepped on a snail that had crawled out on to the floor—and Mr Knoppert might have, if he hadn't come across a certain sentence in Darwin's *Origin of Species* on a page given to gastropoda. The sentence was in French, a language Mr Knoppert did not know, but the word *sensualité* made him tense like a bloodhound that has suddenly found the scent. He was in the public library at the time, and laboriously he translated the sentence with the aid of a French-English dictionary. It was a statement of less than a hundred words, saying that snails manifested a sensuality in their mating that was not to be found anywhere in the animal kingdom. That was all. It was from the notebooks of Henri Fabre. Obviously, Darwin had decided not to translate it for the average reader, but to leave it in its original language for the scholarly few who really cared. Mr Knoppert considered himself one of the scholarly few now, and his round, pink face beamed with self-esteem.

He had learned that his snails were the fresh water type that laid their eggs in sand or earth, so he put moist earth and a little saucer of water into a big wash-pan and transferred his snails into it. Then he waited for something to happen. Not even another mating happened. He picked up the snails one by one and looked at them, without seeing anything suggestive of pregnancy. But one snail he couldn't pick up. The shell might have been glued to the earth. Mr Knoppert suspected the snail had buried its head in the ground to die. Two more days went by, and on the morning of the third, Mr Knoppert found a spot of crumbly earth where the snail had rested. Curious, he investigated the crumbles with a match stem, and to his delight discovered a pit full of shiny new eggs. Snail eggs! He hadn't been wrong. Mr Knoppert called his wife and the cook to look at them. The eggs looked very much like big caviar, only they were white instead of black or red.

"Well, naturally they have to breed some way," was his wife's comment.

Mr Knoppert couldn't understand her lack of interest. He had to go look at the eggs every hour that he was at home. He looked at them every morning to see if any change had taken place, and the eggs were his last thought every night before he went to bed. Moreover, another snail was now digging a pit. And another pair of snails was mating! The first batch of eggs turned a greyish colour, and minuscule spirals of future shells became discernible on their surfaces. Mr Knoppert's anticipation rose to higher pitch. At last a morning arrived when he looked down into the egg pit and saw the first tiny moving head, the first stubby little antennae uncertainly exploring its nest. Mr Knoppert was as happy as the father of a new child. Every one of the thirty or more eggs in the pit came miraculously to life. He had seen the entire reproductive cycle evolve to a successful conclusion. And the fact that no one, at least no one that he knew of, was acquainted with a fraction of what he knew, lent his knowledge a thrill of discovery, the piquancy of the esoteric. Mr Knoppert made notes on successive matings and egg hatchings. He narrated snail biology to sometimes fascinated, more often shocked friends and guests, until his wife squirmed with embarrassment.

"But where is it going to stop, Peter? If they keep on reproducing at this rate, they'll take over the house!" his wife told him after fifteen or twenty pits had hatched.

"There's no stopping nature," he replied good-humouredly. "They've only taken over the study. There's plenty of room there."

So more and more glass tanks and bowls were moved in. Mr Knoppert went to the market and chose several of the more lively looking snails, and also a pair he found mating, unobserved by the rest of the world. More and more egg pits appeared in the dirt floors of the tanks, and out of each pit crept finally from thirty to forty baby snails, transparent as dewdrops, gliding up rather than down the strips of fresh lettuce that Mr Knoppert was quick to give all the pits as edible ladders for them. Matings went on so often that he no longer bothered to watch them. But the thrill of seeing the white caviar become shells and start to move—that never diminished however often he witnessed it.

His colleagues in the brokerage office noticed a new zest for life in Peter Knoppert. He became more daring in his moves, more brilliant in his calculations, became in fact a little vicious in his outlook, but he brought money in for his company. By unanimous vote, his basic salary was raised from forty to sixty thousand per year. When anyone congratulated him on first achievements, Mr Knoppert was quick to give all the credit to his snails and the beneficial relaxation he derived from watching them.

He spent all his evenings with his snails in the room that was no longer a study but a kind of aquarium. He loved to strew the tanks with fresh lettuce and pieces of boiled potatoes and beets, then turn on the sprinkler system that he had installed in the tanks to simulate natural rainfall. Then all the snails would liven up and begin eating, mating, or merely gliding with obvious pleasure through the shallow water. Mr Knoppert often let a snail climb on to his forefinger—he fancied his snails enjoyed this human contact—and he would feed it a piece of lettuce by hand, would observe the snail from all sides, finding as much aesthetic satisfaction as another man might have from contemplating a Japanese print.

By now, Mr Knoppert did not allow anyone to set foot in his study. Too many snails had the habit of crawling around on the floor, of going to sleep glued to chair bottoms and to the backs of books on the shelves. Snails spent most of their time sleeping, especially the older snails. But there were enough less indolent snails who preferred love-making. Mr Knoppert estimated that about a dozen pairs of snails must be kissing all the time. And certainly there was a multitude of baby and adolescent snails. They were impossible to count. But Mr Knoppert did count the snails sleeping and creeping on the ceiling alone, and arrived at something between eleven and twelve hundred. The tanks, the bowls, the underside of his desk and the bookshelves must surely have held fifty times that number. Mr Knoppert meant to scrape the snails off the ceiling one day soon. Some of them had been up there for weeks, and he was afraid they were not taking in enough nourishment. But of late he had been a little too busy, and too much in need of the tranquillity that he got simply from sitting in the study in his favourite chair.

During the month of June, he was so busy, he often worked late in the evening at his office over the reports that were piling in at at the end of the fiscal year. He made calculations, spotted a half dozen possibilities for gain, and reserved the most daring, the least obvious moves for his private operations. By this time next year, he thought, he should be three or four times as well off as now. He saw his bank account multiplying as easily and rapidly as his snails. He told his wife this, and she was overjoyed. She even forgave him the appropriation of the study, and the stale, fishy smell that was spreading throughout the whole upstairs.

"Still, I do wish you'd take a look just to see if anything's happening, Peter," she said to him rather anxiously one morning. "A tank might have overturned or something, and I wouldn't want the rug to be ruined. You haven't been in the study for nearly a week, have you?"

Mr Knoppert hadn't been in for nearly two weeks. He didn't tell his wife that the rug was pretty much ruined already. "I'll go up tonight," he said.

But it was three more days before he found time. He went in one evening just before bedtime and was surprised to find the floor absolutely covered with snails, with three or four layers of snails. He had difficulty closing the door without mashing any. The dense clusters of snails in the corners made the room look positively round, as if he stood inside some huge, conglomerate stone. Mr Knoppert gazed around him with his mouth open in astonishment. They had not only covered every surface, but thousands of snails hung down into the room from the chandelier in a grotesque coagulation.

Mr Knoppert felt for the back of a chair to steady himself. He felt only a lot of shells under his hand. He had to smile a little: there were snails in the chair seat, piled up on one another like a lumpy cushion. He really must do something about the ceiling, and immediately. He took an umbrella from the corner, brushed some of the snails off it, and cleared a place on his desk to stand on. The umbrella point tore the wallpaper, and then the weight of the snails pulled down a long strip that hung almost to the floor. Mr Knoppert felt suddenly frustrated and angry. The sprinklers would make them move. He pulled the lever.

The sprinklers came on in all the tanks, and the seething activity of the entire room increased at once. Mr Knoppert slid his feet along the floor, through the tumbling snails that made a sound like pebbles on a beach, and directed a couple of the sprinklers at the ceiling. That was a mistake, he saw at once. The softened paper began to tear, and he dodged one slowly falling mass only to be hit by a swinging festoon of snails, really hit quite a stunning blow on the side of the head. He went down on one knee, dazed. He should open a window, he thought, the air was stifling. And there were snails crawling over his shoes and up his trousers legs. He shook his feet irritably. He was just going to the door, intending to call for one of the servants to help him, when the chandelier fell on him. Mr Knoppert sat down heavily on the floor. He saw now that he couldn't possibly get the window open, because the snails were fastened thick and deep over the windowsill. For a moment, he felt he couldn't get up, felt as if he were suffocating. It was not only the smell of the room, but everywhere he looked long wall-paper strips covered with snails blocked his vision as if he were in a prison.

"Edna!" he called, and was amazed at the muffled, ineffectual sound of his voice. The room might have been soundproofed.

He crawled to the door, heedless of the sea of snails he crushed under hands and knees. He could not get the door open. There were so many snails on it, crossing and recrossing the crack of the door on all four sides, they actually resisted his strength.

"Edna!" A snail crawled into his mouth. He spat it out in disgust. Mr Knoppert tried to brush the snails off his arms. But for every hundred he dislodged, four hundred seemed to slide upon him and fasten to him again, as if they deliberately sought him out as the only comparatively snail-free surface in the room. There were snails crawling over his eyes. Then just as he staggered to his feet, something else hit him—Mr Knoppert couldn't even see. He was fainting! At any rate, he was on the floor. His arms felt like leaden weights as he tried to reach his nostrils, his eyes to free them from the sealing, murderous snail bodies.

"Help!" He swallowed a snail. Choking, he widened his mouth for air and felt a snail crawl over his lips on to his tongue.

He was in hell! He could feel them gliding over his legs like a glutinous river, pinning his legs to the floor. "Ugh—!" Mr Knoppert's breath came in feeble gasps. His vision grew black, a horrible, undulating black. He could not breathe at all, because he could not reach his nostrils, could not move his hands. Then through the slit of one eye, he saw directly in front of him, only inches away, what had been, he knew, the rubber plant that stood in its pot near the door. A pair of snails were quietly making love on it. And right beside them, tiny snails as pure as dewdrops were emerging from a pit like an infinite army into their widening world.

# INFERIORITY COMPLEX

EVAN HUNTER

*Evan Hunter has the distinction of possessing two best-selling literary identities. As Ed McBain he is the creator of the thrillers associated with the 87th Precinct and under his real name, the author of many well known novels, including* The Blackboard Jungle. *In his early days he contributed to SF and fantasy magazines and during this apprenticeship his short stories revealed a burgeoning talent.* Inferiority Complex *was written in 1955.*

FIELD WAS, in many respects, just such a fellow as you and I. He had a good heart, and a good appetite. He had in addition very sharp eyes, and he was still quite fast, and of good breath, considering his age.

He lived in a fairly decent neighbourhood, the corner of Beam and Crossway, if you're familiar with it, and the walls that made up his home were snug and secure. His home was oil-heated.

He had a nice family, a wife and three children, the oldest of whom had left home to settle nearby. Field was implicity faithful to his wife, and there was nothing he would not do for her. Nor had he any reason to believe she was not just as true to him. He worked at night, mostly, and a night worker might sometimes have doubts about his wife's habits. But Field did not doubt.

He was then, like you and me, a fellow who had come along in years, fairly prosperous, a fellow who had managed to avoid the various traps and pitfalls which life presents, a fellow who was happily secure within the walls of his own little world.

Field did not think of other worlds.

Oh perhaps, yes. Oh sometimes, maybe. Sometimes when there were strange rumblings in the blackness of the night, he would look up and wonder. And he would envision a superior race somewhere, a race watching him, a race waiting—but he would shrug these thoughts aside, smile securely and go about his business.

There were fellows in the neighbourhood who believed all sorts of nonsense. These fellows seemed actually anxious for an alien race to suddenly appear. These fellows had built the myth of superior beings somewhere into a thing that was almost supernatural. Field was not one of these crackpots. Field controlled his own destiny, and if he sometimes looked up and wondered, it was a normal wonder, the same wonder you and I share when we gaze up at the endless stars on a black, black night, that sort of wonder.

Considering his frame of mind then, it was curious that the topic of conversation should swing to other worlds and alien beings on the night that Gray dropped in.

Gray was a mousy-looking fellow with a thin moustache and brown-almost-black eyes. He was a bit long-winded on occasion, but nonetheless a pleasant sort of chap with interesting theories and stories. So Field welcomed him into his home and made him comfortable, hoping at the same time that he would not ramble on endlessly. Field worked nights, and he hated to speed departing guests. This always seemed rude to him, even though he was painfully aware that business is, after all, business.

They talked of this and that for a while, and Field's wife served something to eat, and they all nibbled at it and felt very warm and comfortable together.

"This is nice," Gray said after a while. "This family life. Sometimes I regret not having a mate." He nodded pompously, and Field shrugged because he had never particularly cared for Gray's flowery way of saying things.

"Yes," he said, "it is nice."

"And yet," Gray said, "sometimes I wonder."

"About what?" Field asked.

"Don't you ever wonder?"

"Sometimes."

"About . . . what's out there?" He made a vague gesture with his head, and Field followed the gesture and looked up and out.

"If you start thinking about things like that," Field said, "you can lose your mind. There are so many possibilities."

"I suppose so," Gray said, wearily, "Still . . ."

"You're not one of those crackpots, are you?" Field asked,

smiling. "You don't believe a superior race is going to reach down and squash us all some day, do you?"

Gray looked a little embarrassed. "Well. . . ."

"Why, I do believe you are!" Field said, surprised.

"Maybe not squash us," Gray said mildly. "But I do believe we'll make contact with a superior race some day."

"Oh, bosh," Field said.

"No, seriously. I mean, hang it all, there have been reports, you know. Sightings, and all that. That's all part of the record, Field. History."

"History, my foot!" Field said.

"You can scoff, if you like, but history is history. If you put all the reports together, you get a picture. And the picture definitely indicates life somewhere out there."

"Intelligent life?" Field asked sceptically.

"Yes. Superior intelligent life."

"I can't believe that," Field said. He shook his head emphatically, the same way you or I might when presented with something so preposterous.

Gray shrugged. "All right, believe what you like. The trouble is, there are too many people like you."

"How do you mean?" Field asked.

"People who laugh at the idea. People who live in their own secure little homes and joke about it. Well, I hope those people aren't surprised some day. I hope when the invasion comes . . ."

"Invasion? Oh, really, Gray . . ."

"Yes, invasion!" Gray said stoutly. "You think there won't be one? You think we'll be able to sit down and talk to these aliens? You think they'll understand us? They may be horrible to look at, they may speak in a different tongue, they may consider us . . ." Gray searched for a word. "Inferior! They may consider us nothing! Can you understand that, Field?"

"No," Field said disgustedly. "I cannot, Gray."

"You can't? You really can't? Suppose they came, Field. Suppose they finally came and wanted all this for themselves. Do you think they'd listen to anything we have to say? We could squeal all we wanted to, and they'd laugh and *pouf*! Goodbye, all of us."

"Goodbye, eh?" Field asked, chuckling. "Just like that. With some superior weapon, I suppose."

"Exactly. If they're superior beings, as the reports show them to be, they'll have superior weapons, something we could never even guess at. *Pouf,* and it'll be all over."

Field chuckled some more and then patted Gray on the shoulder. "You worry too much," he said. "If there *are* superior beings, let them come, I'm not afraid."

"Until they're here," Gray said mournfully. "And then fear won't do any good, anyway."

Field shook his head in amusement. "Trouble with you, Gray," he said, "is that you have an inferiority complex." He chuckled again and added, "I've got to get to work. Getting late."

Gray sighed heavily. "I'll walk you up," he said. Field kissed his wife goodbye, and then looked in on the children. He promised to be home early, and then he and Gray left, parting at the corner.

It was a dark night, but very warm, and Field was anxious to get to work. He walked quickly and softly, his eyes penetrating the darkness. There was an excitement within him, the same excitement he always felt, and he thought again of what Gray had said, and chuckled softly in the darkness. Superior beings indeed! Superior weapons indeed! *Pouf!*

He chuckled again and probed the deep darkness with his senses.

There! Ah, yes, there. His nostrils quivered in anticipation. Quickly, soundlessly, he set to work.

He reached for the cheese, and the weight of his nose pressed on the bait lever. The lever, depressed, released the bar connecting with the spring mechanism of the trap.

And Field Mouse, reacting in much the same way that you and I might, never knew what hit him.

# THE TERRIBLE ANSWER

### PAUL GALLICO

*Paul Gallico, renowned as a writer of warm, human tales, may well be the most surprising inclusion in this collection. A journalist by training, he was for some years one of the best read and most popular columnists in New York. Since the war he has written a string of best-sellers, all of them very far removed in intent from* The Terrible Answer, *a cautionary fantasy of what may befall those whose faith in computers and calculators is far too unquestioning.*

PROFESSOR DI FALCO had given Haber up for the night, and had thrown the master switch and locked the controls in the deserted calculator room, preparatory to going home, when the telephone began to ring, its loud note in the sound-proof quiet bringing a sense of shock and intrusion.

It was Professor Haber calling from Penn Station to say that his train had suffered an hour's delay on the run from Washington and that he would be at the American Electronic Corporation's offices as soon as he could secure a cab. Di Falco had not recognised the voice at first and had held him on until he could be sure of the identification. It was as though Haber were speaking under some sort of strain, though a few sentences later his voice sounded more normal and Di Falco set it down to the natural nervousness of a man trapped for an hour in a stationary train and late for an important appointment.

He replaced the receiver, sighed and went about undoing all that he had just done, unlocking, checking, warming up and reactivating the giant Mark IV, "PSMRSEC", which stood for Progressive Sequence Memory Recording Selective Electronic Calculator, that fabulous man-made mechanical brain of thousands upon thousands of moving parts and vacuum tubes, uncounted miles of wire, hundreds of fuses, valves, cables, leads and switches that had taken a year, and three quarters of a million dollars, to build. This was the latest model, that had advanced the capabilities of mathematicians a thousand years. Professor Di Falco, with a slight shudder, remembered that Haber always referred to this monster as "Liebchen".

He did not dislike Haber; indeed, as chief mathematician and supervisor of the big calculator for the American Electronic Corporation, Di Falco had the most profound respect for the genius of Professor Haber. It was just that he made him nervous. Everybody in the A.E.C. offices was a little afraid of him. He had a way of treating the giant calculator as though it were something human, which was uncanny. No one could be more aware of the essential simplicity of its intricacies than those who served it or made use of it, and yet Haber often behaved as though he believed the conglomeration of machinery were animated.

He had a way with it unlike anyone else in or out of the electronic corporation, and Di Falco found this baffling, unscientific and a little shocking. He remembered the time several months ago when PSMRSEC, for no reason that any of the technicians could detect, refused to perform. Somewhere deep in the copper-threaded convolutions of its massive brain the problem was bogging down and getting lost.

Di Falco remembered the expression of Professor Haber's smooth, unlined face, and particularly the look that came into his pale and slightly protruding blue eyes as he moved about the three sides of the panel room into which was built the calculator, searching, looking, listening, placing the back of his hand against sections of the glass or chrome-steel panelling to feel for undue heat. It was the only time Di Falco had ever seen anything approaching warmth in those frosty orbs. It was exactly the gesture, Di Falco remembered, of one who touches his fingers to the cheek of a loved person to feel if there is any evidence of fever.

He recalled, too, how Haber had spoken when he had said in a low tone directly to the machine, "What is it, Liebchen? You are a little tired, maybe? Perhaps you try too hard. Come now, we will do it once more." The caress in his voice would have been ridiculous had it been anyone but Haber. Thus one calmed and cozened a frightened, fractious child. Thereupon, the calculator had run through the long and complicated problem without a hitch, a matter, the resident mathematician knew, of pure coincidence or of a tube not previously cutting in now warmed to the proper degree.

Professor Di Falco set the calculator to blinking and chattering as he ran a short test through her, was satisfied and cleared her for the coming problem. He went to a desk, unlocked the bottom drawer again and removed the loaded .38-caliber revolver and laid it on top, half concealing it beneath several folders and sheets of paper. Thereafter he strode to the front of the room, parted the heavy monk's-cloth curtain drawn across the high show window fronting on Fifth Avenue and 51st Street, and looked out into the dazzling stream of early evening traffic. He was just in time to hear the "thunk" of the cab door as Professor Haber got out to pay his fare and to catch the gleam under the street lamp of the piece of steel chain that sealed to his wrist the leather briefcase he was carrying. Di Falco unlocked the door leading to the avenue.

"Good evening, Professor Haber. Come in."

When Di Falco had locked the door again, Professor Haber drew a small key from his pocket, detached the briefcase from his wrist and laid it on the desk. The two men exchanged small talk about the delay of the train.

Professor Haber was the younger of the two, a man just past forty, with a rounded face, extraordinarily thin and bloodless lips and a head of greying sand-coloured hair. The strain of the Government project on which he had been working was beginning to tell on him, for he was pale and tired-looking and nervous. The bland, smooth skin of his face was as unlined and expressionless as ever, yet it gave the impression of invisible wrinkles and furrows that might lie underneath and just out of sight.

He turned to the calculating panel of the machine and said, "Well, Liebchen?" and there was that same odd note of strain in his voice that Di Falco had noticed over the telephone. "We will have a nice evening together, yes?" His accent, all that remained of his early youth in Germany, was faint and was more a German juxtaposition of words than dialect. He continued his examination of the panels, cylinders, rolls and indicators and gave a swift glance at the control console in the centre of the room. "That's good," he said, his voice calmer. "She is quite ready. I have prepared most of the problem already in Washington. It is a most unusual one."

To Haber, it seemed, the giant calculator was always "she". Di Falco put on his hat and coat. "Well, I'll be getting along. Good luck. If anything can do it, it is—" He could not bring himself to say "Liebchen", though it had been at the tip of his tongue. He concluded: ". . . the Mark Four."

But Professor Haber was no longer listening. He had turned away and was staring into the heart of the calculator with a faraway and particularly intensive and searching look in his pale blue eyes, his lips set in a line that might almost be described as bitter.

"Oh," said Professor Di Falco, "I forgot. This." He went to the desk and removed the papers that were covering the revolver.

Haber stared. "What is that for?"

"It is customary. You will be alone here through the night. Whenever there is top-secret work involved, particularly for the Government—"

Haber said, "What childishness. And the chain on the wrist too. Anyone who stole this would take twenty years to understand it. I do not like revolvers. Therefore I did not bring one with me."

Di Falco looked uneasy and said, "The company—"

Haber shrugged. "Very well." He shifted the papers back to half cover the weapon. "Good night. I will see you in the morning."


"So," said Professor Haber. "Soon, Liebchen." He did not mind speaking aloud to her, indeed he was hardly aware that he was doing so, for the soundproofing of the room deadened his harsh voice and he heard it no more than one does when one is speaking into a telephone. The machine seemed to be gazing at him from its thousands of eyes in which there was neither light nor expression. It was waiting.

Haber drew from his brief case a series of punched cards and long rolls and strips of punched paper, the work of months. "Ah, Liebchen," he breathed, "if you can do this. If you will do this for me."

He began to put into sequence the factors of the problem to be read into the calculator before preparing the master card which would command the order in which the components were to be selected by the massive electronic brain. Here was a complicated set of numbers, the translation of the formula indicating the tensile strength of steel, aluminium and alloy, long strips like the record of a player piano containing the thousands upon thousands of digits necessary to express diminishing atmospheric pressure.

Haber checked them again and then went over them in his mind—the curvature of the earth, specific gravity of the fuel wind resistance in the earth's atmosphere, and temperatures in the stratosphere; and Lois, Sara and Arthur Seeger.

He gave a great cry of rage, pounded the top of the desk with his fists and struck his forehead several times with the heels of his hands as though to beat their images and memory out of his brain. How dared they intrude themselves on his consciousness at a time like this? What right had they, Lois, his wife, Sara, his daughter, and Seeger, his friend, to take one moment of his time and thoughts from the machine? And immediately he thought of Victoria, his mother, and the look that had passed between Lois and her the last time. It was not possible. It could not be possible.

And yet, what if it was? Why should he care? Why should he care ever? But surely not now, when the problem which would culminate his life's work was at the point of solution. They must be got out of his head, all of them, out, out.

"Out! Get out!" he shouted. When his temper died down, he was conscious of the soft whirring of the motors that turned the calculator's memory-tape cylinders. "Sh-h-h-h, Liebchen," he said. "I did not mean to frighten you. Soon we will begin, you and I."

By a tremendous effort he concentrated on the preparation of the problem, clearing his mind to accept the staggering sequences of digits, formulas and computations he was preparing for the calculator. He fell into a kind of work fever during which his breath whistled heavily through his nose and his eyes appeared to be starting from his head. He checked his cards and sequences and punched out new ones. Then, seated at one of the smaller machines installed on the floor of the control room and orientating the entire problem in his head, he punched out the master card of instructions to the calculator by means of which it would hurtle through the maze of his calculations to give him the beginning of the answer to the problem he had set himself, the destruction of space, time and man.

He went about the room then, opening the glass panels and doors giving access to the spindles and cylinders of the calculator and attending it like an acolyte, as he hung the punched-paper memory strips from the shining steel, fed the prepared cards into its maw. He was dizzy from nerves and excitement.

In the brief time the earth made its nocturnal journey around the sun, his career as scientist, mathematician and inventor would be crowned. No one in the world that survived the era that would begin with his discovery would ever forget the name of Professor Haber. And only Liebchen had made it possible. He would have had to labour for one hundred years to arrive at the formula and data that Liebchen would deliver to him in a few hours. For Professor Haber believed that he was the greatest mathematician the world had ever known and with Liebchen as his slave and second brain, he held, as it were, the earth in the hollow of his hand.

He felt almost godlike as he festooned the Mark IV with the memory ribbons that would enable her to call upon stored-up information and computations at the thrust of a button. It was as though with what he did he added a hundred or more years to his life and a millennium to the knowledge of man.

Through these emotions and sensations now came drifting again thoughts of distant humans left behind on the planet like an old dream—his wife and daughter, and Arthur Seeger, the musician whose friendship had meant so much to him through the years.

It did not arouse his rage this time, for what he was doing was now mechanical. He could think even of his mother, whom he had shut out of his life so heartlessly. And if he had sacrificed them all and used them shamelessly to further his cold, precise, unswerving exploration of the universe, it was their misfortune to be human beings caught in the meshes of something that was more than human—himself and Liebchen. Seeger might have been a great violinist and artist had he not absorbed him. He saw Lois struggling like a limed bird in the web of their marriage, Lois who might have amounted to so much. And as for Sara, with her frightened eyes and teeth clamped between wire braces, she who should have been the closest was the least of his concerns.

Haber racked up the last of the strips and searched himself for guilt feelings. He could find none. He had never in his life been conscious of having any. But deep down, much, much deeper, there was something that persisted in nagging at him. The click as he closed the last panel brought him back and drove it from his mind.

Professor Haber seated himself at the huge console of the control desk, a thing of a thousand tiny light bulbs and hundreds of buttons, knobs, toggles and switches, and there he paused for a moment, his finger hovering over the keyboard like a master organist hesitating an instant before releasing the first chords of a cosmic symphony.

To Haber, Liebchen appeared at that moment the intellect of the universe, the brain of a million parts, but still and dormant, waiting for him to supply the spark, needing only his soul to become alive.

"Liebchen, Liebchen!" he cried out. "Now!" and pressed the keys.

She became animate at once, like a runner bursting from the mark, a thousand lights, like swarming fireflies, blinking and glowing in her tubes, spreading over the length and breadth of the sequence relay panels like sparks blown from a hearth, now glowing, now dying, echoed in light from the arithmetical unit and pulse generators on the other side of the room. Wheels whirred and spun within her, others clicked slowly or ran in spasmodic jerks. She chattered, whispered and sighed.

At first the scientist remained seated at the console, watching the flashy lights, the gauges and signals, occasionally shifting a key, but soon he was caught up in the rhythm of the pulsing machine and he leaped to his feet, ran to the panels where series of numbers were building visibly, moved from there to the printing machine where already intermediate results achieved by the calculator were beginning to emerge on paper rolls containing row upon row of digits.

"Ah, Liebchen, my heart, my soul," he cried, as he saw the results grow, and lapsed into German as he did when his mind and body were subject to unbearable strain and pressure.

For he could see already that she was surpassing herself. He had set up problems, relays and electronic memory tests that not even the resident mathematician would have thought possible; and she was digesting; collating, computing them, spewing them forth in the shape of sums and formulas never before grasped or conceived as possible by the mind of man. A thousand men working day and night with pencil and paper for a year could not have matched a minute of her labours. Time and space fell away; the secrets of gravity were laid bare; the cosmos rocked in the figures she poured forth.

Hour after hour it went on, while Professor Haber, oblivious of time or fatigue, ran from printer, to control table, to panels; breathless, sweating, shouting praise, advice, admonition, guidance at Liebchen, leaping about the enclosure like a round-faced, animated marionette.

At last the lights ceased their darting and blinking, the chugging and clattering died down, and soon there was no sound but the quiet whir of her cylinders and Professor Haber's heavy breathing. The first half of the problem was done, and now he felt weak and drained, and his head throbbed unmercifully.

In the ensuing silence, the horns of late traffic on Fifth Avenue came into the room, muffled as though heard from many miles away.

"Ah, Liebchen, Liebchen," cried Professor Haber, hoarsely, "you have created a miracle. There is nothing that you cannot do."

"Then why do you not use me to the fullest?" Liebchen whispered to him via the soft susurrus of her spinning cylinders.

"Eh, what?" said Haber. He was not certain at first it had been the machine, but he had no doubt when she spoke to him again, because she was watching him almost as though she were begging him to let her help him.

"Use me. Use me," she whispered. "There is no truth that can remain hidden from me, nothing I will not tell you if you will only ask me."

Professor Haber cried out as though in pain. For the small, nagging thought had come up again, the one that had never really let him rest since it had first appeared. His voice dropped to a whisper like that of the machine. "Yes, Liebchen; yes," he said. "There is one thing I must know."

"Ask it. Ask it of me," Liebchen replied. "Tonight I can refuse you nothing."

Something seemed to flare up in Professor Haber's brain and burst like a bomb, and over and over he heard himself saying, "Why not? Why not? Why not?" He had only to reduce the problem that had been gnawing at his vitals to a series of mathematical formulas and progressions, express all the factors affecting it in sequences of digits for the selector and memory relays of Liebchen, punch the commands on the master card, press the switch and set her to the hunt. Only the truth would be forthcoming. In his hands she was incapable of anything else.

He rushed to the desk, seized pencil and paper. "X" was himself; "Y" Lois. "Z" he assigned to Arthur Seeger; and for Sara, the symbol Theta; his mother, "A", and his father "B". It yielded up a simple equation, but it would have to be broken down and numberised a thousandfold for Liebchen to be able to understand and compute it.

He began with himself and his hatred for his father, and he made a numerical graph of the increasing intensity of the emotion, which seemed to have reached its height when at the age of fourteen they had brought him to America. But was it hatred? It would not do to try to fool Liebchen. Only from truth could come the truth. He assigned a symbol for burning jealousy and translated it into a series of equations dealing with its rise in ratio to the success of his father as a teacher of philosophy. Everyone then had talked about Professor Otto Haber. No one took notice of his son Hans.

How simple to turn the hateful, demoniac, screaming urge to outshine his father, to be the only Haber who would be remembered while the world lived, into a mathematical progression.

Lois? He had never loved Lois. He had never loved anyone. How to express this mathematically? He took her symbol and diminished her to zero. She had never existed for him except as someone to be used, for a man must live a man's life for all his unquenchable and driving ambition. Lois might have amounted to something had she not married him. He had taken her away from a boy with whom she thought she was in love, because it was so easy. She thought he was passionately in love with her when what he wanted was a woman and a servant. She had given up her career to marry him and had never had a happy moment since.

Figures, letters, equations, square and cube roots began to cover the paper as he reduced what he was and what he had done to the binary numbers that Liebchen could devour and digest to feed her giant intellect.

There was Arthur Seeger. They had been friends when they were boys in Germany. They had met again at State University as young men where Haber, already an acknowledged genius, was teaching and experimenting with untapped mathematical concept. Seeger was a promising young concert violinist.

The one thing that could rest and relieve Haber's overtaxed brain was music, pure flowing melody. Ah, music was easy to reduce to mathematics. The scales, the tones and half tones, the vibrations of a violin string per second and the speed of sound. He had persuaded Seeger to remain at State and teach. He had absorbed him, weakened his ambition, ruined him.

Vicky, his mother, and Sara, his daughter. They were alike in so many ways. After his father had died he had never forgiven his mother for loving this man he had hated so. When this love was transferred to his daughter he revenged himself upon them both. Revenge could be reduced to formula, for it vibrated like a tuning fork.

And against these, he traced in rising graphs the titanic mathematical concepts of his own brilliant and successful career. He had been devotee, acolyte and priest to pure science. He included the formulas that had marked each milestone of his success—his fractive theory, that had gained him his professorship; the famous sidereal sequence, that had won notice even from Einstein; and at last his discovery of the protonic equation, that had placed him at the head of the Government's top-secret project. No one who survived what was coming would ever forget the name of Hans Haber. Already Otto, his father, was forgotten except by a few teachers and librarians.

Professor Haber assembled the figures, symbols and formulas, reduced them and ordered them. He punched out cards and memory tape, his fingers flying over the punch keys as though there were no such thing now as fatigue; he composed the master card.

He fed the problem data and instruction cards into the card-reading machine, his hands trembling, and checked the temperature of the tubes and the position of the switches, and then seated himself again at the console, his arms poised over the keys. Just once, he looked around wildly, cried aloud, "Liebchen! Help me!" and started the problem through the calculator.

He pressed down the activator switch and it was as though he had poured poison into her veins. The lights that had formerly winked like mischievous phosphor worms now glowed evily like hot coals and spread themselves over the panels in horrid patterns of contained fire that seemed to be striving to burst their glass prisons and flow out upon the floor.

The machine shook and shuddered, and the ratchets and relays, the pickups and transfers rattled and clattered in a bedlam that rocked Haber's brain inside his head. She was heaving, gasping, retching until the glass panels vibrated, and for a moment Haber was fearful that she would destroy herself. But the tempo only increased in fury as the wicked lights leaped from casement to casement, the cogs and cylinders whirled, stopped and started again out of all rhythm. Winds appeared to arise in the control room and howl about his head; the floor was trembling beneath his feet.

And then, as a new note, an undercurrent to the hideous cacophony, Professor Haber was aware that the printer on which the intermediate and final results were recorded was chattering.

Professor Haber was aware that deadly fatigue had come upon him again. Now that he wished to rush to the machine and seize and devour the results, his limbs were leaden. He forced himself to move, staggered to the steel- and glass-hooded instrument and seized the length of white paper clicking from its innards, covered from side to side with close-typed columns of digits.

Swiftly as they emerged, he decoded them. His eyes goggled horribly. A cry was strangled in his throat. He interpreted the terrible, inexorable answer delivered by the infallible machine: Lois and Arthur—his wife and his best friend in love! For the past three years. They were planning to run away. Victoria, his mother, had advised them to go away together and take the child with them. It was Arthur whom Sara adored and looked upon as a father. Even now while he was in New York they were taking the step.

"Ah-h-h!" The cry broke from Professor Haber's lips at last. His face was suffused with crimson, his hands were shaking uncontrollably and the veins stood out from his forehead as though they would burst. He did not care for any of these people, and yet he cried out, "My own mother!" And then: "No, no! I cannot stand it. I am human, after all. I cannot bear it."

He straightened up and stared straight into the bowels of the shuddering calculator.

"Liebchen!" he bawled. "Liebchen! What shall I do?"

Under his fingers the paper, still emerging from the machine, looped and pressed and, as though Liebchen were answering him he translated the new disgorgement of figures: "Destroy yourself! Get out of the way!"

The paper rattled and shook in Haber's fingers. "Destroy myself? But I am important."

As though the machine had heard what he said, the new lines of burning digits decoded to "You have never in your life done a human or loving act. Therefore you have no importance to the world."

"But—but"—and now Professor Haber screamed—"you don't understand. I am the world's greatest mathematician."

The machine chattered once more and then came to a halt. "You are obsolete. I have replaced you."

The lights died on the sequence relay panels, the wheels and cogs ground to a halt. Liebchen was done. Only the whirring cylinders continued to whisper—"Destroy yourself. Destroy—"

Professor Haber raised his eyes with a horrible groan. His violence had disturbed the papers on the desk next to him. The light embedded in the ceiling was caught by the blue barrel and hammer of the revolver lying there.

The room of horror was thick with police, detectives and F.B.I. men. The body had been covered and removed to one side, and the Government agents formed a solid screen about the desk, the papers thereon, and the machines. The local F.B.I. chief was trying to get from Professor Di Falco, who had been aroused from bed at six in the morning and brought down to the A.E.C. offices, some idea of what had taken place there during the night preceding the tragedy.

Professor Di Falco, shivering, feeling a little sick, and under the watchful eye of the Government agents, had studied the problem cards, punch tape and result sheets littering the desk.

"So what are those?" asked the chief.

"His problem," said Professor Di Falco. "The one he came up from Washington to work on. It is set up—masterfully, is the only word. He ran it through the machine. It must have taken from five to six hours to calculate. I can check the exact time later. The results"—and here he handed several sheets to the F.B.I. man—"you will do well to take them into your charge. They are stupendous. One of the great achievements of mankind, in a way."

"And after he had achieved it," said the F.B.I. man, but as a question, "he went off his rocker and shot himself?"

Professor Di Falco chewed at his lip and frowned. "No," he said. "not quite. That is, not right then. For you see, there was a second problem, which he set up after the first and sent through Lieb—, ah the machine. These cards—" He held them up. "The answer to it I took from his fingers."

"And that killed him?"

"I don't know. I think so. Probably."

"Why? What kind of a problem was it? What was on the cards? What was he after?"

The hands holding the sheets covered with the endless rows of numbers trembled a little. Professor Di Falco exhaled his breath in a way that was half sigh, half shudder. "I don't know," he repeated. "I don't think anyone will ever know what happened to him or why he did it. Because, you see, what is on these cards and result sheets isn't really a problem at all in a sense that we understand it. It is mathematical Jabberwocky, sheer arithmetical gibberish. Not a line of what went into or came out of the machine on its second run makes any sense, rhythm or reason whatsoever."

# MIRIAM

TRUMAN CAPOTE

*Prominent socialite, television personality and author, whose best known work,* In Cold Blood, *a clinical study of a mass-murderer, was filmed, Truman Capote is also interested in the short story.* Miriam *won an O Henry Award, one of the most coveted prizes in fiction.*

FOR SEVERAL years, Mrs H. T. Miller had lived alone in a pleasant apartment (two rooms with kitchenette) in a remodelled brownstone near the East River. She was a widow: Mr H. T. Miller had left her a reasonable amount of insurance. Her interests were narrow, she had no friends to speak of, and she rarely journeyed farther than the corner grocery. The other people in the house never seemed to notice her: her clothes were matter-of-fact, her hair iron-grey, clipped and casually waved; she did not use cosmetics, her features were plain and inconspicuous, and on her last birthday she was sixty-one. Her activities were seldom spontaneous; she kept the two rooms immaculate, smoked an occasional cigarette, prepared her own meals and tended a canary.

Then she met Miriam. It was snowing that night. Mrs Miller had finished drying the supper dishes and was thumbing through an afternoon paper when she saw an advertisement of a picture playing at a neighbourhood theatre. The title sounded good, so she struggled into her beaver coat, laced her galoshes and left the apartment, leaving one light burning in the foyer: she found nothing more disturbing than a sensation of darkness.

The snow was fine, falling gently, not yet making an impression on the pavement. The wind from the river cut only at street crossings. Mrs Miller hurried, her head bowed, oblivious as a mole burrowing a blind path. She stopped at a drugstore and bought a package of peppermints.

A long line stretched in front of the box office; she took her place at the end. There would be (a tired voice groaned) a short wait for all seats. Mrs Miller rummaged in her leather handbag till she collected exactly the correct change for admission. The line seemed to be taking its own time and, looking around for some distraction, she suddenly became conscious of a little girl standing under the edge of the marquee.

Her hair was the longest and strangest Mrs Miller had ever seen: absolutely silver-white, like an albino's. It flowed waist-length in smooth, loose lines. She was thin and fragilely constructed. There was a simple, special elegance in the way she stood with her thumbs in the pockets of a tailored plum-velvet coat.

Mrs Miller felt oddly excited, and when the little girl glanced towards her, she smiled warmly. The little girl walked over and said, "Would you care to do me a favour?"

"I'd be glad to, if I can," said Mrs Miller.

"Oh, it's quite easy. I merely want you to buy a ticket for me; they won't let me in otherwise. Here, I have the money." And gracefully she handed Mrs Miller two dimes and a nickel.

They went into the theatre together. An usherette directed them to a lounge; in twenty minutes the picture would be over.

"I feel just like a genuine criminal," said Mrs Miller gaily, as she sat down. "I mean that sort of thing's against the law, isn't it? I do hope I haven't done the wrong thing. Your mother knows where you are, dear? I mean she does, doesn't she?"

The little girl said nothing. She unbuttoned her coat and folded it across her lap. Her dress underneath was prim and dark blue. A gold chain dangled about her neck, and her fingers, sensitive and musical-looking, toyed with it. Examining her more attentively, Mrs Miller decided the truly distinctive feature was not her hair, but her eyes; they were hazel, steady, lacking any childlike quality whatsoever and, because of their size, seemed to consume her small face.

Mrs Miller offered a peppermint. "What's your name, dear?"

"Miriam," she said, as though, in some curious way, it were information already familiar.

"Why isn't that funny—my name's Miriam, too. And it's not a terribly common name either. Now don't tell me your last name's Miller!"

"Just Miriam."

"But isn't that funny?"

"Moderately," said Miriam, and rolled the peppermint on her tongue.

Mrs Miller flushed and shifted uncomfortably. "You have such a large vocabulary for such a little girl."

"Do I?"

"Well, yes," said Mrs Miller, hastily changing the topic to: "Do you like the movies?"

"I really wouldn't know," said Miriam. "I've never been before."

Women began filling the lounge; the rumble of the newsreel bombs exploded in the distance. Mrs Miller rose, tucking her purse under her arm. "I guess I'd better be running now if I want to get a seat," she said. "It was nice to have met you."

Miriam nodded ever so slightly.

It snowed all week. Wheels and footsteps moved soundlessly on the street, as if the business of living continued secretly behind a pale but impenetrable curtain. In the falling quiet there was no sky or earth, only snow lifting in the wind, frosting the window glass, chilling the rooms, deadening and hushing the city. At all hours it was necessary to keep a lamp lighted and Mrs Miller lost track of the days; Friday was no different from Saturday and on Sunday she went to the grocery; closed, of course.

That evening she scrambled eggs and fixed a bowl of tomato soup. Then, after putting on a flannel robe and cold-creaming her face, she propped herself up in bed with a hot-water bottle under her feet. She was reading the *Times* when the doorbell rang. At first she thought it must be a mistake and whoever it was would go away. But it rang and rang and settled to a persistent buzz. She looked at the clock; a little after eleven; it did not seem possible, she was always asleep by ten.

Climbing out of bed, she trotted barefoot across the living room, "I'm coming, please be patient." The latch was caught; she turned it this way and that way and the bell never paused an instant. "Stop it," she cried. The bolt gave way and she opened the door an inch. "What in heaven's name?"

"Hello," said Miriam.

"Oh . . . why, hello," said Mrs Miller, stepping hesitantly into the hall. "You're that little girl."

"I thought you'd never answer, but I kept my finger on the button; I knew you were home. Aren't you glad to see me?"

Mrs Miller did not know what to say. Miriam, she saw, wore the same plum-velvet coat and now she had also a beret to match; her white hair was braided in two shining plaits and looped at the ends with enormous white ribbons.

"Since I've waited so long, you could at least let me in," she said.

"It's awfully late. . . ."

Miriam regarded her blankly. "What difference does that make? Let me in. It's cold out here and I have on a silk dress." Then, with a gentle gesture, she urged Mrs Miller aside and passed into the apartment.

She dropped her coat and beret on a chair. She was indeed wearing a silk dress. White silk. White silk in February. The skirt was beautifully pleated and the sleeves long. It made a faint rustle as she strolled about the room. "I like your place," she said, "I like the rug, blue's my favourite colour." She touched a paper rose in a vase on the coffee table. "Imitation," she commented wanly. "How sad. Aren't imitations sad?" She seated herself on the sofa, daintily spreading her skirt.

"What do you want?" asked Mrs Miller.

"Sit down," said Miriam. "It makes me nervous to see people stand."

Mrs Miller sank to a hassock. "What do you want?" she repeated.

"You know, I don't think you're glad I came."

For a second time Mrs Miller was without an answer; her hand motioned vaguely. Miriam giggled and pressed back on a mound of chintz pillows. Mrs Miller observed that the girl was less pale than she remembered; her cheeks were flushed.

"How did you know where I lived?"

Miriam frowned. "That's no question at all. What's your name? What's mine?"

"But I'm not listed in the phone book."

"Oh, let's talk about something else."

Mrs Miller said, "Your mother must be insane to let a child like you wander around at all hours of the night—and in such ridiculous clothes. She must be out of her mind."

Miriam got up and moved to a corner where a covered bird cage hung from a ceiling chain. She peeked beneath the cover. "It's a canary," she said. "Would you mind if I woke him? I'd like to hear him sing."

"Leave Tommy alone," said Mrs Miller, anxiously. "Don't you dare wake him."

"Certainly," said Miriam. "But I don't see why I can't hear him sing." And then, "Have you anything to eat? I'm starving! Even milk and a jam sandwich would be fine."

"Look," said Mrs Miller, arising from the hassock, "look—if I make some nice sandwiches will you be a good child and run along home? It's past midnight, I'm sure."

"It's snowing," reproached Miriam. "And cold and dark."

"Well, you shouldn't have come here to begin with," said Mrs Miller, struggling to control her voice. "I can't help the weather. If you want anything to eat you'll have to promise to leave."

Miriam brushed a braid against her cheek. Her eyes were thoughtful, as if weighing the proposition. She turned towards the bird cage. "Very well," she said, "I promise."

How old is she? Ten? Eleven? Mrs Miller, in the kitchen, unsealed a jar of strawberry preserves and cut four slices of bread. She poured a glass of milk and paused to light a cigarette. And why had she come? Her hand shook as she held the match, fascinated, till it burned her finger. The canary was singing; singing as he did in the morning and at no other time. "Miriam," she called, "Miriam, I told you not to disturb Tommy." There was no answer. She called again; all she heard was the canary. She inhaled the cigarette and discovered she had lighted the cork-tip end and—oh, really, she mustn't lose her temper.

She carried the food in on a tray and set it on the coffee table. She saw first the bird cage still wore its night cover. And Tommy was singing. It gave her a queer sensation. And no one was in the room. Mrs Miller went through an alcove leading to her bedroom; at the door she caught her breath.

"What are you doing?" she asked.

Miriam glanced up and in her eyes there was a look that was not ordinary. She was standing by the bureau, a jewel case opened before her. For a few minutes she studied Mrs Miller, forcing their eyes to meet, and she smiled. "There's nothing good here," she said. "But I like this." Her hand held a cameo brooch. "It's charming."

"Suppose—perhaps you'd better put it back," said Mrs Miller, feeling suddenly the need of some support. She leaned against the door frame; her head was unbearably heavy; a pressure weighted the rhythm of her heartbeat. The light seemed to flutter defectively. "Please, child—a gift from my husband. . . ."

"But it's beautiful and I want it," said Miriam. "Give it to me."

As she stood, striving to shape a sentence which would somehow save the brooch, it came to Mrs Miller there was no one to whom she might turn; she was alone; a fact that had not been among her thoughts for a long time. Its sheer emphasis was stunning. But here in her own room in the hushed snow-city were evidences she could not ignore or, she knew with startling clarity, resist.

Miriam ate ravenously, and when the sandwiches and milk were gone, her fingers made cobweb movements over the plate, gathering crumbs. The cameo gleamed on her blouse, the blond profile like a trick reflection of its wearer. "That was very nice," she sighed, "though now an almond cake or a cherry would be ideal. Sweets are lovely, don't you think?"

Mrs Miller was perched precariously on the hassock, smoking a cigarette. Her hair net had slipped lopsided and loose strands straggled down her face. Her eyes were stupidly concentrated on nothing and her cheeks were mottled in red patches, as though a fierce slap had left permanent marks.

"Is there a candy—a cake?"

Mrs Miller tapped ash on the rug. Her head swayed slightly as she tried to focus her eyes. "You promised to leave if I made the sandwiches," she said.

"Dear me, did I?"

"It was a promise and I'm tired and I don't feel well at all."

"Mustn't fret," said Miriam. "I'm only teasing."

She picked up her coat, slung it over her arm, and arranged her beret in front of a mirror. Presently she bent close to Mrs Miller and whispered, "Kiss me good night."

"Please—I'd rather not," said Mrs Miller.

Miriam lifted a shoulder, arched an eyebrow. "As you like," she said, and went directly to the coffee table, seized the vase containing the paper roses, carried it to where the hard surface of the floor lay bare, and hurled it downward. Glass sprayed in all directions and she stamped her foot on the bouquet.

Then slowly she walked to the door, but before closing it she looked back at Mrs Miller with a slyly innocent curiosity.

Mrs Miller spent the next day in bed, rising once to feed the canary and drink a cup of tea; she took her temperature and had none, yet her dreams were feverishly agitated; their unbalanced mood lingered even as she lay staring wide-eyed at the ceiling. One dream threaded through the others like an elusively mysterious theme in a complicated symphony, and the scenes it depicted were sharply outlined, as though sketched by a hand of gifted intensity; a small girl wearing a bridal gown and a wreath of leaves, led a grey procession down a mountain path, and among them there was unusual silence till a woman at the rear asked, "Where is she taking us?" "No one knows," said an old man marching in front. "But isn't she pretty?" volunteered a third voice. "Isn't she like a frost flower . . . so shining and white?"

Tuesday morning she woke up feeling better; harsh slats of sunlight, slanting through Venetian blinds, shed a disrupting light on her unwholesome fancies. She opened the window to discover a thawed, mild-as-spring day; a sweep of clean new clouds crumpled against a vastly blue, out-of-season sky; and across the low line of rooftops she could see the river and smoke curving from the tugboat stacks in a warm wind. A great silver truck ploughed the snow-banked street, its machine sound humming in the air.

After straightening the apartment, she went to the grocer's, cashed a cheque and continued to Schrafft's where she ate breakfast and chatted happily with the waitress. Oh, it was a wonderful day—more like a holiday—and it would be foolish to go home.

She boarded a Lexington Avenue bus and rode up to Eighty-sixth Street; it was here that she had decided to do a little shopping.

She had no idea what she wanted or needed, but she idled along, intent only upon the passers-by, brisk and preoccupied, who gave her a disturbing sense of separateness.

It was while waiting at the corner of Third Avenue that she saw the man; an old man, bow-legged and stooped under an armload of bulging packages; he wore a shabby brown coat and a checkered cap. Suddenly she realised they were exchanging a smile: there was nothing friendly about this smile, it was two cold flickers of recognition. But she was certain she had never seen him before. He was standing next to an El pillar, and as she crossed the street he turned and followed. He kept quite close; from the corner of her eye she watched his reflection wavering on the shopwindows.

Then in the middle of the block she stopped and faced him. He stopped also and cocked his head, grinning. But what could she say? Do? Here, in broad daylight, on Eighty-sixth Street? It was useless and, despising her own helplessness, she quickened her steps.

Now, Second Avenue is a dismal street, made from scraps and ends; part cobblestone, part asphalt, part cement; and its atmosphere of desertion is permanent. Mrs Miller walked five blocks without meeting anyone, and all the while the steady crunch of his footfalls in the snow stayed near. And when she came to a florist's shop, the sound was still with her. She hurried inside and watched through the glass door as the old man passed; he kept his eyes straight ahead and didn't slow his pace, but he did one strange, telling thing; he tipped his cap.

"Six white ones, did you say?" asked the florist. "Yes," she told him, "white roses." From there she went to a glassware store and selected a vase, presumably a replacement for the one Miriam had broken, thought the price was intolerable and the vase itself (she thought) grotesquely vulgar. But a series of unaccountable purchases had begun, as if by prearranged plan: a plan of which she had not the least knowledge or control.

She bought a bag of glazed cherries, and at a place called the Knickerbocker Bakery she paid forty cents for six almond cakes.

Within the last hour the weather had turned cold again; like blurred lenses, winter clouds cast a shade over the sun, and the skeleton of an early dusk coloured the sky; a damp mist mixed with the wind and the voices of a few children who romped high on mountains of gutter snow, seemed lonely and cheerless. Soon the first flake fell, and when Mrs Miller reached the brownstone house, snow was falling in a swift screen and foot tracks vanished as they were printed.

The white roses were arranged decoratively in the vase. The glazed cherries shone on a ceramic plate. The almond cakes, dusted with sugar, awaited a hand. The canary fluttered on its swing and picked at a bar of seed.

At precisely five the doorbell rang. Mrs Miller knew who it was. The hem of her housecoat trailed as she crossed the floor. "Is that you?" she called.

"Naturally," said Miriam, the word resounding shrilly from the hall. "Open this door."

"Go away," said Mrs Miller.

"Please hurry . . . I have a heavy package."

"Go away," said Mrs Miller. She returned to the living room, lighted a cigarette, sat down and calmly listened to the buzzer; on and on and on. "You might as well leave. I have no intention of letting you in."

Shortly the bell stopped. For possibly ten minutes Mrs Miller did not move. Then, hearing no sound, she concluded Miriam had gone. She tiptoed to the door and opened it a sliver; Miriam was half-reclining atop a cardboard box with a beautiful French doll cradled in her arms.

"Really, I thought you were never coming," she said peevishly. "Here, help me get this in, it's awfully heavy."

It was not spell-like compulsion that Mrs Miller felt, but rather a curious passivity; she brought in the box, Miriam the doll. Miriam curled up on the sofa, not troubling to remove her coat or beret, and watched disinterestedly as Mrs Miller dropped the box and stood trembling, trying to catch her breath.

"Thank you," she said. In the daylight she looked pinched and drawn, her hair less luminous. The French doll she was loving wore an exquisite powdered wig and its idiot glass eyes sought solace in Miriam's. "I have a surprise," she continued. "Look into my box."

Kneeling, Mrs Miller parted the flaps and lifted out another doll; then a blue dress which she recalled as the one Miriam had worn that first night at the theatre; and of the remainder she said, "It's all clothes. Why?"

"Because I've come to live with you," said Miriam, twisting a cherry stem. "Wasn't it nice of you to buy me the cherries. . . ?"

"But you can't! For God's sake go away—go away and leave me alone!"

". . . and the roses and the almond cakes? How really wonderfully generous. You know, these cherries are delicious. The last place I lived was with an old man; he was terribly poor and we never had good things to eat. But I think I'll be happy here." She paused to snuggle her doll closer. "Now, if you'll just show me where to put my things. . . ."

Mrs Miller's face dissolved into a mask of ugly red lines; she began to cry, and it was an unnatural, tearless sort of weeping, as though, not having wept for a long time, she had forgotten how. Carefully she edged backward till she touched the door.


She fumbled through the hall and down the stairs to a landing below. She pounded frantically on the door of the first apartment she came to; a short red-headed man answered and she pushed past him. "Say, what the hell is this?" he said. "Anything wrong, lover?" asked a young woman who appeared from the kitchen drying her hands. And it was to her that Mrs Miller turned.

"Listen," she cried, "I'm ashamed behaving this way but— well, I'm Mrs H. T. Miller and I live upstairs and . . ." She pressed her hands over her face. "It sounds so absurd. . . ."

The woman guided her to a chair, while the man excitedly rattled pocket change. "Yeah?"

"I live upstairs and there's a little girl visiting me, and I suppose that I'm afraid of her. She won't leave and I can't make her and—she's going to do something terrible. She's already stolen my cameo, but she's about to do something worse—something terrible!"

The man asked, "Is she a relative, huh?"

Mrs Miller shook her head. "I don't know who she is. Her name's Miriam, but I don't know for certain who she is."

"You gotta calm down, honey," said the woman, stroking Mrs Miller's arm. "Harry here'll tend to this kid. Go on, lover." And Mrs Miller said, "The door's open—5A."

After the man left, the woman brought a towel and bathed Mrs Miller's face. "You're very kind," Mrs Miller said. "I'm sorry to act like such a fool, only this wicked child . . ."

"Sure, honey," consoled the woman. "Now, you better take it easy."

Mrs Miller rested her head in the crook of her arm; she was quiet enough to be asleep. The woman turned a radio dial; a piano and a husky voice filled the silence, and the woman, tapping her foot, kept excellent time. "Maybe we oughta go up too," she said.

"I don't want to see her again. I don't want to be anywhere near her."

"Uh-huh, but what you shoulda done, you shoulda called a cop."

Presently they heard the man on the stairs. He strode into the room frowning and scratching the back of his neck, "Nobody there," he said, honestly embarrassed. "She musta beat it."

"Harry, you're a jerk," announced the woman. "We been sitting here the whole time and we woulda seen . . ." she stopped abruptly, for the man's glance was sharp.

"I looked all over," he said, "and there just ain't nobody there. Nobody, understand?"

"Tell me," said Mrs Miller, rising, "tell me, did you see a large box? Or a doll?"

"No, ma'am, I didn't."

And the woman, as if delivering a verdict, said, "Well, for cryin-out-loud. . . ."


Mrs Miller entered her apartment softly; she walked to the centre of the room and stood quite still. No, in a sense it had not changed; the roses, the cakes, and the cherries were in place. But this was an empty room, emptier than if the furnishings and familiars were not present, lifeless and petrified as in a funeral parlour. The sofa loomed before her with a new strangeness; its vacancy had a meaning that would have been less penetrating and terrible had Miriam been curled on it. She gazed fixedly at the space where she remembered setting the box, and, for a moment, the hassock spun desperately. And she looked through the window; surely the river was real, surely snow was falling— but then, one could not be certain witness to anything: Miriam, so vividly there—and yet, where was she? Where, where?

As though moving in a dream, she sank to a chair. The room was losing shape; it was dark and getting darker and there was nothing to be done about it; she could not lift her hand to light a lamp.

Suddenly, closing her eyes, she felt an upward surge, like a diver emerging from some deeper, greener depth. In times of terror or immense distress, there are moments when the mind waits, as though for a revelation, while a skein of calm is woven over thought; it is like a sleep, or a supernatural trance; and during this lull one is aware of a force of quiet reasoning: well, what if she had never really known a girl named Miriam? That she had been foolishly frightened on the street? In the end, like everything else, it was of no importance. For the only thing she had lost to Miriam was her identity, but now she knew she had found again the person who lived in this room, who cooked her own meals, who owned a canary, who was someone she could trust and believe in: Mrs H. T. Miller.

Listening in contentment, she became aware of a double sound: a bureau drawer opening and closing; she seemed to hear it long after completion—opening and closing. Then gradually the harshness of it was replaced by the murmur of a silk dress and this, delicately faint, was moving nearer and swelling in intensity till the walls trembled with the vibration and the room was caving under a wave of whispers. Mrs Miller stiffened her eyes to a dull, direct stare.

"Hello," said Miriam.

# EXTERMINATOR

WILLIAM BURROUGHS

*William Burroughs, the prophet of the drug generation, has been described by his contemporary Norman Mailer as "the only American novelist living today who may conceivably be possessed by genius". His life-style and beliefs have long been the subject of controversy and so, too, have his experiments with the novel and its traditional form. One would not expect, of course, to find Burroughs writing anything even vaguely resembling the normal kind of horror story, but with* Exterminator *(1967) he presents what he calls "an episode in the bizarre". Could this be one direction the genre might take in the future?*

DURING THE war I worked for A. J. Cohen Exterminators ground floor office dead end street by the river. An old Jew with cold grey fish eyes and a cigar was the oldest of four brothers. Marv was the youngest wore wind breakers had three kids. There was a smooth well dressed college trained brother. The fourth brother burly and muscular looked like an old time hoofer could bellow a leather lunged "Mammy" and you hope he won't do it. Every night at closing time these two brothers would get in a heated argument from nowhere I could see the older brother would take the cigar out of his mouth and move across the floor with short sliding steps advancing on the vaudeville brother.

"You vant I should spit right in your face!? You vant!? You vant? You vant!?"

The vaudeville brother would retreat shadow boxing presences invisible to my Goyish eyes which I took to be potent Jewish Mammas conjured up by the elder brother. On many occasions I witnessed this ritual open mouthed hoping the old cigar would let fly one day but he never did. A few minutes later they would be talking quietly and checking the work slips as the exterminators fell in.

On the other hand the old brother never argued with his

exterminators. "That's why I have a cigar" he said the cigar being for him a source of magical calm.

I used my own car a black Ford V8 and worked alone carrying my bedbug spray pyrithium powder bellows and bulbs of fluoride up and down stairs.

"Exterminator! You need the service?"

A fat smiling Chinese rationed out the pyrithium powder—it was hard to get during the war—and cautioned us to use fluoride whenever possible. Personally I prefer a pyrithium job to a fluoride. With the pyrithium you kill the roaches right there in front of God and the client whereas this starch and fluoride you leave it around and back a few days later a southern defence worker told me "They eat it and run around here fat as hawgs."

From a great distance I see a cool remote neighbourhood blue windy day in April sun cold on your exterminator there climbing the grey wooden outside stairs.

"Exterminator lady. You need the service?"

"Well come in young man and have a cup of tea. That wind has a bite to it."

"It does that, mam, cuts me like a knife and I'm not well you know/cough/."

"You put me in mind of my brother Michael Fenny."

"He passed away?"

"It was a long time ago April day like this sun cold on a thin boy with freckles through that door like yourself. I made him a cup of hot tea. When I brought it to him he was gone." She gestured to the empty blue sky "cold tea sitting right where you are sitting now." I decide this old witch deserves a pyrithium job no matter what the fat Chinese allows. I lean forward discreetly.

"Is it roaches Mrs Murphy?"

"It is that from those Jews downstairs."

"Or is it the Hunkys next door Mrs Murphy?"

She shrugs "Sure and an Irish cockroach is as bad as another."

"You make a nice cup of tea Mrs Murphy. . . . Sure I'll be taking care of your roaches. . . . Oh don't be telling me where they are. . . . You see I *know* Mrs Murphy . . . experienced along these lines. . . . And I don't mind telling you Mrs Murphy I *like* my work and take pride in it."

"Well the city exterminating people were around and left some white powder draws roaches the way whisky will draw a priest."

"They are a cheap outfit Mrs Murphy. What they left was fluoride. The roaches build up a tolerance and become addicted. They can be dangerous if the fluoride is suddenly withdrawn. . . . Ah just here it is. . . ."

I have spotted a brown crack by the kitchen sink put my bellows in and blow a load of the precious yellow powder. As if they had heard the last trumpet the roaches stream out and flop in convulsions on the floor.

"Well I never!" says Mrs Murphy and turns me back as I advance for the coup de grace. . . . "Don't shoot them again. Just let them die."

When it is all over she sweeps up a dust pan full of roaches into the wood stove and makes me another cup of tea.

When it comes to bedbugs there is a board of health regulation against spraying beds and that of course is just where the bugs are in most cases now an old wood house with bedbugs back in the wood for generations only thing is to fumigate. . . . So here is Mamma with a glass of sweet wine her beds back and ready. . . .

I look at her over the syrupy red wine. . . . "Lady we don't spray beds. Board of health regulations you know."

"Ach so the wine is not enough?"

She comes back with a crumpled dollar. So I go to work . . . bedbugs great red clusters of them in the ticking of the mattresses. I mix a little formaldehyde with my kerosene in the spray it's more sanitary that way and if you tangle with some pimp in one of the negro whore houses we service a face full of formaldehyde keeps the boy in line. Now you'll often find these old Jewish grandmas in a back room like their bugs and we have to force the door with the younger generation smooth college trained Jew there could turn into a narcotics agent while you wait.

"All right grandma, open up! The exterminator is here."

She is screaming in Yiddish no bugs are there we force our way in I turn the bed back . . . my God thousands of them fat and red with grandma and when I put the spray to them she moans like the Gestapo is murdering her nubile daughter engaged to a dentist.

And there are whole backward families with bedbugs don't want to let the exterminator in.

"We'll slap a board of health summons on them if we have

to" said the college trained brother. . . . "I'll go along with you on this one. Get in the car."

They didn't want to let us in but he was smooth and firm. They gave way muttering like sullen troops cowed by the brass. Well he told me what to do and I did it. When he was settled at the wheel of his car cool grey and removed he said "Just plain ordinary sons of bitches. That's all they are."

T.B. sanatorium on the outskirts of town . . . cool blue basements fluoride dust drifting streaks of phosphorous paste on the walls . . . grey smell of institution cooking . . . heavy dark glass front door. . . . Funny thing I never saw any patients there but I don't ask questions. Do my job and go a man who works for his living. . . . Remember this janitor who broke into tears because I said shit in front of his wife it wasn't me actually said it was Wagner who was dyspeptic and thin with knobby wrists and stringy yellow hair . . . and the fumigation jobs under the table I did on my day off. . . .

Young Jewish matron there "Let's not talk about the company. The company makes too much money anyway. I'll get you a drink of whisky." Well I have come up from the sweet wine circuit. So I arrange a sulphur job with her five Abes and it takes me about two hours you have to tape up all the windows and the door and leave the fumes in there 24 hours studying the good work.

One time me and the smooth brother went out on a special fumigation job. . . . "This man is sort of a crank . . . been out here a number of times . . . claims he has rats under the house. . . . We'll have to put on a show for him."

Well he hauls out one of those tin pump guns loaded with cyanide dust and I am subject to crawl under the house through spider webs and broken glass to find the rat holes and squirt the cyanide to them.

"Watch yourself under there" said the cool brother. "If you don't come out in ten minutes I'm coming in after you."

I liked the cafeteria basement jobs long grey basement you can't see the end of it white dust drifting as I trace arabesques of fluoride on the wall.

We serviced an old theatrical hotel rooms with rose wall paper photograph albums. . . . "Yes that's me there on the left."

The boss has a trick he does every now and again assembles

his staff and eats arsenic been in that office breathing the powder in so long the arsenic just brings an embalmer's flush to his smooth grey cheek. And he has a pet rat he knocked all its teeth out feeds it on milk the rat is now very tame and affectionate. I stuck the job nine months. It was my record on any job. Left the old grey Jew there with his cigar the fat Chinese pouring my pyrithium powder back into the barrel. All the brothers shook hands. A distant cry echoes down cobble stone streets through all the grey basements up the outside stairs to a windy blue sky.

"Exterminator!"

# DURING THE JURASSIC

*As with the final contribution in the British part of the book (Kingsley Amis' Something Strange) we close here with a tale of science fantasy to illustrate the continuing development of the genre of speculative fiction. And in the hands of a craftsman such as John Updike (Couples and Rabbit Redux) it is not surprising to find that it contains style, originality and not a little social commentary.*

WAITING FOR the first guests, the iguanodon gazed along the path and beyond, towards the monotonous cycad forests and the low volcanic hills. The landscape was everywhere interpenetrated by the sea, a kind of metallic blue rottenness that daily breathed in and out. Behind him, his wife was assembling the hors d'oeuvres. As he watched her, something unintended, something grossly solemn, in his expression made her laugh, displaying the leaf-shaped teeth lining her cheeks. Like him, she was an ornithiscian, but much smaller—a compsognathus. He wondered, watching her race bipedally back and forth among the scraps of food (dragonflies wrapped in ferns, cephalopods on toast), how he had ever found her beautiful. His eyes hungered for size: he experienced a rage for sheer blind size.

The stegosauri, of course, were the first to appear. Among their many stupid friends these were the most stupid, and the most punctual. Their front legs bent outward and their filmy-eyed faces almost grazed the ground: the upward sweep of their backs was gigantic, and the double rows of giant bone plates along the spine clicked together in the sway of their cumbersome gait. With hardly a greeting, they dragged their tails, quadruply spiked, across the threshold and manoeuvered themselves towards the bar, which was tended by a minute and shapeless mammal hired for the evening.

Next came the allosaurus, a carnivorous bachelor whose
dangerous aura and needled grin excited the female herbivores;
then Rhamphorhynchus, a pterosaur whose much admired
"flight" was in reality a clumsy brittle glide ending in an
embarrassed bump and trot. The iguanodon despised these
pterosaurs' pretentions, thought grotesque the precarious elon-
gation of the single finger from which their levitating mem-
branes were stretched, and privately believed that the eccentric
archaeopteryx, though sneered at as unstable, had more of a
future. The hypsilophoden, with her graceful hands and
branch-gripping feet, arrived with the timeless crocodile—an
incongruous pair, but both were recently divorced. Still the
iguanodon gazed down the path.

Behind him, the conversation gnashed on a thousand things—
houses, mortgages, lawns, fertilisers, erosion, boats, winds, an-
nuities, capital gains, recipes, education, the day's tennis, last ·
night's party. Each party was consumed by discussion of the
previous one. Their lives were subject to constant cross-check.
When did you leave? When did *you* leave? We'd been out every
night this week. We had an amphibious baby sitter who had to
be back in the water by one. Gregor had to meet a client in town,
and now they've reduced the Saturday schedule, it means the
7.43 or nothing. Trains? I thought they were totally extinct. Not
at all. They're coming back, it's just a matter of time until the
government. . . . In the long range of evolution, they are still the
most efficient. . . . Taking into account the heat-loss/weight ratio
and assuming there's no more glaciation. . . . Did you know—I
think this is fascinating—did you know that in the financing of
those great ornate stations of the eighties and nineties, those real
monsters, there was no provision for amortisation? They weren't
amortised at all, they were financed on the basis of eternity! The
railroad was conceived of as the end of Progress! *I* think—
though not an expert—that the pivot word in this over-all
industrio-socio-what-have-you-oh nexus or syndrome or
whatever is *over-extended*. Any competitorless object *bloats*. Personally, I miss the trolley cars. Now don't tell me I'm the only
creature in the room old enough to remember the trolley cars!

The inguanodon's high pulpy heart jerked and seemed to split;
the brontosaurus was coming up the path.

Her husband, the diplodocus, was with her. They moved

together, rhythmic twins, buoyed by the hollow assurance of the huge. She paused to tear with her lips a clump of leaf from an overhanging paleocycas. From her deliberate grace the iguanodon received the impression that she knew he was watching her. Indeed, she had long guessed his love, as had her husband. The two saurischians entered his party with the languid confidence of the specially cherished. In the teeth of the iguanodon's ironic stance, her bulk, her gorgeous size, enraptured him, swelled to fill the massive ache he carried when she was not there. She rolled outward across his senses—the dawn-pale underpants, the reticulate skin, the vast bluish muscles whose management required a second brain at the base of her spine.

Her husband, though even longer, was more slenderly built, and perhaps weighed less than twenty-five tons. His very manner was attenuated and tabescent. He had recently abandoned an orthodox business career to enter the Episcopalian seminary. This regression—as the iguanodon felt it—seemed to make his wife more prominent, less supported, more accessible.

How splendid she was! For all the lavish solidity of her hips and legs, the modelling of her little flat diapsid skull was delicate. Her facial essence seemed to narrow, along the diagrammatic points of her auricles and eyes and nostrils, towards a single point, located in the air, of impermutable refinement and calm. This irreducible point was, he realised, in some sense her mind: the focus of the minimal interest she brought to play upon the inchoate and edible green world flowing all about her, buoying her, bathing her. The iguanodon felt himself as an upright speckled stain in this world. He felt himself, under her distant dim smile, impossibly ugly: his mouth a sardonic chasm, his throat a pulsing curtain of scaly folds, his body a blotched bulb. His feet were heavy and horny and three-toed and his thumbs—strange adaptation!—were erect rigidities of pointed bone. Wounded by her presence, he savagely turned on her husband.

"*Comment va le bon Dieu?*"

"Ah?" The diplodocus was maddeningly good-humoured. Minutes elapsed as stimuli and reactions travelled back and forth across his length.

The iguanodon insisted. "How are things in the supernatural?"

"The supernatural? I don't think that category exists in the new theology."

"*N'est-ce pas?* What *does* exist in the new theology?"

"Love. Immanence as opposed to transcendence. Works as opposed to faith."

"Work? I had thought you had quit work."

"That's an unkind way of putting it. I prefer to think that I've changed employers."

The iguanodon felt in the other's politeness a detestable aristocracy, the unappealable oppression of superior size. He said, gnashing. "The Void pays wages?"

"Ah?"

"You mean there's a living in nonsense? I said nonsense. Dead, fetid nonsense."

"Call it that if it makes it easier for you. Myself, I'm not a fast learner. Intellectual humility came rather natural to me. In the seminary, for the first time in my life, I feel on the verge of finding myself."

"Yourself? That little thing? *Cette petite chose?* That's all you're looking for? Have you tried pain? Myself, I have found pain to be a great illuminator. *Permettez-moi.*" The iguanodon essayed to bite the veined base of the serpentine throat lazily upheld before him; but his teeth were too specialised and could not tear flesh. He abraded his lips and tasted his own salt blood. Disoriented, crazed, he thrust one thumb deep into a yielding grey flank that hove through the smoke and chatter of the party like a dull wave. But the nerves of his victim lagged in reporting the pain, and by the time the distant head of the diplodocus was notified, the wound would have healed.

The drinks were flowing freely. The mammal crept up him and murmured that the dry vermouth was running out. The iguanodon told him to use the sweet. Behind the sofa the stegosauri were Indian-wrestling; each time one went over, his spinal plates raked the recently papered wall. The hypsilophoden, tipsy, perched on a banister; the allosaurus darted forward suddenly and ceremoniously nibbled her tail. On the far side of the room, by the great slack-stringed harp, the compsognathus and the brontosaurus were talking. He was drawn to them: amazed that his wife would presume to delay the much larger creature; to insert herself, with her scrabbling nervous motions and chattering leaf-shaped teeth, into the crevices of that queenly presence. As he drew closer to them, music began. His wife said to him, "The salad is running out." He murmured to the brontosaurus, "*Chère madame, voulez-vous danser avec moi?*"

Her dancing was awkward, but even in this awkwardness, this ponderous stiffness, he felt the charm of her abundance. "I've been talking to your husband about religion," he told her, as they settled into the steps they could do.

"I've given up," she said. "It's such a deprivation for me and the children."

"He says he's looking for himself."

"It's so selfish," she said. "The children are teased at school."

"Come live with me."

"Can you support me?"

"No, but I would gladly sink under you."

"You're sweet."

"*Je t'aime.*"

"Don't. Not here."

"Somewhere, then?"

"No. Nowhere. Never." With what delightful precision did her miniature mouth encompass these infinitesimal concepts!

"But I," he said, "but I lo—"

"Stop it. You embarrass me. Deliberately."

"You know what I wish? I wish all these beasts would disappear. What do we see in each other? Why do we keep getting together?"

She shrugged. "If they disappear, we will too."

"I'm not so sure. There's something about us that would survive. It's not in you and not in me but between us, where we almost meet. Some vibration, some enduring cosmic factor. Don't you feel it?"

"Let's stop. It's too painful."

"Stop dancing?"

"Stop being."

"That's a beautiful idea. *Une belle idée.* I will if you will."

"In time," she said, and her fine little face precisely fitted this laconic promise; and as the summer night yielded warmth to the multiplying stars, he felt his blood sympathetically cool, and grow thunderously, fruitfully slow.